TALES FROM RUGOSA COVEN

Sarah Avery

Dark Quest, LLC
Howell, New Jersey

PUBLISHED BY
Dark Quest, LLC
Neal Levin, Publisher
23 Alec Drive,
Howell, New Jersey 07731
www.darkquestbooks.com

Copyright ©2013 Sarah Avery
Cover Art Copyright ©2013 C.L. Smith

Atlantis Cranks Need Not Apply © 2006 Sarah Avery,
published by Drollerie Press 2009
Closing Arguments © 2006 Sarah Avery,
published by Drollerie Press 2007
And Ria's from Virgo, © 2012

ISBN (trade paper): 978-1-937051-60-0

All rights reserved. No part of this book may be reproduced, scanned or distributed in print or electronic form without the express, written permission of the author.

This is a work of fiction. Names, characters, places and incidents are the product of the author's imagination and any resemblance to any organization, event, or person, living or dead, is purely coincidental.

Interior Art (www.Fotolia.com)
Rose flowers with vintage elements © Seamartini Graphics

Cover Design: C.L. Smith

Interior Design: Danielle McPhail, Sidhe na Daire Multimedia
www.sidhenadaire.com

Contents

Dedication v
Acknowledgments vii
Author's Note ix
Closing Arguments 1
And Ria's from Virgo 115
Atlantis Cranks Need Not Apply 263
About the Author 341

DEDICATION

For all my teachers
of craft and Craft

ACKNOWLEDGEMENTS

Thanks first to Neal Levin of Dark Quest Books, without whom this series might have vanished along with my first publisher. I am grateful also to Deena Fisher of the late Drollerie Press, who took a chance on a novella, an odd form constantly rumored to be on the verge of extinction, and who then asked for a whole series of them. Danielle Ackley-MacPhail has helped me find my footing with a new press and shown me ways to give the book its best chance in the wide world.

Imaginary gardens only bloom when they have real toads in them, and many people have shared knowledge with me as I have tended my toads. Michael Brown of Simplicity Memorial allowed me to pick his brain for hours on the funeral industry and New Jersey's laws regarding care of the dead. Dave Argentar's explanation of how to run an estate sale gave me one of my favorite scenes in "Closing Arguments." For the attorney characters in that novella, I called often on the aid of my father, Bruce Avery, my sister, Prudence Avery Upton, and Renee Cyr Lasko. For medical matters, I relied on Drs. Anne Kaufhold, Jennifer Hamilton, and Dianne Pulte. Marine biology, nautical terms, and sailing conditions on Raritan Bay called for the expertise of Meagan Cummings. Particular thanks are in order to Meagan and my trio of M.D.'s for the improbable physiology in "Atlantis Cranks Need Not Apply." I do not see auras, but one of my protagonists does; without Barbara Brennan's books *Hands of Light* and *Light Emerging*, I could not have written a character who struggles with that particular sixth sense. For the astrological aspects in "And Ria's from Virgo," I referred constantly to *Llewellyn's Astrological*

Calendar. Thanks especially to Lisa Curran-Slaterback, who mailed me the pages for the key months in 2004, when in 2009 I set myself the slightly insane goal of pegging every incident in that novella to real astrological aspects from the time in which the story is set. Maggie Stewart, who has traveled extensively in the Pine Barrens, helped me with the details for that legendary wilderness. Lori Sinatra advised me on New Age retail. Lara Beneshan placed the top bid in a charity auction for earthquake relief in Haiti, winning herself a minor character named after her, and she helped me refine the dialogue so her fictional double would sound at least a little like her. For more reasons than I can count, I wish to thank all the members of several covens in the Blue Star lineage of Wicca that have been active in New Jersey over the years—Clover, Braided Stream, Barleymoon, Balefire, Moonfire, and Torchlight. Two Druid groves, Grove of the Other Gods and Grove of the American Gods, have been hospitable and generous with their lore, as has Vingolf Asatru Fellowship. Two founding members of Vingolf went over all the scenes with Asatru characters, customs, and rituals, and offered me indispensable feedback and suggestions. No doubt I have missed some names that should be on this list. All the book's errors are, of course, my own.

Scenes from all three novellas were workshopped by the Writers of the Weird critique group, affiliated with the Science Fiction Association of Bergen County. In matters of craftsmanship, I wish to thank all the WotW members who offered feedback, especially Pauline J. Alama, George Galuschak, Richard Herr, Patricia Nash, and the group's founder and host, Philip De Parto. David Sklar, who introduced me to WotW and who has since become my primary critique partner, was crucial to every stage of the book's development. So was his wife Rachel Young, without whose enthusiastic support and several rounds of commentary on every draft she could get her hands on—and her stalwart hosting of playdates for my kids and hers—the book might never have been finished.

Above all, I wish to thank Dan Davis, my husband, and our

sons Gareth and Conrad, who have cheered me on, improvised songs celebrating my stories, and made do without my help at times when it truly was hard so that I could get out of the house and write. They're the loves of my life.

 # Author's Note

Read these stories in any order. They appear here in order of setting. "Closing Arguments" takes place in 2002. The events in "And Ria's from Virgo" are pegged to real horological astrology, down to the minute, from 2004. "Altantis Cranks Need Not Apply" is set in late 2005, in a sort of alternate history hurricane season that diverges from ours shortly after Hurricane Katrina.

"Atlantis Cranks" was the first Rugosa Coven story that came to me, just a few weeks after Katrina. How odd that this book goes to press with Hurricane Sandy so recent, and the shore towns where I first glimpsed these characters now a lost world. Some magazine issued a call for submissions, looking for very short tales of psychological horror on the theme of "life interrupted." What, I asked myself, would be the most horrifying interruption to a thinking postmodern Neo-Pagan? The result was nowhere near horror—more a comedy of epistemology, or perhaps paranormal romance as it might be directed by the profane New Jersey filmmaker Kevin Smith, depending on which of my beta readers you ask. And short? Ah, no. The finished novella stood alone, and I did not know if I would ever return to these characters.

Some months later, I helped a friend dig out his late father's house. The old gentleman had become a hoarder in his last years. As I marveled at the heaps of unopened consumer goods, it occurred to me that, to the person who had lived in that house, all those purchases had made perfect sense. But what sense could that possibly have been? "Closing Arguments" began with imagining a supernatural answer to the question. It was the first of the novellas to find publication, so it had to stand alone as well as "Atlantis Cranks" had.

Next I set out to write a short story from the viewpoint of my comic relief character—or at least, that's who she was to me and to her covenmates. But again, her zany beliefs and behaviors made perfect sense *to her*. Her inner life turned out to be deeper and stranger than I had guessed, and it propelled her into predicaments that surprised me as much as they did her. The resulting story turned out to be nearly twice the length of its fellows, more a short novel than a novella. Where its predecessors had taken three months to produce in rough draft, before I had my children, "And Ria's from Virgo" took five years from first notes to final draft—though it is not a coincidence that I began the story a couple of weeks before my older child was born and finished it only when my younger child developed the ability to amuse himself independently for several minutes at a stretch.

The characters in Rugosa Coven have plenty more to say. I don't know if they will ever be done with me. I hope not. They've been delightful company here in my head these past seven years. I can't wait to see what they get up to next.

Closing Arguments

There was no dog, had been no dog for twenty years, but they'd left behind a new dog brush, still in its original packaging, with a receipt of recent date taped to the plastic. It was fifteen years since the last cat they'd kept, but they'd left behind an unopened sack of cat litter. There was no place they needed to be at any particular time, but there were half a dozen alarm clocks in the dining room: two with radios, three in the shapes of various cartoon characters, and one that purported to be a Zen alarm clock, which struck, mechanically, a euphonious handcrafted chime. Charles and Amelia Baines had shared so close a bond all their married lives, they'd hardly needed to speak to one another once their children were grown and gone, and as far as Bob had been able to reconstruct his parents' last year, they'd hardly been speaking to anyone else, but they'd bought several pairs of walkie-talkies. None of those had been popped out of their plastic packages, either. "Is there anyone they *were* on speaking terms with?" Bob Baines asked his sister as he cut one of the walkie-talkies free.

"How would I know? It's not like they were speaking to me, except to lecture me on the phone about money whenever I asked for any." Sophie stepped on one of the squeaky dog toys on her way across the consumer wreckage of the dining room to help him. "And the whole time, they were shopping themselves into oblivion. Figures. Do you really think they'd have brought a pet into this mess? It wouldn't be right."

"I no longer have any idea what they would have done. Look at this." He held up a worn canvas tote bag silkscreened with the Metropolitan Museum's logo. "Look in here."

She waded a few more steps through the dining room and took the bag from him. "One, two, three, four...eight television remotes?"

"I wonder if we'll find eight televisions." It was a stately old house with too many rooms. Eight televisions could easily disappear into it.

Sophie sat down hard on an unopened case of birdseed. "Oh, Gods."

"What?"

"What if the temple room's like this, too?"

Bob slumped into the chair he'd managed to empty. "I can't face the temple room. Soon, but not today. We need to call the coven."

"Not the lodge?"

"If Mom and Dad had been on good terms with their lodge, they'd have called on the old crowd for help. All these fallings out Mom and Dad had—maybe some of them were for a reason."

"We'll have to tell Uncle Florebo the bad news sooner or later," said Sophie.

"And then there's the funeral."

Sophie started to tear up. She pulled a tissue out of her coat pocket to daub her eyes. "Mom and Dad would have wanted it old school."

Bob added yet another item to his to-do list. *Call Theosophical Society, hire hall.* "I still don't think we should invite the fogies in until we have the place cleaned up some."

"Agreed. You want to call the covenfolk, or should I?"

Bob said, "I'll do it. I need some air. Oh, and here. Have a walkie-talkie."

She blew her nose into the tissue. "We'll need batteries."

"Look in that box between the windows. I don't think we'll have to buy batteries for a year or two." Eventually Bob made his way through the kitchen and out into the overgrown garden. Hellebore flowered red and yellow under an impenetrable thicket of rosebushes just in the first green of their spring leaves. *Yellow*

Pages, find landscaper, Bob added to his list, then crossed it out. This garden required the care of a hard-core occultist, someone who knew horological astrology. It would have been important to his father.

So Ria was the first of his covenmates to get the call. Then Amber and Sebastian. Then Jane, who had troubles of her own. He would have liked to call his wife for comfort, but Ricki and the kids were still at church.

Ria arrived with her gardening tools, an astrological calendar, a ten year ephemeris, and a paperback that claimed to be the all-time definitive compendium of magickal herbalism—that last from a New Age press of very dubious reputation. After a quick greeting hug and a moment with the ephemeris to confirm the alignment of the planets, she put her hair up and got to work reining in the hellebore.

"The all-time definitive compendium?" said Jane when she arrived. "Ria, have some self-respect. Those people will print anything. Hey, Bob. You holding up okay?"

"I still can't believe they're gone. I can't believe they fell apart like this. I should keep a running list of all the things I can't believe. What am I supposed to tell my kids about their grandparents? Ricki doesn't want to tell them anything, because then we'd have to disagree out loud about the afterlife again. She doesn't want the kids to see the house until it's less scary, and I don't blame her. I can't believe how fast it all came unraveled. I should have done something. I should have known to do something. But just Winter Solstice before last, my folks were keeping vigil with my kids by the fireplace, same as they used to with Sophie and me. We only missed one Yule, and now it's all over. What the hell happened?"

Jane lit a cigarette. "I brought you a casserole. It's in a cooler in my car."

"Thanks."

"Don't let me forget to give it to you to take home to Ricki."

"I won't."

She sat on the hood of her old Corolla and took a long drag. "Maybe no one will ever know what happened. Bob, I'm so sorry. It's not fair they're gone. It's not fair you have to clean up the mess. Believe me, I know from unfair."

"Sucks."

"Does. What can I do to be useful?"

Bob flipped the pages of his to-do list. "There'll be a lot in the next few weeks, I'm afraid. If we can dig a path from the dining room into the library today, tomorrow we can dig through to the filing cabinets. I'm hoping we'll find the will so I can get it to a colleague before the weekend."

"A colleague? You can't do it yourself?"

"Estate law's nothing like personal injury. Whole other world."

"Fair enough. If you want a hand with the financial docs, too, feel free to ask."

"Yes, your C.P.A.ness."

Jane sucked in another breath of tobacco, then reached back into her car to stub out her cigarette in the ashtray. Once Jane was through the kitchen door, Ria started humming the song about the wicked witch from *The Wizard of Oz.*

The last thing Bob needed was his coven sisters' bickering. He hoped Jane and Ria could keep it to a low simmer, at least until the funeral. "I really appreciate this, Ria."

"If it weren't for the sad occasion, the gardening would be fun. Do you know if they've still got that asafoetida growing in the greenhouse?"

"Considering the mess everywhere else, I'll be surprised if anything in the greenhouse survived. Help yourself to whatever you think you can keep alive."

Ria started singing a Vernal Equinox chant about roots in wet soil, about waking the trees. Bob hummed along while he looked over his to-do list. It was four pages long. *Find will. Phone utilities re billing. Crematorium?*

Sebastian pulled into the driveway in Amber's Miata. Amber herself was bandaged from wrist to shoulder, her pretty face pinched with discomfort.

"New ink?" Bob asked. "But you already had stuff on that arm."

"Sebastian's covering up that old hackwork."

"It wasn't bad," said Sebastian. "She's just running out of blank skin."

Amber leaned over the gear shift to kiss him. "Yeah, but you're twice the artist Big Mike is, any day of the week."

Bob said, "I interrupted you mid-tattoo, didn't I? Sorry."

"When I said call anytime, I meant anytime." Sebastian still had his work voice going—the slightly hypnotic cadence he used to soothe clients while they were under the needle. He came around the car to offer his girlfriend a hand out. "Whatever we can do."

So Bob called all the members of Rugosa Coven into the dining room, where Jane and Sophie had started sorting things into piles: electronics, pet supplies, paper goods. Sophie had opened one of the thirty-odd boxes of tissues. Her eyes were red, and the tip of her nose, too. Bob gave his sister a squeeze around the shoulder.

"Oh, man," Sebastian said as he crossed the threshold from the kitchen. "It looks like the Federation Starship Wal-Mart had a terrible transporter accident."

Amber admired the Zen alarm clock. "There's some nice stuff in here. Diamonds in the rough."

Ria clutched her ephemeris. "They weren't like this. The people I met at your wedding could not have lived this way. Charles and Amelia were...I had great admiration for your parents, Bob. The very greatest admiration. They were adepts of the first water."

"Well," Jane said quietly, "sometimes people change."

By dinnertime, Rugosa Coven had dug their way to the library, and after pizza they surprised Bob by making it all the way to the cabinets. The path into the room had crisp edges, as if shoveled through a two-foot snowfall, beyond which masses of undifferentiated paper roiled. Bob and Sophie bade their covenmates good night and searched for the will.

Fortunately, Charles and Amelia Baines had bought several cases of Post-it Notes of various colors and sizes, with which the Baines siblings labeled the cabinets as they finished them. *Financials,* Bob wrote. *Family Photos. Theosophical Memorabilia, 1881-1930.* There had been a system, once. Its old logic showed itself in the drawers Charles and Amelia had used least since their children grew up, but in the more current cabinets, the logic crumbled. And it seemed that, for about a year, the elder Baineses had been throwing their mail unopened onto the library floor.

"Check it out," said Sophie, leaning over an open file drawer. "Letters to Great-Grampa Frederick from Madame Blavatsky herself."

Bob sneezed. Too much old dust. "We'd better label the file while we still know what it is." The Zen alarm clock chimed nine. "I'm all in."

"Yeah, me too. Give my love to Ricki and the kids. Tomorrow, nine a.m.?"

"I'll bring donuts." Bob took the file of letters home to read. For all that Blavatsky's life had been wild, he could usually count on her prose style to put him to sleep. And he had not slept well since identifying his parents' bodies.

Since Wednesday, every time he made the drive between the old manse in Rumson and his suburban split-level in Holmdel, Bob reproached himself for letting his parents get so isolated. Fifteen minutes away, just fifteen minutes, and the most important year lost.

It was long past the twins' bedtime when he got home, but Susan was still up, still in her Sunday church finery. She clumped down the stairs, her gangly eight-year-old form showing none of the grace she'd hoped to get from ballet. Bob hugged his daughter. "I'm sorry I missed Sunday dinner."

"We should have brought Sunday dinner to you."

"There was no surface to eat it on."

"I can carry boxes as good as Aunt Sophie can."

"As *well* as Aunt Sophie can. Take it up with your mom."

Susan gallumphed away to sulk.

Bob found Ricki folding shirts in the laundry room. She wrapped him in her arms, and he bent to rest his head on her shoulder. They stood like that a long time. "How was church?"

"Susan had her solo with the children's choir."

"That was today? I wanted to go for that."

"There will be other solos. She knows this isn't forever." Ricki took a deep breath. "There was an incident in Sunday school."

"Does Susan think I'm going to Hell again?"

"The twins' Sunday school teacher told them their grandparents are already there. I've had words with her. Reverend had words with her—it's not for us to decide who God's okay with. Your daughter had such nasty words with her, I had to ground Susan from the internet for a week. But for the boys, damage done. They're angry at God."

"This part's in your hands. I gave you my word. But if you want me to tell them what I think, just say so."

"If they ask you anything, it's in your court." Ricki sighed. "Sooner or later, we all hit the first time we're angry at God, but to hit it at four... I hoped the boys would have a few more years."

Bob kissed her forehead. "It'll all work out."

"How was your day?"

"We didn't find the will."

"And after..." She checked her watch. "Twelve more hours. Why did they have to make it so hard for you? What were they thinking?"

"I wish I knew."

Once they'd seen Susan to bed and turned in, Bob sat up beside his sleeping wife, reading Madame Blavatsky's letters with the bedside lamp turned low. The Ascended Masters this, the Ascended Masters that. Bob had little patience for the Ascended Masters. In the fourth letter, old Helena Petrovna recounted to her disciple Frederick Baines how the ancient sage Koot Hoomi had caused a parchment of his observations about the afterlife to appear midair at one of her séances. Bob tried to picture the scene, but every time he came to the manifestation of the parchment, he couldn't help imagining it with a cartoony popping sound, and then he'd crack up. Maybe he was cracking up. Rather than risk waking Ricki with his laughter, he turned the light out and lay staring at the ceiling until dawn.

After making breakfast for his family, he walked Susan to the bus stop. He kissed Ricki goodbye and wished her a good day at the social services office where she worked. Then he buckled his twin sons into their car seats in the SUV and dropped them off at day care on his way to Dunkin Donuts.

At last, he reached the house his thrice-great-grandfather Rodolph Baines had built with his Civil War telegraph profits, the house where his kin had lived ever since. Bob preferred the kitchen door over the grand marble entryway. He was early, so he left the donuts in the car and headed back into the garden.

For a full century, the garden had been a meditation on the zodiac made manifest in stone and growing green. He clambered over the Aquarius patch to reach the yew tree at the far end of the property. The yew was unperturbed by the chaos in the flowerbeds. It bent its branches to form a dome of shade and quiet. Bob ducked and crept in. When he was a child, this place had been his cathedral. Now, he could just stand at his full height in the shelter of the branches. The clay god and goddess figures Sophie had made back when she took up pottery were rainworn and serene, tucked among the roots of the yew. "Lady of the Woodlands," Bob greeted them, "Horned One." He should have brought them something. A donut, at the very least. He had half an hour before he expected his sister, so, for the first time since the terrible phone call from the hospital, there was time for him to tell his troubles to his Gods. He sat himself down in lotus position among the yew needles and let the words come.

"Wisdom," he said, when he'd told them the story he knew they knew. "That's what I need. Common sense is no substitute. What am I supposed to do?"

"Ow! Dammit!" said Sophie, from somewhere in the sidereal clock of the flowerbeds. She limped the rest of the way to the yew tree, her long cotton skirt catching on briars as she came. "Thought I'd find you under here." She sat next to him and slid off her Birkenstocks. "I hope Ria can do something with those rosebushes." She pulled a thorn from the sole of her foot. "Blood offering, anyone?" she said to her little clay sculptures. They didn't take her up on it. "Did you remember the donuts?"

"Yep. To work?"

They took the donuts into the library, and regretted it the moment they broke them out. "Sticky fingers," said Sophie, dismayed.

"Not good with important papers," Bob agreed. Fortunately, their parents had left them a gross of pre-moistened hand wipes. Around noon, he and Sophie found a threatening letter from the IRS about unpaid taxes, a lively anthill, and several files of old newspaper clippings about international art theft.

Buy ant traps, Phone IRS, Bob added to his to-do list when they'd retreated to the living room. "Whatever fallings out Mom and Dad had with their friends, I'm thinking they were irrational," he said. "I'm ready to call in the old crowd. How about you?"

"I think there's an ant in my hair."

"Right. I'm calling Uncle Florebo."

Sophie sat on the floor and pulled a hairbrush out of her battered purse. Bob took that for agreement and dialed.

There was an answer at the first ring. "Smith and Watanabe residence."

"Hi, Uncle Florebo."

"Robert! So good to hear from you. I take it you got my message after all. Your parents might have returned my call while they were thinking about it, but no matter."

"Message?"

"Kiyoshi and I are celebrating our fifth anniversary by registering a civil union with the state. Just when we were thinking we'd move to Boston, New Jersey finally came around. We wanted to invite you and Sophronia, but we never did get your grown-up addresses. You must come. It'll be fabulous."

"I'll be there. But about my parents." Bob had no idea how to go on.

He could hear Florebo's voice catch on the other end of the line. "Something's happened, then."

"They had simultaneous heart attacks while they were out shopping at Target. The manager tried defibrillating them, and everybody knew CPR, but..."

"When?"

"Wednesday night. I'm on leave from the firm, trying to sort things out, and Sophie's between jobs, so we're doing nothing but trying to put things in order back at the old place. We want to arrange the funeral the way Mom and Dad would have wanted it, but we can't find anything in writing to tell us what that would have been. We're hoping you or maybe Aunt Pasca can help us out."

"Simultaneous heart attacks."

"Yes. The county medical examiner said he'd never seen a case like it."

"They were lucky, then. There's nothing worse than outliving your mate."

Bob would have liked to say something about how fondly he remembered Florebo's late partner Simon, but the awful thought of outliving Ricki stole Bob's words.

Florebo sounded awful. "If you need anything, Robert, you just name it."

"We could use your help making sense of the house."

"When's good?"

"Would now be too soon?"

"I'll be right over." Florebo hung up unceremoniously. It was probably the only unceremonious thing he'd ever done.

Sophie said, "So he's coming?"

"Right away."

She put her hands on her hips and surveyed the living room. "Mom would have been mortified."

They cleared the deep chairs in the living room, all of them. There was nothing for it but to put the contents right down on the floor. When the bell rang, the room was bright with dust caught in sunlight. Sophie ran to get the door.

Standing on the colonnaded front porch, Florebo Smith and his betrothed stared wide-eyed past Sophie at the heap of full garbage bags in the marble entryway. Were it not for the shock on their faces, Florebo and Kiyoshi would have been the very picture of a distinguished gay couple in their sixties. "Oh," said Florebo. His eyes were very red.

"Be welcome," said Bob. When had Florebo gotten old?

"They're really not here. They would never have kept the place like this."

Sophie said, "Can I get you anything, Uncle Flori?"

A crashing sound emanated from upstairs. No one had yet attempted to clear a path that far. "The temple room?" Bob guessed.

"All right, then," said Florebo. "Up we go. If I stand still, I'm in danger of thinking."

The grander of the two staircases was blocked up with cardboard boxes. More cases of Post-it Notes, as it turned out. Bob far preferred ferrying those down to the dining room's paper goods pile over attempting the back stairs. The house had servants' quarters—though not actual servants for the past two generations—a servants' entrance, and servants' stairs. These last, Charles and Amelia Baines had used for their clothes when the laundry chute got full to the top—it was from the bottom that Bob had discovered the state of the chute.

Every few boxes, Kiyoshi Watanabe sneezed at the dust, until the stairs were clear, at which point he fell into a sneezing jag that lasted several minutes. "Forgive me, Richard darling," he said to Florebo when he recovered. "I think I have to wait on the porch."

"Quite all right, love. I'm just glad you did the driving."

"Richard?" said Bob. "I never heard Mom and Dad call you that."

"It *is* my name, you know. Did you never wonder why we called your parents Aio and Gaudea? They were our Outer Court names in the lodge."

Bob said, "It never occurred to me to wonder. I got so used to being from the neighborhood's designated weird family, I stopped questioning stuff like that." The marble railing was cold under his hand. He dreaded what he might find at the top of the stairs. "Where did they sleep? With the stairs clogged, how could they have gotten up to their bedroom? Were they sleeping downstairs at the end?"

"*Where* would they have slept downstairs?" Sophie asked right behind him. "No place on the first floor's any better."

"It's as bad as when Ciebo died," said Florebo.

Bob stopped still. "Uncle Ciebo's dead? I thought he just moved to Florida."

"One can precede the other," Florebo pointed out. "It was about a year ago. Kiyoshi and I flew down to help poor Lawrence's children. He had a much smaller dwelling, but it was every bit as full. At the time, I was miffed at your parents that they didn't come to the funeral, but I suppose they were already sliding into all of this."

When they crested the top of the stairs, Bob spotted two of the mystery televisions on the landing. Seven identical shortwave radios had fallen from the top of the larger television. Those radios were the only thing on the landing not covered with dust. "I guess this is our crash." An unwelcome thought was forming somewhere in his mind. "Did Ciebo have the same electronics fixation?"

"He always had, so I thought nothing of it. For your parents, though, it is odd. I never knew them to watch television."

"It's all odd," said Bob. "Find me one thing in this house that isn't odd." He waded through several months of *The New York Times* to reach the door to the temple room. Turning the pressed glass knob, he closed his eyes and took a breath.

The latch clicked. The door swung smoothly—that was a surprise, after all the downstairs doors that had been blocked with piles of purchases. Behind him, Bob heard Sophie and Florebo gasp. He opened his eyes.

The impeccable cleanliness of the temple room, with its jewel-toned velvet drapes and floor cushions, was downright alien after days of dust-coated cardboard in the house's common rooms. Crossing the threshold into the faint lingering scent of good Himalayan incense, Bob felt as if he were walking back into his childhood. Here, his father had tried and failed to teach him astral travel. Here, his mother had instructed him in yoga—Bob's earliest memory was of the cobra pose. Everything was as it ought to be, except that a low table squatted in the middle of the room, surrounded by velvet cushions. On the table was a Ouija board.

Florebo glowered at the thing. Maybe he had the same unwelcome thought Bob was putting together.

Beside the Ouija board, someone had arranged a Montblanc ballpoint pen, a shopping list pad, and a sheaf of official looking paper. Bob guessed right away what that sheaf was. Yes, indeed. "The will," he said. He picked it up and flipped the pages. They were heavily annotated, with numerous changes, all dated and initialed: AB, CB.

The old Theosophist started arguing with the dead. "Decades of practice, the very best training, and still you came to this."

There was a Post-it Note stuck to first page of the will. Charles Baines's handwriting said, *Larry's advice*. Bob asked, "When did you say Uncle Ciebo died?"

That snapped Florebo out of his rant. "It was a year ago at Solstice."

"All these amendments have dates within the past year next to the initials."

"Do they? Hm."

Sophie sat on a pile of cushions to look at the Ouija Board. "It's just an old cardboard Parker Brothers set." Bob winced when he saw her pick up the plastic planchette. "It's the same damn set I bought with my allowance at Toys-R-Us when I was sixteen. Remember the lecture they gave me about refusing to use Grandma's good mahogany talking board?" She sat up straight and narrowed her eyes in imitation of their mother's anger. "'There is a word for this, young lady, and the word is *slumming.* Your father and I have provided you with a first-rate occult upbringing. Why do you insist on squandering your attention on pop culture kitsch and belated hippie activism?'" Sophie laughed. "Oh, Mom. Nobody was more wholehearted about being wrong than you."

Bob knelt by the table and uncapped the Montblanc ballpoint. He scribbled lightly over the top sheet of the shopping list pad to read the indentations of whatever had been written on his parents' last page. The impression of the last shopping list was all in big block capital letters, oddly spaced out as if his father had taken dictation, one letter at a time, from the Ouija board. Bob felt his pulse beating in his neck, and the whole world was red around the edges.

"Breathe, Robert," Florebo said.

"This didn't just happen," said Bob. How thick his own voice sounded in his ears. "Someone did this to them."

Sophie looked up at him with big eyes. "Who?"

"Ciebo." Bob's hand shook, but he showed her the Post-it Note. *Larry's advice.*

"Through a paperboard Ouija set with a plastic planchette?" said Sophie. "He'd have insisted on a full-blown séance with Morse code table-knocking, if he came out to talk at all."

Florebo had an inward look on his face. "Or someone else prodded your parents. Someone who'd prodded Lawrence first. He was only fifty-five. Too young. And for them all to be stripped of their dignity by madness first..." He reached into his jacket pocket and pulled out a cell phone. Two buttons got him someone on speed dial. "Hello, Elizabeth?" he said. Bob remembered his mother calling Aunt Pasca that once. That, and Betsy. "Yes, it is. It certainly has been too long. Far too long. I have to see you with some pressing news. Where are you?" He slumped. "Which Wal-Mart would that be?"

Bob's teeth ground, and he jammed the will into his back pocket. "We're going to get her out of there."

"And do what?" said Sophie.

Florebo held up his hand to quiet them. "And you'll be going straight home after that? Very good. I'll meet you there. No, I really don't mind that your house is a mess. Don't you fret. How about thirty minutes?" He leaned back against the curtained wall. "Why would you need three hours to finish shopping? Have you taken up with a new consort and told none of your old friends? I see. I'll be waiting." He snapped the cell phone shut and closed his eyes. Covered them with his hand.

"We're coming with you," said Bob.

"Damn straight, we're coming with you," said Sophie.

Florebo managed a small smile. "Damn straight? Is that what people say these days?"

Down on the porch while Bob locked up, Kiyoshi said, "What is it?"

"I'll tell you in the car," said Florebo. "Remember how to get to Elizabeth's house?"

"It's been a while, but I think so."

Bob looked over at the driveway, where Florebo and Kiyoshi's sleek little electric car sat. It barely had room for four, and with any luck there would soon be five of them. "You can follow us." It was a good thing he had to stay slow and careful for Kiyoshi's sake, or Bob would have driven like a demon to Aunt Pasca's house.

As it was, Sophie gasped and flinched in the passenger's seat of the SUV. "Slow down, Bob. She won't be home for hours."

Bob said, "Whatever it is, it can't have Pasca, too." She'd baked cookies for all his childhood birthday parties. She'd taught him bawdy songs about Madame Blavatsky. All of the Theosophists who were his parents' world had been disappointed when Bob and Sophie cast their lot with Wicca, but Pasca had gotten over it first. And then Pasca had been kind to Ricki, when

Bob's parents objected to their son marrying a Methodist.

"Um, Bob? If you get us all killed on Route 35, who's going to see that it doesn't get her? Oh, shit." Sophie rolled down her window. "There's an ant in my shirt." She plucked it out of her collar and held it in her hand until Bob stopped at a red light. Pitching the live ant out the window, she said to it, "Blessed be."

Bob turned to wish the ant well, but he noticed just then a yellow Post-it stuck to the dashboard. It said, *All the birds come home to roost.* "Hey, Sophie, did you put that there?"

"What? No. Ricki must have been trying to remind you of something." She ran her fingers through her long hair, searching for more ants.

But it wasn't Ricki's handwriting.

He squinted at street signs, trying to remember where Thornbrooke Drive fell in the grand scheme of Shrewsbury. Sophie pointed and said, "There." Two more blocks, and Bob pulled the SUV in front of the familiar Victorian cottage, with its familiar climbing tree in the front yard. The trunk had put out unsightly shoots, the lawn needed mowing, and the flowerbeds had given themselves over to an early crop of dandelions. Bob's rage woke again, and he ran to the porch to peer in through the windows. There wasn't far to see. Enormous plastic-wrapped packages of paper towels occluded the view.

Bob kicked the porch railing. "Motherfucker."

Sophie glowered at the paper towels and wrapped her arms around herself. "You can stop kicking things anytime, you know. Whatever this is, you're not going to be able to beat it up like it was the captain of the fucking football team."

"I wasn't wrong about him."

"I never said you were."

Bob leaned his forehead against the windowpane. "This can't go on. One way or another, I'll put a stop to it."

Florebo and Kiyoshi pulled up behind the SUV. Florebo rolled down the window and said, "Oh, don't mind us. We'll find Thornbrooke Drive just fine."

"Sorry," said Bob.

Kiyoshi got out and looked the garden over. "I take it back, darling. I believe you."

"I told you so." Florebo didn't sound especially pleased about his vindication.

Bob went back to the car for the legal pad with his to-do list and started a new page. *Salt. New broom. Banishing incense. Asafoetida? Consult Ria re ephemeris.* He had two hours to run down his cell phone batteries, calling the members of his coven.

They were all game for his plan, though Jane didn't believe in Ouija boards or psychic attacks. "Sometimes people just go over the edge," she said. "Your parents' sudden turn for the acquisitive—it looks like garden variety addictive behavior, from where I sit."

"Jane, your house is Addiction Central."

"I found a rehab place that would take him."

"Thank the Gods," said Bob. "So he's agreed to try again?"

"Nils agrees intermittently. I may need a hand getting the spousal unit where he needs to go."

"Whatever you need, we're there."

Jane sighed. "Fine. I'm in. I can lay down a line of salt as well as the next girl. But I still think you should be wary of getting sucked into your parents' delusions. I'm worried about you."

Just then, Pasca drove up in a shiny new minivan and pulled into her driveway. "Gotta go," Bob said into the phone.

It took Pasca some time to get down from the majestic height of the driver's seat. "Bob? Sophie? What a pleasant surprise. Richard, why didn't you tell me you were bringing a party to my doorstep? I'd have insisted we go somewhere tidier. I know how poor Kiyoshi suffers from dust." She looked from face to face and saw there was bad news before anyone could say it. "Pressing business, was it, Richard? Have it out."

"Charles and Amelia..."

"Both?"

Bob said, "Simultaneously," since that part had been some comfort to Florebo.

"Simultaneously? They didn't combust, did they?"

"Heart attacks," Sophie put in.

"I see." Pasca had always been small—she was the first grown-up Bob had seen eye to eye with—but now, beside her massive vehicle, she looked tiny. "We should go out and drink them some toasts."

"No," said Bob, "it really would be better if we went inside."

"But..."

Sophie said, "It can't possibly be worse than the mess we're cleaning up in Rumson."

"I really don't think..."

"It can't be worse than Lawrence's condominium, now can it?" said Florebo.

Pasca laughed a nervous little laugh and looked around as if for someone to back her up. "Surely you understand, Florebo. Or you will soon."

At that, Kiyoshi strode over to the minivan and reached around Pasca to snatch the keys from the ignition. Without a word, he walked past them all to the cottage door and jingled his way through every key on the ring to let himself in. Pasca just stood there, until he sneezed at the dust. "Bless you," she said, in a defeated little voice.

Bob went to her and took her by the hand. "Come on," he said. "Show me."

"Everything will be all right," said Sophie, taking Pasca's other hand. Maybe she even believed it.

While Kiyoshi hovered on the porch, looking in through the open door, the rest of them picked their steps carefully through the detritus in the living room. "I'm sorry there's nowhere to sit," Pasca said. "I needed the space for work." The couch and chairs sagged under the weight of her reference books.

Bob tried not to let on how alarmed he was to see the old alphabetical order of her shelves dissolved. "You're still working? That's good."

She tried to clear them places to sit. "There's not as much demand for my crossword puzzles as there used to be. Can't keep up with the pop culture. The second time Puff Daddy changed his name, I knew I was lost for hip hop. But I do still sell them to the senior citizen magazines, where people remember the Vandellas and *My Mother the Car*."

Sophie blurted out the awkward question. "How do you afford all this *stuff* on a few crossword puzzles a month?"

"I took out a reverse mortgage on the house, of course. I don't have long to live." She was utterly matter-of-fact about it.

"You might have thirty more years," said Bob.

"But I won't. I'll ascend long before then." A little more tentatively now.

"Ascend?" said Florebo. "You? This incarnation?"

"To join the other Ascended Masters."

Bob said, "You need to see a doctor."

Pasca held her head high. "Could doctors have prevented the ascension of your parents, dear? I doubt they've even managed to explain it after the fact. If Aio and Gaudea went together, just slid out of their bodies, you can bet *they've* ascended."

It almost made sense, but Bob looked at the squalor around him and steeled himself. Maybe if she got a preview of what she was headed for, he could turn her around. "Would you come back to Rumson with us in the meantime? We're trying to figure out what to do for Mom and Dad's funeral. If you could put off ascending a little longer, we'd sure appreciate the help."

"Oh, I'm not nearly ready to ascend yet. So much to do! We must reconcile with materiality before we leave it, you know."

"We could go over now," said Bob. Seeing Pasca unhinged like this was almost as bad as seeing his parents dead.

She sighed. "Very well. But would you help me unload the van first?"

Half an hour later, Bob and Sophie carried in the last of the dozen torchiere lamps Pasca had purchased and put them next to the air conditioners and fishtanks. "I think that's everything," he said. "Will you ride with us, or with Uncle Florebo?" He'd learned the parental trick of limiting the options in the question to the ones he was willing to live with. As long as she didn't drive her own van over, he had a handle on her until he thought it safe to drive her home.

While Bob fought rush hour traffic back up Route 35, Sophie kept Pasca talking—about how Blavatsky's *The Secret Doctrine* was at last coming clear for her now that she read it at the start of old age, about how close she was to adapting the humble household radio to receive transmissions from the spirits of the dead, about how pretty Sophie had grown up to be. "And you'd be even prettier if you weren't trying to look like a hippie chick. I was an original, you know. Spent the longest year of my life in Haight-Ashbury, before I discovered the Theosophical Society and came to my senses. It's all very socially conscious, that Guatemalan cotton you're wearing, but it's hardly flattering, now is it? If you're going to indulge in anachronisms, you ought at least to try some good old-fashioned hashish. Nothing like it for astral travel, and one size is equally attractive on all."

"Hashish?" said Bob, trying to sound non-committal.

Pasca laughed. "You young people are at such a disadvantage, having grown up with all that 'Just Say No' claptrap. Nancy Reagan was an enemy of true gnosis, no matter what people say about her astrologer."

When they reached the ancestral Baines home, Jane was already pacing around the garden, puffing away at a cigarette while she searched the ground for something. "You've got a big fat oak tree," she said to Bob as he emerged from the SUV. "You'd think there would be some decent-sized acorns around here somewhere."

Bob went over to confer with her. "You got the broom, then."

"I got everything on the list." Jane leaned against the old oak and put her cigarette out against the sole of her shoe. "Your aunt doesn't look at all like you."

"She's not literally our aunt. We were running out of extended family, so Mom and Dad borrowed their lodgemates."

"She looks lucid enough."

"I think she's been hitting the hashish."

Jane broke out in a coughing fit. "Her?"

"If it was good enough for Coleridge…"

"That's her rationalization, is it?" Jane fished her address book out of her purse and flipped through the pages. "I can phone up that M.D. from Chamomile Coven. He owes me a favor. If he's not on duty, I can get him out here for a house call."

"That must be some favor."

"I got him out of paying the Alternative Minimum Tax last year, despite the mess he'd made of his records. He'll come." As the only Pagan C.P.A. in Monmouth County, Jane was always owed favors she could call in for Rugosa Coven.

"Thanks. Call him. But out of earshot, okay?"

While he gave Jane time to work the phone, Bob gave Pasca the grand tour of the household wreckage. She was utterly unfazed, and settled into the ant-infested library to pore over the Blavatsky memorabilia. With a conspiratorial glance at Bob, Sophie brushed the ants off a footstool and settled in to keep an eye on the old lady. He popped batteries into a pair of walkie-talkies and handed one to his sister before he left her to it.

In the kitchen, Bob cranked the volume on his walkie-talkie to high, double checked that it was on the same frequency as Sophie's, and got to work on the business at hand. She'd buzz him if anything useful came up.

Having found a suitable acorn, Jane jammed it in among the bristles of the new broom. "Wake up," she said to it. "Rise and shine."

Just then, Ria came bounding up the kitchen steps, past Kiyoshi, with a big canvas tote slung over her shoulder. She was dressed all in black and weighted down with silver necklaces and not a few crystals. The moment she opened the door, Bob smelled the jasmine oil on her. "Thirty-seven minutes," she said.

"Until showtime?" Bob set his cell phone's alarm to give him a five minute warning.

"That's when the planets will be propitious. Oh, Florebo! I wasn't expecting you."

The old Theosophist actually kissed her hand. "Annamaria Santini. Still squandering your talents among the Wiccans?"

"Think of her as a bodhisattva," said Jane. "She does."

Ria ignored her, clearing a space on the kitchen table for the mortar and pestle in her canvas bag. "Do we know what we're up against?"

"Not really," Bob said. "Whatever it is that pushed my parents over the edge, we want it out of the house. It's a repeat offender. We can figure out what it is once it's out of our hair."

"Um," said Jane. "No offense to Florebo, but has it occurred to you guys that the thing that pushed Charles and Amelia over the edge was Theosophy? That séances are not the most wholesome form of ritual? People who choose to get mixed up with Theosophy might have a predisposition to fall apart when their glory days are over. I tried reading Blavatsky, and the grandiosity damn near killed me. What happens to people whose spiritual mode *is* the grandiose, once the body starts getting helpless? Power starts in the body, and it ends in the body."

Florebo smiled. "Spoken like a true kitchen witch."

"You got a problem with that?"

"On the contrary, Jane. Your kind of Witchcraft is a blunt instrument, but it'll get the job done."

Ria added the asafoetida into the incense she was grinding. A ghastly smell filled the kitchen, and Bob remembered why the German name for the stuff translated to Devil's Dung. "Blunt," said Ria, "is the word for our Jane."

"Because I told you you were full of shit about having been Cleopatra in a past life?"

"If you really believe power starts and ends in the body, when are you going to quit smoking?"

Her husband being the drunk he was, Jane took it as badly as she could. "If by the word *blunt*, you're trying to imply that it's not just tobacco I've been smoking..."

Bob had to say something. "Would you two please, please, please cut it the fuck out?" It was worse than pulling his sons apart from their little-boy scuffles.

Jane sat on the kitchen stepstool and sullenly wound fresh willow withes around the hips of the store-bought broom to keep the acorn in. Concentrating on a task could usually be counted on to reset her mood. By the time Amber and Sebastian arrived, Jane and Ria were working almost companionably.

Sebastian came in with three sheathed swords tucked under his arm. "Take your pick," he said. "We brought the best of our collection."

The swords were, all three, well sharpened and oiled. Bob could barely lift the largest of them, a fanciful thing with steel serpents coiling around the crosspiece. The smallest was a leaf-shaped blade of bronze, obviously hand-forged. The third was black-hilted and downright austere. Austerity felt right for the occasion. "This one."

"Ah," said Sebastian. "The guy who made that traded it to me for a full back piece. He was five days under the needle for it."

"One of your best," said Amber. "How's the auntie doing?"

Bob shook his head. "Can't get much sense out of her. Sophie's with her now. Hey, let's have a look at that new tattoo."

Where the fresh black linework traced promises of a new image over the old, Amber's left arm was stippled with bright pricks of blood. She beamed. "It'll be gorgeous."

"What is it?"

"Wisteria vines. See? When Sebastian fills the color in, it'll all make sense. We worked on the sketches together for six months."

Bob didn't see wisteria in it yet, but Amber made a good living at graphic design, and Sebastian was the best body modification artist in Red Bank. They knew what they were about.

Just then, the walkie-talkie spizzled to life, and Aunt Pasca's voice rambled faintly through it. "He'd been at it since the sixties," she said, and fizzled indecipherably for a few seconds.

Sophie's voice came through so loudly, Bob jumped. "But...radio waves?" she said.

"Since the dawn of radio," said Pasca. "We've always thought it was just a matter of finding the right frequency. You've got enough of Blavatsky's letters here. See for yourself. Of course, that approach isn't as widely favored in the Society as it used to be, but some of us…"

"Not all of us," Florebo interrupted, and he folded his arms irritably across his chest. Bob wondered if Florebo would have objected like that if Pasca had been in the room to hear.

"…Great advances in the forties, and then the Society's radio researches stalled out for decades. But Larry was really onto something. When I joined up with your parents in the early seventies, they had already been engaged in the project for years. I do wish Florebo hadn't badgered us into dropping it. He was always badgering us into dropping things. And for Charles and Amelia to pick it back up again at the end and not tell me, well, I am a bit stung. We might have made a real breakthrough if we'd been in it together like we used to be." Pasca rambled on about how serious Charles had been, how elegant Amelia always was, and the walkie-talkie cut out. Apparently, Sophie no longer considered the ramble important enough to merit jamming down the transmit button.

Bob said, "My parents thought they could talk to the Ascended Masters on the *radio*?"

Florebo sniffed. "The last gasp of a very old speculation. Vibrations, frequencies—people had a lot of odd ideas in Blavatsky's day. The Society outgrew its founders a long time ago."

"Well," said Jane with a smirk, "thank goodness you Theosophists are all done with odd ideas."

"Said the witch," Ria added.

Bob said, "Don't start." Once the crisis of his parents' death was over, he decided, it would be time to have it out with Jane and Ria about their sniping. Right now, he could not cope with one more thing.

The doorbell rang. "What now?" said Bob.

"That'll be the marker I'm calling in," said Jane. "I got it." Off she went.

"Marker?" Amber asked.

Bob said, "That M.D. from Chamomile Coven. Jon Something."

"Hammill," said Sebastian. "Good guy."

Which was heartening. So Bob followed Jane to the front door, and heard more than he meant to before he turned the corner into the marble foyer.

"How's that going?" a man's voice asked.

Jane said, "We found a rehab place that doesn't use the Twelve Steps, but they don't have an opening until April, practically Beltane, and they're way the hell out in western Pennsylvania. Nils says he'll go, since they don't insist on monotheism as a basis for treatment, but now it's like his own personal Mardi Gras before Lent. He's calling it that. Lent. Like he has no intention of going clean for good. Like, come Midsummer festival, he'll be raising the horn to toast Thor with all the other Norse practitioners. As if Thane Kindred hadn't kicked him out for disrespecting the rites. Like nothing ever happened. And my parents are no help. Serves me right, they say, a nice Jewish girl like me taking up Witchcraft and marrying a Viking wannabe. And they're not totally wrong. What did I think would happen? A woman who marries her old college drinking buddy has no business being surprised if he doesn't stop drinking." Her voice shook.

"Be kind to yourself," said the doctor.

Bob leaned around the corner. "Knock knock."

"Who's there?" Jane said without looking up.

"Interrupting cows."

"Interrupting cows wh—"

"Moo," said Bob. It was good to see Jane laugh. "Susan brought that one home from school. She never gets bored with it."

"Bob, this is Jonathan Hammill. Jon, Bob Baines."

They shook hands. Bob said, "Didn't we meet at festival last year?"

"At the first aid station?" Jon guessed. "Your kid had poison ivy."

"Not one of mine. He was from the next campsite over. My kids are all Methodists. Did Jane fill you in on our little Theosophy problem?"

"Ascended Masters. Now *that's* old school."

"Also maybe hashish."

"Show me to the lady."

When they reached the library door, Sophie stood and brushed an ant off her skirt.

"Oh," said Jon. Everything about him brightened. "I didn't realize you were with Rugosa Coven."

"Have we met?" said Sophie.

His face fell. "Last Midsummer, at festival. At the fire circle."

"Oh, it's you! I didn't recognize you with your clothes on." She glanced at the black bag he carried. "You're a doctor?"

Jane handled the proper, if belated, introductions, and Bob retreated to the kitchen. He tried to avoid having opinions about his sister's love life. Sophie was forever botching it with good men and hanging on too long with unsuitable ones. Advice was unwelcome, which was just as well, since it never did any good. It looked like she'd just botched things definitively with Jon Hammill, so that told Bob to think well of the man.

Before he reached the kitchen, the scent of some earthy essential oil hit him. It was pleasant enough in the dining room, but the kitchen was painfully thick with it. Ria, Amber, and Sebastian had broken out sponges from the econo-pak of five hundred, and were frantically scrubbing down the counters from a bottle labeled *Red Thyme Oil*. Florebo appeared to have fled the room entirely. "What the hell?" Bob said, opening all the windows.

Amber said, "Do you know you have an ant problem?"

"Yeah, we noticed."

"It's such a beautiful old house," she went on. "An actual Richard Morris Hunt should not be permitted to fall to ruin like this. It's a fucking national treasure."

Ruin. Bob's childhood home, where six generations of Baineses had lived, where three generations' ashes were scattered in the garden, and it was sliding into ruin. He hadn't let himself think about it that far, but Amber was right. One bad winter with a bad roof, one nest of carpenter ants (if they were carpenter ants), one spark in the paper-drowned library from the ancient cotton-wrapped electrical wiring, and it would all be over.

Sophie and Jane came into the kitchen, half-whispering to one another. "I'm sure he is," said Sophie, "but the whole point of a festival fling is that it *stays at festival.*"

"I'm just saying, after the way things went with your last serious thing…"

"Wasn't my last serious thing bad enough, without our having to talk about it again?" Sophie grimaced. "What's with the thyme oil?"

Ria said, "Its banishing qualities aren't limited to the ethereal plane. Do you see any ants in this room?"

"I don't see any dragons, either," said Jane. "Impressive all-purpose repellent. Where can I get me a bottle of that stuff?"

"Enough, already," said Bob. His cell phone bleeped, and he remembered what he'd set the alarm for. The planets were nearly in alignment. "Can we get started now?"

Their makeshift procession passed Florebo and Kiyoshi, who were conferring in hushed tones on the back porch. Bob paused to catch them up about the doctor, and Florebo rushed into the library.

Sophie pointed to the yew and said, "Thataway."

Sebastian, who was used to being a spectacle in towns like Rumson, what with his tattoos and piercings, looked around and said, "What are the neighbors going to think?"

"Trust me," said Bob, "we're not the freakiest sight the neighbors have seen on this side of the fence. Mom and Dad used to do workings in the zodiac garden. In full robes and regalia."

They set out across the grounds—Bob carrying the sword unsheathed and Sophie hoisting the much-improved broom over her shoulder. Behind them came Ria with her censer swinging, Sebastian with the bowl of rosewater, Amber trying to keep the candle lantern lit, and Jane, her little black backpack bulging with salt canisters. The coveners dodged rose briars as the sun dipped low, on their way to the yew tree at the northernmost corner of the property. It was a tight fit for six under the dome of branches, and dark until Amber ducked in with her lantern to cast shadows up against the needles.

Bob hadn't even known he wished for this—to bring his coven to the first true temple of his heart. Everything was in readiness. The rainworn terra cotta god and goddess figures seemed to radiate approval. He opened his mouth to speak.

So of course, that was the moment his cell phone went off.

A tinnily digitized version of Peter Gabriel's "In Your Eyes" chorused through the spring evening—his wife's designated ring. "I have to take it before I turn it off," he apologized.

But all his covenmates were scrounging through their pockets to turn off their cell phones, too.

He rested the sword on its tip, its hilt in a wye of the yew, and flipped his phone open. "Hi, honey."

"Dinner's ready. Where are you?"

"Um."

"You forgot."

"Something came up. I am so…"

"It's okay," she said, though he could hear that it wasn't quite. "I just heated up Jane's casserole. Next time you see her, you thank her for me. It smells great."

"I sure will."

"There's dill and caraway in it, and mushrooms, and I think those are buckwheat groats. Good comfort food. I could keep it warm for you."

Bob's mouth watered. He tried to remember the last time he'd eaten. Donuts. Dammit. "I can't. Kiss the kids for me?"

So she did, with loud Bugs Bunny lipsqueaking kisses that made the twins giggle and Susan say, "Mom! Quit it!" Ricki giggled, too.

He could picture them so clearly, all running around the kitchen. "I miss you."

"I miss you, too. The sooner you do what you have to do, the sooner things can go back to normal," she said. "Get on with it and come home."

So Bob powered down the phone and took up the sword. "Hey, Jane. Two thumbs up on the casserole."

She pulled one of the salt canisters from the little black backpack. "There's another in the car. Don't let me forget. Sophie, are you still covered?"

"Full fridge, full freezer. There's just the one of me. Are we gonna do this thing, or what?"

Rugosa's six coveners breathed three slow, silent breaths together. Bob reached into the memory of power that drifted like a permanent fog about his childhood home. It had a temperament shaped by decades of ceremonial magic and hunger for transcendence, but Bob knew it well. He would put it to work, one way or another, to serve what really mattered to him: tribe and territory.

Standing with the sword raised in salute, Bob said, "Spirits of Earth, Guardians of the Watchtowers of the North, I do summon and stir you and call upon your presence, that our Circle be guarded and our rites be witnessed." Sebastian raised his eyebrows in surprise at that—Rugosa Coven's usual ritual style was loose, improvisational, decidedly vernacular, but no one interrupted. Bob went on in the high formal style, enticing the spirit of the place to join him in his purpose.

They walked in procession around the property line, Sophie in the lead, sweeping everything unwelcome out. A step behind her, Bob drew a line in the earth with the tip of the sword. Their covenmates reinforced the line, marking it with earth, air, fire, and water. They all paused at the cardinal points, to call on the Guardians of the other three Watchtowers. The house's façade had a good southern exposure, and the family across the street came out to watch Bob stand on the sidewalk and call the Spirits of Fire. He had to fight the old cringe then, but at least if he was the designated weird neighbor now, it was his own chosen weirdness people were staring at.

Full circle, back at the yew, Sophie called on the Mother of All and the Horned One to join them, and the spirit of the place rippled and buckled in response. Bob soothed it, cajoled it, and stood back while Sophie named the intent.

"We are here," she said, "to banish whatever demands the hoard. Whatever requires the needless things, whatever fosters decay through excess. It may once have been welcome here, but it is not welcome anymore. Whatever drove my parents mad and killed them, whether they invited it or not, we come here to drive that out."

They began their chant with wordless tones, layered tentatively at first, then solidly interlocking, until the coven became one voice together. It was a brash voice they became, defiant, and Bob heard his own grief rise from them all. He filled the spirit of the place with their chant, gave it his instructions to hold the line and keep the wards at the quarters.

By the light of the candle lantern, Rugosa Coven traced their steps back around the line widdershins, to disentangle themselves from the working, and left it in place.

"Anybody hungry?" Sophie asked.

It hit Bob like a blow. "I forgot we forgot to eat."

"Only one thing for it," said Sebastian.

They were all in agreement: "Diner run!"

A distinct electric hum filled the house. In the dining room, Kiyoshi was setting up an air filter. He said, "We found four of these. It's as if your parents knew I was coming."

"Where did you find them?" asked Bob.

"Behind the pallet of ramen noodles."

"Of course. Ramen noodles. Why didn't I think to look there?" Bob looked the empty cardboard boxes over. "Asthma-grade HEPA filters. What next?" He ventured into the library, where Florebo and Pasca were talking old times and Jon Hammill was repacking his black bag. "Diner run?" Bob proposed.

At the Colonial Diner, it took two booths to seat their party. Bob maneuvered to split them so he ended up with Florebo,

Kiyoshi, and the doctor. Sophie caught on to the game, and steered Pasca to join the rest of the coven in the other booth. Theirs was the table of raucous laughter, Bob's the table of hushed gravity. Once the waitress had taken their orders, he turned to Jon and said, "What can you tell me?"

Jon said, "She seems to be in decent condition, for a sixty-eight-year-old recreational drug user. She was so forthright about it, I'm inclined to believe her when she says she only uses the hashish, and that only about once a month. Still, I've given her a prescription for some lab work—liver enzymes, that kind of thing. I doubt she'll have it done unless you press her to. If there are ever results to read, I'll be happy to read them. She's a cool lady."

"And her mental condition?"

"A doctor with a more mundane background might say she suffered delusions or dementia, but really, she's no further out there than my Christian patients who anticipate the rapture in their lifetimes."

Florebo said, "Forgive me if I don't find that a comforting benchmark."

"I'm just saying, she's handling her mortality within her own context, like lots of people do with their religions. If all I had to go on were the history I took and the observations I made, assuming the numbers come back good from the lab, the hoarding behavior would be the only really alarming thing. It's unsanitary, it creates tripping hazards, and she can't afford a hip fracture, but hoarding is nothing unusual with older people. That's my medical opinion, and if I knew nothing about the wider circumstances, that would be my only opinion."

"But..." Bob prompted him.

Jon lowered his voice. "The fact that she's the fourth in her coven..."

Florebo interrupted him. "In her lodge."

"The fourth in her lodge to develop the same hoarding behaviors out of the blue, independently of the other three cases, well, that's pretty damn disturbing, given how the other three ended up. I don't really know what to do with that. In a strictly non-medical capacity, I'd recommend a daily regimen of copal incense to clear the mind, indefinitely, possibly a daily regimen of milk thistle tea for a week if her liver enzymes are unhappy, and a set of wards around her house to keep out unwanted influences. She shouldn't be alone so much. In isolation, people's sense of what constitutes normal behavior can drift. You guys cast good wards, by the way. The whole feel of the house shifted while you were out in the yard."

Over at the other table, Pasca and Sophie were teaching the rest of Rugosa Coven a bawdy song about Madame Blavatsky. Bob smiled and said, "We do our best."

Florebo said, "Kiyoshi and I have a guest room. We could take her on for a few days."

"Thank goodness," said Bob. "Ricki would not be thrilled about exposing our kids to..." A long list came to mind. "Well, the casual talk about opiates, for starters."

The waitress arrived. "Greek salad," she said, and Jon raised his hand. "Eggplant parmigiana, split onto two plates," which she set in front of Florebo and Kiyoshi. "Peppercorn burger, cheese fries, and a side of green beans." There was barely room in front of Bob for all of it. "Are you sure that's enough food for you, sir?"

"It's been a long day," he said, "but that ought to do it."

When she was gone, Kiyoshi said, "We're not bringing Pasca back to our place. Not tonight."

"We're not?" said Florebo.

"Richard, you're the last one left who's not completely around the bend or dead. I mean to celebrate my hundredth birthday with you. There has to be something we can do for Betsy without..."

Florebo said, "It's not contagious."

"We don't know that."

"Even if it were, I know how to live in the company of contagion."

Kiyoshi buttered a dinner roll. "Do you believe in wards?"

"Robert and Sophronia had excellent training from an early age. They're enviable, really, whatever use they've put their talents to."

"Yes or no, love. Do you think they'll keep whatever it is out?"

"Yes."

Kiyoshi said to Bob, "Do you mind if we stay at the old place tonight?"

Bob said, "You can't breathe there."

"We left the filters running. They're big filters."

"There's not a bed cleared off anywhere."

"There are cushions in the temple room. There's the floor. I don't care. In the morning, we'll figure out something else."

Florebo said, "There's no need."

Bob handed Kiyoshi a copy of the key. "In the interest of domestic tranquility," he said. "Whatever you work out is fine with me."

"Thank you," said Kiyoshi.

"You'll sneeze your head right off," said Florebo.

"Worse things have happened."

At the other table, they'd worked the bawdy song into three-part harmony. Bob was glad to hear Jane and Ria laughing together. It happened too seldom these days.

When the last of the cheese fries was consumed and the waitress was tipped in accordance with the din, Bob came over to see Pasca. "I have a favor to ask you."

"Anything, dear."

"Would you stay at the old place with Florebo and Kiyoshi tonight?"

She brightened. "Are you expecting supernatural disturbances?"

He didn't mention that he was sending her to the one place where supernatural disturbances would be least likely. "I don't know what to expect, but I'd take it as a great personal favor."

"Kiyoshi will sneeze his poor head off, filters or no filters."

"I know it's a great deal to ask."

Pasca took his hand. "You can rely on me."

Bob dearly hoped so.

After a protracted round of farewell hugs and a casserole hand-off in the parking lot, Bob finally headed home. Half past ten found him pulling up his own driveway. He shambled into the house, his clothes dust-smudged and speckled with diner grease.

"So," said Ricki as she wandered in from the bedroom, tying the sash on her bathrobe, "did you find the will?"

"What? Oh. Yeah."

"What's the gist? Did they tell you what kind of funeral they wanted?"

"Didn't read it yet."

"I can nuke you up some casserole."

"There were cheese fries."

"I can see that." She stood behind him and kissed the top of his head. "I could take that shirt off you, if you like."

"Laundry?"

"Or whatever."

"I'm sorry."

"What happened?"

"The kind of thing you'd rather I didn't tell you about."

"The kids are in bed."

He had missed them again. "What if my parents' séances actually put them in touch with someone or something?"

She sat across the table from him. "Do you think they did?"

"Mom and Dad thought so."

"Nothing new there."

The minute he told her, she would be creeped out. "Remember my Uncle Ciebo?"

"I remember a bunch of them from the wedding. Was he the one who came to the twins' christening? The gay one?"

"That's Florebo. He says hi, by the way."

"You saw him today, then."

"We went to pay a call on Pasca."

"The crossword puzzle lady."

"Yep." Bob was running out of ways to stall for time.

"I liked her. We should have them over to dinner, if we can get a sitter for the kids. So, spit it out. What happened?"

Bob told her everything—the temple room, the Ouija board, Pasca's insistence on her impending ascension, the wards, all of it. And then Bob braced himself for the I-told-you-so. He was about due to be reminded why Ricki thought his spiritual life was something their children weren't ready to hear about. If she was really pissed off, she'd go into her spiel about how she should never have agreed to let the kids spend Solstices with Bob's parents.

But instead, she said, "Could you put some of those up around our place?"

He blinked at her. "Wards?"

"If you did them discreetly, it would be okay with me."

Time to tell her. "I've been putting up a fresh set every new moon since Susan was born."

"I guess you've got discretion down pat, then."

"I try not to make it your problem."

"It's not a problem."

He didn't answer.

"Not all of it, anyway."

Was this any night to fight it out? He really didn't want to call her on it.

She reached up to take the cookie jar from its perch atop the refrigerator and sat down with two chocolate walnut cookies.

"Can I have one?" he asked her.

"Get your own."

He did. "Ricki, I'm afraid."

"If *you're* scared, what am I supposed to think?"

"You can be scared, too, if you want."

"Do you think the wards work?"

"They're a prayer. If prayers work, they work."

"Okay," said Ricki. "Solomon says, 'Behold, heaven and the heaven of heavens cannot contain thee; how much less this house which I have built.' If Solomon couldn't squeeze the divine into a box, I sure can't. Why not wards?"

"It's a weird universe."

She took his hand. "Weird new universe that has such people in it."

"What do *you* think my parents wanted?"

"A normal life."

Bob looked at her. "These are my parents we're talking about. Remember them? The big name occultists?"

"Think about it. The unmet need is the one that motivates. They had abundance. They had each other. They had two wonderful children and three wonderful grandchildren. They had the house that's been in your family for over a century, and a garden to toil in. They had a circle of trusted friends who believed the same things they did. What *didn't* they have? Normalcy. They sure as heck didn't have that. I can't think of anything else they lacked."

"You're overgeneralizing. I'm the one who wanted a normal life, and I'm sorry I'm not quite cut out for one. But I think they wanted to live forever."

"Nobody gets that, not in the body."

"It's an unmet need. Plenty of people have found it motivating."

Ricki thought about it. "But that still doesn't explain all the *stuff*. Charles and Amelia were eccentric, not stupid. And looking for immortality at a big-box retail chain—that's just dumb."

"Will you read the will with me?"

"Shouldn't Sophie be around for that?"

"She was with me when I found it. I think she'll be relieved not to have to wrestle with it too much." He smoothed the pages flat and flipped through them to the beginning. There were several yellow Post-it Notes stuck to the heavily annotated pages. Funny, Bob only remembered the one sticky about Larry's advice.

One of them stuck to Bob's hand. *There are more things in heaven and on earth than are dreamt of in your philosophy, Bob.*

His first thought was to be offended—in his philosophy, he dreamed of quite a lot. His second thought was to wish his philosophy dreamed of a little less. He did not want to entertain the notion that his parents were pulling the classic Ascended Master parlor trick of manifesting documents out of nowhere.

Ricki pulled her chair up to read over his shoulder, and they parsed the will bit by bit. She came to the handwritten addendum demanding that Charles and Amelia's heirs and assigns burn the mansion down. "Burn it down?!" she said. "They can't have been serious."

"I think they were, but it won't hold up in court." That much about wills, trusts, and estates, Bob still remembered from law school. "Doctrine of waste—common law assumes that stuff is meant to be used. Even if arson were permissible, we couldn't be compelled to destroy the house, as long as it could still be made habitable."

She squinted to read the older version through the amendments. "This will was no prize peach, even before they went crazy. Were they *trying* to pit you and Sophie against each other?"

"It's plain ugly," he agreed, and picked up the phone to call his sister. The ringing started on her line before he glanced at the microwave's clock. Half past midnight. Oops.

Sophie picked up. "Steve, I told you to stop calling. I'm done being your other woman, you lying sack of shit."

"Hi, Sophie."

"Oh. Hi, Bob."

"Sorry to call so late. Can you meet me at my office tomorrow?"

"Oh, right. The will. Yeah. Ten o'clock okay?"

"Ten's great. Good night, Sophie."

"G'night."

Ricki was still scowling at the will. "How could they have been so unfair to her?"

"We are never going to do this to our kids," said Bob.

"Never," Ricki agreed, and they sealed their pact by shaking pinky fingers on it. "How do you suppose we'll split the mansion with her? I don't see Sophie wanting to live there."

"She won't. Once we get the court to agree that she's entitled to a half share to buy out, will or no will, we can buy out her half. Or sell it altogether and split the proceeds."

"You're not selling that house. You'd never forgive yourself. It's your ancestral home."

"Forced to choose between my ancestors and my sister, you know how I'd pick."

"Of course, but would you *want* to live there?"

He thought of the yew tree, thought of the spirit of the place sprawling foggily through the rose bushes, remembered playing hide and seek with Sophie in the secret passages. "But *you* wouldn't want to live there. And, forced to choose between my ancestors and my wife…"

"I'm not making you choose."

"Not tonight, but eventually you would. What if the house is haunted?"

"*You're* haunted, Bob. And if you give up the house where your grandparents' and great-grandparents' ashes are scattered, the house will haunt you even worse."

"Could you really be happy in Rumson, with all those frivolous Manolo Blahnik-wearing women for neighbors? They're exactly nothing like you, and thank goodness you're exactly nothing like them. Besides, doesn't your scripture have some kind of parable about rich men and the eyes of needles? I seem to recall there was a camel involved."

"Look," she said, "week after week, I go to work, and I help the sick get their Medicaid benefits. I help the hungry get their food stamps. I set released convicts up with job training. I shake the system until Caesar renders back. It's as close to the Gospels as I know how to live, and I plan to do it every workday for the rest of my life, until I'm too old and decrepit to haul myself in anymore. Meanwhile, I think God will forgive me if I raise my children in the house of their forefathers. The Old Guy's sentimental about birthrights." She looked at the will and sighed. "It's almost like your parents understood about the camel and the eye of the needle. The amendment where you're supposed to empty the safe deposit box to put the stock certificates on the funeral pyre just blows my mind."

"Can't fault them on thoroughness," said Bob. "This is where my Aunt Pasca's headed. There has to be something I can do for her before she's this far gone. But what? Ask her to move in with us? You wouldn't be any happier with that than I would, or she would."

"You want me to wear my social worker hat for a minute?"

"Yeah."

"Okay. Here's my best guess. Unless you think her situation is so dire it would be better for her to get busted for drug possession than for her to be out on her own recognizance, there's probably nothing the law's going to do for you until she degenerates further. She may be exactly sane enough to refuse all interventions, even if she's not sane enough to get by on her own. A lot of people fall through that particular crack. And without the social worker hat?"

"Yeah?"

"You guessed right, I don't want her living with us. As long as the boys still occasionally surprise us by sticking inappropriate things in their mouths, I don't want any non-child-safe long-term houseguests. Anything else you can think of to do for her, I'm with you for it, but I'm not gambling the kids on her. Four may not be too young for getting angry at God, but it's definitely too young for hashish."

They were both too tired to go on. Ricki stowed the cookie jar back on top of the fridge. Bob had just enough time to get through his ablutions and kiss her good night before he fell into an exhausted slumber.

In the morning, Bob threw together an odd blend of his old routine and his new—he made everyone breakfast, saw Susan to the bus, and drove the boys to day care, as he'd done since he went on leave, but then he got to go back and put on a suit. It was the first time all week he'd worn one, and it felt like a homecoming. In the mirror, he looked almost like his usual self, except for the pallor and the pinched weariness around the eyes.

Twenty minutes of winding roads among horse farms carried him to the county seat, where the streets around the courthouse were chockablock with legal offices. Bob tucked his SUV into his own reserved spot and took a deep breath before he ventured in.

The front door of his office suite bore the firm's logo etched in glass: *Hardenburg, Voorhees, Frelinghuysen, and Baines, Attorneys at Law*. The last names of four dubious scions of old money circled a stylized pair of justice's scales. Bob was the only one of the partners who had to live down his family name rather than coast on it, but the three law school buddies he'd gone into practice with were decent guys. They greeted him with condolences and hailed the return of the rainmaker. The receptionist greeted him with a stack of messages, one of which was from Marc at the practice next door, who assured Bob that ten o'clock would be fine for a bit of consultation about the will. Bob found Penny Marinatos, his young associate, sitting in his chair, at his desk, hyperventilating over the five cases he'd had to drop on her when he got the call about his parents. Poor Penny had cut her teeth on personal injury law as a solo ambulance chaser, and now the thought of taking on a multinational corporation as the lead plaintiff's counsel was doing a number on her blood pressure. Bob spent a while with Penny and his stalwart legal secretary on the Hendrickson case until Sophie arrived.

Sophie showed up in jeans and a t-shirt, wearing a pair of hammer-and-sickle bangly earrings and her usual Birkenstocks. Bob hugged her in greeting and said, "Aren't you laying it on a little thick?"

"What?"

"Nothing. Come on." They walked down the hall to the photocopier so Bob could run off copies of the will. He had to do it one page at a time, so the Post-its wouldn't get stuck in the document feeder. "Here," he said when the first copy was complete. "You'll need this."

"Oh, man." She glanced at the pages. "This is going to take forever."

"Or it might be just fucked up enough to be really simple." He went on hoping so as they crossed the building's lobby to the next suite over, where the friendly neighborhood wills-trusts-and-estates guy had his practice. "Marc," said Bob, "this is my sister Sophie Baines. Sophie, Marc Levy."

Marc shook her hand and gazed incredulously at her Soviet earrings. "Do come in," he said, gesturing to his open office door. While Bob and Sophie settled into chairs, Marc skimmed the will. "Wow," he said at first. And then he came across something that cracked him up. "Sorry, sorry," he said, but it was Marc's habit to be unguarded with his colleagues. By the third page, he could no longer contain his laughter.

"It's quite all right," said Bob. He wished he could laugh at it, too.

Sophie read the will for the first time. Although she kept quiet, her eyebrows kept shooting up in surprise, until finally they just stuck there.

The last page, with its detailed instructions on how to conduct the house-burning ritual, defeated Marc altogether, and he had to dig in his desk drawers for a Kleenex before he could pull himself together to say, "The good news is, once we file our motion in probate court, we can get the amended version thrown out in about two seconds flat. You won't even have to show up for that part."

Bob said, "And the bad news?"

"The courthouse gossip about your family won't be pretty, and this is not the kind of thing people forget. It's not the kind of thing we can contain, either." Bob was used to that, so he moved on with his checklist of questions. Marc had trouble believing there really weren't any remaining blood relatives, but it was true. The late Baineses had both been only children of only children. That left just the departeds' friends in any position to contest the will. Marc scribbled notes.

"Florebo and Pasca?" Marc said. "You guys really *are* the Addams Family."

"Those are, ah, nicknames, sort of," said Bob. "Richard Smith and Elizabeth, um, Adams. No, really. That's with one D. I'm not worried they'll contest the will. Besides, anything they ask for, we're inclined to just give them."

Sophie agreed. "They're what's left of the family, blood kin or not. These past hundred years, we've been too busy communing with the dead to be real interested in propagating our kind. Sick, sad, true."

Just to be on the safe side, they arranged for boilerplate notices to be placed in all the usual Theosophical bulletins. "And now," said Marc, "we wait for our turn in probate court. If you can be satisfied with the original version, we can do the whole thing in motions, you'll never even have to appear in person. If you want to petition the judge to throw out both versions for a fifty-fifty split, we may have to do an evidentiary hearing. Sophie might want to wear a suit for that. Meanwhile, Bob, you're safe playing executor, since you're the one they named for the job both times. Just don't do anything stupid. I'll let you know as soon as we have a court date."

Later, over lunch at Back to the Garden, Sophie said, "I won't wear a suit for them." She poked listlessly at the baked stuffed tofu she had ordered.

"I didn't ask you to wear a suit."

"But you think I should."

"Maybe not today, but when we go to probate court…"

"What, so the judge will think I'm worthy of half of old Rodolph's folly?"

"You have a right to it."

"I don't want it, Bob. I never wanted it. I told Mom and Dad I didn't want it, and if they were only going to listen to me once in their lives, they picked the right thing to hear. It wasn't just the last year that they lived as prisoners of their stuff. All their lives.

It was the first thing I really understood about them, and I don't want to live like that, ever. Keep the house. Sell the house. Burn the house. It's yours to burn. Just don't ask me to live there."

"They left you the beach cottage."

"Downright thoughtful of them. I loved that beach cottage, but if I have to wear a suit to get it, I'll pass."

"You don't have to *own* a suit. Amber would lend you one." Amber had lots of pant suits with long sleeves, for covering her tattoos when she met with stuffy design clients.

"I'd have to wear panty hose. Nothing on this earth is worth a day in panty hose."

Bob took a tentative sip of his wheatgrass smoothie and resolved that, next time, it would be his turn to pick the restaurant. "You're just in a snit."

"It's the biggest snit you'll ever see."

"Nah, Jane and Ria have a bigger one."

"Okay, it's the biggest non-collaborative snit you'll ever see."

"Well, now it's a collaborative one. You're being shortsighted, and your shoes are excessively stereotypical."

"Oh, yeah? Well, you're a meddler, and you don't need an SUV, not even for hauling three kids. Nobody needs an SUV. SUV's are the root of all evil."

"Yeah, some nature-worshipper I am." And since the war had started, he'd had nothing but regret about that damn SUV. "Have you heard from Florebo?"

"No. You?"

"Nope. Give me a minute to swing by the office, and I'll meet you at the old place."

Bob thought he'd just be giving Penny some parting advice on the Hendrickson case—and really, he envied her, because there were few things he enjoyed more than suing Big Pharma. He could have used a good fight right about now, and that defendant could be counted on to put up a big one. But Penny handed him a wad of Post-it Notes and said, "Somebody left you a bunch of messages about the cremation arrangements for your parents. And the hospital called while you were at lunch. The guy was downright snippy, asking how much longer you intend to leave your parents in cold storage, and when you're going to get around to having them picked up. I told him he'd probably hear from a crematory sometime soon. I hope that was all right."

He stared at the top Post-it in the wad. And then pried it up to look at the second, and then the third. It was a veritable serial manifesto about the spiritual benefits of cremation, all in his father's handwriting. "That was just fine, Penny. Could I have the office to myself for a minute? I need to make some calls." At least now there was no question about his parents' wishes. He wasn't about to burn the house down for them, but he could meet them halfway. His father's posthumous manifesto, alas, still indicated a preference for arson. Bob didn't have any particular idea how to choose a crematory, so he phoned Jane up at work.

"H&R Block, Jane Hirsch-Sigurdson."

"Hey, Jane."

"Are you okay?"

He considered telling her about his father's manifesto, but couldn't cope with the impossible *and* Jane's disdain for the impossible at the same time. "Do you have any Pagan-friendly funeral directors in that magic address book of yours?" He could hear her flipping pages.

She lowered her voice, and he was chagrined to remember that she was still in the broom closet at work. "Well, there's a Druid-owned funeral home in Cherry Hill, but a four-hour round trip drive seems excessive. There's an Anubis devotee who hasn't made partner yet at a funeral home in Matawan. That's all I got. The Anubis guy doesn't owe me any favors yet, but he will if I send him your business." She rattled off the name, address, and phone number.

"I'll say you sent me. You sound awful. Are *you* all right?"

"The usual."

"We'll get Nils to that clinic if we have to truss him up in a burlap sack to do it."

"I know." There was a long, awkward silence on the line. He wondered what she wasn't saying. "I have to get back to work."

"Thanks, Jane."

"Back at you." She hung up.

Bob jammed the manifesto into his pocket and hurried to Rumson.

While he drove, he practiced about a dozen different ways to tell Florebo about the Post-its. That was going to be weird enough. He dreaded the possibility he might have to discuss it with Pasca.

She was the one he saw first when he pulled the SUV to the far end of the driveway. Pasca knelt in the garden, pulling weeds, while Ria wrestled a rosebush. The air was filled with a warm, sweet scent, as of burning pine. Granules of copal resin melted in a little incense burner someone had set on the sundial.

"The garden was Dad's empire," Bob said. "I never got good enough at it to be allowed to cut anything. What should I be doing with these roses? They like food or something, right?"

Ria brandished her wicked pair of shears and cut the shoots back by several feet. "Ashes, blood meal, bone meal, hair. They're creepy little bastards. I love them in other people's gardens, but I wouldn't grow them, myself." She peeled off one of the gloves to find a spot where a thorn had pierced it, and she sucked the drop of blood from her fingertip. "I try to avoid cultivating plants that are better armed than I am. Go on in. We've got a surprise for you."

The kitchen was clean. He and Sophie had tidied it, had made it and the downstairs bathroom more or less workable as the first order of business, but now the kitchen was Clean with a big glowing capital C. Although the dining room was still dominated by piles of bulk goods, the paths between the piles had been vacuumed. The library door was closed, and someone had stuck a Post-it on it that said *NO ENTRADA*. The mess in the living room was all compressed into neat stacks. There was not a speck of dust in the place. Bob followed the sound of vacuuming up the stairs, where he found Florebo supervising a team of four Central American women in matching t-shirts silkscreened with a logo that read *Maria's Magnificent Maids*. Bob was inclined to agree that these maids were, indeed, magnificent. There were more Post-its upstairs—*NO ENTRADA* to the temple room, *NO ENTRADA* to the master bedroom, but everything else was open and bright, including the door to the servants' stairs, which were entirely clear. So much for concealing the dirty laundry. "Florebo, you didn't have to do this."

"What's that?" said Florebo. "Can't hear you over the vacuum."

"Thank you," Bob said.

Florebo smiled ruefully. "No need."

They retreated to the temple room for quiet. "How's Pasca?"

"I was able to get her talking. Her interpretation of *The Secret Doctrine* is, let us say, unorthodox. I see now how she went astray."

"How?"

"That doesn't really bear speaking of. No, Robert, trust me about this. Surely you understand what it is to be oathbound."

"We're eclectic witches," said Bob. "We don't do the whole oathbound thing. That's for, well, snobby high episcopagans."

Florebo laughed. "And we Theosophists are the snobs your snobs used to wish they could be. I see. Nonetheless, some things are best respected with silence, and I can't very well win back enough of Pasca's trust to do her any good if I start by breaking her personal confidences. She'll be staying with Kiyoshi and me for a while. If the strip malls of New Jersey are too much temptation for her, we'll just take her to our place in the Catskills for a little detoxification."

"You make it sound so easy."

"It won't be. And that's all right, too."

"Sophie left ahead of me. Did she get here?"

"Oh, she's prowling around the secret passages. I'm sure you can find a flashlight downstairs."

So Bob did, and then picked his way across the paper mess and ant habitat of the library to the tricky bookshelf by the fireplace, which he shouldered open. The beam of his flashlight bounced off a tangle of spiderwebs, beyond which the first hidden room was pitch black. "Hello?"

"Coming!" said Sophie's voice from high above him. "Hang on." He could hear her steps creaking the beams upstairs—the secret passages weren't really very useful for sneaking—and then an abrasive sound he couldn't quite identify. "A new broom sweeps clean," Sophie said. "The spider population is kind of intimidating."

"Fewer ants," Bob pointed out.

"I was starting to get used to the ants." It sounded like she was trying to sweep the ladder steps below her as she climbed down.

"Are you sure that's a good idea?" Bob asked.

"I'll be fine. Ew! Dammit."

"What?"

"I think we may have pigeons nesting in the attic."

Bob dug out the premoistened antiseptic hand wipes and had one open and ready for her when the bristles of the broom came into view through the mass of webs. Trailing strands stuck to her hair, her shirt, everywhere. They spent a few wordless minutes under the ants' surveillance, cleaning her up, before they picked up their flashlights and ventured back in.

It was nothing like his childhood memory of the place. There had been space for everything back here, and now it seemed so cramped and dingy. When Bob was ten and Sophie six, they'd been given permission to play in the secret passages, provided they kept them tidy. It was their only chore, and one that couldn't very well be delegated to the cleaning lady. Here, they'd hidden the things their parents didn't want them stooping to—Sophie's collection of Barbie dolls and, later, romance novels; the boy scout manual Bob bought with his allowance when his parents didn't let him join the local troop; a Walkman with two sets of headphones and a large collection of Top 40 albums on cassette, whose lyrics the Baines siblings had puzzled over through their teens as if in dire need of a Rosetta stone. Later, they'd tried to figure out the steps to the dances all the other kids at school seemed to just *know*. The Achy Breaky. The Electric Slide. Baffling. Taking up Witchcraft had been a major step toward the mainstream for them, and it was as close to the fads of their youth as they'd ever credibly been able to come. The trouble was, they were sincere about the Craft. Nobody had told them they were supposed to be dabblers. Maybe if they'd thought to bring a television back here, they could have accomplished the originally intended transformation and turned out as dull as the neighbors.

None of their old things were in evidence. Instead, there were large, flat parcels wrapped in brown paper. There were wooden crates nailed shut. There were barrister's bookcases, and once Sophie had swept the spiderwebs off the glass doors, Bob opened them to find a large collection of books, some of them obviously rare and precious, and several of those in duplicate copies. Up the ladder and into the room behind the temple, they swept back to the walls and found more of the same. Sophie ripped the brown paper off one of the flat parcels—there were several layers of thick brown paper—to reveal an oil painting in an ornate gilt frame. "I've seen this before," she said.

"What is it?"

"How would I know? I flunked Art History at three colleges."

"What about the other two colleges?"

"Didn't take Art History when Mom and Dad bought my way into Princeton, and by the time they stooped to buying off Rutgers, I just wanted to wait tables. This painting was definitely on the exam at Wellesley, though. I'll never forget it."

"But you just said you forgot it."

"I'll never forget looking up at the projection screen, seeing the black and white slide of this painting, and knowing I was about to flunk. Again. It's kind of pretty, though, isn't it?"

"Yeah, I guess so. We should call Amber. Maybe she remembers stuff from her internship at Sotheby's."

"We could just ask Florebo."

"Maybe not," said Bob. "I asked him straight out about Pasca..."

"He wouldn't tell you, either? Well, at least *he's* fair minded."

Bob knew why she was stung. "The will really sucks. We don't have to abide by it."

"Whatever."

"There's something you need to see." He took the cremation manifesto out of his pocket. "I think Mom and Dad aren't done telling us about their wishes. Penny found these stuck around my office."

"You rate a manifesto," she said when she'd finished reading. "I just get that Talking Heads song on my car radio again and again, interrupting everything. Mom and Dad have no respect for NPR."

"'Burning Down the House?'"

"That would be the song, yes. Maybe I should be glad they stooped to consider my pop culture influences, but really, they made me read *Isis Unveiled* just as many times as they made you. They might have bothered to send *me* a manifesto, too."

Bob had just about forgotten *Isis Unveiled*. Oh, the things his parents had thought were good reading for children. "Anyhow, I guess we have them cremated. Jane knows a guy to call."

"She always does. You wanna take that one, while I call Amber?"

"Yeah." He looked around at the web-wisped gloom, wishing he could make his call somewhere cleaner. Discretion. Dammit. He pulled his cell phone out of his pocket and dialed the number Jane had given him.

"Parr and Sons Funeral Home." The woman on the line sounded distracted.

"Hi, could I talk to Phil Carson?"

"Hold, please."

Meanwhile, Sophie's conversation with Amber seemed to be going all right. "Urgent? Probably not. We'll have to go to court to get the will sorted out. You'll never believe…"

"Phil Carson speaking," said the cheery voice in Bob's ear. "What can I do for you?"

"Jane Hirsch-Sigurdson suggested you might be the man to call."

"Ah," said Phil. "You'll be needing something unconventional, then?"

"We need a cremation for two Theosophists. I'm afraid the hospital's itching to get rid of my parents." Bob couldn't really blame the morgue people. He'd put them off for a week.

"I'm sorry for your loss," said Phil, the good cheer in his voice undimmed. "The hospital guys are big bluffers. Set the date you need, and they'll work with it. We don't have refrigeration on site, so unless you want embalming before the cremation…"

"That doesn't seem very earth-friendly," said Bob.

"Too true. If you're not planning a viewing, you don't need embalming. I don't know much about Theosophy, but I've never yet been asked to accommodate a ritual need we couldn't work with. We get all the weird ones here at Parr and Sons. It's a point of pride. Anyhow, we can't store your parents for long before the cremation itself, so we'll need to schedule transport accordingly. You just work out a time with the secretary, and let me know what you need in the way of artifacts, music, processions. Are you expecting a crowd?"

"No," said Bob. "My parents knew a lot of people, but I don't think many of them will show up."

"You can also do a larger memorial service later. That's the beauty of cremation."

"The beauty of cremation," said Bob. Well, that was what right livelihood sounded like, he supposed. It was a good thing *somebody* loved being a funeral director. They talked price ranges and casket styles, and Bob made an appointment to finish up the arrangements.

"Sophie, are you free tomorrow?"

"I'm always free. And yes, I can go tomorrow."

"What did Amber say?"

"She's got a lot of work to catch up on for her current clients, and we're asking her for something really time-consuming. Next week she's between deadlines. If we can get internet access set up, she says she can figure out at least some of what we've got." Sophie took up the broom again. "I want to get the place in order before she comes."

"Remind me to put internet access on the to-do list."

"So, are we going to tell Florebo anything?"

Bob leaned on the ladder and tried to think. "Sophie, it's worse than the dirty laundry. Something about this is just *wrong*. If he and Pasca know what it is, are they going to tell us? And if they don't know already, maybe we can spare Mom and Dad a little embarrassment. I'm starting to think our parents were terrible friends."

"Do you really think we'll do better at finding out on our own?"

"Maybe. And we can always ask later."

Sophie scrunched her eyebrows together. "Unless anything bad happens to Florebo and Pasca."

That was a big unless, all things considered. They left the discussion hanging there, and when they'd swept up until they could sweep no more, and they'd wiped the pigeon droppings from the wooden ladder rungs, they nudged open the statuary niche in the temple room that was the passages' upper door, and stumbled into the cleanliness to clean themselves up. Maria's Magnificent Maids had worked wonders. Bob and Sophie's childhood bedrooms were thoroughly excavated, and two of the air filters hummed contentedly on the landing.

The Baines siblings broke out a plastic-wrapped set of new towels from the cairn of brand-new linens in the dining room and took turns in the shower that the Maids had just rendered spotless. While Bob waited his turn, he added *Bring spare set clean clothes to house* to his to-do list. He wasn't looking forward to explaining the condition of his suit to his dry cleaner, and he really didn't like having to put it back on after what he'd just put it through.

Despite Florebo's best translation attempts, Bob found it difficult to explain to the Magnificent Maids that he wished to offer them their pick of the bulk goods as a thank-you gift.

Florebo apologized. "The Spanish of Cervantes and St. John of the Cross is not always the most useful Spanish to speak."

"More tip," said Sophie, who had done a lot of waitressing since the last college she dropped out of. She pointed at the dining room, pointed at the Maids, and said, "*Mas tip, gracias.*" That did the trick nicely. They drove off with a van-full of paper towels and ramen noodles, and only accepted one of the six microwave ovens because Bob carried it out to the van himself and insisted.

He spent the rest of the afternoon in the garden with Sophie and his parents' friends, planning the cremation ceremony. Ria took off once she saw there would be raised voices.

Pasca said, "Florebo, you know they need more than a simple cremation."

"Cremation and a traditional ceremony will be quite enough. If it was good enough for Sinnett and Olcott, and for Blavatsky herself, it's good enough for Charles and Amelia." There was no moving Florebo. "We can give them something they'll like, and send them on their way. Amelia always liked Berlioz's requiem, and in his youth, I recall, Charles had a soft spot for the *Bhagavad-Gita.*"

"In his youth," said Pasca. "What about the fruition of his life's work?"

"We are not discussing that."

Bob said, "But you could."

Florebo and Pasca didn't look anyone in the eye, not even each other.

"I like Berlioz," Sophie put in. She'd never been good at long silences.

"Pasca," said Bob, "if you can't tell us *why* a standard Theosophical funeral isn't good enough, Sophie and I may have to side with Florebo about this."

Pasca considered the house and sighed. "It's not for me to reveal this to you. They'll see that it's taken care of, or not. I have my own responsibilities." In the end, she agreed to a traditional rite, asking only that the readings be from *The Voice of the Silence* rather than the *Gita*.

That was half a page of the to-do list checked off, right there.

Bob got home just in time to miss dinner. The twins, Aidan and Brian, ran over to hug him, and got covered with scraps of spiderweb for their trouble.

"What on earth did you do to your suit?" Ricki asked. "You look like you just shambled out of a zombie movie."

"The house is clean-ish."

"Go change. I'll nuke you up some casserole, and you can watch that thing."

"Thing?"

"Go change."

When he got back to the living room, Susan and the boys had been banished to the back yard to run around and let off some steam, and Ricki was fussing with the TiVo remote control. "Got the beginning for you." She scrolled back to the opening of a History Channel documentary about funerary customs through history, part five of seven. Jade grave goods from Korea, chariots from what were probably the graves of the kings of Tara, dramatic reenactments of Viking funerals, ships loaded with everything a warrior could need on the other side. All grave goods, all the time. Bob watched, speechless, until the second commercial break, when he paused the episode.

"Ricki, why am I watching this?"

She leaned her head out of the kitchen, where she was washing dishes. "It was important enough for you to leave me a note about it, but not important enough for you to remember you asked me to record it? Look, I'm picking up a lot of your slack right now, and I don't grudge it, but this is just inconsiderate."

"I left you a note?"

Exasperated, she plucked a Post-it from the fridge and held it out for him. He came over to see it. His father's handwriting was much like Bob's own, but with little barbed recurves on the letters V and S.

Bob took a deep breath. "Do you remember the story of how Blavatsky got busted as a fraud?"

Ricki scrubbed impatiently at the buckwheat groat residue on the bottom of Jane's casserole dish. "Forged letters manifesting in thin air. She wrote them herself."

"I'm wondering if some of them might not have been real."

"Oh, Non-Sequitur Man, thank goodness you've come!"

"I didn't leave you this note, Ricki."

She put the casserole dish down in the sink and looked Bob steadily in the eye. Sighed. "When was the last time you had a good night's sleep?"

"Tuesday. No, I was losing sleep over the Hendrickson case. Sunday before last."

"No wonder you're forgetting things."

"Is this my handwriting?"

She reexamined the note. "Isn't it?"

"Look here. The V in TiVo."

"You've been tired lately."

"Honey, I'm trying to be straight-up with you. No secrets."

"Be straight-up with me when you've had some rest. If, when you wake up, you still want to tell me your parents' ghosts have become big television watchers, and figured out how TiVo works, and have astral access to *TV Guide*, and care enough to ask for any particular show, let alone that cheesy documentary series, then I'll be all ears. I love you. Go to bed."

"It's only seven o'clock." He sounded like Susan, whining for more lights-on time.

"Have it your way." She went back to scrubbing.

Bob got ready for bed. In the bathroom, a Post-it Note was already stuck to the mirror, waiting for him. *You know what we need from you,* said his father's handwriting.

"Grave goods," said Bob. "That's it, isn't it? Our house was your pyramid, and you wanted to take it all with you."

Why do you think we needed the dog brush? said his mother's note, this time affixed to the towel rack. *Goldie's coat hadn't been properly groomed in twenty years.*

That took him aback. "Goldie's there?"

Another note stuck itself to the last one. *Waiting for us, just like we told you she would be when you were a boy. And Mitten the Kitten, too.*

"So." He tried to put aside, for a moment, the thought of his childhood dog. He couldn't help how his heart gladdened. Sophie would want to know about her cat. "Back to the taking-it-all-with-you thing. You can do that?"

Maybe, said Charles Baines's handwriting, on a sticky printed with a repeating motif of kittens with balls of yarn. *That depends on where you're trying to go.*

Bob called back to mind the books his parents had given him to read when he was young. There were so many places to go. "Devachan, Nirvana, Shambala. I thought you had to travel light to get anywhere good."

More kittens with balls of yarn. *That is the orthodox interpretation, yes.*

"And the unorthodox one?"

No answer. Maybe they'd already given it to him, in the notes from his office. If it involved burning down the old manse, he had no patience for it. Bob left the stickies stuck to the various bathroom fixtures for Ricki to find, and went to bed. He was almost as tired as she'd told him he was.

He must have fallen asleep, because now he was waking up. Ricki was waking him. "Wha...?" he mumbled.

"You weren't kidding."

"It would be a stupid thing to kid about."

"What do we do?"

"We hold a funeral, and then they go away." At least, he hoped they'd go away.

"Should I be afraid?"

"Dunno. I'm too tired to be afraid."

"Lucky you."

He rolled over and settled around her, tablespoon to teaspoon, and went right back to sleep.

It wasn't until the next morning, after he'd already seen Ricki off to work and got the kids where they needed to go, that he realized he hadn't told her about his parents' continuing demands for arson. He wasn't about to call her at work to tell her, so he got on with business.

At the Parr and Sons Funeral Home, he and Sophie set the cremation date for Saturday afternoon and chose the nicest of the appropriate caskets.

"There are those," said Phil Carson, "who fill the caskets with objects of significance to the departed. We had a funeral here last week for a Witch—Gardnerian or Alexandrian branch I think—whose coven piled in her Book of Shadows and ritual regalia to go to the fire with her. Which makes sense for your more secretive types. Myself, I hope to reach Anubis with a heart light as a feather. I still don't understand how the ancients reconciled that with bringing along so much stuff."

"Ask my parents, once you've got them," said Bob. "They seem to have opinions on the subject."

Phil made sure they had all the arrangements in writing and gave Bob an itemized receipt. "So you can reimburse yourself from the estate."

Bob didn't want to think about the estate. Later that afternoon, he got word from Marc Levy that they had a date for an evidentiary hearing in probate court the Monday after the funeral.

"That's fast," said Bob into the headset of his cell phone as he drove the SUV down Route 4.

"It's the probate office's little way of saying thanks for the entertainment."

"Great. Just great." His dates for probate court and the funeral meant he still wouldn't be able to see the Hendrickson case through all its phases, but there was plenty he could do to help Penny carry the load.

For the next couple of days, Bob buried himself in work. Initially, he took the time to read the various notes his parents interrupted him with, but mostly they just pestered him to burn down their house, so he gave up on them. Once he recognized the handwriting, the notes went straight into the shredder. "Don't bother me at the office," he told his parents. "I'm busy."

On Saturday, he donned his black suit, and a moment later his lapels were festooned with notes. *It's not too late,* said his mother's graceful cursive. *Once you've disposed of our forms, you can still put the urns in the house when you burn it. That would be entirely acceptable.*

"To you," said Bob. He stripped the stickies off his clothes and went to help his children dress. They'd never been to a funeral before.

Ricki did the driving while Bob stared numbly out the window. He couldn't say he missed his parents, since they wouldn't leave him alone. A person ought to miss his parents, he thought. Today, there was nothing in the place where his grief should have been. What would his children think? What would they tell their therapists, twenty years down the line? *My dad was cold and irritable when his parents died. Cold and irritable, just like they were.* Bob was four years old in his own earliest memory. He hoped his sons wouldn't have a funeral for their firsts.

It was a small ceremony. Despite the pains Bob had taken to post announcements on all the Theosophical online forums he could find, the only attendees were himself and his sister, his wife and kids, his in-laws, his coven, his parents' surviving lodgemates, and Kiyoshi, who had graciously handled all the arrangements for the repast to follow the ceremony. Florebo spoke beautifully of the rhythm of the Great Law, of the cycles of being and non-being, of fulfillment and recompense in the eventual attainment of Nirvana. Pasca read a rather opaque passage from *The Voice of the Silence*. As the caskets slid into the furnace, Florebo said, "Immortal Self found is mortal self lost. Let us now commit their bodies to the swift, clean consumption of fire. So be it." The whole time, Bob kept waiting for his parents to misbehave, to stick a note on someone, to jump up like Tom

Sawyer and declare themselves. Nothing. Maybe they had enough fire now to be satisfied.

The repast was in Florebo and Kiyoshi's apartment in Red Bank. They had the whole tenth floor of their building, with a lovely view of the Navesink River through their windows and plenty of wall space for a collection of large Robert Mapplethorpe prints—photos of flowers so particular and peculiar, Bob thought of them as portraits.

The food was elegant, the mood subdued. Finally Bob had time to say more than *So glad you could be here* to his in-laws. His wife's parents and sister were huddled by the cheese tray, their heads tilted a little to the side to read Mapplethorpe's signature on a portrait of a tulip with ruffly, striated petals.

"Maybe we should be going now," said Ricki's mother.

"Yes," said Ricki's father. "Don't we have a thing to go to?"

"Definitely, that thing," said Ricki's sister. A little apologetically, she added, "It was a lovely ceremony."

Bob said, "Thank you. It means a great deal to me that you were there." He hadn't realized it until the words came out of his mouth. Alas, it meant a thing or two, too, that they were ill at ease with Florebo and Kiyoshi's hospitality. The three Jennets made their farewells only to Ricki and the kids, and then they were off. Off to their thing. Yeah, right.

Once they were gone, Bob saw all at once his dear ones as the Jennets must surely see them. Any one piece of the puzzle might have been all right, but together they were really *out there*—the brace of gay uncles, Ria's crystals, Jane grumbling that her hung-over husband had skipped the ceremony but shown up for the free food, Nils himself in dark glasses and a faint aura of yesterday's bourbon, Sophie in her black cotton sundress with, almost certainly, nothing on underneath. And Amber and Sebastian. Those two, all in themselves, were enough to scare off the Jennets.

Though it was a chill early April day, Amber wore a slinky black dress with spaghetti straps, because the new layer of work on her tattoo was too raw to tolerate being covered. It did look like wisteria now—wisteria coiling up her skin in a profusion of purple flower, under a thin sheen of Neosporin. The school of bright fish racing through their reef on Amber's right arm, the ruby-throated hummingbirds turning aerial capers on her back, and the red Celtic knotwork complete with zoomorphic salamanders that unrolled across her clavicles—all were harmonious with the new piece in ways that they hadn't been with the fading Chinese characters that the wisteria covered. And she was right, Sebastian was twice the artist Big Mike was.

Sebastian was inked all the way up his neck and, in solidarity with Amber, he wore the most conspicuous ornaments he owned in his various visible piercings. His modifications went surprisingly well with his suit, the tie carefully chosen to coordinate with the tribal motif that showed above his shirt collar. Rather than taming him, the suit only made him look broader of beam than he already was. To a stranger, he might have been terrifying.

Not terrifying, apparently, to Bob's children. Brian pointed at Sebastian and said, "With a ring in the end of his nose, his nose, his nose."

"Sorry," said Bob. "'The Owl and the Pussycat' is their favorite bedtime story."

Sebastian got down on one knee to be on eye-level with the boys and recited the whole nonsense poem for them in that voice of his. He could make parking regulations sound consolatory, he could make the lyrics to the Hokey Pokey compelling—Bob had heard him do it. The romantic travails of the owl and the pussycat attained epic scope. And Sebastian was a very good sport when little Aidan gave the gold ring a tug. *There in the wood, a piggy-wig stood, with a ring in the end of his nose.*

There was, for now, nothing Bob needed to hold together, no pleasantry he owed. For a moment to himself as much as for anything else, he headed to the bathroom. Occupied. So he ducked into the guest room to use the one in there, and found, all over Pasca's things, Post-it Notes with dire exhortations. *DO NOT*, said a note on the bureau. Do not what? *DEFY*, said the note on the face of the alarm clock. *HIM*, concluded the note on the closet door.

Bob's heart pounded. He wondered for a moment whether this command was meant for him, but once he thought to look for them, he saw a ball of yellow stickies in Pasca's borrowed waste basket. He uncrumpled and unstuck them, to find a long one-sided correspondence ordering Pasca to do something, whatever it was, that she no longer wanted to do. Bob's father's handwriting warned of a retribution he would not be able to prevent, and his mother's reminded Pasca of a reward, an offer that had never been revoked. There were quite a few wadded-up Kleenexes in the wastebasket, too. Jamming the notes into his pocket, Bob headed back into the gathering and cornered Pasca by the strawberries. "Is there anything you'd like to tell me?"

"Of course, dear. I'd like to tell you how bravely you're bearing up. Your parents should be very proud of you."

"But they're not. You know as well as I do that they're not." He pulled out the fistful of notes. "What are they playing at?"

"Oh. Ha. Um. Florebo, do come have a look at this!"

"Who are they telling you not to defy?" Bob had to struggle to keep his voice lowered.

She took a swig of wine. "No one you need to worry yourself about."

Florebo made his way across the room. The man knew how to project nonchalance. "Nothing better than strawberry season, is there?"

So Bob laid out the most alarming of the sticky notes along the edge of the sideboard. *DO NOT DEFY HIM*. "This would be an excellent time for an explanation."

"We have everything under control," said Florebo.

"Oh, that clears it right up, then."

Pasca said, "No need for sarcasm, dear."

Bob really wished there were something he could hit. "Do not defy who?"

"Whom," said Pasca.

How much more of this was he going to be able to take? Bob forced himself to look at his children. He would not, would not lose his temper in front of his children.

"Robert, we are making progress here," said Florebo in hushed tones. "The estate sale will clear it right up, you'll see. Once the goods are gone, once you make a show of disposing of them, he'll leave us all alone. He'll have to look for an easier target. That's been his modus operandi for centuries. It must be, or he'd have found a way to get what he wants long before now."

"Who?" Bob demanded again.

"Don't take his name into your mind," Pasca warned. "Don't give him more of a handle on you than he already has."

"All right then, what? What is he? Some rough beast, shopping toward Shambala to be born?"

"Just a dead man," said Florebo. "An uncommonly persuasive, persistent dead man."

"At least," Pasca added, "that's our working hypothesis."

Florebo plucked the stickies from the sideboard, crumpled them in his hand. "And if he's just a man, he's nothing we can't handle."

Bob's cell phone burst into song with the chorus of "Penny Lane"—that would be his associate at the practice calling him. Bob tapped the volume button to dump the call into voicemail. Penny could offer him another round of condolences some other time. "Handle *how* exactly?"

But the cell phone rose up singing again. Bob turned the ringer entirely off.

"Our methods aren't so different from yours," said Florebo.

The muted cell phone vibrated frantically in Bob's jacket pocket.

"Go ahead," said Florebo. "If they've called three times, it must be important." He and Pasca saw their chance to extricate themselves, and they took it.

Bob picked up. "Penny, you'd better be calling to tell me somebody's dead or in the hospital. I'm not even home from the funeral yet."

"Remember how opposing counsel on the Hendrickson case kept dragging their heels on the discovery phase?"

"Yeah." It was feast or famine with those guys. Either they were papering Bob to death, or they were sitting on documents they were legally obligated to send him.

"They sent everything today. Fifty banker's boxes of documents, no labels, no index, just *stuff*, and our next court date is..."

"This is normal, Penny. All the big corporate plaintiffs count on bullshit games like this to wear us down. We take on the bullies, and this is what we get. Would you rather go back to chasing ambulances?"

She took a deep breath. "I've got all the legal secretaries sorting things. I've got Dr. Leung on her way in to translate the medicalese. Eric's cutting short his vacation to come in..."

"He is?" If Eric Hardenburg was coming in to cover for Bob, things might actually be dire.

"But the other partners are cramming for their own Monday court dates, and Eric doesn't know the Hendrickson case that well, so it's down to you."

"I don't suppose our motion for a continuance might still be granted?"

"Denied this morning, just like you said it would be."

"Shit." In one breath, he decided to gamble that Florebo was right. "I'll be there in half an hour."

It took Bob nearly that long just to say enough farewells to get out the door. Ricki was unable to conceal her annoyance at having to shepherd the kids through the rest of the day—this day, of all days—without his help. "I'll make it up to you," he said.

"I know you will."

"I will."

"You'd better."

No kiss.

Between worry about the nameless enemy and the sting of the kiss he hadn't had, Bob could barely keep his mind on the road, and only narrowly avoided driving the SUV into a tractor bumbling down the horse farm stretch of Route 520.

At the office, the receptionist's desk was piled high with banker's boxes. The legal secretaries circled around the table in the conference room, sorting and taking notes. Behind Bob's door, Penny and Eric hunched over Bob's desk, their brows furrowed about Bob's case. The back wall was stacked floor to ceiling with boxes of discovery documents. "I see my destiny," said Bob. "I'm fated to drown in paper."

"This is normal," said Penny. "Right?"

"Too normal, lately." Bob took off his suit jacket and rolled up his shirtsleeves. *I love my job*, he reminded himself. *Any minute now, I will love my job.* The photocopies were all dark and smudgy—more bullshit games. Nonetheless, after two hours Bob deciphered a page of handwritten clinical notes that told him just how early the defendant's researchers had noticed the side effect that had landed Geraldine Hendrickson in a wheelchair for life. Six months before she knew she was in trouble, they could have known, if they'd thought about what they saw. The free-floating rage he'd been swallowing for weeks finally had somewhere good to go. "Look at this." He handed the page off to Penny.

Her eyes widened as she read. "Does this mean what I think it means?"

"We are going to nail those sons of bitches to the wall."

And, presto change-o, he loved his job.

Loved it enough, he didn't get out of the office until after the kids' bedtimes. He had just enough time to swing by 7-11 to pick up some roses for his wife before the last convenience store in town closed for the night. The only roses left were kind of wilty, but it was what he could do.

Ricki hadn't left any lights on for him. He was almost afraid to turn them on, dreading more notes from his parents. No need. In the light, his living room looked exactly like his living room.

The refrigerator was clean of unwelcome messages. Bob pulled a vase down from the top of the fridge, cut the rose stems, and set the flowers up on the kitchen table for Ricki to find in the morning.

But, as he discovered when he crept into the bedroom in the dark, trying not to disturb her, she was still awake and sitting up in bed. "Tell me things will get better," she said.

"I'm doing what I can."

"Hm."

"Not all of it is in my hands."

"So, were you the valiant knight at work?"

"I have the strength of ten because my cause is just."

She laughed. Good.

"Things could get better right now," he proposed. "If you're not still mad at me."

"I guess I'd better snap out of it, then. No knowing when we'll have another chance."

Nine years they'd been married, but their long familiarity lost out to the awkwardness of the past few weeks. Before they even got Bob out of his shirt, they were laughing at themselves. Bob said, "You know, in many cultures, head-butting is an act of courtship."

"Get back here, you."

"Ow."

"I'm sorry."

Just when things were starting to go well enough that Bob expected at any moment to be interrupted by his cell phone or the mid-air manifestation of a Post-it Note, there was a tentative knock at the bedroom door. For just a moment, he let himself think that if he ignored the knock it would go away.

"Mom?" said Susan's voice from the other side of the door.

"Go to bed, honey," Ricki said.

"Mom, the boys are crying."

Bob said, "They'll go back to sleep."

"They're crying about Gramma and Grampa."

Ricki said, very quietly, "At least they waited till you got home. This one's yours."

"Um, I need a moment," said Bob.

"Oh. Of course." She chuckled. "Hold that thought. I'll get it."

It was just as well he didn't hold that thought, because within five minutes, all three kids were piled into bed with him. "I'm sorry," said Ricki. "There was nothing else for it." Aidan and Brian blared like sirens, and Susan only held herself together out of pride at being a big girl.

"This is what needed to happen," Bob said. It wasn't what he'd had in mind, but pretty soon he found his children's presence as comforting as they found his. After a few choruses about how there were five in the bed until the little one said *roll over, roll over*, Bob and Ricki arranged themselves as parentheses on either side of the mattress, with the three kids kicking in their sleep between them.

The next day's hearing in probate court was a minor disaster. True to her word, Sophie refused to wear a suit to the evidentiary hearing, showing up in jeans, a t-shirt that proclaimed *Primus Sucks*, and those same damned hammer-and-sickle earrings, and as Marc Levy had predicted, the judge upheld the original version of the will, with its lopsided division of the Baines estate.

When Bob and his sister finally got to lunch, he said, "I should have dressed down to match."

"Nobody would be taken in," Sophie said as she prodded her lentil loaf. They were at Back to the Garden again; Bob found he could refuse her nothing. "Everybody at the courthouse knows you. You could have shown up in a sarong, and the judge would still have upheld the old will."

Bob tried to picture himself saronged in the courtroom. "No, I think things would have gone differently."

"Don't beat yourself up about it. I get to live in the beach cottage. When you move into the old place, I'll only be a ten minute drive away from you. It's cool."

"I'm not sure I'm moving into the old place."

Sophie put her fork down. "What? Is Ricki giving you a hard time?"

"Ricki's been great. Better than I deserve. It's Mom and Dad who are driving me crazy. I'm not sure I want to move my children into a house whose ghosts are determined to burn the place down."

"Oh. Good point." Sophie crinkled her eyebrows. "They're still after you about that?"

"Yep. Maybe after the estate sale they'll give up."

She laughed so hard she snorted her wheatgrass smoothie and had to spend a minute mopping up with her napkin. "If they haven't given up yet, I wouldn't hold my breath."

Sophie went to spend the afternoon in Sea Bright opening up the cottage, and Bob headed to the manse to see how Amber was getting along. The temple room, which had been so sparsely furnished, was claustrophobic and dusty now, full of fine, delicate objects carefully separated into piles. Amber herself sat cross-legged at the little round table in the middle of the room, hunched over her laptop. "Your lame neighbors save the day," she said. "Their wireless network is wide open. Speedy, too. When all this is over, I'll have to set them up with some security as a thank-you."

Bob looked around at the piles she'd arranged. "What's the organizing principle?"

"That heap by the window is stuff too personal for you guys to part with, and if you and Sophie don't keep those things in the family, I'll have to talk some sense into you. This pile by the desk is stuff I'd like to buy from the estate after the appraiser's been through, if you and Sophie don't want it. Did you know you have a Goya engraving?"

"Nothing would surprise me."

Amber laughed. "You speak too soon. Anyhow. That shelf over there is full of stuff that's butt-ugly but that hard-core collectors with no aesthetic sensibility will pay big money for."

Bob picked up a porcelain figurine of a leering jester in purple and green motley. "Someone would pay money for this?"

"It's Royal Doulton. Several hundred dollars, probably. The appraiser will know for sure. The heap of stuff by the door is junk. And this..." She pressed the bronze Shiva to open the statue niche into the hidden room. "This is stuff you probably don't want the appraiser to see." Inside, it looked like the staging area for an incompletely mounted museum exhibit. "Everything along this wall disappeared from European museums onto the black market during World War II. The big figure in the back almost certainly got hacked off the temple complex at Angkor Wat. And that reward the Witchcraft Museum on the Isle of Man still has on offer for the return of the Black Head of Atho?"

"No. Tell me we don't have the Black Head of Atho."

She placed in his hands a horned oaken head, carved with great care for texture but none for representation. Inexpertly inlaid in the wood, tarnished silver limned the signs of the zodiac and several old sigils of invocation. The wood was warm to the touch. It was at once a human face and the face of a bull, caught in an expression of mild surprise. Whatever ardent intent had gone into its making more than balanced out its...ugliness was not quite the word, Bob thought. It was crudely made, but not crude.

"This, I found in your mother's shoe closet. She had a really impressive collection of Manolo Blahniks. Pity I wear a smaller shoe size, or I'd make you an offer for them."

"Mom, what were you thinking?" Bob asked the Black Head of Atho.

A yellow Post-it on the statue of Shiva said, *We were all of us young and foolish.*

Inside the secret room, Amber shrugged. "It was a black spiky thing, so she put it in a closet full of black spiky things?"

"We're giving it back," said Bob. "All of it."

"Of course you are," said Amber. "My old freshman-year roommate from Cooper Union does art detective stuff these days. She can see that it's handled as discreetly as you like. Should I call her?"

"Please. Discretion would be good. I really don't feel like talking to newspapers about my parents."

Amber picked up one of the framed canvases. It was a tiny portrait of a red-haired young man with a large nose and a poufy velvet hat. "What I can't figure out is how they fell from hoarding stolen art and occult treasures to hoarding toilet paper."

"I think they were stocking up for a long afterlife. You wouldn't want to run out of toilet paper only halfway to eternity." Bob clutched the Black Head of Atho—*like a teddy bear,* he thought, but he couldn't bring himself to put it down—and sat by the pile of personal relics Amber was bent on seeing him keep. He shifted them about with his left hand, just to see what they were. "How many autographed copies of *The Changing Light at Sandover* does a household of two really need?"

"If I had one, I'd never part with it," said Amber.

"Yes, but what if you had…six? They were hoarders the whole time, and I never noticed." An awful thought occurred to him. "What if all this stuff's stolen, too?"

"Nah," she said. "Most of the books are inscribed to members of your family, so at least some of it legitimately belongs to you. And the stuff that's not famously missing, well, who would you give it back to? No way to track it to whoever had it before. Give back what you can, and live a virtuous life to make up for the things you can't set right."

While Amber phoned her old roommate to arrange a meeting, Bob took a flashlight into the upper secret room and examined each of the items he'd be giving back, said hello to them and farewell. He was still at it when he heard Sophie come in through the kitchen door, so he clambered down the ladder and through the passage into the library to meet her.

Sophie stood at the kitchen sink, scrubbing her arms past the elbows. She was nicked up all over. "I was attacked by a rose bush," she explained. "It was acting in self-defense."

Bob looked out the kitchen door. Sitting on the porch, its roots balled up in burlap, was a very homely rugosa rose bush, its buds just forming, with a few of last year's withered rose hips still clinging to the canes. There was a trail of beach sand from

Sophie's car to the porch. "For the zodiac garden? It's kind of coals to Newcastle, isn't it?"

"You desperately need something unpretentious around here," said Sophie. "Something *real*. And something of the coven, so the name's a speck of sympathetic magic. The wild rugosa bushes are doing great in the cottage garden. They're just kerblamming out of the sand. I figured, I wouldn't miss one, and it might do you some good. Any cool finds today?"

It was time for Bob to break the news about the collection, but where to begin? "We have the Black Head of Atho."

She looked puzzled. "Should we see a dermatologist about that?"

"No, not the Blackhead of Atho. The Black Head of Atho!" He brandished it at his sister.

"Gah! Put that thing away!" said Sophie. "You'll poke someone's eye out." He set it on the kitchen counter, and she leaned over it for a closer look. "I've seen that before."

"In the shoe closet?"

"No. In an old book. Why would I see it in a shoe closet?"

"That's where Amber found it. Among Mom's Manolo Blahniks."

Sophie stared down at her Birkenstocks. "Do I look like I spend a lot of time digging through Mom's Manolo Blahniks? So, this Head. It went missing, like, in the 60's, right?"

"Yep."

"There's a bounty on it or something."

"A reward."

"We don't need the money. And it's not like the thing's pretty." She considered the horned head in silence a moment. "Besides, he should go home."

Bob said, "A lot of the other stuff's stolen, too."

A Post-it note materialized on the tip of Atho's nose. *I had my reasons*, said their father's handwriting.

"I don't care about your stupid old reasons," said Sophie. "You received stolen property, when it's not like you needed for anything."

"Or they stole it themselves." Bob didn't want to imagine it, but he could now. No sticky note answered him. He'd been a father long enough to know that silence for a confession.

Sophie leaned hard against the marble counter. "That would explain…"

"…The newspaper clippings about art thefts." Bob looked around the kitchen for an answering note. Found none. "Now we have something to ask Florebo and Pasca."

Sophie reconsidered Atho. "He kind of grows on you, doesn't he?"

"I like him."

The Baines siblings gathered up some gardening tools from the porch and found a sunny spot by the yew tree, where they planted the rugosa rose. They ducked into the dome of the tree to rest a moment, and Bob said, "Your Horned One looks kind of like him."

Sophie sat by her clay sculptures. "I guess he does. I wanted to do antlers at the time, but I didn't have the skill for it. Well, whoever made Atho didn't have a lot more skill to work with than I did, did he?

"And Atho's famous."

"Famous for being missing." She stood and yoga-stretched into the king dancer pose. "I should go. I've got a house to move into, a landlord to serve notice to, and a dozen shoreside seafood restaurants to scope out for waitressing gigs. Call me when the estate sale's scheduled?"

"You got it." It seemed only fair to Bob that he should do the logistical heavy lifting, since the judge had awarded him three quarters of his parents' worldly possessions. He hoped Florebo was right that the estate sale would clear up his little haunting problem. Somehow it felt safer to call the appraiser from the shelter of the yew than to make the call anywhere else. Leaning his back against one of the spreading trunks, Bob called the guy Amber recommended and made an appointment.

Even with all the stolen stuff hidden away in the secret passages on appraisal day, the appraiser saw plenty to make him whistle and exclaim. Bob followed him around while he scribbled in his little notebook and snapped pictures of everything in the house. "The Royal Doulton jester!" the appraiser said.

"Tacky," said Bob. "I don't know what they were thinking."

"The finest specimen of its kind," said the appraiser as he turned the figurine, looking for chips and cracks.

What Bob thought of its kind didn't bear saying aloud.

Nonetheless, he was glad to receive, the next day, the appraiser's fax. The more he knew a fair price for, the more of his parents' dubious purchases he could unload. A few internet searches on how to run an estate sale later, he started phoning around to press his friends into service and set a date.

That was enough to set off a whole new round of frantic correspondence from his parents. They sent him a two-foot by three-foot graph paper Post-it, stuck to the office fax machine when Bob stayed late to lock up, on which they reiterated their need for a good house-burning. "What are you so afraid of?" Bob demanded. "Who got a handle on you? Because one of these days I'm going to hunt him down and kick his ass."

His father's writing looped and hooked its way across another sheet of graph paper. *Why do you care so much about that? We were terrible parents.*

"You're the parents I had." Bob thought a moment. "And you did the best you could."

Amelia's note manifested on the cover of the Yellow Pages. *You don't have to soften the blow for us. Pasca and Florebo did better by you and Sophie than we ever did.*

Bob would have liked to disagree, but he couldn't. "Even so."

Just when he thought he was finally making progress in his relationship with his parents, they regrouped and sent him the same sentence over and over again every day until the day his friends gathered for a run-through of the estate sale: *If we matter to you, why won't you help us?*

It seemed to Bob that, if his covenmates were going to move furniture and ride herd over bargain hunters for him, it was the least he could do to tell them the truth about his parents' posthumous agenda. *Perfect love and perfect trust,* that was the Wiccan ideal, and as long as he kept secrets from his covenmates, he fell short of it.

And he tried to tell them, he really did.

On a Friday night, while Ricki stayed home yet again with the kids, Rugosa Coven gathered around the grand dining table in the old manse. The table wasn't entirely cleared off, but it was possible to hold a conversation over the clutter now. Not knowing what else to do with it, Bob had set the Black Head of Atho on top of the pile like a centerpiece. Amber came early to try to set up a wireless network to go with the house's new internet connection, and it wasn't going smoothly. She was still at it an hour later when the rest of the coven arrived and settled in.

Amber smirked and started humming along with the muzak on the customer service line. It was a much-softened version of Twisted Sister's "We're Not Gonna Take It."

"You're kidding," said Jane.

Amber said, "That's what they're playing." She hit the speakerphone button. A hundred and one violinists were not gonna take it anymore. Sebastian joined her in an inexpert Texas two-step.

Ria looked up from her ephemeris. "Why don't you just fix the router yourself?"

"Look, I don't get that deep into the machine. I just make the pretty pictures." A click stopped the music abruptly, and Amber had to duck out of the spin Sebastian had her in to pick up and conduct a hushed conversation with the customer service rep.

"So," said Jane. "What's the big secret?"

Bob didn't know where to start, so he just pointed to the head.

Jane groaned. "No. There's no such thing as the Black Head of Atho. There never was. It's a fake."

Amber covered the phone receiver with her hand and put in, "The Rembrandt's not a fake. Who would collect a real Rembrandt and a real Goya, but a fake Black Head of Atho?"

"Bob and Sophie's parents would, apparently," Jane said. "I wouldn't put anything past them anymore."

Sophie blinked. "We have a Rembrandt?"

"That would be one of the stolen ones, wouldn't it?" said Bob.

"It's just a tiny Rembrandt," Amber said. "It's hardly there at all." With that, she went back to the call. "Yes, I tried rebooting. Repeatedly."

"Stolen. Of course." Sophie started giggling and could not stop.

Sebastian considered the Head. "Ugly little spud, isn't he?"

"Why is it called the Black Head of Atho, anyway?" Jane asked.

Ria narrowed her eyes. "It's a head. It's Atho's. And it's black."

"But why make the color distinction in the name? What color were all his *other* heads? The Black Head of Atho is missing. Fine, we'll just use the Purple one then."

"Jane, you have no reverence to go with your mirth." Ria bowed slightly to the Head. "Show some respect."

"The Puce Head of Atho," said Jane.

Sophie was still giggling. "The Taupe Head of Atho."

Amber hung up the phone. "The Fuchsia Head of Atho."

"The Chartreuse Head of Atho," put in Sebastian.

Bob smiled. "The Plaid Head of Atho."

Even Ria laughed at that one, though she tried not to. "Jane, you bitch."

"What?" Jane patted the Head.

"We have the great good fortune of seeing a lost treasure of the Craft, we're the first of our faith to see it in half a century, fate entrusts us with its guardianship, and how do we greet it? With mockery. Is it any wonder the Craft of the Wise doesn't prosper? I know you think *I'm* ridiculous, and that's fine, but this is not okay. Why are you even here, Jane? I can't figure out why you're here." Ria ran, actually ran, to the back door and slammed it behind her.

"Ria," said Jane. "Ria, I'm sorry!" And she took off through the kitchen.

Bob goggled after them. "Was that an apology I heard?"

"Sounded like an apology to me," said Sebastian.

Amber said, "Burnt offerings are in order. Atho works miracles."

Although Bob hadn't told them nearly enough, he wanted so much for Jane and Ria to put their quarrels behind them, he held his tongue. If he asked Jane to believe in ghosts before that apology got delivered, there would be no reconciliation.

While skepticism and credulity reached their uneasy peace on the back porch, Florebo and Pasca came in the front door. Bob had hoped to separate his two orders of business, to have his coven backing him up when he demanded answers from his elders. He was so frustrated at the thwarting of his plans, he didn't even greet Florebo and Pasca before saying, "Would you like to explain this?"

The Black Head of Atho gazed in bemusement on the old Theosophists.

Pasca tittered nervously. Florebo went pale and said, "Oh, my." He thought a moment and added, "That's not all, is it?"

Sophie said, "There's a lot more in the secret passages."

"So that's where all those things went," said Florebo. "I never quite believed your parents' claim to have buried them."

"Oh, they were buried, all right," said Bob.

"No, in Egypt," Florebo replied. "Aio and Gaudea said they'd taken the whole trove out to Saqqara to make an offering of it. They said they'd buried it all in the sand."

Amber was outraged. "They were going to bury a *Rembrandt* in the sand?!"

"Where our otherworldly contact's tomb should have been," Pasca explained. "Except that he had no tomb. It's a terrible quandary for a dead Egyptian, you know. He lived as an ascetic, and he made a point of telling his children to leave him out for the vultures when he died. Only things didn't turn out quite the way he'd expected. He needed our help."

"He was a con artist," said Florebo. "I suspected, but did anyone listen to me? In three thousand years, a person can get very good at the art of the con." He was getting nowhere with Pasca, so he turned to Bob and said, "It was fun, at first. We thought we were so heroic, stealing a carnelian heart and a lapis eye so that a noble soul could be laid to rest. We were young, we were innocent. And we were only stealing from art thieves, anyway—that's what we told ourselves. But the gang of ex-Nazi museum robbers Menetnashté sent us to raid had more than just Egyptian artifacts. They had crates and crates of lost masterpieces and occult treasures, and we flattered ourselves that we'd see them returned to their rightful owners. Only Menetnashté wasn't satisfied with just the things he'd sent us to get. He wanted it all. That was when I knew he wasn't really an Ascended Master. If he really had ascended, he should already have been in Shambala with Koot Hoomi and old Helena Petrovna, disembodied and content. Why would he care about his own tomb, let alone other material possessions? When Charles and Amelia started collecting news clippings about museum heists, so we could track down the thieves and make off with their hauls before things got fenced, I knew we were in over our heads. Professional art thieves have *guns*. Lawrence was the only one of us who had any experience with weapons, and that in Vietnam. He couldn't abide the sight of a gun. It was not going to go well for us. So, when Lawrence wanted to pursue his radio investigations, I went along. It got us out of the theft business. Or at least, it got most of us out of the theft business. Perhaps Charles and Amelia continued." He turned to look accusingly at Pasca.

"They never said a word about it to me. Menetnashté never mentioned it, either. He just wanted the needful things for the house he was going to have on the far side of the river. It was going to be a large house, he said, and he meant to dwell in it forever, with all of us. He meant to keep it very clean. I suppose there's more than one way to be an ascetic. Well, he said there would be servants to keep it clean, and that sounded like a good deal to me."

Bob filed the name away in his mind and congratulated himself on startling them into mentioning it. Menetnashté. He'd find something to do with it. And then he remembered a stray detail from the grave goods documentary. "Did he say who these servants were going to be?"

"Oh, my." Florebo sank into a chair.

"What?" said Pasca. "Oh. Oh, I see." She looked down at her feet. "I've been an idiot for decades, haven't I?"

Bob brought her a box of tissues and gave her a hug. No wonder his parents were so demanding. It was bad enough to be dead and homesick, but for them, of all people, to be reduced to eternal servitude must be a sort of class anxiety hell. At least it seemed Pasca was pulled back from the brink.

She sniffled into the tissue. "Maybe I should go detox in the Catskills after all. This is so embarrassing. Can we get back to the task at hand?"

Sophie said, "I'll go see how Jane and Ria are doing."

"If I had to hazard a guess," said Florebo, "I would predict that you're not planning on selling off the Rembrandt tomorrow."

Amber laughed. "Step right up, ladies and gentlemen! Dutch Old Masters, priced by the pound!"

"No," said Bob. "We've made arrangements for their return." Shipping that headless Angkorian statue to Cambodia was going to cost him a pretty penny.

Sophie brought Jane and Ria back and said, "We're ready."

"All right," said Bob. "I've done a little homework on how estate sales are supposed to work. We should expect con artists and thieves. If they see that we're paying attention—especially that we're watching the doors and the cash box—the con artists and thieves will probably go looking for another estate sale to hit. So. Sebastian will hold the front door and look menacing. Amber will hold the back door and look menacing. Jane will handle the money. Ria, Sophie, Florebo, and Pasca will hold down one room each and answer any questions about the stuff. I'll float from room to room and try to look like I'm in charge." He handed out photocopies of the appraiser's report, and they walked together through the rooms he meant to open, moving the sale items into the living room, the dining room, and the guest room upstairs. They moved furniture, stuck price labels on things, popped batteries into the walkie-talkies they'd be using, and figured out how to keep the bargain hunters contained.

A good thing, too, because when Bob and his crew returned at seven the next morning, the vultures were lined up literally around the block. A pair of middle-aged women were on the brink of coming to blows over who would be first in line when the door opened. Fortunately, Amber and Sebastian had dressed to flaunt their tattoos, and their piercings were filled with spiky jewelry. Something about facing people who had no fear of pain quieted the crowd. The two of them stood at either side of the front door while Bob fussed with his keys, and the bargain hunters retreated a few steps. The coven and its hangers-on had a few minutes to eat donuts and take their places before Sebastian let the vultures in, twenty at a time, a new one in only when another went out.

Even with so few bodies in so much space, chaos broke loose. The marble entryway echoed shouts as the bargain hunters argued over who had seen which lamp first. An antique dealer tried to badger Bob into selling all the manse's light fixtures. Upstairs, Ria refused to haggle over the Manolo Blahniks. "If you want a lower price on those," she said, as she'd been instructed to, "you can come back in three hours and see if they're still here. If you want to know you have them, right now, the price is as marked. And, oh," she added, "in three hours, Saturn will be quincunx to Venus, and the Moon will be Void of Course after six o'clock. If I were you, I wouldn't wait." Perhaps out of sheer bafflement, the vintage clothing junkie agreed to buy the lot.

Over the course of the day, the estate sale crew caught six well-dressed teenagers pocketing jewelry, three old ladies sneakily peeling off Bob's price stickers and writing lower ones of their own, and a burly furniture dealer who tried to brazen his way through the front door with an end table balanced over his shoulder. Pasca had a good eye for trouble, and was quick to call for Bob on a walkie-talkie. Still, there was no knowing how much tomfoolery went undetected.

Jane sat with the cashbox at a card table in the marble entryway, with Sebastian bristling protectively just a few feet away. She held a long line of impatient shoppers in order mostly through the power of her withering scorn. That scorn was potent enough that, when Sebastian needed a quick bathroom break, they agreed over the walkie-talkies that she could hold the door herself.

Bad idea. The next voice Bob heard when his walkie-talkie piped up was the voice of Jane's husband.

"This is your captain speaking," said Nils. "Please restore your tray tables to an upright, locked position..."

In the background, Jane's crackly voice said, "Give it back, you sonofabitch."

"Motherfucker," said Bob, and he sprinted for the foyer. "Excuse me. Pardon me." Bargain hunters froze in place and gaped wide-eyed at him as he ran. Before he had a chance to think better of it, he jumped right over the pile of televisions and cleared them handily.

Nils was still playing it up for the radio. "American Top Forty, the hits from coast to coast," his voice sang from the walkie-talkie on Bob's belt. "This is Casey Kasem."

Sebastian came pounding down the servants' stairs and fell into step beside Bob. "What the hell is wrong with that boy?"

"That's it," said Bob. "I've had it with him."

"And now a song," said the walkie-talkie, "by four Dublin lads..."

One of the antique dealers waylaid Bob with a Royal Doulton figurine. The jester. "Excuse me," she said, "but I hope you can come down on the price. You know, I can find this piece on eBay for a hundred dollars less."

"So go to eBay, you vulture," said Bob, and he pushed past her.

Nils could be heard around the corner now, as well as over the radio, imitating Bono with horrifying gusto. Like most of the estate sale shoppers, he still hadn't found what he was looking for.

When Bob turned the corner into the marble foyer, he saw Jane struggling dizzily up from the floor, swearing like a Jersey girl at her husband.

"You pushed her, didn't you?" Bob said.

There were wads of twenty dollar bills sticking out of Nils's pockets. "No, I stiiiiill haven't fooooound what I'm looking fooooor!"

Bob and Sebastian each grabbed an arm and dragged Nils out onto the porch. Bob pushed him hard against a pillar and mashed his face into the marble while Sebastian emptied his pockets.

"Guys, chill out, it was a joke."

"Knocking Jane off her feet was funny, was it?" said Bob. It took all his will not to bash Nils's head on the pillar. "That makes everything all right, then. My bad."

"What's next?" Sebastian asked. "Knocking over 7-11's?"

Bob said, "I'm trying to think of a reason not to call the police."

"I wasn't going to keep the cash?"

"Wrong answer, Sigurdson. Try again."

"Um, I'm going into rehab tomorrow?"

"Damn straight you are," said Sebastian.

"And if I'm in jail the day I'm supposed to check in, I could lose my spot in the clinic?"

Bob yanked Nils away from the pillar and shoved him toward the porch stairs. "Get the hell out of here."

So Nils took off at a run. Bob and Sebastian stood at either side of the front door, watching, until Nils found his car halfway down the long block and pulled away, tires squealing.

In the foyer, they found Jane standing stiffly by the cashbox, accepting a handful of bills from a scruffy-looking old man. "Three hundred fifty," she confirmed in a flat voice. "Hey, guys. Sold the jester."

"You okay?" Bob asked.

"I don't want to talk about it. You've got twenty strangers prowling the house. Later."

Sebastian leaned on the doorframe. "I should never have left my post."

"Right," said Jane. "Catheters for everyone. This is *so* not your fault."

The next hour of the estate sale was straightforward and lucrative, until a desperate ant incursion from the library drove the last of the bargain hunters off. Bob patrolled the house to make sure there were no stragglers, and marveled at how much of the stuff had gone. With profound relief, he locked the front and back doors. He flipped back to the first page of his to-do list and wrote *Exterminate!* in the top margin. Surely now he could make finding a pest control solution for the ants his first priority, though he doubted even Jane could find him a Pagan exterminator.

Most of the estate sale crew was in the kitchen, sprawled on the displaced living room couches and chairs, sucking down bottled water and staring, stunned, into space. Jane double checked, then triple checked her tally of the cashbox.

"What's the take?" Bob asked.

"Twenty five thousand six hundred seventy two dollars and thirty three cents."

"Holy fuck," said Sophie. "I don't make that in a year."

Amber said, "I told you those butt-ugly collectibles would go for good money if we advertised right. And I think nearly all the bulk stuff went."

Ria looked at her watch. "Five seconds to Moon Void of Course. Four. Three. Two. One." She dropped her head back on the couch cushion. "Stick a fork in me. I'm done."

Void of Course or no Void of Course, Bob phoned in an order for Chinese food. When he got off the phone, he was the only one Florebo and Pasca hadn't said farewell to yet. When they came to say goodbye, he asked, "Are you two sure you don't want to stay for dinner?"

"It's a long drive," said Florebo. "It would be best if we didn't have to break our journey for the night in some unwarded place. Come see us off?" So Bob followed them out to the driveway in the darkening evening.

Pasca said, "Are you sure you'll be all right without us?"

"Absolutely certain. I'm just relieved that everything's settled and you're okay."

"Everything?" said Pasca. "Is *everything* settled? You've just sold off their grave goods and declared your intent to move into their erstwhile funeral pyre. My dear, everything is not nearly settled. We can stay if you need us."

Bob bent to kiss her on the cheek. "See you next weekend."

She sighed. "Be careful."

And with that, they were off to meet Kiyoshi in the Catskills. Bob watched them go, the last of his elders. He returned to the bosom of his coven, shocked at how alone he felt.

The food didn't help much, when it came. Bob wandered to the fridge for a beer, and just kept on wandering out the back door. He sat on the porch and looked up at the stars. The last of the old guard, gone out of reach, and so terribly mortal.

A few minutes later, Sebastian wandered out after him. "Mind if I borrow your sky?"

"Plenty to go around." They watched the moon rise.

"Some day, wasn't it?" said Sebastian.

"Tell me about it. The second time in my life I raise my hand against another human being, and it has to be now."

"You didn't do too bad. I've had to throw a few drunks out of the tattoo studio over the years, and it's always unpleasant. But sometimes there's no choice but to run somebody off."

"It doesn't bother me that we ran him off by force. What bothers me is that it doesn't bother me. I should have qualms about mashing somebody's face against a stone pillar. What kind of person am I if I don't? And why did he do it, anyway? He could have grabbed the money and gone, but he just stood there and baited us. Was he *trying* to call us out?" Bob took another long drink from the bottle.

"He thinks we're fucking his wife."

Bob sprayed his mouthful of beer all over the porch steps. "Jane?"

"Jane's the only wife he has."

"But she's practically our sister."

"I never claimed it made sense. Look, man, I didn't want to bother you with it when your parents had just died, but last week Nils showed up on my doorstep at three in the morning to tell me to leave his woman alone."

"What did you do?"

"I just stood back and let Amber give him a piece of her mind. She may have a magpie eye, but she's got some warrior soul in her."

"If he bothers Ricki and the kids…"

"Ricki's got a steel spine. I wouldn't worry."

"So does Jane, but look how that went. Why would he think it?"

Sebastian shrugged. "The man is an idiot junkie."

"A drunk, you mean."

"Did you see the size of his pupils? I don't know exactly what he *was* on, but it's not just the booze anymore."

"Oh, shit." But Bob didn't have to feel bad, then, about his one humble beer. "He's pushing her away with both hands. He's got no need to blame it on us."

"No," said Sebastian, "that's exactly why he needs to blame it on us. If he catches on that his wife's not cheating on him, he might have to admit to himself that he's an idiot junkie. He might have to change his ways. And that would be the end of the fucking world."

"Someday that man will put me in the position of having to do him a serious harm."

"If the day arrives, I'm going with you."

Bob wasn't sure how to take that. "You think I couldn't handle him?"

"No. I know the story about that football guy in high school. But let's hope the day doesn't come."

"I wasn't wrong about him, either."

"If Sophie was my sister, I'd probably have done the same. That's not my point."

But Bob never found out what the point was. Jane leaned her head out the back door and said, "Been wanting to thank you guys."

"No big deal," said Bob.

"Bullshit." Jane came out to sit on the steps beside him. "After tomorrow, thank the Gods, he'll be out of my hair for a few weeks, and I can be a person again. I don't know what I've been lately, but it doesn't feel…person-ish." She lit a cigarette. "If I could just get him on the way to recovery, I could walk away, but he'll drown without me, and I don't think I could go back to being alone."

"You wouldn't be alone for long," said Bob. "Any guy would be lucky to have you."

"Yeah, right. Because men love spending time with women who can't stop calling people on their bullshit."

"Any man would be lucky to have you because you love the truth too much to play head games, ever. You're funny. You're a devoted friend. And your address book holds the whole community together."

"It's just horse trading."

"You come to the rescue, and you make strangers into friends."

She leaned her head on his shoulder. "I annoy everyone."

"True, but you'll also help anyone. And you're pretty." The moment he said it, Bob knew he was in trouble. He actually hadn't noticed before. For seven years Rugosa Coven had been a going concern, and it had never once occurred to him. He'd been better off not noticing. Yes, any man would be lucky to have Jane.

"I smoke."

"Like a fiend," Bob agreed. Damn Nils. It might never have crossed Bob's mind to see Jane as anything but his coven sister if Nils hadn't, in effect, told him to. Her hair fell warm across his back. Fortunately, it smelled of cigarettes. Bob resolved to bring his wife flowers at the earliest possible opportunity.

"You know what I hate worse than anything else?" Jane said. "I can save people from being hounded by the IRS, I can save people from jail time for tax evasion, I save people from their own stupidity all the time. I can set things right to the tune of millions of dollars a day, if the right clients walk in the door. But I can't save the boy I married from the bottle, and I can't save myself from him."

"Maybe rehab will take this time," said Bob. And once Jane was out of her damsel-in-distress predicament, maybe the weight of her head on his shoulder would seem sisterly again.

"His body's going to rehab. If his heart's not in it, I might as well be sending him to Vegas."

"Everything will be all right," said Bob.

"So mote it be," Sebastian added.

Bob's cell phone rang. Peter Gabriel's tinnily digitized voice sang on and on about the love that completed him. Bob scrounged into his pocket and discovered another wad of twenty dollar bills he'd have to add into the tally. He threw the wad of bills and the keys to the manse down onto the porch and finally found his phone. "Hi, honey."

"Is it over?" Ricki asked.

"There's just a little mopping up to do from dinner."

Jane stood up and headed into the kitchen. Sebastian followed her.

Ricki said, "Susan sounded great at the children's choir rehearsal for Easter services. You should have heard her. What are the odds you'll have dinner at home sometime this week?"

"One hundred percent." Bob could hear his covenmates rattling around the kitchen, cleaning up.

"Bob, I know there's a lot left to do, but maybe it's time we stopped treating your parents' deaths like an emergency. No matter what we prioritize them over, they're not coming back."

He tried to put Pasca's warning out of his mind. "You're right. Of course."

"It would be a really good thing if you got home before the boys' bedtime. And that's all I'm going to say about that."

"See you soon."

"I'll see you when I see you." She hung up. Well, her patience had to have a breaking point sooner or later.

Bob stared blankly at the moonlit garden. Jane's eyes were very beautiful, a wild speckly hazel, now that he considered the matter. He wasn't going to think about Jane's eyes. But then, wouldn't it have been easier, wouldn't *everything* have been easier, if Bob had settled down with a nice Pagan girl? And what kind of parent was he, walling his kids off from what sustained him, what made his world make any sense at all? Susan's singing happened in Ricki's Methodist world, where Bob, as he really was, would never be entirely welcome.

So this was what Hell was like—Hell was desiring anyone other than his wife, Hell was imagining an existence without Ricki. As advertised, Hell was excruciating. Wouldn't it have been easier to live a life with no notion of Hell?

Easier? Now that was funny. Jane was many things, but easy to live with was obviously not one of them. Bob took a deep breath and ventured into the kitchen.

"All done," said Sophie as she dried her hands on a dishrag. "Go home."

Bob stayed to lock up the house, and then walked out to the yew tree. The moon cast sharp-edged shadows through the branches. He leaned on one of the winding trunks and said to his Gods, "In this lifetime, I've been blessed with three families. Now two of them are fraying at the edges, and the other's nearly gone. One bad day, and they could all fall apart." He listened for any kind of answer. The spring night was turning cold, and the breeze cut right through his shirt, but there was one thing left he had to make sure of.

He closed his eyes and checked the wards—still bright in his mind's eye—and greeted the spirit of the place. It nuzzled against his consciousness like a friendly dog. "Well, that's new," he said to it. "I should call you something. What did they call you?" No answer. "How about Fetch? It may be a different school, but it's still old school." Fetch sprawled comfortably out along the garden and reverted to its familiar form, a sense of suffusing fog. "Good Fetch," said Bob. "Keep watch." He left the old place in Fetch's care and drove home.

When he got there, Ricki said, "The kids are all yours. I need a break." And she headed straight out the door.

"Where are you going?" Bob called after her.

"Walk around the block," she said without looking back, and took off briskly.

Although he would have liked to patch things up with Ricki right away, she needed a break, and Gods knew she deserved one. Susan had the hiccups and was in a foul mood. Little Aidan and Brian couldn't be bothered to greet their father; they were locked into a tug-of-war over their plush stuffed Nemo fish, and before Bob could intervene, there were split seams, there was crying. "How about a story?" said Bob.

"Once upon a time," said Susan, "there lived a girl whose grandparents died. Only they kept sending her letters about pyramids and Kabbalah. Every day at school, she opened her notebook and found another letter. But all the dead grandparents really wanted was things things things, so she decided they were in Hell after all, trying to tempt her. The End."

Bob could barely breathe. "They're sending you letters?"

Susan burst into tears. Her hiccups continued unabated.

"Did you tell your mom?"

She shook her head no.

"Would you show me?"

While Susan dug through her backpack, Bob assured Aidan and Brian that Nemo could be fixed up, good as new. Susan handed him a bundle of letters thick enough to stress the pink elastic hairband she'd bound them in. Bob said, "Can you calm your brothers down while I read these?"

"I take care of them all the time now. I want a raise in my allowance, just for fairness."

"We'll take that up with your mother."

Susan upended a box of Duplo blocks on the living room floor with a great clatter and set about building a pyramid complex. Brian and Aidan quieted down and started sticking blocks together apparently at random, while Bob sat on the floor with them to read the letters.

Dearest Susan, said his mother's script, *Since your father is neglecting your education, your grandfather and I must take it upon ourselves to see to it that the family expertise is carried on.*

Oh, no. Ricki was going to be furious. Furious and terrified. "Did you read these letters?"

"Duh," said Susan. "You didn't really listen to my story, did you?"

He tried to find some upside, any upside. "Your grandparents loved you. They love you still. They would never do anything that they thought would hurt you." Whatever else was true, he thought that was. He remembered the first time his parents had seen Susan, the first time his mother had held her. "They always meant well."

She started sniffling again. "You're gonna go crazy like they did, and Aunt Sophie, too, and then we'll all be orphans, and what's Mom going to do when we're orphans?"

Bob decided this was not the best time to explain what the orphaned state actually entailed. "I'm an orphan," he said. It was the first time he'd thought it. He put an arm around his daughter. "Your Aunt Sophie and I are not going to go crazy."

Susan finished her pyramid. "Why don't you believe in Hell?"

Suddenly, Bob's self-pity of an hour before seemed trivial. "The universe is kind," he said. "Bad things happen in it, but I don't think it's a rigged game."

"You don't think God gets mad?"

"We do, so I don't see why the Gods couldn't. Still, I'm just not buying Hell."

"If Gramma and Grampa could have bought Hell at Wal-Mart, they would have."

Bob laughed. "Yeah, they probably would." He flipped through the letters. Mixed in with instructions on conducting séances in the table-rapping style, there were exhortations, some of them none too subtle, to burn down the ancestral home before Bob could finish selling off the grave goods. "Did they ever send you these letters when you were anywhere other than school?"

"No."

"You're sure?"

"Yeah."

Ricki's key turned in the latch. Susan looked at the letters, looked at her dad. Suddenly, Bob knew if he asked her to keep the letters a secret, she would. He could spare Ricki animal fear and ontological angst. But Susan would never forget, and Bob was not going to start lying in his marriage, especially not today. "Kiss your mom good night," he told the kids. "Ricki, we need to talk."

"Why, yes. Yes, we do." Ricki hung her coat on the peg and then leaned back against the wall, her face tight.

"It's not my bedtime!" Susan protested.

Bob said, "You can read quietly in your room until it is."

Susan waded through the plastic blocks and, a little grudgingly, kissed her father good night. "Don't forget about my allowance."

"Thanks for reminding me."

Aidan and Brian cried at being parted from their blocks, but Bob did eventually get them through the tooth-brushing stage and into bed. They let him off easy, with only one pass through *Where the Wild Things Are*.

Back in the living room, Ricki knelt on the floor, picking up toys, collecting them in a Rubbermaid tub. "If we raise Susan's allowance, she'll just spend it on candy and soda."

"Can she handle one more dollar a week? That is, if she's really been helping you more with the boys." Stalling wouldn't do any good. "Ricki, there's something you need to see."

They read the letters together sitting on the floor with their backs against the arm of the couch. She didn't say a word the whole time she was reading them.

"The implications..." Bob began when he saw that she had finished.

"I can't think about the implications. It has to go away. Do you have a thing you can do to make it stop?"

"Maybe. The wards don't keep my parents from sending *me* notes. But then, the wards do seem to be keeping out whatever pushed them. I mean, you haven't been experiencing a sudden urge to stock up on paper towels, have you?"

She laughed nervously. "No, but every time I notice we're out of something and write it on the grocery list, I wonder, is this it? Am I going over the edge yet? Worrying about going crazy is driving me crazy."

"You want to hear crazy? I envy Susan. I don't merit actual letters, and they don't bother writing dates on the Post-its they send *me*."

"Grandparents spoil their grandkids," said Ricki. "It's the way of the world." She got back up to finish collecting the blocks. "I wonder what they'll want next, now that it's too late to burn the stolen stuff and the estate sale stuff. They only send her letters at school? Not at home?"

"Where are you going with this?"

"If you wanted to put some kind of ward on *them*, on the kids, something portable..."

"There are no guarantees."

"And if you did it while they were asleep, you wouldn't have to explain it to them." It cost her to ask him. She might never ask him again.

"Are you sure?"

"I'm sure. And in the morning, I'll tell Susan she has another dollar a week." She ran her hands through her hair. "I'm so tired. I'm just so tired."

So Bob went to the twins' bedroom and guessed how best to do the working for them. He looked around the room for something important to them to latch it onto, and he thought of *Where the Wild Things Are*. He called on the Wild Things of Earth, Air, Fire, and Water to watch over his sons. The stodgy old Ascended Masters wouldn't stand a chance anyplace where the Wild Things were, especially if a Wild Rumpus began.

Susan was awake, scowling at her book. Bob came into her pink bedroom and sat on the foot of her bed. "Still weepy, honey? Your mom and I talked it over…"

"It's not that," she said. "I just finished Narnia." She threw *The Last Battle* at the wall, and it bounced off her Eowyn poster. "Susan doesn't get to go back. The world ends, so she's lucky she didn't have to see everything in Narnia die. But how's she supposed to know she's lucky, if nobody comes back to London to say? The story ends without her, and she never finds out. It's not fair."

Bob was just as glad she didn't go for the Book of Revelation stuff in that last novel, so he didn't correct her. "You finished the whole series? It's only been two weeks."

"Mrs. Benjamin said I was precocious. P-R-E-C-O-C-I-O-U-S. She made me look it up in the dictionary. It's still not fair."

"No, it's not. Come here." He patted the edge of the bed, and she came to snuggle up next to him. "Bless your feet," he said, "that you may walk a safe path. Bless your hands, that your works may be virtuous. Bless your heart, for it is the first temple. Bless your voice, that it may speak truth and be heard. Bless your mind, that you may recognize wisdom and choose it." Silently, he added, *And bless her, Lord and Lady, for she is Thy child.*

"Are you supposed to be doing that?"

"Your mom's mellowing out about it. I wouldn't have offered, but she asked."

"My head is all tingly."

"Talk to your mom about it in the morning." He tucked Susan in. "Sleep well."

Bob would have liked to take a few more things up with his wife, but she was already asleep. He knew the measure of her exhaustion: she hadn't even managed to get her socks off first. The moment he lay back to back with Ricki, he remembered Jane. Jane saw through everyone. She would see through him, too. With her speckly hazel eyes. Dammit. Whatever this thing was, he had to snap out of it fast. He knew the reason he couldn't put her out of his head was precisely that he needed to. Finally, he commanded himself not to think of an elephant, again and again, until all he could think of was elephants. With the lullaby scene from *Dumbo* running on infinite repeat in his head, he fell into an exhausted sleep.

The phone rang. Six a.m. Rang again. Ricki got to it first. "Yeah?" she mumbled by way of greeting. "I'll get him. Say again? Are you sure?"

Bob snapped awake. "What is it?"

Ricki touched her fingertip to his lips to quiet him. It had been so long. For several minutes, she bent her attention to listening. "Okay," she said to whoever it was, and hung up. "You're going to Jane's house."

"I can't," he blurted.

She looked at him quizzically. "They were supposed to start the long drive to rehab by six. Jane packed Nils's things for him when he wouldn't, so he slapped her around until she locked herself in the bathroom. She was whispering into the phone to tell me she needed help. She was spooked enough to whisper, Bob."

"Ricki..."

"Oh. I see. But you haven't done anything about it yet. Have you."

"Of course not!"

"Then you get your ass over there and you get our friend out of her jam. I'll work the phone tree while you drive. And when you get back, you're mine for twenty-four hours. No estate business. No calls from the firm. No astral plane bullshit. Just us. Got that, mister?"

He kissed her hard, and then got up to dress. Ricki had Sebastian on the phone before Bob's shoelaces were tied.

In the driveway at Jane's house, her old Corolla's doors hung open. The dashboard emitted a forlorn repeating ding, and Bob considered closing them just to shut it up, then thought better of alerting Nils to his presence. The car's feeble dome light and the early rays of morning showed a back seat full of luggage. For the first time, it occurred to Bob that he might be too late. Not again. He ran the last few steps to the door and barged right in.

Nils, who was leaning against the locked bathroom door to shout at his wife, swiveled his head around when the front door slammed. "I knew it."

Bob opened his mouth to deny the unspecified accusation, but a long string of profanity came out instead. Every word he'd ever thought about bad drivers on the Jersey Turnpike poured out of him as he chased Nils into the bedroom—a wrecked room, strewn with suitcases and shoes and the shattered remains of a lamp and bedside table. Bob grabbed Nils by the scruffy hair and dragged him into the living room. It occurred to him that there were walls in the living room. He could beat Nils's head against a wall or two. What a relief that would be. A relief and a horror. Bob watched himself drag the luckless drunk, but there didn't seem to be a way to stop. Maybe he wouldn't be able to stop this time. *I'm going to kill him,* he thought. *This is it.*

Sebastian charged in through the front door, and Bob shoved his burden at his friend, hurled Nils from himself as fast as he could.

The tattoo artist grabbed Nils, grappled him and held him still. In that soothing voice of his, Sebastian said, "Sigurdson, you are one crazy motherfucker, but you have picked for your crowning screw-up the one day in the lifespan of the universe when Bob is crazier than you are. So I'll tell you what: you're going to go to that clinic and sign yourself in now."

"Fuck you," said Nils.

"Or else I'll hand you back to Bob. Consider your options carefully," he said, as he might have while urging a client to be very sure before commissioning a permanent body modification. Which, Bob thought, Nils sort of was. "Look at him. Actually frothing at the actual mouth."

"I am?" Bob wiped his mouth. He let Sebastian's patient intonations calm him.

"That's something you don't see every day. You can go to the clinic quietly, and I can keep talking him down, or you can pull some bullshit stunt to set him off again, and I can wash my hands of you. What'll it be?" Either way, it sounded like the most reasonable transaction in the world.

Nils Sigurdson lifted his chin in an unconvincing imitation of self-respect and looked Bob up and down.

"Please," said Bob, "just go to the fucking clinic. You weren't always an asshole. What happened to the guy who decided he'd rather have a fishing trip for his bachelor party when his brother offered strippers? Can't everybody just put it all back like it was?"

"No," said Jane's voice through the bathroom door. "We can't put it all back like it was."

From the kitchen, Amber chimed in, "Jane, can I just say your timing sucks?"

Bob hadn't even realized Amber was in the house. "What are you doing in there?" He stepped into the kitchen to see that Amber, Ria, and Sophie were huddled together, hiding around the corner.

Sophie answered him. "Making sure nobody went for a knife. We came in through the back while you boys were thumping around."

"A knife." It hadn't even occurred to Bob. How had his life come to this? He was a respected litigator.

Jane ventured out of the bathroom. "Oh, Gods. Tell me nobody went for a knife." The imprint of an open hand was just purpling into bruise on her left cheek.

None of them could take their eyes off that hand print.

"I'm going," said Nils.

Bob closed his eyes and thanked the Gods.

"On one condition."

Amazing how fast the rage rushed back.

"Jane, you have to quit smoking."

She laughed. "Oh, hello kettle, this is the pot speaking."

"I bet I can stay clean longer than you can stay quit."

"I'll take that bet," said Jane, and she stepped right up to shake her husband's hand.

It took them half an hour to get every last cigarette out of the house. Jane couldn't bear to watch as her covenmates chucked the cartons of Marlboros into garbage bags. "Hey, Bob," she said. "Just in case you're still thinking about burning down that damn mansion…"

"I'm not."

She handed him her good Zippo lighter—gold-plated, engraved, the works. "Please take it. I can't keep it. None of this will work if I've got it."

Odd as he felt about taking something so important from her now, he wouldn't sabotage Jane. Especially not about this. And besides, Ricki had a plan to save him. He pocketed the Zippo.

"Thank you," she said. "And also, thank you."

"I hope I never have to do that again."

"Working on it."

"Will you be okay?"

Jane smiled. "Paisley Head of Atho."

None of them trusted Nils to behave on the long drive—not even Nils himself—so it was clear that a group pilgrimage was in order. Sophie asked, "Do you think we could fit everything into the SUV? I have to admit, it makes a good coven carpoolmobile."

Bob was desperate to beg off. Ricki was waiting for him. "Seven adults plus luggage, without the roof unit installed, with an eight hour round trip minimum? And I'm guessing it's more than ten hours, really. That's at least one body too many, even once I take the boys' car seats out of the back."

"We could caravan." Ria suggested. "Mercury's not retrograde for two more weeks."

"No need." Bob handed the SUV keys to Sophie. "Trade you? I've got estate stuff to do."

Sophie dug her keys out of her pocket and hugged him. "You didn't damage the guy, and Gods know he was asking for it. You don't have to feel bad about what happened."

He did, though. Nils hadn't been nearly wrong enough about him. "I just want to go home."

"It's okay," said Jane. "Thank Ricki for me, will you?"

"I mean to."

When they had the boys' car seats removed and all the luggage and passengers loaded up, Bob stood on the sidewalk waving goodbye.

To his puzzlement, all the CDs in Sophie's car were Three Dog Night albums. Well, why not? Three Dog Night was a relic of the mainstream Seventies childhood they hadn't had. "Shambala" was cued up in the car stereo, and the drive home gave him time to listen to it twice.

"Back already?" said Ricki when he came to kiss her in the kitchen. "I was guessing you'd all take off across Pennsylvania."

"They all did. I needed to come home. Ricki, I could have killed him."

"But you didn't. Have a cookie."

Despite everything, he couldn't help feeling better. "Is this some kind of positive reinforcement trick?"

"You ain't seen nothing yet."

"What about the kids?"

"My mom's covering for us."

"All right, then," he said, and stood to follow her upstairs. "Bring on the conditioning."

Three hours later, they came up for air.

"That's more like it," said Ricki. She cast about the bedroom to see where they'd flung the blankets, then wrapped herself up with him.

"You've been so patient these past few weeks. With so many things. Sometimes I wonder why you ever got mixed up with me."

"Because you cared about all the same things I did, but the ways you thought about them kept surprising me. Because many waters cannot quench love's fire. Because it's better to marry than to burn, and by the time that ecumenical retreat was over, I knew that if I walked away, I'd burn for you for the rest of my life. So here we are." She rested her head on his chest. "Best choice I ever made."

"Best choice I ever made," he agreed.

They slept a little and woke thirsty. Ricki got up to refill the water tumbler she kept on the beside table. She turned on the bathroom light and let out a squeak of alarm. Glass shattered against tile.

"Are you okay?" He was up in an instant.

"Put your slippers on, honey. Broken glass."

In his slippers and nothing else, he hurried to the bathroom. Every surface but the floor was covered with Post-its. The floor was covered with shards of the water tumbler. Bob picked Ricki up and set her bare feet down in the bedroom, then stepped back into the glare to see what his parents had to say for themselves.

Upon examination, it turned out to be an itemized list of complaints, numbered one to at least seven hundred eighty six, one complaint per sticky. Bob plucked a few off the walls at random: *503 we object to threats posed to our living descendants; 197 efforts to attain the Sephiroth Binah have proved more difficult than advertised; 31 everything here is vibrating at the wrong frequency; 622 will someone please turn down that white light?*

"Mom, Dad, why couldn't you just reincarnate like normal people?"

A large pink note manifested midair with a cartoony popping sound and affixed itself to the bathroom mirror. Charles Baines's handwriting said, *It turns out to be a matter of misplaced fealty. We could use a champion. Are you up for a little trial by combat?*

"I tried that this morning. It was awful."

His mother's reply singed as it stuck to a light bulb. Bob plucked it off and read, *But you won. Well done.*

"I wouldn't call anything well done that involves frothing at the mouth."

Clunking up the stairs in her clogs, Ricki carried the broom and dustpan precariously in one hand and a small vacuum cleaner in the other. "Why can't it be over?" she said. "Is this *ever* going to be over? I want our life back. I want you back. It's really not more complicated than that."

"Maybe I can end it," said Bob as he swept the glass into the dustpan she held.

"Anything," she said. "Just make it stop."

"You're in charge for twenty more hours. Your wish is my command."

"Well, you're the one who knows what needs doing."

He plugged in the vacuum cleaner. "*Know* is too strong a word. But there's something left to try."

Once the glass was cleaned up, they dressed, and he told her his plan while they drove to the manse. She said, "Are you sure about this?"

"No, but it can't get any worse."

Up in the temple room, he searched through his parents' supplies. They had boxes of strike-anywhere wooden matches, bought in bulk, and a little Himalayan incense left. He lit a wand of it and set it into a stand on the little table. "When this stick burns down, light the next."

"What else?"

"Just be here with my body."

She was trembling. "What if something goes wrong?"

"Call Ria first. This is right up her alley."

Ricki's laugh had a slight hysterical edge. All these years, she and Jane had been of one mind about Ria's ceremonial magic proclivities. "I wish she were here. Ria, of all people. How about that. Maybe we should wait until they get back."

Bob looked at his watch, then took it off and tucked it into his wife's purse. Watches were counterproductive for trance work.

"It's a long way to Shesequin. I'll be surprised if they're back before midnight. And this is for me to do."

"If you fail, then what? Do I go tell Sophie there is another Skywalker?"

He kissed her. "If you feel like praying, that can't hurt."

"I don't even know what to pray for."

"You'll hit on the right thing. You always do." He did a couple of yogic sun salutations to loosen up, and then settled into lotus position on the floor.

She pulled a cushion up next to him. "Is it okay if I touch you?"

"Please," he said, and her knee resting against his was the last sensation he noticed in the material world.

Bob started with the simple visualizations his father had taught him. A solid brass ankh rotating in empty black space. The opening petals of a single rose. A candleflame, the inner arch of its greater heat sheltered by the yellow arch of brightness. Bob pictured himself stepping through the gate of flame, and then he stood behind his body where it sat. It was night-dark in the temple room, and a crescent moon shone through the window. He'd left at two in the afternoon—it couldn't possibly have taken him that many hours to slip to the astral plane. Maybe he'd done it wrong.

"Astral travel never was your strong suit," said Charles Baines. "Goodness knows, I tried to teach you."

"Thanks for the encouragement, Dad." Bob turned around, and his parents stood before him, dressed in discordant combinations of store-brand clothes with the tags still attached. Goldie, his old retriever, stood beside them, wagging contentedly, holding her chewed-up old brush in her mouth. Mitten the Kitten hovered above them, fluttering an enormous pair of white wings and lashing his stripy tail.

"Wings?" said Bob.

"A lot of the cats in the afterworlds have them," Amelia Baines said. "It takes some getting used to."

It occurred to Bob that he ought to hug his parents, or something, but they didn't seem all that interested. He accepted Goldie's brush, wiped her astral saliva on his astral jeans, and brushed her coat. "What the hell are you guys wearing?"

Amelia stiffened. "They were on sale."

"You were the most stylish woman in Rumson, not two years ago."

"I had misplaced priorities."

"And then you misplaced them even worse."

"Maybe so," she conceded. "Why, indeed, could we not reincarnate?"

"Like normal people," Charles added, with some distaste.

Amelia raised an eyebrow. "Like most of your relatives. If it was good enough for Frederick Baines, it ought to have been good enough for us."

Bob reached up to scritch Mitten behind the ear. "Dad, you're just going to have to get over yourself."

"No shortcuts to a right and proper ascension." Charles sighed. "We did our best. Maybe next time around. So, shall we to the garden?"

As they descended the grand marble stairs, Bob readied his mind for the trial by combat his father had asked of him. "Where's Uncle Ciebo? I'll spring you all at once, if I can."

Charles looked away, his jaw clenched.

Amelia said, "After Larry's daughters were done selling off his things, it was clear Menetnashté was angry enough at being let down, he wouldn't take Larry over the river with him no matter what else happened. And then Larry's younger daughter, the Mormon one, had him posthumously converted. The moment he was offered an invitation to some other afterworld, he took it. At the time, we thought him irresolute. We were sure you wouldn't disappoint us. Menetnashté was determined not to be disappointed again, too. He started binding us to the river, keeping us from looking in on the other afterworlds, pressing us to press you, to press Susan. Menetnashté has a particular regard for firstborns. Just as well, I suppose. I don't think Sophie would have borne up as well as you have. We knew we were in trouble when you declared your intent to give away his art collection, and then you sold off the basics, too. Menetnashté stopped watching what he said around us, and we realized that *we*, of all people, were intended to be the servants in his house. Our house. Yours. Soon he started talking about feeding us to the crocodile, making us take his place in the river."

"It occurred to us then," said Charles, "to wonder why, after three thousand years, we were the only followers he had accumulated. I think, though, that we weren't. We were just the only ones left. Florebo was right about everything. Won't he be smug when you tell him?"

"Crocodiles," said Bob. He and Susan had watched a lot of shows on the Animal Planet channel together last summer, but Susan preferred series with kittens and puppies. Now Bob wished he'd seen more episodes of *The Crocodile Hunter*. What would Steve Irwin do? All Bob could remember from the episode previews was that Steve Irwin had spent a lot of time narrowly avoiding getting bitten by poisonous snakes. "I am so screwed."

"Not crocodiles, exactly," said Amelia. "Ammit, in fact, the crocodile goddess."

"You do have an advantage," Charles pointed out. "You're alive."

"Yeah, for *now*."

His parents looked at each other ruefully. His mother said, "We've botched things badly, I'm afraid." She pulled a large pad of Post-its out of her pocket. "I need a pen, Charles."

He had a whole handful of identical Bic ballpoints. "Pick one."

She pulled a pen at random and started sketching something. "If you can get there, you'll be needing a boat."

"I'm a father of small children," said Bob. "I have no business fighting crocodiles. I'm not my own to throw away anymore."

"Nonsense," said Amelia. "Would I ask you to throw anything away? What do you remember about *The Book of the Dead*?"

"That you preferred the most discredited translation ever. I'm not fighting crocodiles for you. I have three kids to raise. You got yourselves into this..."

"We got you into it, too," said Charles.

"...And you're going to have to get yourselves out. What?"

Amelia sighed impatiently. "Do you want this finished, or don't you? You'll need a boat. Here's a boat."

"It's a *picture* of a boat, Mom."

"This method worked for the Pharaohs. It will work for you. Answer all the boat's questions, and you'll be able to lure Menetnashté out into the Field of Reeds."

Bob looked at the yellow Post-it with its rough sketch of a reed boat. "Answer all its questions. Right. Have you heard a word I'm saying?"

"When he's done with us," said Charles, "he won't stop at Pasca and Florebo. He's had a look at you. And we let him get a look at Susan. If we could fix this on our own, we would. But we can't. Over there, we're just two more dead people with hearts heavier than feathers."

They'd arrived at the kitchen door, and Fetch stood just on the other side of the screen, nose to nose with Goldie. They were both wagging like old friends reunited, so Bob opened the door to let his dog out. Charles watched the spirit of the place rolling in the flowerbeds with her and said approvingly, "It's yours, Bob. This house was never going to belong to Menetnashté. Not like that."

"So you want me to lure this guy into a field of reeds..."

"No, not a field of reeds," said Amelia. "The Field of Reeds."

"Fine, The Field of Reeds, and then what?"

His parents couldn't look him in the eye.

"You have no idea, do you?"

"Not as such," said Charles.

Bob had to ask himself then whether his parents were capable of betraying him to their patron. He looked hard at them, at the pathetic shades they'd become—all the more pathetic for the shreds of dignity they still had. They'd lied to Florebo, they'd kept secrets from Pasca, they'd been prepared to destroy every physical trace of the Baines family legacy, and they'd played havoc with the orthodox tenets of Theosophy they had claimed to espouse. It was the humility that decided him, because they weren't very good at it. Death had humbled them after all. If they'd been faking their humility, they'd have made it look graceful.

"So," he said, "I bring the fight to him."

His father tugged at a price tag on his sweatshirt. "That, or you can break the wards and let him in. Which I don't recommend."

"No," Bob agreed, "he's not getting in." But that meant that Fetch and the wards had kept Menetnashté out. Maybe his case wasn't entirely hopeless. "Are you sure I'm not just in phase one sleep, with wonky alpha waves?" That was how Jane would have explained it all, but he wasn't in Jane's universe now.

"You'll have to come with us," said Amelia. "If we stand still here long enough, we'll be pulled back."

Charles said, "Just hang on to us."

So Bob tucked his right hand into the crook of his mother's arm and his left hand into the crook of his father's, and they waited like that for a while. Fetch padded up and dropped Goldie's brush at Bob's feet, and as soon as the cat and dog huddled with the little family group, Bob blinked his eyes and found himself standing on a low hill surrounded on all sides by marsh. It was a bright, hot day, or seemed to be. Slender green stalks topped with feathery tufts of paler green rose a man's height above the water all around him, but he could see where the reeds gave out and the river deepened. "You're right, Mom," he said. "This really is the Field of Reeds."

Amelia handed him her sketch again. "Remember what I told you?"

"Answer all its questions."

"Good. Now, go get him."

Not having a better idea, Bob obeyed. He carried the Post-it to the water's edge and laid it down there. In an instant, a crescent-shaped reed boat bobbed on the water, the horns of its prow and stern rising nearly as high as he was tall. A long black pole rested inside. What would the boat ask him? Bob thought, absurdly, of the hours Ricki had spent with him all those years ago, drilling him with flash cards for the bar exam. It was too much to hope that the boat would ask him about the legal doctrine of adverse possession. Probably it thought about riparian rights. Bob's scores had tanked on the riparian rights section. "Hello, boat," he said.

"What is my name?"

"Boat," said Bob.

The boat sighed. "Try again. What is my name?"

"Reed boat?"

"Oh, for goodness sake." The boat waggled its prow at him. "What's the name of that?"

The boat was a crescent. "Horn of the Moon," he said.

"That's better. Not right, but good enough. What's this?" The boat hopped on a little wave, and the pole bounced before landing back in its proper place.

Bob stared at the pole until something came to him. In function, it was just a long, long leg. "Betty Grable," he said.

"Isn't this fun?" the boat asked, and that was another question to answer.

"Not especially," said Bob, "but I'm glad you like it."

"At least you're a good sport." The boat paused to consider its next question. "You really do have to tell me my name."

Bob thought about his many reasons for coming here. "Vengeance," he said.

"Nope," said the boat. "Come on, one more try."

"Protection," he said.

"Whose?"

"Theirs."

"That's close enough. Climb in."

He hadn't tried surfing since college, but he remembered enough to balance, with the pole's help. After a few nervous moments of tippiness, Bob stood in the stern of the boat and pushed off. "Where am I going?" he asked the *Protection*.

"Beats me," it said. "You're in charge of this part."

"Where is Menetnashté?"

"Oh, him. You have the power to give or deny him what he wants. He'll come to you."

So Bob poled idly among the reeds, narrowly avoiding clumpy little islands, keeping to the narrow channels where the water moved faster and the papyrus stalks thinned a bit. He was tall enough to see over the green tufts, not that it did him any good.

When Menetnashté came, he came silently from behind. Bob only realized he'd been overtaken when his poling brought the boat no headway, and he turned to see that his enemy stood on an island, gripping the aft horn of the *Protection* in his hand. Bob knew him by the con artist smile on his face.

"It's a pleasure to meet you at last," said Menetnashté. "I'm sure we can work this out in a way that's agreeable for all concerned."

"Get your hand off my boat."

"Have it your way." Menetnashté grabbed the horn of the crescent with both hands and jerked it to tip Bob out. While Bob spat murky water and struggled to his feet, Menetnashté kicked him hard in the chest and shoved him back into the marsh. Bob tried to tackle him, but couldn't get any kind of footing. Where was Betty Grable? Bob reached for the pole, a long leg to kick his enemy with, but Menetnashté had grabbed it first, and down it came on Bob's shoulder.

He knew then that his own strength was not enough. The image came to him of his wife holding his empty body in the temple room. That was sufficient to keep Bob getting back up, but not to keep him from getting knocked down again. He hadn't come here to die.

A mouthful of mud. Funny, he didn't remember falling on his face. The pole was coming down again, he could hear it cutting the air. Bob rolled aside. He hadn't come here to die, but it looked like he was going to.

A boy scout would have been prepared, he thought. His thoughts were nonsense. He prepared for the end with a self-blessing. *Bless my feet, although they brought me here.* The pole hit the ground with another muddy thwack in the spot where

Bob's head had been a moment before. *Bless my knees, that knelt in reverence and buckled in mirth.* The next blow landed across his back. *Bless my seed, that brought forth life.* What would Ricki tell their children? *Bless my heart, which was a temple to my Gods.* He would have blessed his hands, but they were busy pushing down at the earth, pushing him up to his feet. He would have blessed his voice, which had won him his wife. He would have blessed his mind, but it was clouding, growing distant. *My heart, which was a temple to my Gods.* A temple inhabited. *Bless me, Lord and Lady, for I am Thy Child.*

Bob watched himself stand, watched himself charge headlong at Menetnashté. It seemed to him that he floated a foot or so above his own head. What a strange sensation it was. He watched himself slam into the ancient ascetic and draw blood on him. Should people bleed who had been dead three thousand years? But there Menetnashté was, bleeding. Bleeding, and crawling away into the marsh. Bob willed his body to follow, but instead it bent down to the river to drink. In the good green taste of the water, he was within himself again, in good company. Something wordless and benevolent suffused him.

When the water stilled, he caught sight of his reflection. Two horns curved smoothly from his temples forward to a wicked pair of points. Two thoughts came together, both unbidden: *So this is what the snobby high episcopagans mean when they talk about Drawing Down the Sun,* and then, *Ricki's not going to like this one bit.* The moment he considered their implications, the horns vanished. A wave of dizziness swept in from nowhere, and the wordless other mind left him. He was just beginning to realize that he'd disarmed himself and ought to be afraid, when Menetnashté caught up with him and pulled him onto his feet. Not an improvement over kneeling, no. The ascetic hit him in the gut a couple of times, then slung him into the reed boat and climbed aboard to stand in the stern, poling them toward the middle of the river.

Bob lay on his side, curled around himself. He breathed careful yogic breaths to keep the fear and rage at bay while he listed his assets. A moment ago, he'd had full invocation of the Horned One, but it seemed he couldn't hold it. He still had with him the astral forms of himself, his clothing, his wallet, his wedding ring, and, in his jeans pocket, Jane's gold-plated lighter. Quietly, he reached into his pocket for it, and quietly he pulled it out. He willed it dry, and it dried. Just to be sure the boat would catch quickly, he plucked at the reeds a bit, roughened them with his fingers.

"What is my name?" whispered the boat.

"Sacrifice," Bob whispered back. He'd never had to kill anything before. "I'm sorry."

"Sacrifice," the boat mused. "That's a good name."

The fire caught readily, and Bob had to scramble away from it, backward into the pointed prow. If the crocodile goddess was going to get him, she'd get his captor, too. That had to be good enough. The *Sacrifice* was done for. Bob dove from the smoke into murky water and made for the shallows.

Coming up for air, he saw the *Sacrifice* burnt to the waterline, and Menetnashté clinging to the boat's still-buoyant remains, kicking frantically for shore. Bob had to remind himself that the old con artist was already dead. How else could he have survived the goring and the fire?

And then Bob saw what put his foe to flight. Ammit was massive—she could only have been Ammit. The crocodile goddess was far too large to sneak up on anyone. Her eyes, her ridges, though they were all of her that rose from the river, were nearly as high as the boat had been. Bob dove, hoping her gaze would fix on Menetnashté, and stroked his arms hard through the water until his lungs burned. In the thick of the reeds again, he could stand, and the water came only to his chest. His steps squashed through muck and submerged roots. More than once, he felt the brush of some swimming creature against his legs, and he bit his tongue to keep from crying out in surprise. To lose his pursuers, he lost himself

At last, Bob stumbled up onto a hummock where the ground was nearly dry. The little rise was, he thought, maybe ten feet around, but at least it got his feet out of the river. If he could just get to the highest point on the hummock, he might be able to see far enough across the Field of Reeds to come up with some sort of plan. It would be dangerous—being visible across the Field might attract Menetnashté's attention, or Ammit's—but Bob hated feeling blind. Fortunately, it looked like there was a clear spot ahead.

His right foot thumped into something soft. *Someone* soft.

Someone large.

Slowly, Bob looked down to find a massive human figure curled comfortably among the reeds, with a golden pair of scales laid down beside him. The clear spot Bob had been making for was a circle of broken papyrus stalks around a sleeping man who happened to have the pointy black face of a dog. Or a jackal, perhaps. The man scratched drowsily at his doggy chin with a bare size seventeen foot.

Bob had just kicked the local god of death. It seemed like a very good time to let sleeping gods lie. As he backed slowly away from Anubis, the god lifted his muzzle and sniffed at the air, then turned to look right at Bob. "You're not one of mine," said Anubis. "What are you doing here?"

"I, ah, well."

Anubis stood to his full height and took another whiff in Bob's general direction. "You're not even dead."

"Um, I'm sorry?" Bob heard footsteps thumping hollow on the springy wet soil of the hummock. Menetnashté. "Is *he* one of yours?"

"Oh, no," said Anubis. "Not him again."

Menetnashté charged Bob, stopping short only when he saw Anubis before him. The dead con artist slid to a precarious halt on the mud, but kept his footing. "You," he said to the god. "You have no power over me."

Anubis yawned. His long, narrow, doggy tongue curled, then slackened. "Go to Ammit," he said.

"Have you ruled on the matter?" Bob asked. He glanced at the pair of golden scales that lay on the broken reeds. "Officially?"

At that, the ascetic and the god began to dispute over obscure points of law and theology. They argued heatedly for some time, until Bob began to wonder whether they had forgotten he was there. It seemed to be a question of jurisdiction. Certainly, Anubis had no doubts about what the proper ruling ought to be. Bob made bold to ask Anubis, "What would have to be different, for you to be able to decide this case?"

"He would have to believe in me."

"But, but, but..." Bob sputtered. "We're looking right at you."

"Not the same thing," Menetnashté declared. "Not at all."

"I don't suppose my parents count as believing in you?"

Anubis sniffed at the air, his nose pointed back the way Bob thought he'd come from. "Definitely not."

"All right." Bob wracked his memory of *The Book of the Dead*. "I wish I could ask Phil Carson."

Pricking up his ears, Anubis said, "Phil Carson?" The corners of his mouth rose in a slight smile, and his tongue lolled out.

"Phil Carson prepared my parents' bodies for burning. *Your* Phil Carson."

More sniffing. "Then he sent them here."

Menetnashté's back stiffened. "They would have come in any case. They came for me, and we *will* cross that river."

"The other side is not our territory," said Anubis. "By all means, go if you can. I'm not closing it to you."

"Go if you can. That all sounds very open-handed, but you know perfectly well..."

"Hold on," said Bob. "One of Anubis's devotees sent my parents here."

Menetnashté snorted derisively. "Unorthodox methods."

Anubis nodded a rueful nod. "Hardly anyone does it properly anymore. Things just aren't what they used to be."

"But surely the intent counts for something," Bob said. "If the lightness or weight of his heart determines a man's fate, regardless of how well he followed the laws in life, why should intent not be a factor in your deliberations? And Phil Carson's intent is to be pleasing to you. If my parents' case isn't in your jurisdiction, then whose is it in?"

"Mine," said Menetnashté.

"Oh, now hold on right there," Anubis said. "Who died and elevated you to the godhead?"

"They obeyed me as if I were a god, and they're not the first."

"They may have once," said Bob, "but they don't anymore, and no one else does, either."

"Then there *is* no legitimate jurisdiction," Menetnashté said, and crossed his arms over his chest, as if that settled anything.

"But Phil Carson…" said Bob.

"I don't see the relevance," said Menetnashté.

Anubis said, "It bears consideration."

For what seemed like an eternity, the three of them went around and around like that. Bob knew his case was weak, but he didn't have much else to go on. There was something more, somewhere, he was sure of it. If he could just buy time, he'd figure out what it was. Meanwhile, all he could do was flog his one pathetic point with every bullshit rhetorical trick he had. How mortifying—he was trying a case before a god, for Gods' sake. Too bad he hadn't taken the time to bone up on *The Book of the Dead*.

"But," Menetnashté protested, "there's not a scrap of evidence that *I* ever venerated Anubis. I lived an ascetic, I died an ascetic, and I ordered my body cast to the vultures."

"Not ever?" said Bob.

"Not ever!"

What had Florebo said? Ignoring his adversary, Bob turned to the god. "What would possession of a lapis eye signify?"

"Protection from evil," said Anubis. "What's your point?"

Dead end. Bob tried again. "What about a carnelian heart?"

Anubis's ears pricked up. "A carnelian heart, you say?"

"I don't have one," said Menetnashté. "I never did."

Bob grinned. "I can name five witnesses who will all agree that one Menetnashté, resident in the Field of Reeds, commissioned them to procure for him a lapis eye and a carnelian heart. I put it to you that this man had sufficient belief in you to require a carnelian heart amulet, and that he went to considerable trouble to obtain one."

"Five witnesses?" said Menetnashté with a menacing smile. "If you'd like the living witnesses to join the dead ones here, I can arrange that."

"So you admit there *are* witnesses," said Anubis.

"I never said…"

"But you did," said Bob. To the god, he said, "I am prepared to base my case on the testimony of the late Charles and Amelia Baines, formerly of Rumson, New Jersey." He had doubts the moment the words were out of his mouth. He was about to break the cardinal rule of cross-examination, asking questions when he had no idea how his witnesses would answer. Oh, well. Too late now.

Anubis barked, and the elder Baineses materialized on the hummock.

"Nice trick," said Charles. "How's the trial by combat going, son?"

"I got my ass kicked."

"You don't look well," Amelia agreed.

"Mom, Dad, I need you to tell the truth." *For once.*

Menetnashté looked a bit frantic. "You can't possibly take the word of these pitiable latecomers."

"Why not?" said Anubis, with a gleam in his eye.

"Did you or did you not," said Bob, because that was one of his favorite ways to wind up for the pitch, "procure a carnelian heart amulet for the defendant…"

"Defendant?" said Menetnashté.

"For Menetnashté, at his explicit request."

Charles and Amelia looked at one another, and Bob waited to see which of them admitted to the theft first. It was his father. "We did," said Charles.

"And how did he present his request?"

Amelia said, "As a matter of the greatest importance, because his children had disposed of his body improperly."

"Is that what happened?" Anubis asked Menetnashté.

"That's what I said at the time, but my intent…"

"Do you imagine," said Anubis, "that I have never had occasion to weigh the heart of a hypocrite?"

"I…" Menetnashté stalled out right there.

Bob held his breath and waited for it.

The ruling came rather more abruptly than he expected. Anubis opened his jaws and grabbed Menetnashté by the neck, then shook him until it broke. The jackal flung the body to the ground so hard it bounced. Anubis said to Bob, "I'll be weighing the heart in a moment. You three might want to get going. Latecomers are so squeamish."

"Yes, your honor," said Bob.

"But…" said Charles.

"Yes, your honor," Bob repeated, and he wrapped a hand each around his parents' elbows to turn them back to the Field. They hadn't even reached the water yet when he heard Anubis bark. In a blink, they were somewhere entirely different.

Bob and his parents floated in space, surrounded by a swirl of vibrating colors. The place looked like a rejected special effects experiment from the earliest days of the music video.

Amelia looked around and said, "This must be Devachan."

"I expect we'll be here for some time," said Charles, "if we're to reincarnate like normal people."

"I wonder if we'll get to stay together, after everything we've done wrong." Her voice quavered.

Charles took her hand. "We'd better. Fifteen hundred years of contemplation will not be long enough, my love."

Bob didn't want to say a word. Their devotion to one another was the only thing they'd done right. Ever, really. He wanted to remember them like that. Rather than give them another chance to condescend or command, he called on Fetch to pull him out of this no-place into the place that was his home.

Next thing he knew, Bob lay on the grass by the rugosa rose he'd planted with his sister, and the spirit of the place was nudging him with the idea of a nose.

Apparently, it was possible for an astral body to ache. Bob's was a mess. He was muddy, bruised under the mud, bleeding through some of the bruises, and quite possibly fractured somewhere in his rib cage. Leaning on Fetch all the way, Bob shambled across the garden, through the kitchen and up the servants' stairs, then around to the temple room, where his physical body still sat in perfect repose by Ricki's fretful form. When he woke, she greeted him with kisses.

"Did you do it?" she asked.

"It's done." He regretted the boat again. "We can go back to worrying about day care schedules and choir rehearsal carpools now."

She laughed. "My valiant knight."

"I hope you're up to driving."

The ache quieted once he was in his body, but it didn't quite leave him. It didn't leave him when Ricki got him back to Holmdel, or after he'd slept the night through. It wasn't until the next afternoon, when Ria came over at Ricki's request to examine Bob's aura, that he felt any better.

"Wow," said Ria, when she'd assessed the damage. "You've been somewhere interesting. What was it like?"

"Work. Only more so."

"Fine, don't talk about it if you don't want to. Just hold still, okay?" She placed crystals carefully on him—to retune his chakras, she said—and sat by the bed humming. In the tunelessness of her hum, Bob let his mind drift until it found the thing that still troubled him. He could see it, could almost name it. She hummed herself hoarse for a couple hours, and when Ricki hollered that it was time for dinner, Ria took the crystals off. Much better. "See?" she said. "Told you so."

That night after the kids were in bed, Bob held onto his wife. "Ricki, I owe you an apology," he said.

She kissed the top of his head. "For what?"

"I've been thinking about how you used to worry, when we first got married, that we wouldn't end up in the same afterlife. I was such a jerk. What if you were right? I get the Summerlands, or reincarnation, or both, whatever, and you get Heaven, and we don't get each other."

"You know what I did today?"

He held onto her tighter. "Please don't change the subject."

"While you were lying around under a pile of crystals, I cleaned all your parents' Post-it Notes out of the bathroom."

"Oh."

"I sorted the stickies into categories on the kitchen table, because how often do you get a preview of coming attractions like that? And a lot of their complaints were about travel restrictions, that Menetnashté wasn't letting them visit the other afterlives anymore. Which means there's travel. Which means I'm not worried. My yoke is easy and my burthen light."

"This whole thing doesn't tweak your faith?"

"I tweaked my own faith plenty when I settled down with you. Now it's your turn."

"My turn, huh? Yeah, I guess it is."

He didn't feel all the way to right for months, though. Not on the day Amber's art detective friend came to the manse with an unmarked van to take away all the things that needed returning. Not even on the day he and Penny settled their big case out of court for a sum that answered Geraldine Hendrickson's paralysis. It wasn't until the day the moving truck pulled up in front of the ancestral home with all the contents of the little split-level, and the movers carried Bob's new life into his old one. At sunset, his kin and his coveners joined him in the garden. Together, he and Sophie scattered their parents' ashes at the roots of the hungry roses.

And Ria's From Virgo

Ria reached the therapist's office at 1:56 p.m., right on time for the Moon to form an auspicious sextile with Uranus. Filling in the new-patient questionnaires took most of two hours. By the time Ria was sure she was next in line to see the doctor, not only did she have to worry about getting to her coven's Full Moon Circle on time that evening, but she suspected the Moon would nearly be trining Jupiter when the shrink first saw her. Moon trine Jupiter tended to bring out excessive optimism in Ria—excessive and short-lived. And what if she got in a car wreck, speeding to the shore for ritual?

She knew just where the car wreck would happen, too. That exit ramp off Route 36 was a deathtrap, and there were so many SUV's on the road these days. The movie of the collision she was certain to get into played in her head, and then it played again. Again. The fouth time, she dug into her capacious purse for her jar of homemade jasmine hand lotion. She dipped a knuckle in and slathered the lotion from the back of her left hand to the back of her right, careful to avoid besmirching her fingertips. It wouldn't do to leave lotiony fingerprints all over the therapist's office. Now that her chapped, cracked hands were well moisturized and the scent of that costly first-pressing jasmine oil surrounded her, she could hope to hold it together through the session without excusing herself to go wash them. *I may be losing my mind, but at least I smell good.*

At 5:15, with the Moon very nearly trine Jupiter, the receptionist finally leaned into the waiting room to say, "Annamaria Santini?"

Ria stood and smoothed her long black skirt. Her hands itched. On that exit ramp on Route 36, the SUV was slamming into the side of her car again. Silently—and, she hoped, unobtrusively—she touched each of the pendants in her profusion of silver necklaces as she crossed into the therapist's office. *Slam.* She watched the front airbags deploy too late to save her. Touched the pendants again, this time in the proper sequence. *Slam.* Her car didn't have side-impact airbags. That Hummer was going to pulverize her. *Slam.* And if they airbags did deploy, *they'd* probably kill her. It happened to people sometimes, therefore it would happen to her.

"I'm Dr. Bradley," said the therapist, a small, sharp-faced woman in pastels.

Who knew what this pastel-wearer would make of Ria's professionally Gothic wardrobe? Probably that the patient was about a decade too old to have any excuse for it. Dr. Bradley returned Ria's assessing gaze, eyebrows high in mild surprise.

Nonetheless, the therapist reached to shake Ria's hand, and for once Ria didn't hesitate to reach back. Here, of all places, she didn't need to conceal or explain away the condition of her hands. If she had to rub sanitizer on them after a handshake, well, at least she'd made it into the office first.

As they settled into their chairs, Dr. Bradley flipped through the sheaf of new-patient questionnaire forms. "So, it seems you've already tried to diagnose yourself."

"I was reading on Wikipedia…"

Dr. Bradley made no effort to conceal her distaste.

"…About obsessive-compulsive disorder," Ria went on. She considered defending Wikipedia as a layperson's starting point, but checked her watch. Moon and Jupiter, trining, with all the false hope that angle entailed. Ria was so tired of false hope. "Anyhow, whatever I have, I've had it all my life, but now it's getting worse." On the exit ramp from Route 36, she floored the gas pedal rather than yield to a bright yellow Hummer. "I used to fight it by gardening, to force myself to get into the dirt, though I had to wear gloves. Being around the plants' auras relaxed me when I concentrated on them. I got really knowledgeable, and I even enjoyed digging sometimes." Bright yellow Hummer. Ria tried to blink it away. "Now I've missed the whole spring planting season, and I haven't been able to..." The accident was going to be all her fault. "Pardon me. I haven't been able to touch my gardening tools since last fall." Maybe she should take the long way to Sandy Hook, avoid Route 36 altogether. No, that would be avoidant behavior, and Wikipedia said avoidance would just feed into her disorder. She'd been a fortuneteller long enough to know these pictures weren't any kind of prediction, but once they got started, it was hard to turn them off. Lately, the harder she tried, the more they stuck.

"The problem with Wikipedia..." Dr. Bradley began.

"I don't believe everything I read on Wikipedia," said Ria. After all, Wikipedia dismissed astrology as a pseudoscience. *If astrology is as useless as all that, why do people keep paying me to do their charts?*

"You may be right about the OCD, but it may not be your only problem, or even your main problem. Your questionnaire answers do suggest obsessional ideation with poor insight and..."

"Poor insight?!"

"I'm sorry. It's the jargon of the field, not a personal judgment."

"I had the insight to show up at a therapist's office, didn't I?" Fuck it. Ria picked at a cracked spot on the back of her left hand. The flash of sensation lifted her out of the accident.

"Yes. Yes, you did. I'm concerned, though, about all the ritualizing behaviors you describe."

A tiny meniscus of blood rose in the crack on Ria's hand. She picked harder. "*All* the ritualizing behaviors? They're not all...like this."

"Well, yes. All of them."

"If you lump all my ritual habits together, that just shows you don't know much about ritual." Maybe Ria shouldn't have chosen the first shrink to try from the phone book by doing numerological analyses of their names. Maybe some of the others would have been nicer. Now that she made bold to look, she didn't much care for the shape and shade of this one's aura—prickly, with an unfortunate preponderance of orange.

The therapist appeared to be sizing up Ria's numerous necklaces with their numerous amulets. "Ah. And how long have you believed you were a witch?"

"Wiccan," Ria answered. She always used the more politically palatable term for her religion when filling out forms. "I said I was Wiccan." She twisted sideways a little to pluck her purse strap from the back of the overstuffed chair. No point in staying to find out what Dr. Bradley thought of Ria's profession. "Twenty-three years. And how long have you *believed* you were a mental health professional?"

Dr. Bradley did not urge her to stay, did not apologize, so Ria slammed the door to the therapeutic inner sanctum on her way out. *Bigot.* She slammed the outer office door—*Bitch*—and felt a little bit bad for the receptionist, who hadn't done anything wrong. It was a long way down the hall to the building exit, but Ria slammed that door, too. *Waste of money.* Lacking insurance, she'd had to pay up front. Now she was that much further from buying the shop.

The shock of summer heat after the office's aggressive air conditioning dizzied Ria. Air rippled over the asphalt from the front door to the spot under a scraggly little parking lot tree where she'd tried to shade her car. Poor little parking lot tree, it fought a losing battle. Heat rippled over all the ornamented surfaces of the Saturn sedan, too. Her car was a rolling amulet. The shells, buttons, and beach glass Ria had spent the past six months gluing on had protected her—so far—from collisions, but not from the June sun.

She opened all four doors, rolled down the windows, and ran the AC a few minutes until the vents gushed cold before she got in. The dozen little figures glued down in her dashboard shrine smiled upon her. "So much for the festival," she told them. "Looks like we're staying home." It was hard enough keeping her covenmates from figuring her secret out as it got worse from week to week. If she went camping with them, with the dirt and bugs and sticky sunblock, everyone would see how bad off she was. She'd tried to stall on the decision, tried to laugh it off—*the planets are aligned unfavorably for camping*—but now that the therapist she'd been counting on to fix it had turned out so badly, she couldn't imagine pulling herself together in time to go.

Her aura was all out of kilter. The energy field of her solar plexus chakra felt like it was rotating the wrong way round, and her third eye was squinched shut. It was going to take time and concentration to fix the damage. She couldn't even begin yet. Ria sat in the driver's seat with the air blasting right at her while she rubbed her hands down with more sanitizer. The sanitizer stung like blazes.

The merge onto Route 36 turned out to be completely clear. Not a Hummer in sight.

On fair warm-weather evenings, Rugosa Coven liked to hold their rituals on the beach. Ria muttered incantations against bridge collapse all the way across the Highlands Bridge until the road touched down in the sandbar town of Sea Bright. A few blocks south on Ocean Avenue, across the street from the seawall, stood the teal beach cottage where her covenmate Sophie lived. Though Ria's psychiatric appointment had started late, she'd ended it so soon she was early to Circle.

A U-Haul truck took up nearly all of Sophie's driveway. That was odd. Sophie had moved in all her worldly possessions a year ago when her parents left her the place, and Sophie had never been big on owning stuff anyhow—she was a classic Pisces. Moving day for her had taken the coven maybe two hours on a Saturday, before the traditional pizza and beer thank-you for carrying furniture.

Yet here the U-Haul was, its back wide open, unsealed boxes thrown heedlessly in. Either someone hadn't given a damn, or someone had been in a mortal hurry.

Jane, then. And Ria was betting on mortal hurry.

She heard her coven sisters before she saw them. Two voices drifted up from the cottage's basement and out through the chocked-open kitchen door.

"What's with the waterline on the wall?" said Jane's voice.

"On spring tide nights the basement gets pretty damp," Sophie said. "Oh." An awkward pause. "I guess we shouldn't have put your electronics in the basement, huh?"

Jane laughed her gallows-humor laugh. "They can't do worse here than back at my place with Nils."

Ria was going to have to offer to help—anyone else would offer to help—so she needed to pick out a task she could do. Quick, before Sophie and Jane could get up from the basement and ask. She looked over Jane's mess of boxes and found one labeled *Wedding Linens*. It was full of tablecloths and placemats, still in their original packaging after five years. Jane had once expected her life with Nils to include entertaining dinner guests. Well, that box would do for carrying, and it would give Ria an excuse to avoid the damp basement. Come to think of it, tonight would be a spring tide night

She leaned her head in the kitchen door and hollered, "Hello down there!"

"Hello up there!" Sophie hollered back as she clomped up the basement stairs in her Birkenstocks. To Ria's great relief, Sophie was not too sweaty from hauling boxes, nor too cobwebby from clambering around her basement. Wiccans generally tended to be huggers, and Sophie, a latter-day hippie chick in the beach blonde mode, was a hugger and a half. She was still clean enough that Ria could hug her back without thinking too hard about germs.

Her voice low, Ria said, "What happened?"

"The usual things, I think," Sophie whispered back. "Just, this time Jane did what she should have done ages ago."

It wasn't much of an answer, but there was no asking for more, because here Jane came up the stairs.

Her aura had never looked worse.

Oh, Jane herself looked fine, with her dark hair in its corkscrew curls catching the wind off the ocean. Anyone but Ria would have said she was doing better than she had in months.

But Jane's aura had apparently been in a brawl with a grizzly bear. Her throat chakra was unsprung, her root chakra was torn, and her heart chakra oozed prana. Her entire etheric layer was a mass of astral bruises, and her ketheric template appeared to be blistered. Blistered—that was a new one on Ria, and she'd seen a thing or two in her professional capacity. Injuries like Jane's would take years to mend—even with regular crystal rebalancing, which Jane was unlikely to do—and they might never mend completely.

Not going to say a word about it, Ria admonished herself. Jane wanted to make Wicca respectable, wanted to respect herself as a Wiccan, which seemed to require getting tied up in knots of angry embarrassment about all things New Agey. *It would be no kindness to set her off, today of all days. Let her talk first.*

"Hey there, Cleopatra," said Jane, and greeted Ria with a hug. It was a good, weary hug, trusting.

Ria wished it hadn't come with a side order of sarcasm about her past lives. She tried to make light of it. "Hey there, Galileo." She gave Jane an extra squeeze before letting her go. "Are you okay?"

"Okay enough to throw some boxes in a truck. I could use some help getting them back out, though." So she didn't want to talk yet about what the last straw had been. Fair enough.

Good thing Ria had already picked out the boxes she could touch without flinching. "Where do you want these, ah…linens, it looks like?"

"The basement."

Oh, shit. "Are you sure? They're pristine."

"They're wrapped in plastic. It'll keep the damp off them until I figure out where to go next."

"Of course," said Ria. Of course she'd have to go down there. Why should her luck get any better? She was going to slip on the damp stairs and break her neck. Her brain ran the short film—

slip, oops, bump, bump, oof, bump, crack. Mercifully, this time the film was too comical to deter her. *And the part of Annamaria Santini will be played by Buster Keaton.* Amusement got her down the stairs, but once she found herself in the middle of the squelch of salt and sand on the cracked concrete floor, her heart started pounding. *Salt is pure,* she reminded her heart, and she reached for the liturgy she'd memorized in the first coven she'd belonged to, years ago. *On this altar, salt is the symbol of purity.* She'd forgotten so much of the beautiful, formal ritual style they'd had. She missed Oakbridge Coven, sometimes. *May the salt of the law bless and consecrate...* What came next?

Sophie's basement shelves were filling up with Jane's household goods. There was still room for the box of linens on a shelf higher than the whitest of the rimed waterlines ringing the walls. Ria kept distracting herself with the puzzle of the half-forgotten liturgy—*bless and consecrate this sacred temple to the Gods*—as she stepped from one slightly less damp spot to another, back to the wooden stairs. Heading up, she got a view she'd been spared on the way down: in the open spaces between the risers of the steps, thick spiderwebs glimmered with water droplets.

Ria ran for daylight, up and out and bang into the broad chest of her coven brother Sebastian. The tattooed spikes and coils of an intricate tribal pattern crept up his neck above his shirt collar, right at Ria's eye level.

"Oof," he said, and dropped the overstuffed duffel of Jane-things he'd slung over his shoulder. "Ria, are you all right?"

"Fine. I'm fine."

"You're about to faint." It wasn't a question. Sebastian spent his workdays tattooing and piercing people. He'd seen plenty of fainters.

When did I break into this sweat? Down in the basement? On the stairs? Just now? "I don't feel very well." Her voice sounded distant in her ears. When did the rumble of breaking waves on the far side of the seawall get so loud?

"I'm getting you out of this humidity." Sebastian set one beefy hand on each of Ria's shoulders, turned her around, and steered her through the cottage door, past the kitchen, and into Sophie's room. A window-mounted air conditioner hummed, fluttering the batik tapestries with which Sophie had decorated dorm rooms at a dozen colleges before dropping out for good.

Sebastian was saying something.

Ria's ears rang. "What?"

He turned on his work voice—soothing, resonant, hypnotic. "When's the last time you drank any water?"

There was no one else to hear them. "I think I'm having a panic attack," she whispered.

"Doesn't mean you're not dehydrated. A glass of water won't make it worse." He leaned out through the door and called toward the kitchen, "Amber?"

"Yeah, honey?" Amber's voice called back.

"Water for Ria, please?"

"Right on it."

Sebastian leaned into the air conditioning. "Ria, you just sit down and rest."

"But..." Actually, she was relieved, but a better person, a well person, would have protested, so that's what Ria did.

Amber clacked into the room in a pair of very tall shoes. She wore no jewelry in her numerous piercings today but for a tasteful pair of pearl studs. The pearls wouldn't have been all that surprising, but they were in Amber's earlobes, where just anybody might have put pearls. Her purple hair was pinned into a once-graceful chignon that was starting to unwind under the weight of her perspiration. She carried two big glasses of ice water and handed the fuller one to Ria. "Hey, sweetie," she said. "You look as bad as I feel." Amber flumped down on the edge of Sophie's bed and shucked her suit jacket with a relief so great her newly freed tattoos seemed to sigh with it. "Remind me never to visit the snobby design clients on heat wave days."

Ria held the cold glass between her palms. The air conditioning vents jetted their chill at a spot right between her shoulderblades. *Drink it. Just drink it.* But what if Amber had been too rushed to wash her hands before touching the glass? What if Sophie had washed the glass carelessly?

It was time, past time, for Ria to put her aura in order.

She set the glass down on Sophie's bureau. "Give me a minute, would you, Amber?"

Amber would. None of the protests about dehydration any of the others would have offered. "Squawk if you need anything," Amber replied, and turned her attention to a tangle of jewelry she was pulling from her sleek handbag. She filled her piercings back up with spikes and studs while Ria concentrated on her own seven chakras.

She pulled the warm light of the Earth up through her root and the cool light of the stars down through her crown. The remaining five energy vortices, spaced evenly along the hara line that was her aura's spine, she rebalanced by visualizing a rose whorling open where each chakra spun. The aura's several outer layers and templates shook loose like clean sheets on a summer clothesline.

Ria opened her eyes.

There was Amber in lotus position, her underlying expression all tranquility, with bits of finely crafted silver and steel bristling from her nose and eyebrows. She said, "You look about a million times better."

Ria said, "You look about a million times more like yourself."

"Now are you going to drink that water, or aren't you?"

Ria downed it all in under a minute, so she wouldn't have a chance to think about the glass again.

Outside, a car door slammed so hard the cottage's windows rattled.

Amber and Ria looked at one another. "Bob," they said, and got up to greet him.

The last of their number had finally arrived. Bob Baines, direct from the courthouse and still in pinstripes, ran across the cottage's small, scruffy yard to where his sister Sophie stood just inside the big metal box of the U-Haul and tossed out unsealed Hefty bags of what appeared to be winter clothes.

"Is everyone okay?" Bob asked.

"No one's physically injured," said Sophie. "Define 'okay.'"

That gave Bob pause. Ever the big brother, he said, "It's not too late for law school, Sophie. You don't have to wait tables your whole life."

Sophie laughed. "I'm freer waiting tables than you are litigating."

"What the hell happened?"

There was still the U-Haul to explain. Ria and Amber leaned out the door in case Sophie let more details slip for her brother than she had for them.

"Jane will talk when she's ready. Go change out of your suit, for Gods' sakes."

By the time Bob had fetched his beach clothes from his SUV and clambered through the front door—and then over the foyer-full of beach towels, flip-flops, and shade umbrellas—Ria and Amber were attempting nonchalance in the living room. They were on a roll, chatting about the latest New Age and occult books at the shop where Ria told fortunes.

Eyebrows tight with worry, Bob hung each layer of his suit carefully on a peg in the foyer, stripped down to his boxers, and threw on a t-shirt and shorts. One of the pairs of flip-flops in the pile turned out to be his. The rubber soles squeaked each step across the cottage floor, until he settled onto the couch between Ria and Amber, and asked, "Did you guys get any more out of them than I did?"

No point pretending they hadn't listened in. Ria shrugged at Amber.

"Less," Amber replied. "And I barely got a look at her stuff before the heat got to me. I don't think she packed real well."

"Her aura's shredded," Ria said. "I've seen some auric injuries in my time, but nothing like this."

Bob took a couple of calming deep breaths. "Must not punch coven sister's husband over shredded aura. Must not punch coven sister's husband over shredded aura." In his teens, he'd had occasion to take a swing at a couple of Sophie's troublesome boyfriends. Jane's husband was worse than anything Sophie had ever dragged home, which was saying something. Bob took another deep breath. "You could do that thing with the crystals."

Ria doubted Bob's endorsement of her crystal regimen would be enough to persuade Jane. Bob's aura had been completely trashed after his and Sophie's parents died. Even Bob's very Methodist wife had agreed: Bob needed fixing, and Ria fixed him. That had been one of her finest repair jobs. The constant maintenance that Ria's own aura required at least paid off for the people she helped. *Nothing like driving a junker to make you a good do-it-yourself mechanic.*

But would Jane see it that way? Ria sighed. "She'll never go for it."

"Nah, probably not." He stood to join the bucket brigade line that Sophie, Jane, and Sebastian were setting up to pass Hefty bags of clothing from the truck into the spare bedroom. Jane's bedroom, now. Ria and Amber filled in the line. The rhythm—grab, turn, pass, turn, grab, turn, pass—freed Ria's mind, which then decided Jane's aura was a puzzle, one far too intriguing to put down. How would Ria fix it, given the chance? Grab, turn, pass, turn, grab, turn, pass. Tourmalinated quartz crystals on the heart chakra, or a hand-polished lump of snowflake obsidian? There were arguments to be made for both treatments, and before she could stop herself, she'd put the question to Jane.

The trash bag Jane was slinging toward the pile in her room flew wild, hit the wall, and poured sweaters all over the floor. "Tourmalinated quartz crystals? Tell you what, Ria: let's skip my heart chakra and put those *quartz crystals* on my credit history. That'll take seven years to recover. Or on my bank balance, after I blew the good start I'd made on retirement savings to get Nils through rehab *three times*. Or we could put quartz crystals on my reputation at the office. How about my reputation in the Pagan community? I've called in so many favors from so many people to save his sorry ass, I've got none left to call in for saving my own. After the spectacle he made of himself at Pagan Pride last year, everybody knows what kind of man I cast my lot with. Fuck. What box did I put my Nicorette patches in? Anybody see them? I'd do anything for a cigarette except smoke one."

Quietly, while the others scrounged around in the open boxes, Ria touched the amulet she wore for finding lost objects and concentrated on her third eye chakra. "Where's your toiletry bag, Jane? The toiletry bag is where I'd be if I were a Nicorette patch."

"Bathroom, unless it's still with the bathrobes." Jane upended a duffel bag. A pantry's worth of ramen packages and half-used jars of peanut butter tumbled out. "Fuck. Wrong duffel." She headed for the kitchen.

Just as well, because that gave Ria a chance to close herself in with the bathroom sink and wash her hands. She counted to one hundred, scrubbing her palms together under hot water. Should have kept her mouth shut about the aura thing. Why couldn't she shut up when she knew perfectly well she was pushing people's buttons? She never screwed up like that with divination clients, but with everybody else... She'd have to try another therapist, because she could not go on like this. After she found the box of Nicorette patches in the toiletry bag, she washed her hands to another count of a hundred before venturing back.

Jane was standing right outside the bathroom door. "I'm sorry, Ria. It's not your fault I married an asshole."

"Have a Nicorette patch." There was little enough she could offer that Jane would accept.

But Jane didn't accept those, either. Not quite. "I really thought I was done with these. They're the lowest dose and everything. I got through a whole week with no nicotine at all, and then... I just hate to go into ritual space with this poison in my system."

Ria did not point out that Jane used to, as a matter of course, suck down two cigarettes right before casting Circle. "Do what you have to do to make it into Circle, and ask the Gods' help once you get there." It was what Ria did, and usually by the end of the liturgy it worked well enough to get her through drinking a sacramental sip from a shared cup. The Wiccan ideal of entering Circle in a state of perfect love and perfect trust was too much to ask, but on a good day the ritual could move her, if only for a moment, into perfect love and perfect trust before it ended.

Thank goodness for Sophie. At the first mention of Circle, she picked her way into the foyer and flung fallen beach towels off the covered picnic basket she used for her ritual kit. "Time to go, people," she said. "If you want to clear the air, do it where the air is clear. We need to go to the beach now. Should have gone before we got snappish."

"But..." Ria waved a hand over the mess they'd be leaving.

Sophie shrugged. "It's not bad, for moving day. The truck's empty, so it's all improvement from here. We can order pizza for post-ritual feast. C'mon!" With that, she was off, and the rest of Rugosa Coven could follow her or not.

"All improvement from here," Sebastian said. "That's a nice reality. I'm in." His gravitational pull got the stragglers moving. Ria tucked a Nicorette patch in her pocket and followed.

The Friday night traffic on Ocean Avenue was slowed to a stop. Only when the narrow peninsula's one long road was choked like this was it really safe to cross. Once on the far side, the coven clambered up the rickety aluminum stairs over the concrete and aggregate seawall.

Cresting the top, Ria caught sight of the Full Moon just risen over the Atlantic, its reflection a straight path across low waves to the horizon. So lovely. It was just past sunset, the Moon still trining Jupiter, an arrangement of the planets that brought out the unwarranted optimism in everyone, and sometimes fostered a little progress to go with all that hope. Ria allowed the shining waves to fill her with joy. There would be other moments, later, for nursing the sting of Jane's mockery. Her crown chakra spun wide to welcome the stars.

Down on the dunes, Sophie was looking for a good spot to set up the altar. There was poison ivy to pick past. There were rugosa roses, plain and fragrant, last year's bulbous rose hips still clinging to the canes. Though the coven had taken its name from the beach rose, they also knew from experience not to get barefoot too soon on the sand. It wasn't enough just to get beyond the reach of thorns and itches; too close to the water, bare feet were likely to squish into beached jellyfish. A Full Moon was a great help. New Moon rites on the beach ended with flashlights and first aid kits.

Ria's footsteps clanked down the seawall steps and carried her to the good spot Sophie had found. Somebody must have raked it level for volleyball. The two coven sisters spread the altar cloth and anchored it against the wind with smooth river stones. Most of Sophie's rit kit was specialized for windy beach rituals: she kept her candles in foot-tall glass chimneys, she favored a butane lighter over matches, and her wand was a piece of found driftwood. The tools and symbols of earth, air, water, and fire were all in the basket. As was usual for her, Sophie made to put the chalice in the east, facing the ocean. And, as was usual for *her*, Ria pointedly moved the chalice to the western side of the altar.

Sophie picked the chalice up. East.

Ria swapped it with the incense burner across the altar as if she were castling chess pieces. West.

"Oh, for fuck's sake, Ria," said Sophie. "There's an ocean right here. It's in the east. If Paracelsus had lived on our side of the Atlantic, he'd have put water in the east, too."

"But Paracelsus wasn't, and he didn't. We may not be traditionalists, but we are carrying on a tradition that incorporates the finest ceremonial and Neoplatonic…"

"That's fine," said Sophie. Her voice was trying for graciousness, but she'd never been that interested in the outward forms, not of etiquette any more than of old-school ceremonial magic. "Whatever. But you get to priestess tonight. I am not going to stand with my back to the ocean and invoke the spirits of water to come to me from the west. You do lovely rituals. I'm too tired from moving boxes to exercise my hostessly prerogatives, anyhow."

"Oh, I didn't mean to…"

"No, really. You're always welcome to use my altar tools, you know that. I'm sure Bob will be cool with priesting opposite you. Hey, Bob!"

"I really didn't mean to..."

Bob, who had been gazing across the water, turned and said, "Yeah, Soph?"

"You mind a change of plans? How are you for priesting opposite Ria?"

"Cool." He came over to confer about the rite, then glanced down at the altar setup. "Ah. Chalice in the west. So, you want to do this old-school, Ria?" It was a specialty of his. Bob and Sophie's parents had been serious occultists. While Sophie emphatically preferred postmodern kitchen-witchery over ceremonial magic, Bob was comfortable with both styles.

Unprepared as Ria felt to priestess, she knew none of her coven sisters favored the classical precision she liked, and if she wanted the Full Moon celebrated her way, it was her responsibility. They were almost twenty-three hours past the real full of the Moon as it was, because Friday was easier than Thursday. No amount of Ria's advocacy for tighter astrological timing could outweigh the imperatives of the work week. That ongoing argument didn't bear thinking about, not right before entering sacred space. A lot of things didn't. "I'm still feeling a little jangly," she admitted.

"Who isn't?" Bob pointed out. "Will you come breathe with me? I was thinking I'd go stand with my feet in the surf. There's a lot I'd like to wash away."

Ria left her shoes by the exact edge of the raked-flat rectangle on the sand and followed Bob to the water, watching for jellyfish as she went. "Good, clean sand," she mumbled to herself. "It's all good, clean sand."

Bob's aura rippled along its outer edges, dislodging tiny spots of blackness that Ria always thought of as sticky, though of course they had no real texture. The surf rolled up to his knees, then away, then up to his knees again, carrying the loosened spots away.

She'd have liked to compliment him on his technique, but that could wait. She tucked a handful of her skirt hem into her waistband and stepped into the surf. The first wave was a shock of cold. Retreating waves pulled sand granules from under her feet. Matching her breath with Bob's, she stood just far enough away that their auras would not quite touch. Her solar plexus chakra was shooting forward those long tendrils again, the ones that poked at the auras of everybody around her. No wonder Jane had gotten snappish. On the inhalations, Ria pulled her tendrils in; on the exhalations, Bob shed the residue of his anger—as a litigator, he got angry for a living, even on good days. Ten breaths later, they turned to face one another, nodded, and left the water's edge to pace their way back to the altar.

Candlelight burned steady in the glass chimneys, not least because Amber positioned herself carefully to be a windbreak. Sebastian, Sophie, and Jane arranged themselves to fill in the southern arc of the Circle, leaving space for Ria and Bob to either side of the altar in the North. Someone had filled the chalice. Jane looked like she could make it half an hour without that Nicorette patch. Everything was ready.

Ria took up the long driftwood wand and dug a shallow line in the sand as she circled her companions:

> *Thrice round, thrice round*
> *That in this space the Gods be found*
> *Thrice about, thrice about*
> *To keep misfortune well out*
> *Thrice spin, thrice spin,*
> *Good fellowship for all within*

It was a bit of the Oakbridge Coven liturgy she'd never been able to let go. That oldest layer of her training came through in everything tonight—in the calling of the four elements, the welcoming of the God and Goddess, in the blessing of the wine and cakes. Even the impromptu prayer-spell to bless Jane with healing and safety felt like an echo of the coven Ria had lost years ago.

Somewhere down the shore, in Ocean Grove or maybe Asbury Park, Oakbridge Coven would probably be celebrating the Full Moon right now, too. They'd been as addicted to weekends and as lax about lunar precision as Rugosa Coven was. Ria had told them and told them...

Focus. That was not a thing to dwell on mid-ritual. *Be where you are, do what you are doing.* It was time to bid farewell to the elements, to the God and Goddess, and to open the Circle she had cast. This was just the moment when most people got sloppy, but Ria believed in practicing good magickal hygiene: whatever you call in, you ought graciously to see out, and whatever you build, you ought carefully to dismantle and put away when its work is done. A Circle properly cast and then forgotten could siphon energy out of its caster's aura for lunar cycle after lunar cycle. She'd seen it happen.

Bob followed her lead through the farewells and anchored the energy while she paced the Circle widdershins, scuffing her sand-line open with her foot every third step. The space that had been their temple was just a stretch of beach again. When she stood at the head of the altar in the North, she said,

Round the Waning and the Waxing,
Round the Year-Wheel's span,
Merry meet, and merry part,
And merry meet again.

There. And the spirits of Water had lodged no objection whatever to being called in the west.

After a round of post-ritual hugs, Jane said, "Um, Ria?"

"Yeah?"

"Do you still have that..."

"Nicorette patch?"

"Yeah."

"Where do you want it stuck on?" Ria concentrated on Jane's aura and placed a little bet with herself. The blisters on the ketheric template were, now that she considered them, about the shape of a Nicorette patch. "Have you been favoring the front of your left shoulder?"

Fortunately, Jane had also been tugging the collar of her shirt to suggest exactly that spot, or she might have snapped about the aura thing again. Looked like it didn't even occur to her.

"Yeah. I should vary it more. The directions say to put them on different places, but..."

"How about here? Right-handed person like you, I bet you never think to tuck it behind your right shoulder." It aligned with a relatively undamaged stretch of the aura, one that could take a little hard treatment if it spared the rest of the system.

Jane untucked her shirt and shifted the collar a bit to give Ria a shot at her shoulderblade. "Would you do the honors?"

Ria peeled the backing off the patch and smoothed it into place, and found the temptation to do something about that unsprung throat chakra irresistible. The tiny chakras in the palms of Ria's hands were still wide open from priestessing, and as she stepped away, she lifted the unsprung, drooping coil of Jane's throat chakra back into place.

Jane's eyes flashed wide. "What did you do?"

"I..."

"I didn't ask for *that*, whatever it was."

The snappishness was getting on Ria's last nerve. "If you don't believe in auras, why do you care? In your universe, I didn't really do anything."

"It's my aura to disbelieve in. You could have asked. I'd have said no, but still, you *should* have asked."

Which was a fair point. The only thing to say to that was sorry. Ria's hand found its way to the hematite pendant, her amulet for calm, and she drew a breath to apologize.

Jane beat her to the forgiveness, sort of. "It was a beautiful ritual. A rare treat. Like nothing I'd have thought of. After an effort like that, a person needs a chance to come back down to earth."

"Hey!" Amber called from where she stood at the top of the seawall. While Jane and Ria hadn't been paying attention, the rest of the coven had packed up the rit kit and headed back for the cottage. "I'm ordering pizza. We're all starving up here. Can you two stop bickering long enough to prefer some toppings?" The top of the seawall was the only spot in Sea Bright that got reliable cell phone reception, and Sophie forgot to pay the bill for her landline as often as not.

"Mushrooms!" said Jane.

"With broccoli!" Ria added.

"And sausage!"

"No!" Ria counterproposed, a little frantically. Who knew what went into a pizza joint's sausage? "Ham!"

"Fine," Jane agreed. "Priestess's prerogative."

"Thank you." It seemed they'd put the aura thing behind them for now.

"Maybe if we eat some actual food, we'll stop biting each other's heads off," said Jane. "Low blood sugar and all that."

"Here's hoping." But Ria wondered what Jane would be able to say now, after that half-finished repair to her throat chakra. Greater ability to speak her truth might not be an improvement for the people around her.

Back at the cottage, over mushroom, ham, and broccoli pizza, Jane broke down entirely. Covering her face with her hands left trails of tomato sauce.

Amber and Sophie wrapped her in their arms, and Sebastian started the coven on a calming chant.

The chant carried them until Jane wiped the tomato sauce from her cheeks and said, "He left all the kitchen cabinets hanging open."

The chant fell away. They stared at her, boggled.

"Well, you wanted to know what the last straw was," she went on. "After the drinking and the shoving and the smacking and the broken furniture didn't drive me off, what could possibly have done it, right? And I made it through all that, and gave him his three shots at rehab, and here we all were, holding our breath and waiting for the bullshit to start again. So what finally makes me pack my bags? The goddamn kitchen cabinets. Why couldn't I have left over something smart? Why did I have to leave over petty shit like that?"

It didn't seem all that petty to Ria.

"Because," said Bob, "the bullshit *would* have started again, we all know that. Some part of you saw it was better to leave today over petty shit than to wait around for a major disaster. You've spared everybody the fallout. Well done."

The awful film started rolling in Ria's head. Somehow it was a shock every time the projector started back up after a break. In the awful film, disaster found Jane despite her escape. The disaster came in a dozen different forms simultaneously, and Ria flinched from the things her brain found for her to fear. Worse, she couldn't help feeling as if her anger at Jane might *make* something bad happen.

Sebastian noticed right away. "You okay, Ria?"

"Um." Would it be helpful to anyone for her to name her fear? "It just occurred to me that leaving Nils might make him more dangerous. Sometimes that happens. Sorry. Probably everybody's thought of that, but..."

Apparently they hadn't.

"Well then, I can consult the cards when I get home," she said. That was her main comfort when she was alone.

Jane rounded on her. "Is there anything you don't believe in?"

"Vampires. There are definitely no vampires." Ria had spent her twenties searching for them. If they'd existed anywhere, in any form, she was sure she'd have found them. Maybe they could have fixed whatever it was, this thing she wasn't supposed to diagnose for herself. "Is there anything you *do* believe in, Jane? Is there any magic left in the world for you?"

Jane took a deep breath, and when she answered, it was with that slowness she got when she was listening to herself, trying to figure out what was true. "There's plenty in the ocean. In the dolphins, in the wind through the rosehips. I believe in nature. Make that Capital-N Nature. And my inner jury's still out about Dion Fortune's definition of magic as change of consciousness in accordance with will."

Bob smiled. "Just like you, Jane, to have an Inner Jury when the rest of us have an Inner Child."

Jane would take that kind of ribbing from Bob, would take it with good grace, but Ria knew how prickly Jane would have been if she had said the same thing. As for change of consciousness in accordance with will, that was the one definition of magic Ria knew to be false. *If will were enough to change consciousness, would I be like this?*

"Ria even believes in polyamory."

Amber said, "Oh, now wait a minute," just as Sebastian said, "There's no call for that."

"Come off it," said Jane. "You two like to think of yourselves as polyamorous, but how long has it been since either of you used the open-relationship clause? Polyamory works for you guys because you're not actually practicing it."

Ria said, "Polyamory works for me better than monogamy has worked for you, Jane," and she instantly regretted it. Jane was only mean when she was hurting. Which happened a lot lately, but still, responding in kind didn't help any.

Everyone fell silent.

She tried damage control. "Not that polyamory actually works *well* for me, I'll admit. I have my disasters. They just haven't required U-Haul rentals so far."

Not much of an improvement. Jane was barely avoiding tears.

"Well, I just totally fucked up," said Ria. "Maybe I'd better call it a day before I do anything worse." She couldn't even blame it on the planets this time—the aspects were favorable, though that could only carry her so far.

Sophie was gearing up to say something about it being not such a big deal.

Jane steamrolled right over her. "Yeah, maybe you should."

"You were already feeling ill when you arrived," Sebastian pointed out. "It's no wonder if, after strenuous priestessing, you're not firing on all cylinders. Are you okay to drive home?"

"As okay as I am to do anything else."

Halfway through making her farewells, Ria realized she wasn't the only one leaving. Her departure seemed to have signalled the end of the whole coven's evening. Probably she should have felt guiltier about that, but mostly she was relieved. It was almost as if the lateness of the hour really had been the problem, almost as if everyone were simply tired. There were the usual parting hugs with everyone, even Jane.

Pretending nothing had happened was no way to go. Ria blurted out the first idea she had for making amends. "We should get together next Friday. After a big thing like Jane escaping from Nils, we shouldn't wait around for the New Moon before we convene again. And we weren't even sure we were going to meet for the New Moon, with Midsummer Festival the same weekend."

"Oh, hey, speaking of festival," said Amber, "have you decided if you're going? I was just filling out the form to request a cabin."

"Um. Probably not going." Damn pastel therapist. "The hot weather has been knocking me for a loop this year. Don't know how rustic I can go before something dire happens."

"Next Friday sounds like a good idea," said Bob. "A week into your new life, Jane, you'll have a much better idea of what support you need from us."

Jane daubed at her eyes with the pizzeria's napkins. "You guys are the best."

"I can host," said Ria. "Please, allow me to host." And that settled it.

The drive home was uncommonly free of doom visions, mostly because Ria kept replaying the moments when she'd said stupid things. Fine. If she had to suffer, she preferred that her suffering be substantive. She'd been such a jerk. *They just haven't required U-Haul rentals so far.* What kind of thing was that to say?

Once she reached her quiet Red Bank side street and the cheery yellow bungalow her grandmother had left her, the state of her garden caught her up short. Long June days had sped the chaos she'd given up fighting even before the Spring Equinox. Just when had the stalks of wild horseradish and amaranth grown so tall? She had to crick her neck back now to see the tufts of seed. It was a testament, she supposed, to the care she used to take of the soil, that the weeds prospered so. No stranger would guess, looking at the garden now, that the inside of the bungalow could have passed the most stringent white glove test. She would have to come up with some excuse for this mess before next Friday.

If she couldn't get her ailment in order soon enough to keep the amaranth from seeding the whole yard, there was hardly any point in recovering her meager sanity before winter, was there?

In the divination room at the back of the occult supply shop the next day, candles burning on her altar, Ria threw quick three-card Tarot spreads for herself while she waited at her reading table for her next client. She'd lost count of how many three-card spreads.

"Did I remember to turn off the stove?" Ria asked the cards.

Yes, said the first card.

Get a grip, said the second card.

And while you're at it, honey, said the third card, *don't give up on seeking professional help, even if the first one was a dud.*

And then the whole three-card spread had its collective say: *How many times a day do you really need to ask about the stove? The parking brake? And your hands! Enough with the handwashing, already. Insurance or no insurance, you need a therapist.*

The deck had been her confessor for over twenty years, since the day she admitted she wasn't a Catholic anymore. Nobody could blame the cards now if they wanted to share the job with a shrink.

She read with the same old Rider-Waite deck she'd learned on in her teens. They'd survived coffee rings during the years when she gave free readings at No Ordinary Joe's. They'd survived being cried on by any number of college girls with bad boyfriends. They'd survived a house fire, though they no longer smelled of smoke. They'd even survived immersion in the Atlantic, the day Ria fell off a rain-slick jetty with her backpack full of ritual gear. Hers were hardworking cards with two decades of well-paid consultations behind them, and if they occasionally presumed on their familiarity with their interpreter, she wasn't inclined to complain.

The phone rang. And rang. Ria poked her head into the shop

from the divination room. "Morgan?" she shouted at the back of his balding head with its squirrelly gray ponytail. He was standing right next to the ringing phone, not picking up, nor did he turn around to acknowledge her. "Are you going to get that?" It was probably her client, who was now five minutes late. If the girl arrived seven minutes later than she already was, there would be a new planetary alignment to worry about, one that might be ill-suited to the reading. The thought of giving a poor performance made Ria want to wash the bad luck off her hands.

But Morgan leaned across the glass counter with one of the old regulars, fiddling with his ponytail and lamenting about how the internet had eaten up the occult supply business. "Time was when the only way a newcomer to the Pagan scene could find a coven was to come to the local shop, check out the notices posted on the corkboard, take a class or two. These days..."

The phone went on ringing.

Ria stomped out past the corkboard with its diminished crop of notices, touching nothing as she went, past the astrology calendars, past the fingerprinty bins of crystals and dusty jars of herbs, past the hanger rack hung thick with cloaks, right up to the counter, where she glared at Morgan. "Are you going to get that?"

"You could get it yourself," he said, glaring back. "It's probably your client." His aura shifted, swelled tall, and tried to press down on hers from above.

She glared at the old black phone, a rotary dial relic that had been there longer than either Ria or Morgan. She glared at it, and the fluourescent lights in the shop's drop ceiling reflected, rainbowed, in the oily sheen of fingerprints all over the receiver.

Who knew what germs lurked there?

Never had Ria been able to pick up that phone. Morgan never sanitized it, so Ria couldn't touch it. He wouldn't ask why, and she preferred not to explain. It was embarrassing enough without labels.

The phone gave up.

When I buy this shop, I will make sure the fucking phone gets answered, even if I can't answer it myself. Ria did the math in her head again for the bajillionth time—it was such a familiar tally, she did it four times fast to calm herself. Six more months, and she'd be able to offer Morgan seventy-five percent of what he said the business was worth. He was tired enough to take it. Unless, of course, she had to pay a therapist's full fee for months instead. That could scramble her nest egg over high heat.

Did I remember to turn off the stove?

Just as she was about to go back to her cards and ask them, the phone rang again.

Morgan looked at Ria, looked at his commiserating old regular, and sighed. His aura deflated as he picked up the receiver and said, "Transcendence Perfection Bliss of the Beyond, how may I help you?" Paused. Looked incredulous. "Ria, it's a personal call."

Ria's friends knew better than to call her at work. She never took calls when she was reading for a client—it happened to be true, and that was the excuse she gave to the people who mattered most to her—and she could not, could not pick up that filthy phone. "Who would call me here?"

"Only one way to find out," said Morgan. "I'm not about to take a message when you're *standing right there.*"

There was not enough hand sanitizer in the world, no paper towel thick enough.

Morgan started humming the *Jeopardy* theme.

"Could you just rest the receiver on the counter, handle down, ears up?" She tried to keep the wheedle out of her voice. How Ria hated the wheedle, every time she heard herself do it.

"You have got to be kidding me."

She might need to explain this time. There would be no passing it off as concern with inauspicious astrological aspects. "I'm not kidding. Please, Morgan." Tears burned in her eyes. *When I buy this store, the fucking phone will get sanitized daily. Hourly. It will be my fucking phone.* "Please. Just do it."

He set the receiver gently down, just as she'd asked. "Oh, man. You've got it bad, don't you?"

Ria couldn't deal with him or his regret right now. She bent and twisted to be near the receiver she couldn't touch, both hands busy coiling her long black-dyed hair out of the way of the counter, which surely had its own bacterial population. "Hello?"

"How's my favorite ex-girlfriend doing?" said the phone-crackled voice of Franklin Lear, trying too hard to sound jocular.

"You know better than to call me at work, Frank."

"Nobody's stopping you from getting a cell phone."

"Just because other people are willing to fry their brains with radiation doesn't mean I have to join them. Why couldn't you leave me a message at home?"

"I need to see you right away. I need your advice."

Which meant Ria would probably get laid, which she hadn't since the last time she and Franklin broke up. But it wouldn't mean only that. Things with Franklin were always messy, though he himself was fastidiously, metrosexually clean whenever he wasn't out doing research for a story. "So come see me, Frank. You know where I am. Goodbye." She straightened, but couldn't bring herself to touch the phone to hang it up.

Franklin's crackly voice said, "Wait! Ria!"

Grimacing at the thought of putting her face near the receiver again, Ria intended to bend and hear him out. Couldn't make herself do it. She marshalled faded memories of her childhood ballet classes and hitched her skirt up a bit, then lifted a well-shod toe to click the call off. Done. The dial tone droned its demand for the receiver she couldn't put back in the cradle.

When she'd smoothed her skirt with the requisite four strokes, she realized Morgan was standing behind her, tapping his hand on the glass case. He probably had no idea about his hand. The man had a blissful lack of physical self-consciousness that Ria had always envied.

The shop door swung open, jangling its cluster of tiny bells.

"That was quick," Ria said before she even looked over.

But it wasn't Frank. It was her eleven o'clock appointment, a classic undergrad complete with sorority sweatshirt. "Sorry I'm late," said the girl. "I hope I haven't messed up your schedule."

Ria looked at her watch. Half an hour late, in fact. "Come on back. I'm expecting someone, but he can wait."

In the back room, Ria stood with her client before the little altar and said, "Before we begin, we need to perform a small act of purification. Dip your hands into this bowl of consecrated water and concentrate on clarifying your intent." The water was, in fact, consecrated with a dash of antiseptic tea tree oil, and a few nicer-smelling oils to camouflage it. Knowing that the cards would be handled by hands that had been properly cleaned certainly helped Ria clarify *her* intent. Ria allowed herself a bit of hand-washing, too, in her own separate bowl, and said her pre-Tarot prayer before sitting down to the cards. "Truth be shown, truth be spoken, truth be heard."

Had the girl been on time, Moon quincunx Venus would have called for discrimination in affairs of the heart, but now the Sun was trine Neptune, so Ria expected the cards to be optimistic about the girl's love life. Most days, she'd have called that a refreshing change. Tarot readings for college girls usually required lots of Kleenex. Between bouts of weeping, the girls would look at the plain-talking cards and say, *But I loooooooove him.* And Ria would look at the little icons of infidelity, addiction, or general ass-hattery and say, *I know, but he won't be ready to love anyone for a while yet.* Happy girls with happy loves did not seek out professional fortunetellers.

Today, with Frank on the way, Ria would rather have done the usual undergrad reading. At least then she wouldn't have felt like such a freak. Of course, she'd still *be* the freak who would need to spread her cards out under ultraviolet light at the end of the workday, to cleanse them of her clients' touch.

This girl had applied to medical school to please her parents, and to law school to please herself. Divorced parents, it turned out, who agreed on very few things, so medical school would be a rare chance to satisfy them both at once.

The surface question was a cakewalk: *Please yourself, kid, it's your life.* If the surface questions were the only ones that mattered, Ria wouldn't have needed cards or star charts or any of her other stock in trade. But the questions her clients thought they were coming to ask were sometimes the least of their troubles. Ria started with a classic ten-card Celtic Cross spread, adding clarification cards wherever the client wanted more detail. Clever girl, good questions, and Ria would have been happy to keep branching more clarifications off the initial spread until all seventy-two cards in her deck had their say, if Frank hadn't barged in.

He stuck his head in the room—his bald-shaved head. Looked like he'd finally decided to lose the rest of his hair on his own terms. It suited him, though perhaps he'd put on a little weight since she'd seen him last. He smelled faintly of laundry detergent. "Oh, sorry! Didn't mean to..."

"I told you I had an appointment." Sweetness and light, sweetness and light. She would not let him derail the rest of her client's reading.

"I just thought..."

"Well, hold that thought another thirty minutes." She hadn't heard from him in six months. She wouldn't let him rush her now. Frank backed out the door, and she closed it decisively with her whole body weight.

The girl started reaching for her book bag. "Maybe I should..."

"Not at all. We just need to refocus." Ria stood and turned to her altar. She held a small disc of fine charcoal to a candle flame and blew gently on the lit edge a few times before setting it down in her censer. Here, in her territory, she burned only the best incense, her own homemade, which she ground and blended with ingredients from a perfumers' supply company in San Francisco—none of that crap Morgan sold in the shop up front would do for Ria's altar work. There was a time when she'd used ingredients from her garden, too, but last year's dried flowers and leaves were nearly gone, and until she could get her hands back into her gardening gloves, if not into the dirt, she couldn't bear to grind the last of those with her mortar and pestle.

Copal, sweetest of the conifer resins, burned clear with oils of oakmoss and basil. She could trust the copal not to turn acrid on the charcoal, so she released the blessing she'd bound in it and turned her attention back to the client.

"Nice," the girl said. "I feel about ten I.Q. points smarter."

Ria smiled. *Still got the moxie.* "Now, about your parents' divorce."

They didn't quite go through the whole deck, but most of the cards found a question to address. The girl availed herself of Ria's box of tissues after all, but over a break-up half her lifetime ago, which was a nice bit of novelty in a sorority girl reading. After the client had gone her way and Ria had cleaned the cards with non-bleaching sanitizer wipes, she would have liked a chance to throw a few three-card spreads about Frank and his burning question, but before she had the chance, he planted himself across the table from her.

"I need to find something. The magazine's on the verge of going big this time, but our competition already got picked up by the chain bookstores." Bleach-stained jeans and a worn t-shirt with his magazine's logo fading across his chest—that was as much thought as he'd given to meeting his ex.

"Good to see you, too. I've been fine, thanks for asking." If Frank hadn't missed her, Ria wasn't sure she wanted to hear about the latest circulation figures for *Bizarro Jersey*. He'd been polyamorous for as long as she'd known him, and she'd been his secondary or tertiary lover off and on over that decade, but ultimately it was the magazine, not the long series of fiancées, that Frank seemed to care about most.

"Hauntings and abandoned mansions make for okay articles, but a cover story about the Jersey Devil would be just the trick. Something with fresh pictures, real pictures."

"And I'm guessing your last fiancée didn't work out."

"True, but I don't need GPS coordinates to locate *her*. Can you tell me where to look for the Jersey Devil, or can't you?"

"Let's start with *whether* to look."

"It's got to be somewhere in the Pine Barrens."

"Have you read your own historical pieces? The rampage of 1909? The Jersey Devil is not a creature you want to find. It's not a creature you want to get found by, either."

"Is this about our breakup?"

"If this were about our breakup, I'd graciously relinquish you into the arms of the Jersey Devil, just like I've relinquished you into the arms of...how many other girlfriends is it now? I've lost count. No, Frank. You don't have to persuade *me* the Jersey Devil is real and lives in the Pine Barrens. I know it's true. And I don't want you to get torn to pieces."

"But *could* you do it? Theoretically?"

Ria sighed. "Map and pendulum. That's the method I use for finding apartments for people, or helping them decide which house to make an offer on. It'd probably work for this, too. If I were willing to do it."

"If it's a matter of payment, I've already given Morgan the usual fee for your time."

Now if she refused, she'd look even more unprofessional to Morgan that she already did. Odd as Ria's profession was, she practiced it to the highest standards.

What would the highest standards say about helping a person get into a situation that could kill him seriously dead? She turned to face her altar, sprinkled another pinch of incense on the little charcoal disk, and tried to connect back to all the other oracular priestesses in history. This wasn't her first incarnation on the job. What had she known in the temple she remembered in dreams? *The seeker is responsible for his question, and for what he does with his answer. You are responsible for seeking the truth, and for getting out of its way when you recognize it.*

She nodded in acknowledgement to the altar, then opened the cabinet beneath it for her maps and pendulum. When she turned again to face Franklin Lear, her eyes teared up.

"You should go easier on the incense," he said, handing her a tissue.

"Be careful out there," she replied. "You ever learn to shoot a gun?"

"Would you shoot the last of the snow leopards? Would you shoot..." Apparently he couldn't think of any other endangered species. "Ria, why are you being so hard on me? Do you want me to leave?"

"*I'm* being hard on *you*?"

"Yeah. You kind of are."

She played it all back in her head, starting with the call on the phone she couldn't touch. That had pissed her off, but it wasn't as if she'd ever told him the truth about why he shouldn't call her at work. She'd interrupted him, hung up on him, put him off, kicked him out of the room, and mocked the failure of yet another engagement. Probably there was more that would wake her up in a sweat of mortification when she remembered it in the middle of the night. "I kind of was. I'm sorry. I don't want you to leave. But I also don't want you to go."

"To the Pine Barrens?"

"I'd feel a lot better about asking the pendulum where to go if we asked the cards *whether* to go first." The backs of her hands itched so hard they burned.

"If there are reasons not to go, I don't want to know about them. I've made up my mind."

Isn't that what you said last time you dropped me for a primary lover who wanted you to give up polyamory? "I won't press you to accept a reading you don't want."

"I would just become another of your cautionary tales about people who ignore the cards' advice. We'll both be less annoyed if I don't ask the cards in the first place."

So she spread the big state map over the table and smoothed its creases, then smoothed her skirt four strokes, and took a deep breath. Her pendulum was a six-inch length of silver chain with two heavy beads of turquoise, one at each end. She held the irregular, lumpy bead between her fingertips and dangled the carved, pointed bead a few inches over the map. She chose a starting point at the center of the Pine Barrens, an expanse of state park green shot through with bogs and creeks—and shot through with an invisible network of summer camp scary stories and high school dares. If New Jersey's collective unconscious resided anywhere, it was in the Pine Barrens. The carved bead hung still.

"Ask," said Ria.

"Where is the Jersey Devil?"

The pendulum rocked slightly, then swung in a wide circle before following a definite pull to the southeast. Ria let her hand drift down the map, and the rotations tightened around a spot where a tiny unnamed tributary joined the Mullica River. The polished bead stopped abruptly there and felt so heavy, the rough bead Ria held between her fingertips nearly slipped from her grasp.

"That's your spot."

"You've really come through for me, Ria." He beamed. Perhaps he had confused a run-in with the Jersey Devil for a free trip to Disneyland. "Can I take you to dinner?

Restaurant kitchens were full of rats and roaches. Not all restaurants, maybe, but enough, and how could anyone be sure which were which? It occurred to Ria that the pizza the coven had ordered just last night might have come from an unsanitary kitchen. She should have thought of that at the time. No, actually, thank the Gods she hadn't.

"Maybe we could eat in?" she suggested. Either of their home kitchens could be trusted.

"All the better. I'll cook you something spectacular. My place at eight o'clock?"

Ria knew what she would see in the horological charts of her ephemeris, but double-checked the page for the day anyway out of pure wishful thinking. Moon in opposition to Mars, 8:28 p.m.: high energy, but not cooperation. The warning of Moon quincunx Venus was completely superfluous: discrimination required in romance.

If this could even be called romance.

But it wasn't like she had any other prospects. "I'll be there with bells on. Do you have…um…?"

"Yes, and plenty of it."

"I'll bring the wine."

Good as his word, Frank had so many kinds of latex barriers that one bottle of wine was enough for Ria. She'd brought two bottles, just in case. The food he cooked in his rather Spartan one-room apartment was probably okay, but she was so anxious until the wine kicked in, she barely noticed what she was eating, let alone whether it was any good.

He seemed to think her latex fixation was a kink, bless his heart, so he kept trying to make a show of enjoying the barriers. They both got a laugh out of the squeaking of the male condom against the female condom, though that wasn't really a moment when they'd been craving laughter. He was a good sport, she had to give him that. A good sport, and persistent. If only she could bring as much enthusiasm to bear about him, about anyone, about the whole endeavor. No wonder she had no other prospects. Maybe she should have opened the second bottle of wine.

"Will you stay?" he asked her in the shower afterward.

"You really want me to?"

"I'll make breakfast."

So she gave him a good scrubbing, which he seemed to appreciate, and they settled in for the night.

She dreamed of the temple where pilgrims had come to hear her speak as oracle. Lately she'd been trying to dream into the memory of the name she'd worn in that life, or the name of the deity she'd served. Still no luck on those tonight, but she did step into a courtyard in her bare feet. Very young feet. By the cool of the stone and the dew on the grass, she guessed it was early spring. White flowers filled the courtyard. What were those flowers called? The ones with the funny upside-down looking blossoms. Not columbines, the other ones, that sometimes the grocery store sold in little pots. One more name she woke without recalling.

Over an early breakfast Frank went melancholy, though the pancakes had turned out just fine.

"I have something…awkward to tell you, Ria."

What would it be this time? Seeking serious involvement with some monogamous other woman, again? About to be a father, Gods forbid? "Whatever it is," she said, "better to know than not to know."

"Remember the girlfriend I broke up with right before we got together?"

She remembered too many candidates for that description. "Which time we got together?"

He scratched his head like he wasn't sure, either. Great. "Three years ago, maybe? Yeah, back in 2001. Cindy. The kindergarten teacher."

Oh, no. No, no, no. He was about to tell her he'd picked up some sort of disease. He looked so mournful. Why hadn't the cards warned her? They warned everybody else about that kind of thing. She should have insisted on even more latex. Shouldn't have joined him for dinner at all. "What about her?"

"She hexed my refrigerator."

"What?"

"She hexed my refrigerator. The same refrigerator I gave you later, when I tried moving to New York to take the magazine national."

"For the past three years, I've been living with a hexed refrigerator?" It seemed unlikely that she, of all people, could have been eating out of a malefic major appliance for that long without noticing. So this was what it felt like to be Jane. Ria considered phoning her coven sister as soon she got home, considered telling her, *I finally get it!* But there Franklin was, still mournful. "Well, I told you that girlfriend was too mired in pop culture. Of all the things to hex! At least if Zool pops out of the produce drawer, I'll know who I'm gonna call." And then, bubbling up under her confidence—the fear, the pictures, a beginning.

"As if *you* would need to call anybody. Now that you know, I mean. I kept telling myself I didn't have to break it to you, that your house had protections prepared against that sort of thing. But while you were with your client yesterday, I got to talking with Morgan ..."

"Talking with *Morgan*?!"

"How else did you expect me to kill half an hour?" Frank said. "I've already read practically every book Morgan carries, and local occult supply shops are great places to get leads on stories for *Bizarro Jersey*. No leads this time, and he carries our competition instead of us. Anyhow, Morgan's worried about you. You're off your game. And I thought right away of the fridge."

Three years. She breathed deep, considered her escalating series of symptoms, and…since the fridge came to live with her, only the past year had been really bad. High school, two decades back, had been far worse, and she could hardly blame the fridge for that. "What kind of angry ex-girlfriend puts a two-year time delay on a hex?" The part of her brain that was flashing pictures of death by food poisoning chimed in, *Bitch.*

Frank communed with his pancakes while he considered. "One who isn't very good at hexing things? One whose hex ends up with the wrong person, in a house with lots of protections on it?"

"I scrubbed that thing out like you wouldn't believe, just as soon as it was installed. How do you *know* it was hexed?"

"Cindy told me at the time that she'd done it, but I didn't quite believe her. Yesterday Morgan said he remembered selling her the black candle…"

"The black candle?" Fuck. All the candles at Transcendence Perfection Bliss of the Beyond were high-quality beeswax. Oh, except for the soy candles Morgan stocked for the most committed lifestyle vegans. Maybe it would be a wimpy hex, if Cindy had bought soy. Morgan carried the black candles because lots of perfectly nice Pagans used them to honor the New Moon, but every once in a while some spell junkie would get a bad idea.

"…And that she'd mentioned something about a refrigerator. All I can say is, I'm never purchasing an appliance with a woman I'm not married to, ever again."

In one way, it hardly mattered whether what's-her-face actually had hexed the refrigerator, or how well: now Ria would be unable to rest until she'd cleansed it ritually. Or maybe until she'd gotten rid of the thing. *Wasn't it bad enough when microbes were the only worry in my fridge?*

"Thanks for the pancakes and all that, Franklin. Sounds like I need to get home and do some cleaning." She waited for him to think of offering to help.

"Got to pack for the Pine Barrens," he said. "I need to be out and back before layout time for the next issue. I'd have shot better photos if I'd made it there in time for the full moon. If I want any moonlight at all for night photography, that means leaving today. I'm sorry about the fridge, Ria, I really am. And thank you again about the map thing."

Time to go, before her composure melted completely. She hadn't expected to spend the night, so she hadn't brought anything with her but the wine and her purse. "Get home safe, Frank. Call when you're back and tell me whether you got killed."

"Will do. Hey, no kiss?"

"Oh, all right. For luck." She could count on him to taste of Listerine, any time of the day or night. Even right after pancakes. How did he do that? He was irreplaceable.

Later that morning, every window open to clear out negativity, Ria knelt on the pink linoleum her grandmother had favored, scrubbing the vegetable bin. The Moon was in Aquarius, so it was no surprise to see her schedule disrupted by urgent causes. So far she'd found no trace of black wax, and no auric trace of a hex. Any spell stubborn enough to last three years would have had at least a wisp of an aura about it.

Meanwhile, a fridge's worth of groceries, which she could ill afford to replace, waited already packed up for disposal in a cooler on the back porch. If Ria could just persuade herself before the perishables perished that there was no hex, she could save herself a couple hundred dollars. The fridge's and freezer's inner cavities were chanted clean, top to bottom, and scrubbed with a blend of hyssop leaves, tea tree oil, and borax salts that Ria had charged with her purifying intent.

The *inner cavities* of the appliance. Not enough.

Ria reached her arms around the hulking thing and scooted it carefully away from the wall, out of its alcove of vintage pink cabinets. Every Solstice and Equinox she vacuumed the dust off the refrigerator's coils. If her covenmates were to be believed, that environmental virtue verged on the puritanical, but beyond vacuuming, she'd never done anything else to the coils.

Any shrink would say the whole exercise in cleansing the fridge was one big symptom already, so at this point, Ria figured she might as well go for broke and do the coils a couple weeks earlier than usual. Why not get a side order of energy efficiency with her main course of crazy? She dragged the vacuum cleaner from the front closet to the kitchen.

The coils were like a refugee camp for displaced dust—it got driven out of the rest of the house so routinely, it had nowhere else to hide. A few loud moments finished it. Ria knelt to examine the back of the fridge closely for the first time.

Bingo.

Blobs of black stuck to the copper. Ria leaned close to smell it. Beeswax, definitely not soy. She'd handmade enough of her own devotional candles to be very sure. It had no trace of an aura, but even so, Ria was not about to touch it with her bare hands.

One benefit of keeping an impeccable personal shrine was that Ria already had a large bottle of solvent on hand just for candle drippings. Latex gloves withstood the solvent just fine. Chanting steadily as she scrubbed with paper towels, Ria visualized the surface of her aura as a bubble of quicksilver mirror, reflecting the hex back at its source.

So much for the contaminated groceries. Ria tossed them, cooler and all, along with the now-waxy paper towels, into the big trash bin outside. The bin was already inscribed with sigils of containment for physical contagion. It took only a moment to recharge the sigils against contagion of all kinds.

When that work was done, Ria went to the basement to strip off her black clothes—black to absorb ambient negativity before it could reach her skin—and threw them all straight into the washer with several drops of the tea tree oil blend and set the machine on high. She showered, scrubbing her skin red under very hot water, and dressed in a fresh uniform of gothic black.

Maybe with the fridge hex out of the way, she could finally make some progress at saving her life.

The psychiatrists' offices would all be closed on a Saturday, which made the phone calls easier. She worked her way through the list, listening to each of their voicemail greetings before deciding where to leave messages. Voices weren't as easy to diagnose as auras, but they would have to do. One sounded too mean, another too nasal. A couple had incomprehensible accents. This one was too cold. That one gave too much rambling detail. She crossed through a third of the names, then called again to leave nervous messages for the other two thirds. *New patient, no insurance, sliding scale, panic attacks, please call soon. Please.*

Two hundred grocery dollars further from making Morgan an offer on the shop, Ria arrived at work early for the eleven o'clock opening time. Dammit, dammit, dammit.

Morgan was two steps ahead of her, pulling his keys from his jeans pocket. "You've got a noon Tarot appointment," he told her. "Housewife with a toddler in tow. Good luck."

What was a toddler but a walking ball of germs held together with saliva and endowed with opposable thumbs? "You could have said no about the toddler."

"You told me you needed cash. I believed you. You're welcome." The lock clunked open. He held the door for her as the little brass bells chimed.

"Did you know the whole time that my refrigerator was hexed?"

Morgan looked almost apologetic. "I knew Frank had a crazy ex-girlfriend. What's new about that? If I'd known the fridge went to live with you, I'd have mentioned the black candle. Why couldn't he just give you flowers?"

"He was moving to the world's dinkiest apartment. I wasn't. Noon, you said?"

"Yep."

Ria had time before her noon client to move all the breakable relics on her altar back from the edge, to swap out the charcoal discs and loose incense grains she preferred for a less hazardous stick incense, and to tie the low cabinet of altar tools and divinatory implements closed with a piece of string looped back and forth around the knobs. She put a few extra drops of tea tree oil in her purification bowl for the querent's handwashing. Too bad she couldn't justify asking the kid to wash his hands, too.

When the toddler came, she was ready.

For people with such cheery futures, the mother and son were awfully contentious. The cards answered every worry with assurances that the terrible twos were almost over and everything was about to get much easier.

Meanwhile, the child pulled all the astrology reference books off Ria's shelf, wiped his nose on her skirt, and knocked the stick incense onto the floor, where its smoldering red tip left a molten mark on the carpet. No wonder the mother was at wit's end.

Are you sure they'll be okay? Ria asked the cards silently.

A three-card clarification gave the iconic equivalent of a philosophical shrug: *Joy takes many forms.*

The instant she saw her client off, Ria ducked into the bathroom to scrub hand sanitizer into the spot on her skirt where the little boy had wiped his nose. Then she spent a good ten minutes scrubbing her hands under hot water, hyperventilating. Any hope she'd allowed herself that cleaning up the hex would solve all her woes, she scrubbed away, too.

Over the next two days, Ria played phone tag with the shrinks willing to call back an uninsured sliding-scale case, and she crossed off the names of the ones who couldn't be bothered with her kind. Even the ones willing to consider her weren't all worth keeping on her list—this time she checked with the cards about every candidate before setting appointments.

It would have been faster to ask Jane to search her little black book. Accountants were rare in the Pagan community, so Jane had rescued a lot of people from tax bewilderment over the years. The little black book was deep in skills, names, and favors owed. Ria could not bear to ask.

When she was where the next shrink's office address led her, she wished she had asked. *Prosthetic Limb Building*, said the dusty letters in the dustier front window. It looked as if no one had been making or selling prosthetic limbs in there for a long time. A disinfecting wipe from Ria's purse made it possible to touch the door handle. Inside stretched a long, windowless hall of tiny offices, some with plaques on the doors naming the small businesses and cheapskate medical practitioners within. Mike Dillard, Suite 178.

There was no receptionist, and no space for one, in Suite 178. In a tiny windowless waiting room packed tight with poorly assembled Ikea furniture, Ria found a stack of paperwork waiting with her name on it. Probably a violation of that privacy law. *Should have asked Jane.* But the astrological aspects were favorable, energizing to one's personal charm, so maybe this Dillard guy wouldn't write Ria off. *I hope his charm is more energized than his office's is.* Her knock on the door of the inner consultation room got no answer.

After the ninth time her brain made her watch the film of her chair collapsing under her, she flipped the thing over and tightened the Allen bolts as far as her bare fingers would let her. Finally, she could concentrate on the forms.

Same damn paperwork. She should have asked for the questionnaires back from Dr. Bradley and saved herself two hours. Maybe two hours times several, depending on how many more of these people used the same standard assessment thingies.

Eventually Mike Dillard, the clinical social worker, bothered to show up at his own office, carrying an excessively aromatic salami sandwich, which he proceeded to eat while he looked over the questionnaires. "I notice you didn't mention any history of sexual violence."

"Um, no. I don't have one. I'm here about obsessive-compulsive disorder."

"You wrote very little about your childhood."

"I spent a lot of it washing my hands, and a lot of it trying to cover up that I'd been washing my hands. Your ad said you did cognitive-behavioral therapy."

"I've done trainings about that, but really, we need to get to the root emotional cause of your problem. What happened to you?"

"OCD happened to me. Gods, isn't that enough?" Ria didn't want to think of anyone with an actual history of trauma having to dig into it in this dismal place, with this dismal help. "Please, can I have my forms back?"

"I'm required by the state to keep them for my records."

Filling them all out again somewhere else would be a lot better than staying. She sighed, reached for her purse, and walked out. She did not offer payment. He did not chase her to ask for it.

At the shop, she told Morgan she'd be out again for a chunk of the next day. "Third time's the charm," she assured him as the two of them stood puzzling over the wall calendar.

"Just tell me you're not dying of cancer."

Of course, it was a possibility. Ria's brain flashed a burst of cancer fears—what if her hand sanitizer was carcinogenic?

"Because," he went on, "I might be able to help a little with a thing like that. We could do some kind of fundraiser for hospital bills, put something in the newsletter…"

"No," said Ria. "Thank you, Morgan. It's nothing life-threatening."

"Tell me it'll get better."

"I'm working on it."

"I had to turn away two walk-ins while you were off missing your posted hours this morning."

"And you can't afford that any better than I can." Her hand found her prosperity amulet. Against her thumb, the Roman coin's worn emperor wore smoother. "It's a problem. I'm solving it."

"You're the best in the county, Ria. I need you here. Do what you've got to do, and then, for the love of all the Gods, get back to work."

"I will. But I'm out tomorrow from four until five-thirty."

"The after-school rush? You're killing me." He popped the cap off a white-board marker and wrote *Ria Out* in the square for the date. "Killing me."

Between divination clients all afternoon, Ria intended to write up astrological charts for clients who'd placed online orders. Instead, she dusted everything in the back divination room, and scrubbed the small window behind its privacy blinds. *At least I don't ask my walk-in clients to fill out forms. And when it's my shop, I'll put in a skylight.*

The next day's shrink kept a gleaming office in a very swanky building in Little Silver. The ladies waiting ahead of Ria in the queue wore the kinds of clothes she had only ever seen on magazine covers. She couldn't stop staring at their shoes. They glanced at her and looked abruptly away, sour turns to their perfectly lipsticked mouths. That these women were willing to be seen here *by one another* probably meant the psychiatrist herself was a conspicuous consumption product, one whose idea of sliding scale could not possibly slide low enough. The framed picture over one row of chairs was a Picasso pastel sketch, and when Ria crossed the room to confirm her suspicion that it was not just a reproduction, the woman sitting under it muttered, "Yes, it's real," with a heavy suggestion of *Duh* in her voice.

Ria didn't bother with the forms, never presented herself to the slender receptionist. She managed to avoid running for her car until she'd made it out of the building, called that a victory, and chanted a self-blessing as she sat in the driver's seat, rubbing hand sanitizer into all the red cracks of her hands.

Skipping the forms and interview altogether got Ria back to the shop two hours before her earliest scheduled reading. And then she got a sense of what it must have been like for the cheated-on among her Tarot clients to walk in on their cheating partners.

A very blonde peasant-built woman stood across the counter from Morgan. Was he flirting with her or what? Just as Ria got within earshot, he said, "I hear Thane Kindred won the games at the Jersey Althing this year. So, is it like the original Olympic games?"

Thane Kindred. The peasant-built woman would be an Asatruar, then, a reconstructor of the old Norse faith. Blonde as she was, it wasn't surprising. Ria wondered whether the visitor had been part of the pro-Nils faction or the anti-Nils faction. She braced herself for a wave of Reconstructionist snobbery—Asatru could claim a clearly unbroken paleo-Pagan lineage, was in fact one of the official religions of Iceland—but instead Ria got a wave of Minnesota Nice.

"The Olympics? Um, no. For the Battle at Sea event we had a vigorous round of canoe tag, and pretty much everybody got dunked. Once all the menfolk got cleaned up, we had a Win Back Thor's Hammer Contest." The woman chuckled like Morgan ought to know what that entailed.

Blank stare.

"Sorry. Long saga short, this giant stole Thor's hammer and he'd only give it back if Freya married him. Freya said, heck no, sorry Thor, you're on your own, so Thor had to dress up as Freya and cover his head with a veil. Must have been a big veil and a really stupid giant, because Thor wasn't much in the girlish figure department. So."

Ria didn't get it. "So?"

"So, all the guys from all the Kindreds had a cross-dressing competition, judged by acclamation votes by all the women. Oh, and we had ax-throwing, too, but that came first in the day. Couldn't very well do ax-throwing after Win Back Thor's Hammer, which involved, you know, drinking." She paused, almost coyly. "I came in first at ax-throwing this year."

Ria's brain was stuck on the Win Back Thor's Hammer contest, picturing Nils in a wedding dress. Nils drunk as he'd been at the Pagan Pride march last summer, reeking of bourbon, hiding bloodshot eyes behind sunglasses, a three-day growth of stubble on his face. A sequined veil would not much improve him. *I could have gone my whole life without imagining that.* She really hoped her obsessional ideation didn't put it on heavy rotation.

Morgan said, "You've got to put the ax-throwing thing in your bio for the newsletter."

Uh-oh. "Newsletter?" said Ria. Had she been beaten to the purchase by this Minnesota Nice Valkyrie? The bottom fell out of her day.

"Ria, this is Kim Kjeldberg, our new Rune reader. She'll be taking divination clients when you're out."

Kim reached for a handshake.

Promising herself a good handwashing as soon as she could sidle off to the bathroom, Ria reached, too. It was just the sort of handshake Ria would have expected from a cheerful champion ax-thrower.

Morgan went on. "Kim, meet Ria Santini. Does astrology, Tarot, pendulums, past life regressions, you name it."

The handshake went lukewarm then, and not on Ria's side. So maybe there was a little Reconstructionist snobbery after all.

"Morgan," said Ria, "I'm not out that often, and it'll be less often soon."

"I had to do something," said Morgan.

Kim checked her watch. "Look at the time. I'd better be going. Morgan, when you and Ria have had a chance to talk…"

"I've made up my mind, Kim. Come in for your first shift Friday afternoon."

Friday was always a big money day. Of all the time slots to lose.

The Valkyrie turned, abashed, to Ria. "Good meeting you." And got herself out only a little less quickly than Ria had from that awful shrink's office.

Morgan's weight thudded into the chair he kept behind the counter. He leaned his head back against the wall, eyes closed. "I had to do something."

"You did."

She would have to do something, too. In the back room, she opened the pages of her ephemeris. The new constellation of her circumstances would reveal what she needed in those columns of times and aspects. The planets kept their courses. She would find whatever in their turnings she could turn to advantage.

There it was. Perfect. Coming up fast, almost too fast, and if she missed her moment there wouldn't be another lined up as auspiciously for a week. Fortunately, she had a bit left of her best batch of prosperity incense. Her need was dire, and what she needed right now was so small—just enough of a boost to remind Morgan why it was good to have her on hand.

The Moon conjoined Venus at twelve minutes past noon, saturating the world with extravagance. The lunch hour rush filled the funky little eateries of Red Bank, and today a long stream of well-fed impulse shoppers wandered into Transcendence Perfection Bliss of the Beyond. So many of them wanted readings that Ria set up a table in the front window and did quick three-card spreads, ten dollars a pop, until the last of the customers drifted back to work.

In the sudden two o'clock quiet she helped Morgan straighten up the crystal bins. "So," said Morgan, "you, too?" He gestured to the scattering of coins on the floor behind the counter.

"Money on the floor brings money in the door." She smiled at the old folk spell. "Yeah, me too. Basil and cassia with a pine needle topnote. And some very good timing."

"If only it worked this well every day." Morgan was always trying different prosperity spells.

"If anything worked *every day*, I would be out of a job altogether."

It had seemed like such a good idea, that offer to host an extra gathering of the coven on Friday. The house was ready—the house was always clean enough to host the Queen of England on no notice—but the garden!

The sight of her gardening gloves set off hyperventilation. Digging without them was out of the question. No way could Ria afford to hire a landscaping crew to restore actual order. She ended up hiring a neighborhood college kid home for the summer to come in with a mower and a weed whacker. Indiscriminate. Of course. Ria suspected going in that the best she could hope for was that the kid would distinguish between shrubs and everything else, and that duality was indeed the best she got.

On Friday night, Bob arrived first. The courthouse had been closed that day. His SUV was full of his kids' beach toys. He shook sand off his flip-flops, then stood in the driveway, blinking in astonishment at the state of the yard.

"Your ornamental hellebores," he said. "Your asafoetida."

"I'm on a big simplification kick," said Ria. "You know, the New Simplicity, all that."

"But...your medicinals and aromatics, too? What's up with you?"

"I can't win, can I? If I keep a well-ordered magickal garden, I'm a New Age freak. If I just hire a neighbor kid to mow the lawn I'm...I don't even know what. There is no pleasing you people."

"You people?" Bob smiled. "Since when is this coven uniform enough to get lumped together as *you people?* Sophie and I are fifth-generation New Age freaks. Our ancestors started expecting the Age of Aquarius around the end of the Civil War. Please, dear heart, wait to pick a fight with Jane until Jane actually gets here. On second thought, please don't pick one at all. Sophie called me this morning, spooked by who knows what and very keen to put a protection spell on the beach cottage."

"Come on in," said Ria, a little sheepishly, and he followed her into the pink kitchen. "We can set the altar up early. What did you bring for feast?"

He set his covered dish on the counter. "That green bean casserole with the cream of mushroom soup. I know it's a cheat, but the kids needed a beach day, and I couldn't leave the kitchen too messy for Ricki to deal with alone with the kids."

"Fifth generation freak my ass," Ria chuckled. "You're more normal than you know."

"You really think so?" He brightened.

"You're a respectably employed, stable, married, monogamous father of two-point-seven children."

"There were three of them last time I counted."

"If you set out to have a second child and get twins by accident, you should get a karmic discount for wear and tear on the planet. It's not your fault you have three kids when you were aiming for two. So, two-point-seven."

"Foot in mouth. I don't usually mind it, but when it's about my kids... Maybe you should quit while you're ahead, Ria."

"Sorry."

He rubbed his hands over his face and closed his eyes, just for a moment. She thought she was about to get one of his bursts of temper, but when he spoke, it was with weary grief. "You're driving a wedge between yourself and the rest of the coven, and it breaks my heart to see it. For a while now I've wanted to talk it over with you. If anybody else were doing to you what you're doing to yourself, I'd..."

"You'd beat the crap out of them?"

"I'd think about it, anyway. But it's not some outside enemy. It's not even Jane, not really. It's like there are two Rias, one who's my trusted friend and coven sister, and one who's a passive-aggressive loony out to sow discord in my family of faith. Half the time, I don't know which of you I'm talking to. I can't be a knight in shining armor and protect you from yourself. That trick never works. Please, Ria, pull your shit together. I don't want the coven to lose you. I don't want to lose you."

Ah. Ria remembered conversations like this from the end of her time with Oakbridge Coven. "I don't know what to say."

"Honestly, I don't, either. I just had to say something."

The shrinks had to fix her. Right now, if she could just find something to *do*, something familiar, she could get through the evening without tears. "You want to get the altar started? I need to fetch some incense from upstairs."

He put a hand on her shoulder in an awkward attempt at comfort. "Get whatever you need."

So she retreated to her aromatics workshop, where she had not set foot in weeks. The last dried leaves and flowers from her own garden, the last bottled decoctions, from when she still had the will to dig in the earth—all those things were running out. She'd stocked up on perfumer's-grade essential oils, too, in more prosperous years, so there was plenty to work with, but the end of her homegrown supply had made the room too sad to bear.

The door was cool to the touch. The air, when she turned the knob, held its perfectly maintained sixty-five degrees, thanks to the most expensive window-unit air conditioner in the house. Chemical potency was magical potency, and she didn't want her supplies losing their virtues to heat. Heavy shades covered the windows to protect the essential oils from light strike. The only bright lamp in the room clamped onto to her work table, where mortar and pestle waited for her. There wasn't even any dust to clean off of them.

Ingredients, ingredients. She ran a finger along the shelf. She needed peace, grounding, trust. She needed to refrain from being a jerk. If only she had avoided saying something cutting to Bob about his children, he wouldn't have felt the need to give her a talking-to. She needed Spanish amber resin—too gummy for jewelry, but a gorgeous scent for burning, as long as whoever tended the censer scraped it off the charcoal before it turned acrid. She searched the shelves for sandalwood. The amber resin needed oomph, and sandalwood was all oomph. Powdered was the only form she had it in. Not her favorite form, but sandalwood trees were endangered, so she hadn't bought new in years. The blend needed a topnote, a bright scent to balance the warm ones. Not jasmine. Jasmine gave Jane headaches. Though in petty moments Ria contemplated jasmine as a means of revenge, Jane with a headache was even worse than Jane without. *And I was trying to refrain from being a jerk. Right.* She settled on orange blossom essential oil. After a few rounds with the mortar and pestle, the oil had glued the sandalwood powder to all the blobs of amber resin. Pieces that small would burn fast, but the scent was divine. Peaceful. Joyful.

By the time Ria got back to the living room, all the covenmates had arrived. She ran the gantlet of hugs through the kitchen. Why did all the people Ria loved have to do so much hugging?

Bob had the altar nearly set up. Ria handed him her little bowl of incense to set in the eastern quarter. "Nice," he said, holding it to sniff. "That'll burn beautifully."

"It'll burn too fast, and it'll go bitter."

"Nobody here is a beginner. I'm pretty sure every member of this coven could walk, chew gum, and tend incense at the same time."

Ria didn't realize she was about to sigh until the big melodramatic sigh puffed out of her.

"Are you really up for priestessing?"

"Not even a little bit."

"Stay here."

She tried to look like she was meditating while he ventured back into the kitchen full of hugs. Something was going on in there, something she should have noticed.

Jane's aura stuck out through the doorframe so Ria could see it around the corner. Who would have thought that aura could look any worse? Its core seemed to be trying to escape Jane's body by climbing out through her head. Ria made a bet with herself about the physical posture she'd see if she came around the corner to see Jane herself. Yep, standing pigeon-toed, arms tight across her chest, as if she were squeezing her soul from its mortal frame.

"What happened?"

"Creepy stalker sonofabitch," said Jane.

Sophie added, "Nils was going through our trash last night. From the noise, we thought he was a raccoon, so we went out with a flashlight." She flipped her hair with a little more nonchalance than she could quite mean. "Creepy stalker sonofabitch, that pretty much covers it."

Amber looked up from the edible flowers she was arranging on the salad she'd brought for feast. "Why the *trash?* Do you suppose he was looking for something specific?"

"Does it matter?" Sebastian asked. "That wouldn't really affect the creepiness index."

"It might matter," said Amber. "I mean, he could have tried to break into the house, or steal Jane's car, or spraypaint something rude on the wall. Of all the creepy things he could have done, he chose trashpicking, which you'd think would be the least attractive of his options."

For once, Jane looked more scared than angry.

"Not helping, Amber," said Bob.

"So," Ria ventured, "I hear the beach cottage needs some kind of protection magic—"

Jane was about to say something Janelike.

"—or something to make you feel protected, or better at protecting yourselves, whatever. You can argue about how to do it, or the exact reasons you need it, but can you really say you'd turn your nose up at prayers of protection from people who love you?"

That melted Jane. She leaned her head on Ria's shoulder. "Oh, Cleopatra."

"I wish you'd stop calling me that."

"But you said..."

"I was Cleopatra *the Third*, not the famous seventh one. I ruled jointly and well with my husband Ptolemy, and never once crashed my empire. Do I come across as a minx to you?"

"A *minx?* No."

"I just hate to be misrepresented, is all."

Sebastian was trying not to laugh. He covered his mouth with a beefy hand a moment, then said, "Good to know Nils hasn't knocked us off our game. So, protection magic."

Sophie sat at the kitchen table and started arranging potluck dishes into some sort of schematic diagram. "There was that thing we did to ward my parents' house—well, Bob's house now—when our folks died. It's not a perfect fit for this occasion, but it got the job done."

"Now that was a beautiful working," said Amber, satisfied at last with her edible flower arrangement. "We need something more portable this time, something decentralized, to be wherever Nils might find Jane or Sophie."

"Or any of you," Jane said. "His anger was kind of all-purpose by the time I packed out. Why not glue the spell to the man himself? Make it a sort of restraining order? Why glue a protection spell to six people, and all our homes, and all our workplaces, if the source of the problem is Nils."

"Threefold return," said Ria. "If we do a working to limit his freedom, that limitation will rebound on us three times over. If we do a working to protect ourselves, there's no karmic rebound."

"Three times over," mused Jane. "I always wondered, why not two and a half? Why not six?"

Bob said, "Surely the gist is good enough: don't do stuff to other people you wouldn't be willing to live with yourself. I don't need quantitative studies to justify that sentiment. Anyhow, Ria wasn't sure she felt up to priestessing. Any volunteers?"

"Got no sleep last night," Sophie admitted. "Not after waking up to our not-a-raccoon."

"And I'm right out," said Jane.

"I'll do it," said Amber. "Sebastian, could you pass me my..."

He handed her a jewelry pouch out of her feathered vintage handbag.

"Thanks." She started swapping out the relatively understated studs she wore in her various piercings on office days for a set that seemed to be made from...

"Are those animal claws?" asked Ria.

Amber beamed. "This one time, on a road trip in the Rockies? I passed the most amazing roadkill. It was a whole bear, pretty recent. Well, how often do you get a chance to work in the medium of bear claws? So of course I had to pull over. The flies were extreme, and it took a while to get the claws out, but it was totally worth it. Clean-up was a bitch. Turns out animal claws are pretty easy to mount as jewelry. There. How do I look?"

"Honey," said Sebastian, "should I call National Geographic, or Frank Frazetta?"

She kissed him. "You wanna priest this circle?"

"I'll defer to Bob. He's more warrior than I am."

"Please take it on," said Bob. "I've never gotten over roughing

Nils up that time he hit Jane. You don't want me flinching out of guilt in the middle of a protection spell."

"You got it," said Sebastian. "Okay, let's talk mechanics."

Ria broke out some chips and salsa. "This could take a while." And it did. They all followed Sophie's lead with the casserole dish diagram, each covener represented by the food he or she had brought. In keeping with the fierce mood Amber's claws cultivated, Ria opted to be represented by the salsa, which was extra hot. Utensils allowed them to model the energy patterns they would envision. They laughed long and well, all of them, as they circled Jane's pyrex pan of sweet kugel with a haloing ring of table knives. By the time they were ready to cast the circle the chips and salsa were much depleted, but Ria felt exhilarated, useful, like part of something. Only after she'd lit the incense did she realize she hadn't washed her hands in almost an hour. *This is what that Dr. Bradley will never understand about ritual. If I could feel every day like I do right now, I'd be well.*

The auras of the six coveners pulsed in unison, raising energy in chant.

Sebastian drew the raised energy toward him and the tendrils of his solar plexus chakra spun it into a cord of brilliant gold and silver. At the loose end of that cord Amber flew, fearless. Flowers of lightning crackled silently across the bubble of her etheric template. That was what priest and priestess could do when they worked in perfect love and perfect trust.

What her fellow coveners saw when they looked at it, Ria never knew. They felt it, though. She heard it in their song.

Their work and worship completed, they opened the circle and stepped from it still shining with the traces of their spell into the gray of Ria's mere living room.

The feast table was as merry as they'd ever kept it. Perhaps they were protected even from one another—Ria dared to hope she might be protected from herself. Not until the kugel dessert did she begin to count how many times she chewed, to count her bites, to work numerological analyses of each tally, and to align the numerology in her head with what she remembered of the day's page in her ephemeris. The wild energy of Rugosa Coven loosened its embrace, and the hell of details flooded in to take its place.

The auras faded from her sight. Amber asked something about making a pot of coffee, her tattoos still crackling with that light Ria had seen in circle. "Coffee, yes. Go ahead." Wisteria vines coiled up Amber's left arm so vibrantly Ria could smell the blossoms, with their odd scent combination of cold burnt cork and spice and honey. She knew in an instant how she would formulate the fragrance to express that tattoo.

If my own arts can't save me, maybe Sebastian's can.

It was an entirely new thought. For some people, a physical ordeal with a side order of aesthetics was just the thing. Why not?

"Sebastian," she said, "theoretical question: what effect would seeking body modification have on a recently completed protection spell?"

"Would it void the warranty, you mean?" He chuckled. "Depends on the motivation and the modification. You got something in mind?"

"Maybe."

All the covenmates' heads swiveled to stare.

"It's just an idea."

"Ooh! Tell all!" said Amber, washing her hands after taking the bear claw ornaments from her nasal piercings. Thank goodness for the handwashing. "You come up with such beautiful things."

Tell all. All. What if she did? Everything about her illness, right now? It wouldn't be beautiful, but it would be true. *I hate to be misrepresented,* she'd said just that evening. No one misrepresented Ria more completely, more constantly, than she herself.

"She's not ready to talk about it," Sebastian said. "You can see that."

The moment he said it, he was right. The moment before, would he have been? *I almost told them.* And once she'd put it to herself in those words, the choice was already behind her. A wave of grief.

"Come to my studio tomorrow," he said gently. "Or whenever is good for you.

She nodded.

While she washed dishes with Jane and Sophie—the last guests to go home, perhaps nervous about what they'd find there—it occurred to Ria that she had never given any thought to what kind of modification she might get, how she would want it to look, what forms of pain she wished to withstand. The practical aspects, she was not ready to talk about. Only the why, and that only almost.

Sophie fired off the dishwasher without pushing the button for the sterilize setting. Ria noticed too late to fix it. She'd have to run those dishes all over again.

On the porch she said her farewells to the unlikely housemates. It would be bad magickal hygiene to second-guess their spell by wishing Sophie and Jane safety, or luck, or anything that would lead the universe to doubt the intensity of their collective ritual will. Instead they talked of the future, as if they were sure it would come, and Ria gave them a casserole to take home. What was a major life transition without casseroles from one's friends, after all?

Jane said, "I've developed the most beautiful packing list for midsummer festival. It started as an exercise to teach myself Java, but now that it's done, I really like it."

Sophie stared incredulously. "You wrote your packing list in Java? Why can't you just throw some sarongs and condoms in a messenger bag and go?"

"Tenting this year. I haven't done any real camping since before I was married. I think I've forgotten how. Nils always wanted to bunk in the Asatru cabin. That's where the party's at."

"Oh, hey," said Ria. "You know anybody named Kim Kjeldberg?"

"I miss Kim," said Jane. "We parted badly last time I saw her, but that's so with a lot of Thane Kindred. Different reason for each of those people. Why do you ask?"

"She's picking up some rune reading gigs at Transcendence Perfection. Is she going to run me out of a job?"

Jane laughed. "Do I look like a Tarot deck to you? I don't know. But she's a good egg. You could come right out and ask her."

"Speaking of things I could come out and ask," said Ria. "That packing list. I love a well-designed organizational tool. Could I see it sometime?"

"So you can check it against your ephemeris," Jane suggested. "The Javascript would probably accommodate all the planetary aspects. Wait. Sorry. I didn't mean to be sarcastic. Okay, well, I didn't *plan* to be sarcastic. That's the kind of crappy way Nils would have responded, a put-down to repay every compliment."

"It's nearly midnight," said Ria. "Take the lasagna, hug me, and go home." Hugs were easier to manage if *she* decided when they would happen. Good hugs, as that sort of thing went. Then Ria stood on the porch waving as Jane's venerable Corolla turned the corner and zipped off to Sea Bright.

The moment Ria stepped back into the kitchen, her aura itched. Something tickly brushed her about two feet out from her skin. It was such a slight sensation, like an ant running across her arm. Only she couldn't quite pin down where the tickle was coming from. Near the refrigerator, perhaps.

Where the curse had lurked for years, unnoticed.

Ria turned and backed out of the kitchen, crossed the perimeter of the ritual space her coven had made of her living room. A circle recently cast and dismantled would be quick to recast, should she need it.

The tickle could be anything. A consecrated ritual tool forgotten by one of her covenmates, maybe. Or a colony of especially vigorous bacteria from one of their kitchens, stowed away in a potluck dish. It didn't have to be a curse.

The phone rang. Ria had no desire whatsoever to pick it up, but the Moon was trining Mars. It was a time to be cheerful and harmonious, dammit.

Caller ID said it was Bob. Maybe he would apologize for the talking-to before ritual. Ria hoped not. He'd been right, and if he apologized she would have to say so. She picked up.

A child's wail burst from the receiver.

Ria recoiled from the sonic assault. "Hello?"

"Just a moment, kiddo, I'm on the case," said Bob's voice. "Ria. Hi. Apparently one of the twins put his favorite toy in the thermal bag I brought the green beans in. Or maybe he didn't, it's hard to get a straight answer out of a hysterical four-year-old. They put things in the weirdest places. Could you look for it? It's a small plush seagull."

"His favorite toy? Something he carries with him constantly?"

Bob sighed. "He sleeps with it, talks to it, throws stuffed animal tea parties for it. We thought it was a good growing-up kind of sign when he started leaving Squawk in odd places, but instead it's just a pain in the ass when he turns out to need Squawk after all, and then we have no idea where to look."

A toy that beloved would have its own aura. Just a little, faint one, and some practitioners would call it a sloughed-off fragment of the child's aura. Ria avoided children too well to have a professional opinion on the point. Still, she sent a tendril from her solar plexus chakra venturing into the kitchen to investigate. The little aura gave off a sort of flavor, a sweetness as of butterscotch lollipops, that she was quite sure would not accompany a curse.

"It's here."

"Oh, thank Gods. Aidan, good news! Aidan. Look at me. Take a deep breath." The wailing continued unabated. "Sorry, Ria. One of us will come by to pick it up. Thank you."

A child's toy. A four-year-old child's favorite toy, with all the nose-wiping germs that entailed. And it was loose in Ria's kitchen.

"I'd have had better defenses against the curse," she muttered as she picked up her cooking tongs. Maybe she could avoid touching the plush seagull with her hands until Bob or Ricki showed up.

Now that she was searching for the thing, it was annoyingly hard to find. Auravision was exhausting to maintain now—she had exerted it so much during the ritual—and she'd never seen the toy with her actual eyes.

"Here, seagull-seagull-seagull!" she called, before she realized how nutty that would sound. What if it was Ricki who showed up, instead of Bob? Ricki was the kind of social worker who did something for homeless families, and soon-to-be-homeless ones. Ria had never been clear on what. It wasn't therapy, but social workers usually had a bit of psychology training. Much as she liked Ricki, Ria had been avoiding her since the malady had taken its turn.

The seagull wasn't under under the dish-drying rack. She nudged the tongs around the kitchen, poking into any space she could think of where a small toy might lurk. At last she found it pinned between the tile backsplash and the big glass jar of sugar Amber had dipped into to season her coffee. Ria tipped the jar with one hand and snatched the seagull up in her tongs just as the doorbell rang.

Of course she forgot to swap Squawk out of the tongs and into her bare hand before going to answer the door.

There was Ricki on the porch, already opening her arms to hug Ria in greeting. She noticed the kitchen tongs, and her eyebrows shot up. She chuckled. "What did Squawk get into this time?"

"A hard-to-reach spot," Ria said. A simplification was not a lie. Just when she thought the risk of a hug was past, Ricki embraced her after all.

"Thank you for finding... Um, sorry. Have I offended you, Ria?"

"Of course not." Ria handed off the toy, tried not to look too glad to be rid of it. Ricki deserved better than to think she'd done something wrong. "Come on in. I was just cleaning up from circle."

The kitchen would pass for clean, with normal people. Ricki looked around as if the last of the mess were invisible to her. Considering what kinds of people she worked with, it probably was. She must go into the most squalid kitchens in the county, shake hands with people who could not afford soap. *Stop it right now, brain. I will not categorize my friend as dirty. My virtuous friend who helps the poor, when I can't even look at them. I will not.*

Ricki was saying something. Something about an argument Ria couldn't even remember having.

"...And ever since, it seems like you've been avoiding me."

"Um." So whatever argument it was, it must have happened after the symptoms kicked up. "It wasn't that big a deal."

Ricki took a deep breath. "I'm so glad to be able to clear the air about this. Actually, my problem isn't with the divination. My problem is that you're basically practicing psychotherapy without a license. I get the impression you have a knack for it, but when troubled people come to you, a knack may not be enough."

Ria thought of Dr. Bradley, the pastel-wearing bigot. "And training always is?" She scrubbed the tongs with antibacterial detergent.

"Not always. Of course not. But I do serve my clients better for having had it. Anything I can do to help clean up?"

"No, thanks. I've got it." Scrubbing gave Ria an excuse to break eye contact when she needed to.

"What do you do when a person comes in for a reading and you see right away that something is seriously out of whack in his head?"

Takes one to know one, Ria almost joked. "I've urged a lot of querents to seek professional mental help. Some of them even do it." A glimmer of a thought came to her. "I just wish I knew any specific therapists to recommend. I have this client—well, actually, I read cards for her for free—I think she may have OCD. She's had no luck finding someone Pagan-friendly who can treat her, and I don't know what advice to give. Do you know anybody?"

"If you're giving away your professional services to her, she must be really broke. Does this client have insurance?"

"Not a speck of it."

"Then she'll need a sliding scale that slides really low. Okay, try Adam Edelstein. He's in the phone book. He's a good guy, and he's been willing to work with some flat broke people I've sent him from the housing projects. Tell him I sent...your client?" Ricki looked surprised to have figured it out, but she only missed one beat. She smiled a rueful, tender smile, and Ria saw all over again why Bob loved her. "Dr. Edelstein has the highest standards of confidentiality. And if there's anything else I can do to help *your client*, anytime, you just let me know."

The Saturday morning walk-ins at Transcendence Perfection Bliss of the Beyond brought three consecutive clients seeking reassurance of spousal fidelity, followed by a narrow, nervous man in a beautifully tailored suit. He closed the door carefully behind him before he said, "I hear a rumor you have a working crystal ball."

"Very funny, stockbroker." She was going to have to throw him out.

He turned pale. "Investment banker, technically. How did you know I was coming?"

"I didn't. Only stockbrokers ask for a working crystal ball. Stockbrokers, and one time the quirk-beat columnist for *The Wall Street Journal.*" It was all Franklin Leary's fault, for running an article about her in *Bizarro Jersey* when he was short of other stories. For just a moment, she hoped Frank had been eaten by the Jersey Devil. "Yes, I have a working crystal ball. No, it won't pick winning stocks for you. I hope you paid Morgan in advance for my time. Now go away." Why couldn't it have been another anxious spouse? Ria was so good with anxious spouses.

"But..."

"If my crystal ball were the right tool for getting rich on stocks, I might still choose to tell fortunes for walk-ins off the street, but *I would own this shop by now.*"

He pulled a money clip out of his pocket, peeled off three hundreds, and slapped them on the table. "I apologize on behalf of my entire profession. *Now* can I ask you a question?"

She stared at the bills. "Apology accepted. Please accept mine."

"Where do I have to run to get away from him?"

Ria was very glad just then to have a kickass protection spell covering her. "A crystal ball is exactly the right tool for your question. One moment. I don't get a lot of requests that actually call for it." Her sphere was in the very back of the cabinet under the altar. She knelt to reach around the spell candles to extricate it, loosed its silk wrappings, and placed it on a cushion on the table.

The banker arched his fingertips together. "I thought it would be bigger."

"It's big enough." She settled into her chair, rested her elbows and palms on the table, and slid into a concentration exercise she hadn't tried in two years: open the chakras, project the sigil out onto the inner eggshell surface of her aura's ketheric template, follow the sigil into the stone. The steps rushed back so fast, she had only a moment to congratulate herself on how solid her old practice must have been. Then she became a tiny chip of herself in the center of the sphere.

A concrete building from some awful, boxy architectural movement of the 60's loomed before her in beige. It seemed familiar and vaguely chilling. She sent her voice back across the void to her body. *I've seen this place before. It's a huge office complex. Why am I so sure I know it, when I can't remember anything I might have done here?*

The client's voice boomed back, *Did you ever watch the X-Files?*

Ooh, I loved that show!

They used to use a real street shot of FBI headquarters, he said. *Is that it?*

That's it! How did you guess?

It's what I was afraid you'd say.

Ria blew out the sigil as if it were a birthday candle with the very best wish, and blamm-o, she was back in her body.

He hunched over the table, face in hands. After a moment he massaged his temples, opened his eyes, and said, "I was never here."

"Of course not. Need a good luck talisman?"

"Hell, yes."

"This one's on me."

In her box of assorted crystals was a good-sized chunk of tiger's eye, something to watch the guy's back while he slept. She blessed it with salt and smoke, flame and water. With a tiny brush and clary sage essential oil she painted onto it the astrological sign for Mercury, patron of thieves and messengers. "Keep it in your pocket when you're awake, put it where it can watch over you while you sleep. Do the right thing, whatever that is."

"The right thing. Right."

Ria knelt to tuck her crystal ball back into the cabinet. When she looked up, he was gone.

She hadn't noticed she was holding her breath until she sighed it all out. Leaning her forehead on the cabinet was quite comfortable, really. Maybe she'd just stay down here a while and wait out these shakes. The reading for the investment banker was as close to true danger as she ever wanted to get.

A rough voice, half forgotten, said from the door, "Hi, Ria."

She pivoted her head where it rested against the cabinet to find Nils Sigurdson. His slumping, embarrassed-to-be-tall frame stood in the back hall, the toes of his broken down dress shoes just brushing the threshhold of the divination room. He wore a threadbare and not recently washed version of his old professional wardrobe from when he used to sell mobile phones. That was more of an effort than she'd seen him make since the funeral for Bob and Sophie's parents two years back, though really he could have stood to be cleaner then, too. There was a chemical smell about him that she couldn't quite place, so maybe he was cleaner than his shirt. Maybe not. He badly needed a shave, or remedial lessons in beard maintenance. He badly needed.

"Hi, Nils."

"Not going to ask how I am?"

"You've looked better. You've looked worse." She stood, straightened her skirt, and rested a hand on her talismans. "What brings you to Transcendence Perfection Bliss of the Beyond, of all places?"

He choked out a small laugh. "When you put it that way, it does sound like a good question. There are things I need to ask Jane."

"I won't be your go-between. Her all-purpose answer for you is *No*."

Every fiber of him tightened slightly. He stepped across the threshhold into her sanctum and closed the door behind him.

"It must be convenient," he said. "I talk, and nobody has to listen to me. Nobody has to think, even, about *whether* they're going to listen. I'm a big drunk, so anything I say must be bullshit. Simplifies your life, right? I bare my soul, and you tune me out to consider your meal planning options for the coming week."

Familiar as that experience was to Ria, she considered how smoothly the complaint came. "I'm not the first person you've said that to. Not even in those exact words."

He no longer looked embarrassed to be tall. She'd never realized quite how tall Nils was. He stretched straight, then drew back as if to launch himself bodily at her.

And launched himself instead at the wall right beside her. Deity figurines toppled off her shrine. He stepped back and hurled his body back at the same spot on the wall. His head hit with a sickening crack. The crack turned out to be the aging plaster, which dented and flaked in a halo around his forehead.

Ria's brain tried to ignore the immediate peril to wonder, *Has that old plaster wall ever been tested for lead paint?*

Nice try, brain, she replied.

She backed away from him around the table, working her way toward the closed door. "You can't really have come to ask *me* to be your go-between, anyway," she continued, keeping her voice light as she could. "How much credence would Jane give anything *I* said?"

"You're the one I can reach," he said. "Can't ask Sophie without violating the restraining order about Jane's dwelling. Bob and Sebastian are right out, and when Amber's not in Manhattan, she's home with Sebastian. That leaves you."

He'd thought too much about this. Jane had been right to cover everybody in the protection spell. The restraining order was news to Ria.

On the other hand, beating his head against the wall seemed to have calmed him some, or the spell was working, or both. *What would I have done when I was temple oracle?* A temple oracle would have had bodyguards, or staff, or somebody to back her up. Speaking of which, why hadn't Morgan bothered to look in on her after all that thumping? Still, the memory from the temples where she had served came clear in answer: *I would have offered him his future, for good or ill. Especially for ill.*

She held her Tarot deck toward him and said, "Sit down. Shuffle. Stay a while." She could wipe the cards down twice afterward to make up for skipping the purification.

"Seriously?" The invitation stunned him more than the wall had.

"You could get some ice for your head first if you want."

His gray shirt was flecked with white plaster dust. Blood trickled from his left eyebrow. "I'm fine." He took the cards and sat in the querent's seat to shuffle them.

Fine? Ria wondered what the alcohol content of that blood trickle would have to be for Nils to feel fine. While he shuffled, she set her altar in order and steadied herself by lighting fresh incense with vanilla and lavender essential oils, almost as good as a tranquilizer dart.

Shuffling distracted him long enough for Ria to get a look at his aura. His root chakra had blasted a hole through the bottom of his etheric template. It looked less like a cracked eggshell than in cases she'd seen before, more like a steel hull ripped by torpedos. The whole auric body was a cloud of murky purple—if a cloud could be patched with black duct tape. What were those black stripes, anyway?

The cards also knew he wasn't fine, of course. As Ria placed the first ten carefully in the opening spread, each card shouted suffering. She winged her fingers wide and laid them down over the spread. *Hush a moment. Get it together.*

She could almost hear the click as ten cards became a single story. The deck tried again. *The worst he's ever seen, worse than you can imagine, and he's years from either shore of it.*

"Nils, I don't think any answer Jane could give you will fix this."

"Fix this? Not what I came for."

"What, then?"

"I just want to know if she threw out our handfasting cords."

"Ah." Ria remembered the wedding, Jane and Nils laughing and kissing as they joined their left hands and then struggled, each one-handedly, to tie the joined hands together. "You haven't had a formal handparting ritual. Of course."

"Did she burn them, or landfill them, or throw them in the ocean? She could have left them behind, I could have untied them or... I don't know. But why take the handfasting cords with her, of all things, if *she* was the one leaving? And it kills me that I have to ask one of you people, that I can't just ask her. I'm sick of you all telling me I don't really love her. It's not true, dammit."

Ria looked down at the cards. "Nils, what idiot would tell you you don't really love her?"

Nils let out a bitter breath that failed to be a laugh. "Your illustrious coven brothers. Bob and Sebastian showed up on my doorstep last night to tell me what I'd been putting her through. They were all, 'That's not love,' and 'If you loved her blah blah blah.' I went through rehab *three times* for that woman. Do you have any idea what rehab's *like*? Just because it didn't take, that's no reason to say I didn't try it out of love."

Four of Wands, reversed. Two of Cups, reversed. Ace of Cups, reversed. Ten of Pentacles, reversed.

A whole world of love turned upside down, and the Devil trump upright at the center of it all. *Practicing psychotherapy without a license, huh? I can't do worse than those licensed bozos I've been seeing.*

"Look at this," she said, pointing to the Devil.

"Now you're going to tell me I'm fucked up because I'm possessed?"

"No. Really *look* at it. Not just the word written on the card, not just the big bogeyman in the middle of the picture. Look at the man and the woman chained to the Devil's throne. The Devil represents the most fucked up thing in your life. What if the most fucked up part of your life isn't your drinking? What if it's your marriage? What if you have to kick your addiction to having a fucked up relationship with Jane before you can kick your addiction to anything else?"

"She tried so hard to help me."

"Did it work?"

Nils closed his eyes.

Ria pulled a tissue out of the box and held it ready.

Eyes still closed, he said, "It's never going to work, is it?"

"I'm just the card reader. It's your life. The way things are going right now, if you don't change direction radically, permanently, I'm guessing no. And even if you did, not for a long time." She proffered the tissue to him.

He needed it. "Just the cords. Can you tell me just about that?"

The opening spread didn't, so she flipped down three more cards. *Hidden in the place of refuge. Don't ask her directly.*

"They're still in the beach cottage," said Ria. "Maybe you can have your lawyer ask her lawyer about them. A proper handparting would do both of you good."

He cleaned himself up with the tissues and, bless him, tucked them in his pocket. Ria hated having to clean up the crying clients' tissues. "Haven't got a lawyer," said Nils. "Can you picture anything more pointless than me fighting her in a courtroom? Better to lie down and take it, skip the waiting." He stood to go. "Thank you, Ria. I don't know what to do about those cords, but I'm glad she hasn't destroyed them."

"You're still in there," said Ria. "The guy I used to be glad to see at community barbecues. You're not all...dissolved away."

"Try telling that to, hell, to any number of people. They'll be as eager to hear you out as they are to hear me. I'm sorry. About a lot of things. About the dent in your wall. I'm sorry."

"It's all right, Nils. You're not the first suffering person who's set foot in this room. Be well."

"Be well."

He pulled the door open and nearly walked into Kim Kjeldberg. She looked every inch the champion axe thrower.

"Ria, you okay?" Kim asked, her eyes pinning Nils where he stood.

"Everything's under control," said Ria.

Kim raised her eyebrows. "As soon as Morgan told me who was thumping around, I came to the door to back you up. But your voice sounded relaxed enough, so I didn't want to bug you. You sure you're okay?"

Nils said, "Hi, Kim. Been doing fine, thanks. You?" His voice cracked.

"You're bleeding. Go clean yourself up, for Frigg's sake." Perhaps her Minnesota Nice was vacationing back in Minnesota.

"Just for the record," Nils said to Ria, "rehab would have been easier if Thane Kindred's form of worship hadn't been basically a kegger with occasional prayers."

"If that's how you see our rites..." Kim began.

"Mockery is not the best help you could have offered a recovering alcholic."

"Recovering, my ass."

He stretched tall again, turned his back on the women, and strode for the shop's front door. Slammed it behind him so hard the strand of bells flew off, arced high, and landed with tangled clinks in a display case of chalices.

Never had Ria seen Nils Sigurdson so open in his grief. She could hardly bear to imagine him walking the fine streets of Red

Bank dirty, bloody, weeping, and, for once, plastered *literally*.

That is, until she figured out what was missing from her reading table. The fretful investment banker's three hundred dollar tip. Nils had piled his tissues over it and pocketed the whole thing.

"Now *that* I should have seen coming," Ria muttered.

"Seen what coming?" said Kim. "Because it all looked like a surprise to me. I've seen him drag himself through some painful shit, but I have never seen him cry. What did you say to him?"

The Asatruar woman could not possibly be asking Ria to violate her querent's confidentiality, could she? Asatrufolk had a different definition of honor from Ria's, but they cared an awful lot about it.

"I gave him a reading," Ria replied, her face as neutral as she could make it.

Kim smiled. "Didn't mean to pry. I think we'll get along just fine. Which is good, because I'm about to ask you an awkward favor."

"You picked a suitably awkward day to do it. The Moon squares Mars. Compulsion and emotional thinking. Come in and tell me about this favor."

She stepped in, and that was when Ria noticed the box Kim carried. A slightly battered cardboard box labeled in black Sharpie with Norse runes so hastily written, Ria had to wonder whether the ancient alphabet had a cursive form.

"My divinatory shrine stuff," Kim explained. "On paper, this room belongs to Morgan. In Morgan's mind, this room is generic fortunetelling space, for whoever he brings in to use it by the hour. But I open my eyes, and I see a temple you've been building with the keenest purpose for…how many years?"

"Coming up on six years as my full-time gig. Before that, I had mundane part-time jobs and did readings here off and on, oh, since I was just out of high school. Three different owners since then, and none of them short-timers."

The blonde woman sat at the reading table, her box held steady on her lap. "All this stuff on the walls and counters, it's not me. If I try to think of this room as mine, the incense feels like fakey-fake perfume, the deity figurines feel like false advertising. But they're not, of course, when you're presiding in here. If there were a square foot of space somewhere in this room where I could put my little clay Odin and pour him a couple ounces of mead for a libation, and a few inches of shelf space for my reference books, I'd give better readings."

And why would I want that for my competition? Ria wondered.

It must have showed, because Kim said, "Whatever territorial struggle Morgan has set us up for, the people who walk in off the street with troubles deserve the best from whoever meets them at this table."

If Ria had been a hugger, she'd have hugged Kim right then. "Let's see what space I can free up." She had laid out her current shrine after a Feng Shui binge, two obsessive collapses ago. The prospect of moving anything significant made her twitch. She was actually twitching under her left eye right now, dammit. This was no time to lose her composure, not when Kim Kjeldberg might become an actual friend. "Should Odin go in the northeast corner of the room, for where he comes from, or where the desktop fountain is in the west, since he'll be getting libations?"

"We don't fret as much as you guys about compass directions," said Kim. "I'm thankful for whatever space you offer."

After twenty minutes of arranging and rearranging furniture with Kim's help, Ria was ready to phone that psychiatrist Ricki had suggested. If only it weren't Saturday. Kim's patience held, but couldn't last much longer. Ten mortifying minutes more, and Ria had the fountain plugged into a new outlet and humming away. "Would Odin be happy under the window?"

"It's perfect, Ria. It's all good. Thank you."

How well Ria knew that tone, the one people used while they congratulated themselves for not yelling. "I really appreciate you asking first, Kim. Technically, you didn't have to do that."

Kim appeared to be weighing her thanks. She must have reached some kind of conclusion. "You should come to the Seidhr."

"The seethe? But I don't want to be a person who seethes." Jane did enough seething for the whole coven.

"Not the *seethe*. The *Seidhr*." Kim pulled a book from her box. *Seidways*, it was titled, and handed it to Ria. "A whole bunch of Kindreds are getting together to hold one next weekend. It's an open thing, Wiccans welcome, everybody welcome. We've even got Lara Beneshan coming in from Arizona."

"Lara...?"

"Oh, come on, you've heard of her. She's a Lakota-trained shaman. At Thane Kindred, we're trying to reconstruct a lost shamanic part of an indigenous religion, so somebody who's part of a living, unbroken line that still has most of its shamanic practices may be able to give us some pointers." She set on the little stand in the corner a clay figure whose one distinguishing feature was a beard. Odin, it must be, because she set a miniature drinking horn in a wooden stand before him and filled it from a hip flask.

Ria waited a respectful moment before saying, "I thought you guys already claimed an unbroken line, through Iceland."

"Yeah," said Kim as she turned to the bookshelf with an armful of books, "but some rituals mentioned in the sagas and Eddas fell out of practice centuries ago. The shamanic stuff was probably the first to vanish. You can learn a lot from the thousand-year-old texts, if you can limp through the Old Norse. But sooner or later, if you really want to understand *Seidhr*, you've got to roll up your sleeves and give it a try."

"And here I thought you were a Reconstructionist snob." Ria pulled the disinfecting wipes from her cabinet and set about cleaning her cards, two passes for each trump.

Kim smiled back. "Reconstructionist, yes. Snob, I try not to be. The real Asatru snobs don't approve of Seidhr, because it hasn't been handed down intact. They're not pleased with my reading runes for money, either. Anyhow, you have your snobberies, too."

"Hey, I just did a reading for Nils Sigurdson."

"Maybe snobbery is the wrong word, at that."

With the box emptied and the Odin shrine in order, Kim

Kjeldberg sat quietly across the reading table from Ria and polished her wooden rune tiles with lemon oil. Before they knew it, both fortunetellers were humming along with the Blackmore's Night album Morgan was playing up front in the store. Kim wiped the last excess lemon oil from tiles and fingers, and threw herself a quick reading.

"Hey, Ria. You need to borrow my cell phone."

"I do?"

"Yeah. I'll go make a quick Starbucks run while you make your call. You want some coffee?"

"No need. Um. Thanks."

And with that, Kim was off.

It was one of those smartphones that did a million things, including emit brain-frying radiation. Ria wasn't at all sure how to use it, and she was not keen to venture into Morgan's territory for the phone book. She wiped the phone down with antiseptic and noticed Kim had left it open to her search engine. Ria finger-typed *Adam Edelstein psychiatrist New Jersey* and was delighted that she had only to tap the phone number once to call him. So this was why other people were willing to court brain cancer. It almost made sense. She made ready to recite her usual spiel—sliding scale, OCD, soon—at the voicemail prompt, when an actual live human picked up at the other end.

"Monmouth Family Care," said a man's voice. "Can I help you?"

"Oh. Ah. Yes. You're in the office on Saturdays?"

"I take it you'd be a new patient."

"Maybe."

"Not all my clients can get time off work midweek. I'm out Mondays and Tuesdays for my days of rest. Just think of me as a Broadway theater and it's easy to remember."

She found herself smiling. "Ricki Baines said you'd be good to call about OCD and sliding scales."

"Ricki's right, as usual. I've got a cancellation about an hour from now. How soon can you get here to fill out..."

"The forms. Of course. I'm histrionic, with obsessional ideation and poor insight."

He laughed. "I'm sorry. I know they're tiresome. But I really do need you to fill them out one more time."

So when Venus trined Neptune, Ria handed the phone and her workshift off to Kim and drove the amuletmobile to Avon-by-the-Sea.

Or you could drive your car straight into the ocean, her brain pointed out as she drove south. *It would be easy, anyplace in Jersey. Turn east, keep going.*

"How sick do you want to be?" she asked aloud. "Seriously, is the prospect of being well that scary?"

There's a public boat launch in Neptune City, in that little inlet. The pavement goes right down into the water, and the tide's nice and high right now. You could be entirely submerged before anybody in the park noticed you didn't have a boat. Oh, I made a picture—check it out!

Now Ria knew exactly what the cabin of her car would look like with water over the dashboard and rising.

"Screw you. I am going to take so many pills, you are never going to torment me with this shit again."

Pills are good, too, said her brain. *Take lots and lots. Here's how you look lying dead on the kitchen floor. Do you like the trickle of vomit? I thought that was an especially nice touch. Here, look at it again.*

A bright yellow Hummer in the right lane honked long and hard at Ria for drifting into its path. The only part of the driver she got a look at from her low-slung car was the middle finger.

This shrink will be no better than the others, Ria's brain went on. *He'll sneer, or indulge some ridiculous unrelated theory, or have a reception room full of famous people who make you want to sink into the floor. Go home, Ria. You're already all that you can be, Gods help you. Go home, before you lose the longest-running paid gig you've ever had. Who would go to you for fortunetelling when they could have Kim Kjeldberg? Oh, and remember what you looked like lying dead on the kitchen floor? Allow me to re-*

mind you. I'm trying to decide if that's a better picture than the old one with the Hummer. How do you like this new car crash? Because if you go about five miles an hour faster and start drifting in your lane again, that middle finger is up ahead waiting for you.

Ria pulled over in the parking lot of a boarded-up laundromat and unwrapped the black silk from her Tarot deck. With trembling hands, she searched out the Devil trump and laid it, pointing upside down, in the passenger's seat. She crossed him with the guardian angel on Temperance, crowned him with the surety of the Star, and dug under his roots with the smiling woman taming her lion on Strength.

That held her as far as Avon-by-the-Sea. When she stood at last outside the doctor's door, she could hear, just barely, the breaking waves. Her silver talismans bit into her palm, she held them so hard.

He opened the door before she worked up the nerve to do it herself. "You can hesistate in here, where it's air conditioned," he said. "No sense suffering ninety-degree weather on top of everything else. I'm Dr. Edelstein."

"Annamaria Santini. Ria. Bring on the forms." She got to circle different numbers this time for the suicidal ideation questions. That wasn't quite enough novelty, though, to fend off her brain's constant replaying of her failed meetings with the other shrinks. *I can't believe I actually mentioned Wikipedia.* Maybe she should have changed into a less gothic outfit. Or bought one—nothing she owned would have been normal enough for that first pastel doctor.

Three questionnaires and some other patient's appointment later, Dr. Edelstein invited her into the inner room. A silk scroll of Chinese calligraphy hung on the wall behind him. No diplomas. An arrangement of two perfect globe chrysanthemums was the only thing on the austere black desk.

Ria struggled to be curious about the Zen vibe of the inner sanctum, but she'd been stewing in the anteroom too long. She didn't hear whatever pleasantries he offered as he accepted the forms from her hand and settled in to read them. The big squishy chair that was obviously intended for patients had nothing of austerity about it. Oh, perfect chair! She closed her eyes involuntarily. When she opened them, she saw what the chair aimed her at, something that had not been visible from the entrance, and gasped.

A red demon with tusks and a tasselled spear cavorted in a brush painting on another silk scroll. Fire leapt and spiralled behind him as he rolled his yellow eyes at her.

Dr. Edelstein looked up from the papers when she gasped. "He's a little unnerving, isn't he? My teacher at the monastery told me that's what enlightenment looks like to the ego, the moment before it happens. And lo and behold, the moment before my one tiny flash of enlightenment was a lot like that."

"You're not at the monastery now." Ria was a little shocked at the cattiness in her own voice.

He shrugged. "I let go of my attachment to being a Buddhist monk. So, it looks like you're ready to be done with your OCD. Are you at peace with taking medication for it?"

"At peace? Did you even read those questionnaires? I'm not at peace with anything."

"Anything, to include coming here to see me." His face was unreadable.

"Look, smug boy, I've had my enlightenment. I've seen into the hearts of the Gods, I've seen thousands of futures for thousands of people, I've seen into a hundred of my own past lives. I've conversed with the spirits of the dead and gazed on the bare auric souls of friends and strangers. None of that made me sane, but none of it was crazy, either."

"Wow."

She couldn't tell whether it was irony or true astonishment in his voice.

"And another thing: I didn't come here to be cured of my faith, or my personality, or my livelihood. Even if you could cure me of fortunetelling, where would that leave me? Unemployable or hypocritical, take your pick. I've never made a real living at anything else. What am I supposed to do now? Take the SAT? It's a couple decades late for that."

He smiled. "What's the one thing you most wish I understood?" Damn, he'd have made a fine fortuneteller.

She fixed her gaze on the silk demon. His tusked smile was more jaunty than cruel. What enlightenment looks like to the ego. All right, it was Edelstein's familiar deck of images, his trump to interpret for her. "I like the outer forms of the life I've made for myself. I just don't want to suffer all the time. I want to do mostly the same things and feel okay about them. I want to turn off the terrible pictures in my head. Oh, and to not annoy my friends as much. It sounds like so little, but I've never been able to have it. Can your drugs get me there?"

The psychiatrist said, "Probably. There are side effects. There are always side effects."

It was like asking a boon of the faeries in the old tales. There would be some terrible price to pay, some piece of her soul. "Like what?"

"Diminished libido, for instance, if we start with the first-line drug for obsessive-compulsive disorder."

Ria laughed. "I don't usually have a sex life anyway. I haven't attempted a real romantic relationship in three years, and living without a libido would have made that a lot easier." It was hard enough to conceal her malady from her covenmates—concealing it from lovers was just more work than she'd had it in her to do, after last time she lost Franklin. She didn't really have him back now. Just as well.

"And you'd probably have some digestive problems for a few weeks."

"That's it?"

"That's the common stuff. If you want to worry about the rare stuff, you could have a paradoxical reaction to Paxil and become an axe murderer."

Ria laughed nervously. "Would I still feel a compulsion to wash the blood off my hands afterward?"

"I'd have to reread the Paxil axe murderer case studies and get back to you on that."

"Okay. You'll do. You're not fired yet."

"Are you going to say the thing everybody says, about not wanting a quick fix?"

"I have been struggling against these idiot visions since I was six years old, every way I could think of. You're the second to last resort. If this fix works, even if it works before sunset, there's nothing quick about it."

"Second to last resort? What's the last?"

"Extreme body modification. I've never had a tattoo or anything, but I'm ready to try ritual branding."

"No wonder the side effects list didn't faze you. If Paxil doesn't work out, please consider changing prescriptions before you resort to ritual branding."

"I'll consider anything."

"That can be a strength." He opened a desk drawer and pulled out a little paperboard box whose cheerful colors and earnest fonts could only have emerged from a Big Pharma marketing department. "Here's a free starter pack. It ramps the dose up slowly, to manage the side effects. If this drug works for you, I can probably get you a price break from the manufacturer."

She held the box among her talismanic pendants, speechless.

He passed her a second parcel. "In case of emergency, I'm also giving you a couple of Xanax samples. This stuff kicks in fast, you don't need it to build up in your system. You can save it for the day when you really, really cannot face something on your own. I'm going to ask you to hold off on it, though. If we possibly can, we need to find out whether Paxil is the right drug for your everyday OCD symptoms first. Read the cautionary inserts thoroughly, then call me with all your questions. All of them, seriously."

But when she got home, it was her cards she consulted.

Yes, said the deck. *Finally. And don't worry about lack of libido. Give this stuff a year or two, and you'll really be relationship material for the first time ever. Bonus!*

"Oh, come off it. You always tell the college girls never to date a mentally ill person, that sooner or later they all want to get off their meds."

Actually, said the five clarification cards Ria laid down, *we're revisiting our position on that. There's about to be a huge breakthrough. Ten years down the line, it'll change everything about psychopharmacology. Not that you should wait around for it. Open the starter pack, already!*

Ria made a mental note to invest in Big Pharma. She'd have to ask Bob which companies his clients had had least cause to sue. Maybe if that Wall Street guy made it back alive from FBI headquarters she could barter services with him.

The third day with no change, she thought the whole thing was a bust.

The fourth day of the pills, she woke up with an overwhelming urge to buy a pink dress. Not sorority girl pink, but a pale sakura pink. A color that would be at home in a Zen brush painting. For decades, ever since she read that black clothes would absorb negative energy before it could reach her skin, she'd been in a nigh-nunlike habit of gothery. What if all her favorite black garments were absorbing negative energy *and keeping it?* What if she herself was emanating negativity and her black clothing was trapping it inside? She knew this was an obsessional train of thought, but for the sake of its kernel of novelty, she decided to run with it.

The town of Red Bank had its avenue of elegant boutiques leading to the riverfront. A desire to wear an actual color seemed worthy of celebration, so Ria ventured into a few fancy shops to look at the clearance racks. An hour later she stepped back out on Broad Street overdressed to an extreme that only her unrepentantly gothic hair and makeup allowed her to pull off. Pink chiffon swooshed and draped just as pleasingly as black. Who knew?

The bells of Transcendence Perfection tinkled as she opened the door. Morgan looked up from his newspaper and his mouth hung open.

"Any schedule changes?" she asked.

He seemed to be having trouble closing his mouth.

"What, don't you like it?" She gave a little spin.

Morgan finally managed to say, "If you had some urgent reason to start checking stuff off your bucket list, you would tell me, right?"

She was about to make some wisecrack about the planetary aspects, and only then noticed she hadn't checked her ephemeris at all that morning. "I'm feeling uncommonly well, Morgan. You?"

"Apparently I'm suffering hallucinations. No schedule changes. See you when I wake up." He turned resolutely back to his newspaper.

In the back room she nodded in greeting to Kim's Odin, lit copal and rose incense at her own altar, and settled in for a morning of sorority girls. All of them regulars, these girls carpooled down from the university. They squeaked with delight at the pink dress. More enthusiastic squeaking determined the order of their turns in the back room, where each sank alone into seriousness. Problem boyfriend, parental illness, too-good boyfriend, grad school applications, and finally a cluster of boyfriends who had just figured out one another's existence. It was stuff Ria saw every year. She knew it as thoroughly from reading for decades of girls like these as if she had gone to college, herself.

Something was about to surface in memory, something she should have remembered days, maybe weeks earlier. No, it would have to wait until she had finished reading for her clients. The last girl had gotten entangled with a married professor and needed, at the very least, Ria's full attention and full box of tissues.

Franklin Lear. She must not think of Franklin Lear.

He'd gone into the Pine Barrens just after the Full Moon to have good light for his photographs. Since then the Moon had waned, was nearly new, and had been useless for photos or wilderness tracking for several days. So where was Frank? Anything might have happened. If not the Jersey Devil, some Piney with a shotgun and little patience for trespassers might have done for him. He should have called by now. She should have called him. With all the worry her OCD had forced her to expend over hand sanitizer, she'd lost track of someone she cared about who might be in actual danger.

She had only a half hour break between the carpooling sorority girls and a pair of big tippers. Not long enough to go home and call. The shop phone still looked unutterably foul. For just a second, she even considered buying a cell phone, but her brain slammed her hard with warnings of cancer and the possibility that Nils Sigurdson might be working as a cell phone salesman again—he'd be waiting in whatever storefront she walked into.

The shop phone rang.

She was running toward it before she knew she would run.

Morgan picked up. "Transcendence Perfection Bliss of the Beyond, how may I help you? Yes, I ordered five pounds of clear quartzite points. I'm still waiting for the delivery."

Ria retreated to wipe down her cards and, instead of throwing short spreads for herself, she arranged them into a nice clean spell. Frank had told her he would call. She wanted him to remember he'd said so. What he did after remembering was his business. She took great care that the spell be the karmic equivalent of mailing him a postcard—nothing that smacked of love spells, which always backfired hideously.

Two trophy wives from Rumson and their big tips later, Ria ventured out to the shop floor to catch some sunlight from the front windows. There was Frank, leaning against a wall next to the calendar and reading a very small, cheaply printed booklet. He was so immersed, she got close enough to see that it was the manual for a satellite phone before he noticed her. When he did, he sputtered with astonishment.

"Pink?"

"I see you're not dead," said Ria.

"Is that how you dress for mourning?" He smirked at his own cleverness.

And it did make her smile. "If you like, I could reserve this for your funeral. I take it you're going back to the Pine Barrens?"

"What? Oh, the satellite phone. Yeah, that's what I came to ask you about."

Is it, now? "I've fielded weirder readings this week."

"I especially like the way the sparkly beading on the neckline contrasts with your combat boots. Are those real Swarovski crystals?"

"Screw you."

"No, I really do like it. You look..." He considered. "You look spectacularly bizarre."

From the founding editor of *Bizarro Jersey Magazine*, that was as high a compliment as she expected ever to hear. Which meant she was probably going to get laid. Apparently four days on Paxil hadn't killed her libido yet. "Come on back to the divination room."

The map he spread over the reading table was much marked up, its edges soft with wear. One corner had been torn and reattached with what Ria discovered, once she flipped it over, was duct tape. The map shed pitch pine needles and bits of sand. There were probably deer ticks hiding in the creases, too, just waiting to jump out and give her Lyme disease.

Frank said, "I asked the wrong question. Before I even finished packing, I asked where the Jersey Devil *was*. By the time I drove down there, it had already moved on. I should have asked where *I* would *find* the Jersey Devil. Can we try the pendulum again?"

As long as I don't have to touch that filthy map. "Sure." She gave her incense burner another pinch of copal and rose. "Looks like you had a strenuous trip. Is that really the only question you want to ask?"

"Absolutely. Wait, no. Did you find Cindy's curse on the fridge?"

"Yes. Cleaned it out and bounced it back."

"Well, that explains a few things."

Ria cringed. "What did I do to her?"

"Nothing she didn't have coming. Now, on to the devil I *can* sell pictures of."

Ria pinched the rough turquoise bead between her thumb and middle finger. At the other end of the pendulum's silver chain the smooth, pointed bead hung over the river-shot expanse of green. "Ask."

Before he'd finished saying the words, the swinging bead pulled her hand south, rotated in a few nice round circles, and stopped dead over a spot just a few miles inland. Frank's handwriting marked the spot with the words *ghost town abandoned papermill.*

"Of course," said Frank. "It *would* be lurking in a place I've already done two feature articles on. The background of the photos will be stale for my audience. Well, at least I know my way around."

"Isn't that the place you broke your ankle that year?"

"Only because…yes. Okay, yes it was."

"Only because of the collapsed brick walls and roofless old cellars you can't see until you've fallen into them. Which won't have changed any since the last time you went. Have you thought about what will happen if you break your ankle and then have to flee from the Jersey Devil?"

"Then I'll die doing what I love. Some people die climbing Everest, some people die bringing medical relief to disaster areas. I can't think of a better way to die than chasing a good story everybody half knows but nobody will believe without my pictures."

That was the thing about Frank, the thing she'd recognized as heroic the first time she ever met him. He had come to the shop two owners ago, sample copies of an ambitiously glossy zine tucked under his arm, offering the whole world reasons to believe the endangered lore that Ria had dedicated her life to.

She said, "Did you bring any latex with you?"

"Here?"

"Here."

There was his smile again. "Not as much as you tend to like. Our options will be limited."

"I can work with that."

She wasn't able to make her peace with using the floor, or her reading table. Up against the wall was ergonomically challenging, but the best available option. The Swarovski crystal beading on the dress's back neckline gouged the paint on the wall. She tried to keep her voice down, for discretion's sake. Must not have done too well at it, since Morgan cranked the volume on the Dead Can Dance album he was playing up front, far louder than he could usually stand. Frank's kisses, astringent as witch hazel, might be the last she'd ever have from him. Might, for that matter, be the last kisses she'd ever want, if her faerie bargain with the Paxil turned sour.

Afterward, Frank said, "I should offer to repaint that wall."

"It needs replastering anyway" said Ria. "Meanwhile I'll hang something decorative and devotional over the scratches."

She was not at all chagrined at the range of personal cleaning products she kept in the cabinet. Her stockpile of hand wipes seemed like brilliant foresight.

Frank finished straightening his shirt. "Something's going on with you. What is it?"

"Come back alive and find out," she said. "Though I can't promise a repeat performance."

"I should tell you. This is a bad time to mention it. I'm sorry. I, um. I've sort of met someone. On one of those online dating services."

"You've *sort of* met someone." He'd sunk to a new low this time, dumping her for a woman he hadn't even seen. She would not let this get to her, not in front of him, not again.

"It's time I settled down, Ria. If I ever want to start a family, I can't wait until I'm ten years older than any woman who can still have kids. I don't want to be that creepy old guy trawling for twenty-somethings."

"Why be *that* creepy guy, when you're a perfectly good creep already?"

"I earned that." He sounded so reasonable in breakup mode. Breaking up with Ria was always the reasonable thing to do, especially when they weren't exactly together in the first place. "Look, you've never wanted to have kids. That's never going to change. I never want to pressure you about it. So. I've sort of met someone who does."

"But not in person yet. Online." Was that the wheedle she heard in her voice again? Fucking wheedle. She would not ask him to stay. Let it be anger in her voice. Righteous anger—that might entail some dignity.

"Ria, do you want to be a mother? If you do, neither of us has forever to wait around about it."

"No. I want you to be a good sport about latex, smell of Listerine, and fuck me good and hard against the wall. Maybe I won't want that much longer, though." She hoped not.

"I'm sorry. And maybe this courtship won't come to anything, either. None of the others stuck."

"I'm not interested in being your consolation prize anymore. Go to the Devil."

"Thank you," he said with almost disarming earnestness as he folded his map on his way out the door, "for telling me where to find him."

The sorority girls had left Ria with half a box of tissues. She went through most of them before she found the right page in her ephemeris. The Moon was Void of Course, of course, all day. Should have checked. Purchase nothing, choose nothing, begin nothing when the Moon is Void of Course. If only she had consulted her ephemeris—well, he would still have been chasing his electronic woman, but she could have protected herself better from giving a damn. And she wouldn't have been wearing this ridiculous pink dress.

Perhaps mental health was overrated.

When she'd pulled herself together enough to face Morgan, she went up front. Maybe it was the tears, or the headache that always followed tears, but Morgan's aura seemed to be in some kind of weird double vision. It was like trying on her grandmother's bifocals, only sideways. "You might want to call in Kim Kjeldberg for the rest of the day."

Morgan nodded. "You're in no condition to advise anybody on their love lives. Go home and take care of yourself. Give me the word and I'll ban him from the shop."

"But his magazine..."

"I will not allow him to make your last weeks on earth miserable."

"I'm not dying. Honest, I'm not."

"Whatever. I'll call Kim. Take a hot bath or something. It's too bad you'll never want to wear that dress again. It's not every woman who can rock evening wear over combat boots at ten in the morning. Ballsy, that's what it is. I'll miss that about you. Oh, Santini, of all the fixtures that came with the shop when I bought it, you're the shiniest."

"Thank you? Morgan, it's really not that dire."

"Go home, or I'm in danger of reminiscing about days of yore."

But once she got out of the shop, she felt light and relieved. Morgan's folly was good for one thing: it put her actual problems in perspective.

The summer sky stretched endlessly blue, cooler than the weather had been in weeks. Now that she thought of going home, she wasn't sure she could face how pink her dress would look among the vintage tiles and cabinets of her very pink kitchen. Ria decided a walk would do her more good than a bath. A walk with window shopping—and *only* window shopping. Surely she had learned her lesson about buying anything important when the Moon was Void of Course.

She remembered her lesson all the way down Harding Road, and into the cheaper blocks of Red Bank far from the boutiques and the funky, edgy, alternative shops just around Broad Street's corners. She remembered until her brain started stewing again over Frank's online almost-girlfriend. And once she started stewing about one thing, she was stewing about everything. Having an imaginary argument with Jane about the familiar accusation that Ria was humorlessly gullible—apparently that was worse than other varieties of gullibility—was far more pleasant than thinking about the humbling blunder she'd subjected herself to with Frank. Just where the zoning shifted and local character gave way to classic Jerseyan strip mall hell, Ria was about to turn back, get her car, go home.

She saw them through the window at Odd Lots: stacks and stacks of inflatable holiday lawn sculptures. Santa Clauses, Easter Bunnies, jolly snowmen, Uncles Sam, Menorahs, and giant graduation mortarboard hats, $9.99 apiece.

"When," Ria muttered, "am I going to see *my* holidays get tacky mass-produced lawn ornaments?"

And then it came to her. She laughed aloud. Laughed hard enough, joyfully enough on the street that the shop clerks looked up, startled, through the window.

She came back with her car and bought thirteen of the lawn inflatables, figuring $9.99 was a fair price for the fan apparatus that did the inflating. Once she got them home, she opened up one of the jolly snowmen and calculated its volume—astrology had kept her arithmetic and geometry skills sharp. Multiplied by thirteen, that told her how much gray polyster she needed to buy. It would delay the shop again, but oh, if she could pull this off, it would be so worth it. Nobody could call her gullibility humorless after this.

As she busted out laughing again in the tangle of disassembled Santa Clauses in her living room, it occurred to Ria she ought to be more upset about Frank, so she phoned Dr. Edelstein.

He said, "Side effects already, on Day Four? Technically, you're still at a subclinical dose."

She told him about the impulse shopping, the laughing jag, neglecting the ephemeris, and—because he was so far into his Zen he might not hold it against her—about the scratches on the wall and how they got there. "If this is a subclinical dose, I'm a little afraid of what will happen when I ramp up to the bigger pills in the starter pack."

"Would you wish undone any of the surprising things you did today?"

"I regret…"

"Not regret. Wish undone. It's a little different. Sit with it a second."

"Oh." She sat with it for several seconds. "I don't." She was as surprised at that as at any of the things she'd done.

"Then maybe they're not side effects. Maybe they're the desired effect. Maybe you want a relationship with your ephemeris that doesn't resemble prison. Whatever you decide to do with your regimen next, we now know you respond to Paxil. It certainly didn't fall flat."

So Ria set up the sewing machine she used for gothing up her black clothes and started sketches for her project. For once, it was a project that wasn't about avoiding anything, and it kept cracking her up, long into the work.

The week flew by. While her covenmates spent their evenings packing and cooking in preparation for festival, Ria spent her evenings at her sewing machine. When she had a prototype to inflate, she duct-taped it to the pump, and the noise from the fan filled her living room. How envious her previous incarnations from Neolithic Britain would have been, after their lifetimes of labor on Stonehenge, to see the easy rise of her first standing stone. One down, twelve to go.

She was going to need a lot more duct tape.

The next time the shop phone rang for Ria, Morgan covered the receiver with his hand and said quietly to her, "It's time you got a cell phone. Honestly, with as little time as you have left, how much can the health risks matter now?"

She would have argued with him about her longevity prospects, but she thought she might be able to touch the phone. She wanted to know, far more than she wanted to set anybody straight. Ria reached out her hand—yes!—and held the germy receiver right up next to her face. "Hello?"

"It's Amber. Can you get to Jane's old place right away?" Ria's coven sister's voice was tight and rushed. The engine of her little red convertible rumbled in the background.

"Yeah. My lunch hour client bailed on me. Jane's *old* place? What would any of us want to see Nils about, ever again?" Oh, no. "Jane can't have gone back to him?"

"He broke into Sophie's house and stole all Jane's clothes. Jane's gone to steal them back."

So much for the protection spell. If it had been breached at the beach cottage, it would be in tatters everywhere else.

And, in the wake of that fear, Ria's brain muttered to her, *All your fault*. So much for the Paxil victory, too.

She tried to shake it off. "How far down the coven phone tree are you?"

"Sophie and I divvied up the calling," said Amber. "We've got everyone now. Can you pick up Sebastian? I'm driving straight from the office."

"Consider it done," said Ria

The old black phone clicked a couple of clicks, then blared its dial tone. Ria dropped the receiver on the counter. No way was she going to touch it to hang up. She'd just figured out how this was, in fact, all her fault. *It wasn't Jane's clothes Nils wanted. It was the handfasting cords. I told him they were in the cottage. I told him not to ask Jane for them directly. What did I think he would do with that advice, in his condition?*

The front door swung open with the chiming of a dozen tiny bells. Ria did not turn to look.

She said, "Morgan, I'm out of here. If any clients..."

"Oh, no," said the investment banker she had sent to FBI headquarters. So he'd survived the week despite turning informant. Good for him. He stood in the doorframe, wearing an impeccable suit and the expression of a man condemned. "Tell me you're not leaving."

"Can't stay," said Ria, running to the divination room. She extinguished her incense, scooped her Tarot cards into their black silk wrappings with one hand, grabbed her bulky black handbag in the other, and headed for the front door at a run.

The client tried to catch her on the return swing. "I could really use some help." He pulled a money clip from his pocket and started peeling bills from it.

She didn't want to know how much he was offering. "Sorry. Coven emergency."

Morgan's aura looked like it was about to boil over, and there was that weird auric double vision again, as if she were viewing him through an incorrectly calibrated stereopticon. The client's face—had he been so gaunt last time?—went ashen. His aura was split, too. Ria turned her head from side to side, trying to get a better fix on him. His outer projections were rigidly perfect, but the chakras within spun in full reverse at the highest speed Ria had ever seen, a case study in concealed terror.

The phone blared its dial tone, its receiver still lying ears-up on the glass counter.

Ria stopped, breathed, put a hand on the banker's shoulder as much to steady herself as him. "Wait in the divination room. I trust my backup. She'll do right by you. Morgan, please call Kim Kjeldberg and tell her I would be personally indebted to her if she'd come in and help this gentleman."

"She's got her freelance editing gig. She can't just drop everything..."

"Personally indebted, Morgan. Please tell her that. She'll come."

Ria pushed gently past her client and fled Transcendence Perfection Bliss of the Beyond, sprinting for her car. She would let herself regret the money later.

The Saturn's ornamented door creaked open, and Ria swung her bag into the passenger seat—then she remembered she was supposed to pick up Sebastian, and pitched the bag into the back. The Saturn started with a rattle, rattled all the way to Sebastian's studio. Now she definitely needed more duct tape.

Sebastian waited on the sidewalk, his massive frame blocking out the neon in the storefront windows. Above his studio door, backlit brushed steel letters proclaimed *Sebastian Geck Body Modification*.

Ria reached over the stick shift to pop the passenger side lock, and Sebastian folded himself into the seat.

"Thanks for the lift," he said. "Hazard of living walking distance from work."

"No problem." At a red light, Ria stole a glance at her watch. Moon conjunct Mercury, temperamental actions and words. "Do we have the first clue what we're walking into?"

"I don't, anyway. If Nils is home and he threatens any of us, it could come to fisticuffs again. I hope not. Bob felt so bad after that other time, and I'd just as soon not take a turn hitting anybody."

"Sebastian, you stick people with tattooing needles every day. You pierce people with giant pointy piercing thingies. You *brand* people, for Gods' sakes." Green light. Ria caressed her dashboard figure of Hekate, Lady of the Crossroads, and accelerated into the intersection.

"Only after I've made sure they really mean it when they say it's what they need. And they pay me enough so I can afford some very expensive small business insurance. Watch out! No, on your right. I don't think my liability coverage extends to defending my coven sister from her ex."

"Yeah, well, if Nils decides he really means it about needing a punch in the face..." The three hundred dollars Nils had stolen from her would have covered, more than covered, the weird things she'd been buying lately.

"Ria, I have a feeling he got beat up plenty, long before Jane ever met him. He learned his bullshit *from* somewhere. I really, really don't want to jump on his karmic dogpile."

Red light. Ria breathed deep and took stock of her aura. Its root and crown chakras were rotating in the wrong direction, but the traffic light changed before she could relax into reorienting them. Her brain started making pictures of what could go wrong. *Oh, don't,* she told her brain. *Please don't.* How many days since the last pictures like this? She wasn't even sure.

Nils could have a gun, her brain suggested. It was a valid point. *Jane could already be dead, and you would be as much to blame as if you'd shot her yourself. You might find her body looking like this.*

"What is it, Ria?" Sebastian asked.

"Obsessive-compulsive disorder," she said. One confession could cover for lack of another. "Maybe if I could just get this

OCD thing under control, I wouldn't have to settle for being Franklin Lear's perpetual secondary."

"And maybe," said Sebastian, "you wouldn't have to settle for Franklin Lear, period. You two are no good for each other. Well, obsessive-compulsive disorder. No wonder you didn't come see me at the studio. Bodily fluids and all that."

"No, I love your studio. You and your apprentices practice such perfect sterile procedure, it's clean in there as in my own kitchen. And I covet your autoclave. It's just…I thought I was making headway against the OCD. I found a shrink, I'm taking pills and everything. But now it's snuck up on me and dragged me back. If the pills can't help me, what's my best treatment option: piercing, branding, or ink?"

"Dear one. I'm so sorry. This is not a thing I can fix. I could help you mark your desire to change, help you call into being the opportunity for change, or seal into your skin a change you'd already accomplished, but what you're asking for isn't in my scope of practice. Tattooing a college seal on a person doesn't make him a graduate, tattooing a girl's name on a guy's arm won't make her love him. A lot of people have come to me over the years asking me to fix their lives with ink. Body modification is magickal, yes, but not like that. You get it with your clients, too—people who want you to fix their lives with Tarot or astrology. You know the limits of the magickal arts. Hey, you know the speed limit, too. Do you need me to drive?"

The Saturn was chasing down a pickup truck far faster than she'd meant it to. She braked and let the following distance back in, wiped her eyes at the next red light. Too bad the Xanax samples Edelstein had given her were home in her kitchen. She'd never leave the house without them again.

"Do you need me to drive?" Sebastian asked again in the hypnotically gentle voice he used in his work. "I truly wouldn't mind." Those few words rinsed the topmost layer of misery right off her.

"No, I'm okay. We're hurrying for a reason." *And it's all my fault.*

The weeds and unmown grass around Nils's house were so tall, the place would have looked altogether abandoned except that a coven's worth of cars converged in front of it. Ria's own garden mishaps were nothing compared to this yard—wild amaranth stalks, taller even than Sebastian, had gone to seed. Ailanthus saplings raced the amaranth for sunlight. Nils's poor landlord would need a chainsaw, or perhaps a flame thrower, to clean up after the inevitable eviction.

No hope of seeing into the windows. It would be the perfect place to leave a body.

Bob's SUV screeched around the last corner, stopped with a lurch in front of the house. With no word to anyone, he burst from his car, flinging off his suit jacket into the weeds and rolling up his shirtsleeves as he charged for the door. His aura blazed silver and scintillant, as it must have in the many lives he had lived as a knight.

Sebastian sighed. "Here we go again." And he ran in after Bob.

Last time around, Ria had huddled in the kitchen with Sophie and Amber, waiting for the thumping to subside. Not now. The three of them strode straight and tall for the front door. Ria wondered why Sophie and Amber did. She knew she was responsible for this mess, and she meant to look squarely at it.

Every surface inside the living room was covered with clothing, as if someone had sprayed it from a firehose. In the middle of the floor knelt Jane, stuffing her things into garbage bags as fast as she could.

"He's not here?" Ria asked.

"The guys are making sure he's not hiding anyplace." Jane didn't look up. Her hands were barely steady enough to hold the bag open. At least her aura hadn't sustained any new damage, unless that double vision thing counted. "I can't figure it out. If he wanted me to come back, this wouldn't do it. And if he wanted to do something with my clothes, why isn't he here doing it?"

Ria knelt to help her. "Unless he was looking for something else." *I should tell her. It would be as big a relief for her as for me.*

But I don't inform on my clients.

Amber pulled another garbage bag from the roll at Jane's side. She held it open and Sophie started flinging things in. "Was anything else missing?" Amber asked.

"He pulled the drawers right out of my bureau. Looks like he threw them in his car still full and fled before he even started going through them. He was in more of a hurry than we are."

Bob's voice drifted down the hall. "No sign of him here."

Sophie said, "He left plenty of signs at my place."

Uh oh. "What do you mean?" asked Ria

Sophie popped open her cell phone to show a photo of the beach cottage's kitchen door defaced with a red spray-painted bindrune. The basic magickal technique was instantly recognizable, but Ria wasn't fluent enough to recognize which individual runes had been combined into the tangle of symbols on the door. Only at the second long look did she notice that the door's mundane lock had also been smashed and wrenched, probably with a claw hammer.

If she'd had a cell phone, Ria would have dialed Kim Kjeldberg right then. Morgan was right about the phone thing. *Still all your fault,* her brain grumbled. "So that's how Nils got through the protection spell."

Amber looked over Ria's shoulder at the picture. "Spray paint? He broke my beautiful working with spray paint? That is one ugly-ass bindrune."

Jane said, "I'm just as glad it was spray paint. If he'd used a brush, I'd have had to wonder if it was blood, and then whose blood it was, and by the time I touched it to find out it was just paint, I'd have been a total basket case. Whereas now I only need a partially enclosed basket." She laughed a broken glass laugh. "Stupid question of the day: does anybody have a cigarette?"

"No," they all said.

"Fuck this." Jane stood and headed for the bedroom. "I know where Nils keeps his."

Bob planted himself in the hall between her and the bedroom. "I am not going to let him poison you."

"It's my..."

"No. He's not allowed to stalk you, rob you, or give you cancer. Not at a distance, either. He doesn't get to do this shit anymore."

Behind him, Sebastian said, "Bob, if you're looking for someone to be angry at, Jane is the wrong target."

"Damn straight," said Jane.

"Jane," Sebastian pointed out, "Bob doesn't make a fair target, either."

"Plus," said Amber, "if you light up, this place will smell even worse. Doesn't it smell bad enough now? What has Nils been burning, anyway?"

Ria's mouth said, "Handfasting cords," before any part of her mind kicked in to stop it.

Jane raced back to the living room and upended the ruins of her bureau drawers. "Cheap Ikea crudboard," she muttered. "Handfasting cords. That's exactly what he wanted."

From the kitchen, Amber said, "It's coming from in here. What were your cords made of?"

"Um, they had a layer of silk on the outside, but the core was probably polyester. It's hard to find a really thick cord with just silk content."

Sophie said, "It does smell exactly like a waitress uniform after a run-in with a stove."

Soon the whole coven was in the kitchen, a tight fit they hadn't attempted since Jane stopped being able to host rituals there, before Nils's rounds of rehab. The fan over the stove churned at its top setting. In a cast iron frying pan on the stovetop a blackened coil of plastic still smoked slightly.

Bob said, "In the kitchen? What is wrong with that man? If you absolutely have to burn plastic, you do it outdoors."

"Indeed," said Amber with a dark smile, "he might have asphyxiated on the fumes in here. Can't have that."

Ria said, "The weeds are too high in the yard. He'd have started a brushfire and taken half the town out with him." Her brain showed her the evening news story that would have run, with dozens of innocent families burned out of their homes, or burned up in them, and all her fault.

Jane poked the crumbling mass of her handfasting cords with a spatula. "He's melted them together. I untied them, I was going to give his back to him, and now he's fused them chemically. Sonofabitch."

This was exactly why Ria cared about magickal hygiene. Things conjured should be properly released, things built properly disassembled and stowed when their work was done. Jane should never have kept both cords, and certainly shouldn't have kept them together, once she decided her marriage was over.

"If you believed in them as more than a symbol," Ria said, "you'd really be in trouble."

She'd meant it to be helpful. She'd been looking on the bright side, even envying Jane a little. The moment the words came out, she knew what expression would be on Jane's face.

Yes, there it was. That special combination of wounded and livid.

"Do you hear that?" asked Sophie.

Someone was knocking on the front door.

"Nils," said Jane, "would not knock. He lives here. If you can call it living."

"Hello in there?" called a woman's voice. The screen door banged. "Greetings and salutations, covenfolk of Rugosa."

Jane laughed with relief. "Kim, is that you?"

Kim Kjeldberg leaned her head into the kitchen. "What on earth are you people burning?"

"It wasn't us," Ria said.

"Ah, then we're all just breaking and entering."

Bob said, "He started it. How do you think Jane's clothes got back to this house?"

"I don't mind it at all," Kim assured him. "One good turn deserves another. Speaking of which, Ria, I took care of your person. Your person has rather taken it to heart about doing the right thing. Very brave. And after that reading I cast some runes about you, to see if you were okay and where you were, so here I am. Oh, introductions." Most of the coven knew her only by reputation.

Before long, Kim was puzzling over the bindrune photo on Sophie's phone. "You guys must have put some serious protections on the cottage, for him to pull out the big guns like this. It's cunningly done, but he would have to be off his head to try it. It's a straight-up breaking and entering combination, shouldn't do *you* any lingering harm, as long as you get the physical locks replaced."

"Locksmith's already working on it," said Jane. "I know a guy."

Kim smiled. "From your black book."

"A little mom-and-pop hardware shop, Reformed Order of the Golden Dawn folks. They do good work."

Ria decided this would be a bad time to recommend a psychiatrist for Jane's black book, though Edelstein was worthy.

"No harm *to you*," Kim mused. "To him, though, and to all of us in Thane Kindred, this is a big deal. He's screwing around with our communal luck, to say nothing of his own. Magic this nasty, right out in the open, will definitely come back and bite somebody. I wish I knew exactly what he was attempting with the molten cords."

Jane sighed. "I should do *something* about them. In the back of my head, I'll always worry that I'm more bound to him than before. I'd like to leave him a little bindrune note right here in the kitchen, that I'm done with him and he's done with me."

"Well," said Ria, "if anything ever called for kitchen witchery, it's fixing a spell he worked in a frying pan."

While Kim considered what runes to combine and how, the coven searched the kitchen for spices. Nils didn't keep them where he used to—in fact, the kitchen didn't seem to be much used for food anymore—but eventually Sebastian found a full canister of cayenne pepper on top of the fridge.

"Perfect," Kim said. And with a suspiciously tiny spoon the coven's search had turned up—Amber thought it might be a coke spoon, she'd had such a thing when she was young and stupid in college—Kim cayenned a bindrune as intricate and finely lined as any monastic sand painting, all across the expanse of the cast-iron pan.

"If he uses that spoon to snort anything now," said Jane, "the cayenne residue will serve him right."

"Shh," said Kim. "This is harder than it looks. I'm not thrilled about having to rush it, either."

Bob kept watch at the front door and Sebastian at the back in case Nils came home. No sign of him. The women of the coven finished gathering Jane's clothing into bags and loading them into her old Corolla.

At last Kim proclaimed her rune complete. "Okay, Jane. You're divorced now. Congratulations on your divorce. Whatever the State of New Jersey has to say about it, your remaining legal proceedings are just formalities. All of you, speak of the marriage-that-was only in the past tense, think of it only as over. Make the spell's job as easy as you can. Go home. Have dinner." She sat at the one structurally stable chair that remained of the kitchen's dinette set.

"You're staying?" said Ria.

"At least until Nils gets home."

Bob said, "Not alone, you're not. I'll tell my wife I'm needed here a while longer."

Kim shook her head. "Thank you, but it's not necessary. This is Thane Kindred's business now."

"Then I'll just stay until your people arrive to back you up."

Sebastian said, "Bob, I'll stay. Don't keep Ricki and the kids waiting for family dinner."

Ria's brain tried to stop her, but she blurted out, "I'm personally indebted to you, Kim. Personally indebted. I should stay."

"I'll call on your debt at the Seidhr, Ria. Nils listens to you, and I mean to invite him, as a parting gift. He needs a good look at his Wyrd."

Sophie said, "Isn't he weird enough already?"

Amber said, "He seethes enough already, too."

"Not the seethe," said Ria. "The Seidhr. I'll be there."

Kim smiled. Under the shimmering surface of Minnesota Nice, the Nine Worlds turned. "Would you go to my Odin shrine at the shop? Drink him a toast with the mead in the horn. Pour the last drops from the horn as a libation on my behalf, and rinse it gently. I won't be waiting here alone."

The coven went outside to huddle together among the cars and confer. No one was happy about leaving Kim there for Nils to find.

"On the other hand," said Ria, "crossing paths with one of us could provoke him to be even more violent, and obviously we can't count on our protection spell anymore."

Amber pulled a makeup compact from her purse and started smearing green eye shadow in broad streaks across her face. "If I can't hide in weeds this tall, I'm not trying."

"Honey, purple hair," Sebastian pointed out.

"Right. Ria, can your Tarot deck do without its black silk scarf until tomorrow?"

Ria apologized to the cards as she unwrapped them. They wouldn't mind—they were far less fussy about such things than she was.

Sebastian reached into Amber's compact for a fingerful of green shadow. "If you stay, I stay."

Jane said, "Circle around from the sides. Don't leave a trail behind you into the brush that he can see from the front walk. And move your car, too. He'll recognize the Miata for sure."

Everyone turned to look at Bob.

"What? I'm perfectly happy for someone else to do the honors this time."

Sophie kissed him on the cheek. "I take it all back about anger management class."

"So," said Ria, "we were going to skip circling for the New Moon this week, what with festival starting tomorrow."

Amber and Sebastian paused from painting one another to look incredulously at her. Sebastian said, "This is not a great time for a ritual."

Ria sighed. "We already had one, just not one we planned. But it might be wise to do a new protection working tomorrow, before you all drive off to camp."

"You're definitely not coming?" said Sophie.

"I owe Kim my help at her oracular thingy on Sunday. Plus, I really want to see how it works." It beat admitting an inability to cope with gnats and germs.

Jane said, "As long as we try a new method for the working, one he hasn't already broken, it might be reassuring. We talked about meeting at Amber and Sebastian's place to caravan. Is that a plan?"

"It's a plan," said Amber. She had swapped the bear claw ornaments into all her piercings.

"Definitely National Geographic this time," said Sebastian, who looked fit for a tribal cover portrait, himself.

Ria stayed until she was certain they were safely invisible in the brush. The tips of their auras flickered as wind brushed the amaranth stalks—flickered in split vision.

She arrived at Transcendence Perfection Bliss of the Beyond just as Morgan was locking up for the evening. "Mind if I do a little altar work?" she asked.

"Whatever you need to do," he said. "Are you and yours okay?"

"Will be, I think. Thank you for calling Kim in."

"I should thank you," said Morgan. "Never have I seen so satisfied a tipper. There's an envelope for you in your incense drawer. Enjoy it while you can."

It turned out to be a hundred dollar bill, which was a pretty good tip for having refused to do a reading. She suspected she'd lost his business to Kim for good, if he was so glad to be referred to the rune reader. Anyhow it would pay for the fabric Ria needed to finish her inflatable Lawnhenge.

She sat drinking with Odin in the divination room. A slight dusting of incense ash had fallen on the surface of the mead in his horn—a fine, dry blackberry mead that no God need scoff at. He didn't seem to mind the ashes, and the Paxil allowed Ria to concur. She drank the horn down to its last drops for libation, toast by toast, as she gave thanks for her fellow coveners.

All the coven's cars parked in a row in front of the flagrantly painted Victorian on Reckless Place. All but Ria's leaned heavy on their shocks, packed full for festival: tents, banners, coolers, incense, drums, glitter. Sophie's messenger bag of condoms and sarongs sat open on the passenger's seat of Jane's Corolla. The Miata's trailer hitch hooked up to a U-Haul trailer full of tattooing equipment. Ria's brain compiled an exhaustive list of what it would have insisted she pack, had she been well enough to go. Useless brain.

If the Miata and the trailer were assembled, that probably meant Amber and Sebastian had survived their vigil in Nils's yard. Nothing to dread about going into the house. Nothing at all.

The couple sprawled, sleep-deprived, on the huge leather couch in their living room. Under a wall hung heavy with a display of antique knives, Amber looked nearly naked, for all her clothes, with no ornaments in her piercings at all.

Sophie bounded over to greet Ria. "Finally! We've all been waiting for the story. They're too tired to tell it more than once."

So Ria sat on the ottoman by Bob's feet and fidgeted with her silver amulets. "How bad was it?" *All my fault.*

Amber said, "Oh, hey, your silk wrappings." She bundled them tight in her hand and tossed them across to Ria. "Thank you."

"The story!" Sophie protested. "Tell us!"

Sebastian rearranged his bulk among the cushions. "Nils took his sweet time getting home. He was mighty surprised to see all his lights on and his door wide open. He walked right past our hiding spots, calling Jane all the way. Kim came to the door. He was pissed as hell to see her."

Amber chuckled. "That woman really knows how to put on the brass brassiere. He gets all in her face, swearing like beach trash from Seaside Heights, and she just says, 'Who did you expect would clean up the mess you left at their door? You thought the cords would burn and you'd be free, didn't you? And then how did you plan to recover from that little miscalculation?' So he hangs his head like he's getting called into the principal's office, and he goes to the kitchen to take his lumps."

"They were in there a long time," said Sebastian.

"I fell asleep, twice," Amber admitted.

"But he woke us up all right," Sebastian went on, "yelling from the porch about how he was going to call the police on us for trespassing. 'I don't know who you are, but I see where you're hiding, curled up in the grass like dogs!' So I yelled back something like, 'You don't seriously want the police to come to your house, do you? Because they might not stop their search with your front yard, and they wouldn't stop their questions with us.'"

"Actually," said Amber, "we were kind of worried because, you know, camouflage face paint."

Jane flipped through her little black book. "I know a guy in the Red Bank Police Department, he's a Hellenic Reconstructionist. He's who I called for advice about with the breaking-and-entering report for the beach house."

"Yeah," replied Sebastian. "We know Mike Moros, too, but I wouldn't want to put him in the position of having to stand up for us when we were coated in sparkly green eye shadow and—Nils had a point—trespassing. Fortunately for us, Nils couldn't see us well enough to know we were bluffing, and he knew it was me by the voice, so he backed down. I told him we would go when Kim went, so she went, and that was it."

"Well," said Amber, "that was it with Nils. Kim was not overjoyed with us for staying when she'd asked us not to. But what were we supposed to do? She thanked us, sort of, and then we couldn't stop apologizing. Very weird."

"Ah," said Ria. "She saw something coming in the runes, maybe."

Jane buried her face in the little black book. "I'm not going to say it. I will not be ungrateful to my insane fortuneteller friends."

What did Jane have to be grateful to Ria for? For telling her husband where the cords were? Ex-husband, ex-husband. *I do not inform on my clients.* "Kim's not insane. She knew where to find me. I didn't tell her where I was going."

"I would have an easier time taking your divination seriously," said Jane, "if you hadn't made that big deal about Nostradamus and the Y2K bug."

"A misinterpretation of Old Provençal verse. Could have happened to anybody."

Jane's aura, dizzyingly doubled, clouded over in gray and dark orange swirls. Ria couldn't look away from it.

"What?" said Jane.

"Is it just me, or does eveybody have two auras lately?" She could not turn the auravision off.

"Well," said Sophie, "you're looking kind of green right now, but I don't think it's your aura."

Sebastian sat at attention. "This is what you were telling me about in the car?"

"Side effects of my...new dietary regimen. I think so."

"Maybe a steak would help," Jane suggested. Had she meant to make Ria feel queasier? "What did you need to go on a diet for, anyway? You look perfectly fine."

"It's a spiritual thing."

Bob said, "Fasting can be dangerous. Please, tell me you're not endangering yourself."

"My doctor okayed it." The half-lie did not improve her composure. How had the conversation become all about her? Everybody could see she was getting weirder and weirder.

"Hey, lay off, guys," said Amber. "A spiritual fast can be a really beautiful experience. So, is it about anything in particular, Ria?"

Ria blurted out the first thing that came to mind. "The land is sick!"

"You do live in New Jersey," Sophie pointed out. "It's been sick all our lives. Longer. What's up *now* that's different?"

Oh, fuck it. How far afield would Ria have to go to not talk about Nils's reading? "The land spirits are getting extra unhappy..."

"Which land spirits are these?" Jane asked. "Like, fairies?"

"In the Pine Barrens," said Ria. She wasn't sure where she was going with that, but maybe all Frank's talk of his expedition would give her something to work with.

"Fairies of the Pine Barrens," said Jane. "Seriously?"

"Why not?" Ria demanded. "There are fairies. Some fairies are land spirits. The Pine Barrens are land. Ergo, the possibility of fairies of the Pine Barrens." And now that she put it that way, it sounded pretty convincing, didn't it?

"That's enough," Bob said gently, to all of them. "Ria, call your doctor about this fast, please. You're hurting yourself. And let me drive you home. Sometimes fasting and driving don't go so well together."

"But you're supposed to be caravanning to festival."

"We can swing by your place on the way out of town," he said. "And there are enough extra drivers to get your car home, too."

"Ooh, can I drive the amuletmobile?" Sophie asked.

"Damn," said Amber, "I was about to ask."

Ria handed her keys to Sophie just because that was the shorter reach. Amber called shotgun, and the two of them praised the dashboard pantheon all the way to the end of Reckless Place.

In Bob's SUV, Ria buckled her seat belt and adjusted the seat as far away from the airbags as she could get it. How many times had she seen herself killed by airbags?

"Do you need someone to stay behind from festival?" asked Bob. "None of us would mind, if you need help while you rebalance your fast."

"No," said Ria. "I'll cook up some red meat. Nobody should have to miss out because of me."

And she did make herself a steak for dinner that night, if only to lower her load of lies by one. She had a new all-my-fault, a fresh one grown just that day: the coven had parted company without doing their protection spell. In their rush to get Ria safely home, the whole reason they had gathered had been forgotten.

The next day, Ria spent all her breaks between Tarot clients drawing diagrams of her inflatable henge. She would have to position the nylon menhirs just right to get the first sunlight of

Solstice morning to stream through the arch that was her crowning achievement in inflatable design. She ventured to the front of the store only to flip though a book on Stonehenge to doublecheck her recollections of the stones' orientation.

Morgan said, "If you're too tired for your sunlight breaks, it's okay to take the day off. Kim would pick up Saturdays."

"Do I look tired?"

He considered, and said with surprise, "You look like a person with something to look forward to."

"There you go, then."

At home on Saturday night, Ria dug up her brass sextant, a museum replica, from back when she tried writing her own ephemeris from scratch. The homegrown ephemeris would have been a lovely exercise in continuing professional education, if she'd lived somewhere with less light pollution than New Jersey. The sextant was the right tool for tonight, though. She found it in the shelves under the main living room shrine. And wasn't this a fine time for a bit of incense and a moment of devotion, to bless her absurd but ardent endeavor? She lit a disc of charcoal, sprinkled benzoin and rose on it. *Hear the words of the Star Goddess, the dust of whose feet are the hosts of heaven, whose body encircles the universe.*

Ria's old notebook yellowed in the sextant's protective box. That year she'd drawn a flow chart of all the steps for adjusting the sextant, and she needed it even more now. Without it, she would never remember how to correct for her height above sea level, and turn the knobs just so for the bending of light through the air. She consulted the pages of her current store-bought ephemeris and set out for the garden with her folded-up inflatables and a handful of little plastic tent stakes.

Standing in the yellowing stubble of what had been her flowerbed of aromatics, she followed the flow chart: turn the brass knobs, find the stars, notate. A humid day had turned to a hazy night—Ria could sight only the brightest bodies through the reflected glare of a thousand suburbs. She knelt to adjust the bases of the menhirs, pinned them down with the tent stakes, and stood again to peer through the tiny telescope. The sky seemed to be getting cloudier. With her luck, she'd have a thick gray sunrise and no morning light to play with.

The grass grew slick. Tiny droplets clung to gray nylon. Dewfall, of course. The air compressors' manual claimed they were all-weather, so despite the damp she duct-taped them to her handiwork and hooked them up to her all-weather extension cord. She hurried back to her kitchen door to shelter from a clammy drizzle, and hit the switch on the power strip.

Thirteen nylon megaliths rose in a ring. The thirteen fans whirred. She chanted over their drone.

On Solstice morning, Ria rose before dawn and looked out her bedroom windows with dismay. High winds blew the menhirs to a most un-menhir-like diagonal, from which they irregularly bobbed back to verticality. How was she supposed to mark the sunrise now?

It was 5:05 a.m. She had twenty-one minutes.

The Moon would go Void of Course an hour after that, and then it would be doubly pointless to try.

She stuffed herself into clothes and clogs, then clomped down the stairs two at a time. As soon as she turned the knob of her back door, it flung itself open with a bang.

Ria ran too late to steady the most ambitious of her pseudomegaliths, a trilithon arch that bridged between two compressor fans. A gust caught in the dolmen as if in a sail, and the nylon ripped free of the duct tape. Down the street it blew.

Ria grabbed her duct tape roll off the kitchen counter and gave chase. "Dammit, dammit, dammit," she muttered, then shut herself up. It wouldn't do for the neighbors to think damnation had a place in her religious chants.

A rosebush two blocks away put an end to the pursuit. A poorly pruned rosebush. So much for the trilithon arch. Not that the sun was going to burn off those clouds any time soon. Ria plucked the gray ruins from her neighbor's rapturous flowers, pricking her hands more than once.

I am a failure at Neolithic astronomy.

Hadn't she started this whole project intending to prove she had a sense of humor about her Paganism? Joy, all right, she sometimes had joy. She had taken so much of it in sewing her henge, she'd wanted it actually to do something. So maybe she was gullibly humorless, or humorlessly gullible, after all.

Ria spent the rainy morning patching the menhirs. She decided not to clean up the bloodstains from her struggle with the rosebush. She wouldn't begrudge so small and accidental a sacrifice. *We needed the rain. If I'd listened to my garden, I'd have known to pray for some.* One nylon panel needed to be replaced altogether. Ria hummed and chanted, seam ripper in hand. *Welcome, beautiful rain.*

That evening, just before she had to drive to the Seidhr, the rain let up. She had time, barely, to duct tape the mended menhirs to their tiny compressors and pump up the henge. It looked like the clouds might clear by sunset. Had she not been personally indebted to Kim Kjeldberg, Ria would have been tempted to stay and observe the last light of Solstice day through her handiwork.

Moon in Leo: the best and worst time to throw open a big event to all comers. There would be spectacle, Ria had picked up that much about the ritual. There would, inevitably, be ritual drama, too, and not just in the theatrical sense. The Moon, when in Leo, would shower an occasion in glory, and bring out the craving for recognition in everyone.

As she drove the amuletmobile across town, Ria seriously considered popping one of her precious Xanax samples. Nils Sigurdson would be at the Seidhr. She would, to discharge her debt to Kim, have to deal with him somehow.

Thane Kindred had hired a hall from the local Unitarian Church. Ria knew the place. She'd tried to be a Unitarian last time she was between covens. It was a lovely building—all masonry, plate glass, and well polished dark wood. Guests gathered in the fellowship hall while the practiced seidhrworkers prepared outside in the sanctuary garden.

Ria knew a few of the guests, too. Most of the established covens on the shore were represented, as well as the Druid groves from up by the university. There were people she had seen around the shop, or at the Pagan Pride march, or long ago at festival when she had been well enough to enjoy festivals.

Each of those people had an aura, and each of those auras flickered double. The crowd dizzied her. Just a week ago, she'd needed to decide to concentrate on auras to see them, and now it was always hard to turn the auravision off. She struggled to look through the energy bodies, to slow her own vibrations enough to resonate with the church's good granite walls, or at least the potted ficus trees.

Anybody she greeted would probably hug her, so Ria hung back and listened to the chatter. She found a table set up with cheese cubes and chips. That was something to concentrate on while she assiduously refrained from mingling. The conversations wove a repeating jacquard of remarks: *I've never been to one of these oracular things before. You're Lara Beneshan? Couldn't make it to festival this year. That's Lara Beneshan? I thought she'd be... Taller? No, not taller. This is my first Seidhr, too. Hey, why aren't you at festival?*

No way in Helheim would Ria want to discuss why she wasn't at festival this year, and she had nothing else to add to the weft of conversation until it reached the volume of an embarrassed yelp right behind her.

"*You're* Lara Beneshan?" said yet another voice. This one sounded cheated, too. All right, now Ria had to look.

She was only a little surprised to find that the Lakota-trained shaman Kim had flown in from Arizona was a blue-eyed blonde. Lara was shorter than the most blatantly Nordic members of Thane Kindred, and slight-boned as a bird, but Ria would have guessed by the look of her that she was Asatruar, chasing the ways of some Scandinavian ancestors. Well, it took a lot of ancestors to make a person, she supposed. Bloodlines were full of surprises. Or maybe Lara had followed a calling from a past life.

Ria hesitated an instant about examining the woman's aura, but the hesitation evaporated before she could decide anything. Double vision again rushed in on her, and she had to lean her weight back on the nearest bulletin board full of peace activism flyers before she could concentrate. Ah. There was no need for that cheated tone of voice she kept hearing. This was the aura of an adept: a vast wound in the heart chakra had scarred open, not over. Through that gouge poured sunlight. In Ria's experience, no two shamans' auras looked quite the same, but the best of them had beautiful wounds.

The shaman turned to face Ria, cocked her head, and then stuck out her tongue. "Caught you looking," she said with a chuckle.

"Sorry. I didn't mean to pry."

"Hey, at least *you* won't think I'm here under false pretenses. I get that a lot." She considered Ria's amulets. "I take it you're a guest, too?"

"Ria Santini, from Rugosa Coven. We're eclectic Wiccans." She almost reached out to shake hands, but flinched. Well, if she couldn't be real with a shaman, who could she be real with? "Sorry, I have trouble touching people."

"You apologize a lot."

"Do I? That's a new thing, then." Maybe it was the meds. "I seem to be falling apart. More than usual, even."

"May I examine you?"

"Please."

Sunlight through the wound, yes. And there was movement in the sunlight that poured out of the woman, but Ria couldn't see into the doubled glare to figure out what the movement was.

"Well," said Lara, "I've never seen anything quite like that. I specialize in soul retrieval, and I thought you might have some broken-off bit that needed bringing back. But no. The problem is that you've got two souls at the moment."

"I can't be pregnant." Could she? Ria was so careful with the latex, and she was pushing forty.

"No, I've seen plenty of pregnant people. It's weirder than that. Or Wyrder, as our hosts might say. It's like you have a funhouse mirror bisecting you, and you're looking out from both sides."

"That's what everybody looks like to me. Um, in auravision."

"Auravision's not one of my gifts. What can you tell me about it? And, hey, where did you find those cheese cubes? I've been so busy managing other people's shock at my whiteness, I haven't found a thing to eat."

So Ria was back at the snack table with a mouthful of gruyere when Nils slunk into the fellowship hall. He shied away from light fixtures and settled into the shade of a potted ficus. What had he done to his sleep cycle, to get freshly hung over at nine o'clock at night? Drunk, Ria had expected, but not quite this.

Lara followed Ria's gaze across the room. "Wow. He could keep me busy retrieving soul parts for weeks. Who thought it would be a good idea to expose a person in that condition to an oracle?"

"Kim did."

The blonde shaman's eyes widened. "I hope she's right."

"I have to say hello to him. I owe Kim a favor."

"Must be a big favor. No offense, but I think I'll stay outside the blast radius for now. Good luck."

Nils didn't quite register Ria's approach until she was nearly sharing the shade of the ficus with him. He said, "I shouldn't have come. These aren't my people anymore."

"Do you have any others?" Ria asked.

"Nope."

"Then you might as well be here."

They stood silently together, the broken leftover people watching all those whole people mingle. Well, the whole people plus Lara, who was something better than whole.

The duct tape on the bottom of Nils's aura was sticking to one of Ria's bisected aura halves. Ria watched in horrified fascination as an energy tentacle from each of her mirrored solar plexus chakras ventured tentatively out and poked Nils right in the gut.

"I suppose," he said, "I ought to take some comfort in the company of the only person on earth my wife hates as much as she hates me.

"Jane doesn't hate *me*, exactly," said Ria. "She just hates the person she thinks I am."

Nils bent double laughing. When he could speak, he said, "Oh, Ria. Now, *that*? That is fucked up."

"Think what you like."

"I didn't say you were wrong. I just said it was fucked up. More so if it's true."

Across the fellowship hall, some booming-voiced man called for attention. "Please gather for the procession to the high seat," he said. He said a great deal, too, about how to put questions to the Seidhkona—that must be Kim—but Ria lost most of it to Nils's grumbling. Well, she was the designated Nils-sitter, so she supposed being underinformed was part of the debt she was repaying Kim.

Nils and Ria drifted back and back toward the end of the procession. Only a stern woman who had clearly volunteered to shoo out the stragglers was still behind them by the time they stepped out of the air conditioned glass and masonry into the damp summer night. The procession snaked toward the center of the sanctuary garden, which was really more of a minimally tended woodlot with a circle of cleared and graveled ground in the middle. The trees breathed back the rain that had fallen all afternoon. Ria's heavy black bangs clumped together with sweat and clung to her forehead.

In the center of the clearing, Thane Kindred had built a slightly raised plywood platform, maybe four feet by four feet. A folding chair from the fellowship hall was the only thing up there. A ring of tiki torches burning citronella lit the glade. The torch nearest Ria still wore its WalMart price sticker. *That's it? That's their worship space?* Ria's brain wanted so much to be disappointed, but she reminded it of the unlikely shaman, and it settled down.

Only when the booming-voiced man held his ceremonial hammer and called on Thor to ward the place of Seidhr did Nils stop his grumbling. For the first time in years, Ria saw him reverent.

Odin, who knew wisdom's price, and Freya, who wept tears of gold, joined the ancestors and land spirits to protect the people. So said the holder of the hammer, and so it was. Thane Kindred rumbled into a well practiced rune chant for protection. Ria knew the runes only a little, but when she shaped the name *Algiz* in her mouth to chant with her hosts, she saw shining a shape, a straight line raising what might have been its arms.

A cloaked form stepped forward from treeshadow. She bore a tall rod of brass, a distaff with a tuft of wool caught in its tines. The wool reflected the flickering tiki torches. Ria thought a flame frozen in place might look like that wool. The cloaked woman's doubled aura twisted and flickered, too, stretching high and low into the Nine Worlds. She leaned on the hammer-bearer's arm to climb to the high seat. He lifted the hood from her face for her.

Kim's face was there. Kim herself dove down through the root chakra of her aura.

The hammer-bearing attendant spoke, and more than she heard his words, Ria saw rising through the plywood platform a white ash tree, its branches raised like joyful arms. She followed—everyone in the glade followed in procession—down through the heartwood of the tree to its roots. The roots drank fate from a well. The world-tree Yggdrasil sweated fate out, changed, through its leaves, and the Wyrd rained down again to the well's depths. White water, white tree, white rain. How did Ria see any shape in all this endless whiteness?

Kim's voice echoed, white, in the well. "What would you ask?"

Someone spoke. "How can I make amends to my mother?"

"You have little time," said the oracle. "Go home to her hearth while she still warms it. Dwell there while you can."

So many questions. There were careers to pursue or abandon, cancers to excise, autistic children to rescue from well-intentioned educational plans.

A mumbling black cloud hovering near Ria said, "The bottom of the Well of Wyrd is a long way to travel for a Dear Abby column."

Nils's voice knocked Ria back from the otherworld. A folding chair rested atop a plywood platform, surrounded by WalMart tiki torches, on gravel in a minimally tended woodlot. A hundred assorted Pagans stood sweating on a brutally humid night, faces turned up to Kim Kjeldberg, who sat tranced out of her mind on a mass-produced high seat. That heavy cloak couldn't have been making her job any easier.

Ria struggled to retrace her journey to the roots of Yggdrasil. No going back.

"What would you ask?" said Kim.

Ria wanted suddenly to know about her auravision problem, her antidepressant regimen, the higher dose looming before her in the sample pack. How could she ask about it in front of all these people?

Silence.

The hammer-bearer said, "Anyone who would ask, ask now."

Ria started in before her brain could stop her—too fast to choose her words. "Should I take more drugs?"

Nils's head swiveled around. "What?"

"For my illness," Ria corrected herself. "There are side effects."

"For your illness?" said Nils. "You didn't say 'medication.' You said 'drugs.' I've thought a lot of things about you. I never thought you were a hypocrite."

Kim stood from the high seat and held the brass distaff high.

"Son of Sigurd, strain to hear it: a curse I wield from the Well of Wyrd. You'll be a good man—not may, not might. You shall, though long your will yet balks. What strength only suffering can teach, you'll suffer. You'll squirm, you'll flee, you'll cry to Asgard: Can I not die now, was this not enough? Though you drag yourself down every ditch, though you heap harm and harm upon help, you will learn until lore and law forge virtue to call down Valkyries from Valhalla."

Nils smirked. "Nice alliterations. Did you practice that in front of a mirror?"

The Well of Wyrd boiled up through Kim's aura in colors that were not colors. She spoke a word—Ria never knew what it was—and searing light blasted from her mouth. Nils recoiled. Ria fell. Gravel scraped into her scalp.

She was back in the ocean the day she fell off the jetty—wave after wave ground her against rocks until the lifeguards dragged her out. What a sunny day that was, a gorgeous day to drown.

"Stop that," said Lara Beneshan's voice. The wiry little woman dragged Ria through the sanctuary garden and leaned her back against a tree. Ria had to look away from the magnificence of the wounded aura. "The oak says he'll help if you let him. I have to go to Kim now. I can't carry both of you." And she was off.

Ria reached back to touch her head where it leaned on the tree bark. She seemed to be bleeding from the scalp.

Thank you, said the white oak. *It's not something I would ask for, of course, but the blood is a very classic gesture.* It was in some kind of chemical conversation with the roots of its nearest cousins, all of whom agreed that blood made greetings with humans much easier. A maple tree on the far side of the sanctuary garden muttered, *Better theirs than ours,* but none of the oaks seemed to pay it much mind. The white oaks were formal, stately, courteous.

You'll be going to the cavern, of course, said the tree at her back.

"I will?" Ria was surprised to hear herself answer aloud. "What cavern?"

This one.

Rough rock overhead, and footing worn smooth by a thousand years' use. She stepped barefoot toward the tripod chair. As she had been taught, she adjusted her white robes as she took her place there. She wore a garland of white and purple flowers from the courtyard in the upper temple. Acrid fumes rose from cracks in the cave floor. Her attendants bore torches. Those smelled acrid, too.

Just a few months it had been since she first came here, yet already the fumes had changed her. The girl who used to stare sullenly at kings who had walked months on pilgrimage to beg her advice, that girl was gone. Now she inhaled her god and spoke him back out. She was the smoke's oracle.

The white oaks were thirsty. *For water,* they assured Ria. They were embarrassed about how much they had appreciated her blood. *The rain last night was delicious. Please advise your Gods that we need more like that.*

On the far side of the grove, two burly Thorsmen disassembled the high seat and its platform. Kim sat on solid ground before it. Her attendants passed her a mead horn to drink from, and Ria could make out the familiar voice, hoarsened, raising a toast.

Ria herself was in no condition to help, and it looked as if nobody needed her. Indeed, she seemed to have been forgotten altogether. The crowd had drifted from the grove to the parking lot. Already a line of tail lights and blinking turn indicators formed just at the edge of Ria's vision. Time to take her place in that line.

Halfway across the parking lot toward the amuletmobile, Ria spotted a couple making out. The woman had the man pinned to a car—how did they stand it in this humidity? They kissed so greedily, Ria would have liked to look away. None of her business.

Wait a minute. Was that Nils? Yes, definitely Nils, and damned if that wasn't what's-her-face, the kindergarten teacher, Franklin Lear's fridge-hexing ex-girlfriend. Ria shuddered at the mercilessness of the Threefold Law colliding with the mercilessness of Wyrd. Out of pity she blessed the couple in her heart as she picked up her pace across the parking lot.

Sealed in the Amuletmobile, Ria cranked the air conditioner. Maybe she should have tried to dismantle the hex rather than reflect it back to its source. That would have been more compassionate. But if the catastrophically unwise embrace she had just witnessed was the hex's reflected image, what had it done to Ria in the years it lurked in her kitchen?

She gnawed at the worry, and the worry gnawed back at her, all the way home, until Ria decided the gnawing was worse than the double vision. If her previous incarnation as temple oracle had relied on toxic fumes to get the job done, who was Ria to turn her nose up at antidepressants?

The first day on the higher Paxil dose was a queasy one. The second involved an embarrassing number of trips to the bathroom for dry heaves, which rather dimmed her credibility with her walk-in clients and elicited appalling sympathy from Morgan. The third day, she tentatively called Kim Kjeldberg in to cover for her at the shop. Kim's throat was hoarse, but she was otherwise recovered and happy to take the shift. The fourth day, Ria stayed home and consulted the Tarot cards on her own behalf.

Travel clean-up party employment, said the cards.

"What?" said Ria. She tried another spread, a Celtic cross layout with clarifications.

Nightmares vacation money. Oh, and the Devil.

A gibberish answer meant she'd asked the wrong question, but the cards got less and less coherent. The Devil trump was the only card the deck wanted to emphasize.

"Should I even keep asking?" Ria asked.

Ace of Swords, reversed. Sorry, chica, can't help you today. Go ask somebody else.

Ria phoned Dr. Edelstein to beg mercy.

"The side effects will get better in a couple more days," Dr. Edelstein said.

Ria, who was lying on the bathroom floor with a cool damp washcloth on the back of her neck, said, "I'm not going to live that long."

"How are your obsessive symptoms?"

That was when it occurred to her that she ought to be skeeved out about lying on the bathroom floor. "Better. Oh, fuck. Excuse me a moment." More heaves. A chance to breathe. "False alarm."

"Are you able to rehydrate between bouts of vomiting?"

"I think so."

"Take a Dramamine with some extra-diluted Gatorade and, if the Dramamine works, give the higher dose one more day. If you're still throwing up overnight, stop the pills and call me."

Which meant Ria was going to have to ask someone to bring her a Dramamine. A big box of Dramamine. A gross of Dramamine. Maybe she should buy stock in whoever made Dramamine while she was at it, because she was still lying on the bathroom floor, and it still wasn't skeeving her out. Yay Paxil.

"Okay," she said. "This sucks, but even now, it still sucks less than the OCD. Gotta go."

"You call me if you need to," Dr. Edelstein insisted. "Don't you hesitate."

"Right. Thanks. Hanging up now."

"Good luck."

It was time, and past time, to call some live human being to come actually to the house, for Dramamine at the very least, because there was no way Ria could drive out to get it. And what if she stopped being able to rehydrate herself? Ria weighed that worry and was surprised to find it reasonable. The trouble was, anybody she called would want an explanation. Would deserve one, would otherwise guess at one. Best to tell the truth, but who could Ria stand to tell?

Bob would overreact. Sophie would be ineffectual. Jane would be Jane.

Sebastian already knew, of course. But calling him would mean Amber would find out.

Amber would categorize Ria's predicament as either beautiful or ugly, and that would probably be the end of it.

Ria dialed. Waited through the ringing. Rearranged her

washcloth to get a cooler spot in contact with the back of her neck.

"Sebastian?"

"He's in Florida. Jesus, Ria, you sound like shit."

"Florida?"

"His best friend from high school's taking holy orders at a monastery down there. But the guy's a Franciscan, so it's cool. What's going on?"

"Not feeling well. Need Dramamine. And Gatorade. Oh, fuck." More heaves.

"I'm on my way." Click.

She stepped down from the marble floor of the temple complex into the cool courtyard garden. White cyclamen flowers crooked their necks down like swans. Above, framed by the courtyard's portico, clouds shone gold, lit from beneath by a sun rising at the horizon she could not see, and would never see again. She tucked her robes close about her, not wanting to knock the dew from the blossoms. Her robes reeked of the cavern, reeked of the fumes that brought visons. Reeked of the gift of her god. She did not remember falling, but a moment later she lay crushing the cyclamen beds, the bright scent clear, petals soft against her face. Voices called out, "Pythia, can you speak? Send for help, the young Pythia has fallen!" The voices murmurred worry. Ria thought she heard mention of plague.

An old woman ran through the courtyard and knelt beside her, crushing cyclamen blooms under her knees. "Ah." She nodded. "You again."

"Me?" said Ria.

"You as you will be, but not soon. Why do you not speak to us when she calls you from the cavern?"

"She?"

"The Pythia, you as you were. Are, to me. In the cavern, it would be easier for you to give us whatever warning you have come to give."

"I haven't come to warn anyone. I just want to know who I was."

The old woman leaned back a moment, tilted her head to assess Ria. "Ah. Of course you would want to know. The bright line through your soul-colors splits. People always look back when the bright line splits. Why should it surprise you that I see the soul colors? I taught you, and will teach you many times. The bright line splits. Tell me again what that means."

Apparently Ria really had been this woman's student before, because the answer came, and it was one she'd never read in her New Age books. "My aura is dying and being reborn within the same incarnation. Oh, that means I get to keep my same old body! Good. I was getting worried about that. It was pretty dried out when I left it." She tried to stand up, but the young Pythia's body remained dizzy and weak.

"Do you truly have no warning for us?" the old woman asked, gently helping Ria back down. "When you're not coming from as far, you usually have something to warn us about."

"Be picky about your soul-healers, but don't be preemptively rude? I don't know. All the hardest things in this life have been in my own mind. I don't really know anything useful about great world events, and I don't have my divinatory tools here. Um. Wash your hands with soap as often as you can? Boil your drinking water?"

"Boil it?"

Ria considered. In Jersey, that would have been overkill. But here, now, among people whose lives would play out centuries before the development of germ theory? The advice felt rational, even if she was giving it through the body of a previous incarnation to her…spirit guide? "Definitely boil it. That and the handwashing can slow down a plague."

The old woman smiled broadly. "You see? Help and a warning after all. Thanks, my girl. Go home. You've done well."

Ria had no idea how long it took Amber to get there,

presumably by way of a drugstore. Maybe Ria had slept a little on the bathroom floor. She didn't remember sleeping, but she didn't remember not sleeping. She remembered...

The bright line splits. Ria concentrated hard on Amber's aura. The whole world was one big broken stereopticon again—she must be seeing Amber with both of her energy bodies, the new one she would keep, and the old one that was dying. Amber herself looked perfectly normal, bristling with spikes through all her piercings, the positively baroque tattooed rendering of a wisteria vine coiling up the arm that held the plastic shopping bag. *Rite Aid Pharmacy*, promised the shopping bag, and Ria hoped fervently for the right aid. Or for aid for her rite, if she could get over her heaves enough to mark her passage ritually. "Rite Aid." She giggled a little at her own lame pun.

"Oh my Gods," said Amber. "Gatorade. Gatorade *now*."

"Dramamine first," said Ria. Chewable tablets. Vile. The Gatorade was ambrosia of the Gods. "More."

"If that tastes good to you, you must really need it. I wish you'd called sooner. I'd still have come if you *weren't* at death's door, you know. Any of us would. *Any* of us."

Ria meant to say something appreciative, or at the very least something like, *I know.* "Mmph," she said, her mouth full of Gatorade.

"You should probably slow down a little."

The wisteria blossoms in Amber's tattoo were blowing in a breeze that seemed to affect only her left arm. The reef fish on her right arm darted merrily through their coral fans. Her aura snapped into unity.

"I feel much better," said Ria.

"You're stuck with me all day, better or not."

Dramamine bought time for Gatorade, and Gatorade bought time for Paxil. Sleep came, dreamless this time, and Ria woke on her living room sofa to see Amber staring out the window, sketching Lawnhenge in her design notebook.

"What time is it?" Ria asked.

Amber smirked and kept sketching. "What, can't you read

your own henge?"

"It's five past Solstice. I was hoping for something more specific."

"Time for dinner, if you're up for the won ton soup I had delivered. Or just the broth. Your call."

"Oh, won tons. My Gods, I'm hungry. Can you bring a mug to the couch?"

When Amber turned to fetch it, Ria caught a distinct fluttering among the hummingbirds inked on her back. Perhaps this new energy body would have an advantage or two over the one Ria had just shucked. Or the dehydration was making her hallucinate. Too soon to say.

"Here you go," said Amber, and she sat on the other end of the couch with a mug of her own. "So, was it food poisoning? Or do I need to worry about catching norovirus?"

"Sebastian didn't mention?"

"No. Oh, no. Tell me Frank Lear didn't get you knocked up."

For a second Ria was unsure again. Counting days against cycles was something her brain could do very fast, though, so she settled the question. "No, it's not morning sickness. I'm finally taking meds for my OCD. The side effects are supposed to get better as my body adjusts."

Amber's spoon fell with a clank back into her mug. "You have OCD?"

Ria laughed. And laughed. "You don't think the way I live is crazy?"

"I don't *care* if it's crazy. I think the way you live is beautiful. And who among us isn't at least a little crazy? I haven't been quite right since I got struck by lightning at the age of sixteen."

"You got struck by lightning?"

"Oh come on, surely you've noticed I'm not quite right. I told you all about it. I wouldn't have thought you'd forget a story like that."

"Lost conversations happen to me all the time. I probably looked like I was listening, while I tried to pretend my brain wasn't showing me some horrible film again and again. Passing for anything like sane takes up a lot of my attention."

"Ria, you're better than sane. Sane people don't make art."

Ria looked around at the agonizingly pristine living room with its dozen little devotional spaces and their nervous offerings. "Is this *art?*"

"You want my professional opinion?" Amber turned toward the shrine to Brighid over the fireplace to make some kind of point about it, but before she could say what it was, she drifted half out of her body with delight at the presence of beauty. She sat there reexamining the details until Ria realized Amber had forgotten she was going to say anything at all.

"Should I take that as a yes?"

Amber drifted back from whatever inner plane she'd gone to. "And Lawnhenge isn't half bad, either. You could make a little chunk of money selling them on eBay, and not only to Pagans. How much time did it take to make?"

Ria tried to tally up the hours. Fewer than she would have guessed, actually.

"I could help you price it appropriately, it you want to make a cottage industry of inflatable standing stones. It's a brilliant work of design."

The old habit of calculating how much more Ria would have to scrimp to make an offer on the shop tried to reassert itself, before giving way to a recollection of joy at the sewing machine. "I could try that. Something new."

"New is good," Amber agreed. The salamander zoomorphs that coiled in a knotwork of flames along her clavicles capered and shot their red tongues out to taste the air.

New was good. Shaky and fragile, but good. Ria rose Friday morning, made it through her ablutions with only a few breaks to sit down, chewed a Dramamine tablet just in case, and ventured out into the world. She drove around her block at five miles an hour, twice, to make sure she wouldn't be a menace on the road. Good enough. She doubted she had the stamina to do readings, but she wanted to show her face at the shop before she lost any more shifts. Fridays were Kim's now, fine. Ria needed to keep Saturday and Sunday or she was sunk.

The moment she turned off the amuletmobile's engine in its downtown parking space, a wave of fatigue pulled Ria under. She thought she'd fall asleep right there in the car, on a ninety degree day with all the windows shut, and her too weak even to turn on the air conditioner. There was no way she was going to put up with dying now, not after what she'd just fought through, so she shoved herself out of the car and clung to a parking lot tree for a few minutes.

She didn't dare drive herself home.

The nearest storefront with air conditioning was a cell phone provider's, from the same company that handled her landline. That would do for a cosmic sign.

Sure enough, Nils Sigurdson was in there putting the hard sell on some guy who wasn't sure he wanted a qwerty keyboard. Nils glanced over at her. His embarrassed-to-be-tall slouch deepened until she wasn't sure she'd be the first of them to topple over.

Ria found a chair under a cold vent in the ceiling and closed her eyes to wait there for a salesperson. She didn't expect Nils to have the gumption to speak to her. The torpedo wound in his aura wasn't the least bit improved. The black strips that had put her in mind of duct tape had been replaced by gray-green scarring, not quite opaque—less baffling, but harder to fix in the long run. The only good thing about his aura was that Ria saw just one of it. The effort of examining him forced her to grip the sides of the chair to avoid falling off.

Here came Nils in a natty new button-down and a fabulous tie. The three hundred dollars he'd stolen from her must have run out before he could replace his shoes. "Are you okay, Ria?"

"Just who I wanted help from," she mumbled before she realized she was saying it out loud.

He covered the tie with his big hand. He knew exactly what she'd been assessing. "Look, I said I was sorry. I really needed this job. I can pay you back, just give me a few months." The wheedle. Poor bastard. He lowered his voice. "I'm not the best person to consult if you're suffering Seidhr aftereffects. I'm sorry about that, too."

"Actually, I came to buy a phone."

"A cell phone? Seriously? You?"

"No hard sell, Nils. Something simple, with not so much radiation."

"I don't think radiation levels are in the comparison charts they give us."

"Try."

He tapped keys a while at one of the computer terminals and phoned some kind of corporate office. Ria closed her eyes and leaned her head back against the plate glass window. Whatever Nils told his fellow salespeople sufficed to get Ria a few minutes of peace.

"Okay," he said quietly as he sat in the chair beside hers. "A smartphone is right out. No GPS or email or any of that stuff. Calls and text, that's it."

"Do I *have* to text?"

"Nobody can make you use that feature if you don't want. I've set you up with the least gimmicky contract available and every coupon code I could dig up. It just about wipes out my commission on the sale, and you won't have to pay anything for three months. And by that time, maybe I can make it right about when I came to the shop."

"Call it even," she said. He wouldn't make it right about the money, not for years even if the curse of virtue came true. He might mean to, he might try to sooner, but there was no point in setting herself up for aggravation. "You've probably just saved me that much, anyway. Where do I sign?"

"Right here. It's the best I can do for now."

She wanted desperately to change the subject. "Do you have a water cooler? I could really use some water before I try driving home." She signed the papers and leaned back against the window.

When she opened her eyes, she was looking at a plastic cup, full, speckled with condensation. Heavenly cold.

"Drink deep," said Nils. "May you never thirst."

Ria's first call on her new phone was for a taxicab. Her second call was to Amber, asking her to help get the amuletmobile home. Her third call, as she rode back to her bungalow, was to Morgan to tell him she wouldn't be in on Saturday, but Sunday might work.

"You're alive!" Morgan's voice shouted from the cell phone, so loud the cab driver startled.

Ria said, "Um. Yes."

"Now we see why I'm not the one who tells fortunes for the walk-ins. All my divinatory methods told me you would die on Thursday."

"I sort of did. But I feel much better now. Could you turn down the stereo? That just got really loud."

"Can't. You don't turn down the Hallelujah Chorus. See you Sunday, Santini. Glad to have you back."

The restorative powers of won ton soup and nearly two solid days of sleep worked wonders. The higher dose of Paxil kicked ass. It probably didn't hurt that the Moon was entering Scorpio. Ria woke Sunday feeling the way she suspected normal people did. She opened her kitchen knife drawer and no warning visions tormented her. She opened and closed it again a few times. Nothing. "Thank you," she said to the air. "Thank you, thank you."

The minute she was decently dressed, she ran out to the yard barefoot and stuck her fingers in the dirt. She dug at the weeds. It was like archeology, exposing the outlines of her old garden beds. By scent she found the asafoetida reasserting itself from its rhizomes. Never had she been so glad to breathe a smell so foul. Most of her medicinals, aromatics, and magickals were putting up new growth—that was the bed where she'd taken the greatest care with soil composition. It would be work to bring them back. Good work.

"Thank you," Ria whispered to them. "I won't leave you again."

She resisted the temptation to return to work in the pink dress. For just a moment she considered culling her tangle of silver necklaces with all their amulets. No, she had put effort and intent into consecrating each one, and if she did retire any, she would not do it rashly. She tightened the laces on her combat boots and set out. The hem of her skirt caught in the boot tops. She had forgotten to straighten it.

It seemed a good day for a personal ritual of thanksgiving, so Ria loaded her main ritual tools in the car and figured she'd go to the beach after work. Summer weekends were crowded on the shore, but if she went up to the one nude beach on Sandy Hook she'd be able to find parking. Let other people's modesty be her gain.

The drive to work was hazardous for fresh reasons today. At every red light, Ria kept checking pedestrians' auras to see if they doubled, and then she'd miss the green until somebody honked at her. "I'm well," she told her dashboard Gods. "I think that's what this is. Am I well?" The Gods smiled, as they had always smiled on Ria.

Morgan greeted her at the shop door with a bouncing hug before the brass bell even rang. "Are you back? Are you really back?" He pinched her shoulder, perhaps to test for corporeality.

"I'm really back."

He put the Hallelujah Chorus on again and sang along with the tenor line. Ria was not a big fan of the monotheistic lyrics, but she appreciated the exuberance and joined in with the alto line she'd learned in high school choir. The first of the day's Tarot clients, a young gothling still in the professionally unimpressed stage, walked in to find them belting out the umpteenth blast of the King of Kings and Lord of Lords part.

"Wow," said the gothling. "It really is Transcendence Perfection Bliss of the Beyond in here. I'll never make fun of your name again."

Two readings later, Ria was still transcendently, perfectly blissful. She drifted to the front window for a sunlight break between clients. She was about to ask Morgan what divinatory methods he'd been using when he thought he'd received the exact date of her demise. It was hard to get that kind of precision out of anything other than Ouija boards, but most of the spirits who liked communicating through those were nothing but trouble.

The phone rang. Ria picked it up, because she could. "Transcendence Perfection Bliss of the Beyond."

"Thank God it's you," said Franklin Lear. "I need you to come to the Pine Barrens right away, to that place you found on the map."

"Are you all right? What happened?"

"I'll tell you when you get here."

"You'll tell me right now whether you're all right, or I'm calling 911 for you."

He sighed with an exasperation that conveyed perfectly across the distance from his satellite phone straight up into low earth orbit and back down across all the networks of North America. "I wasn't harmed at all."

"By what?"

"Just come, okay? And bring yourself some bottled water. It's a hike from the end of the road to the abandoned papermill."

"No."

Long silence. "No?"

"You have a magazine. Your magazine has a staff. Call one of them. You're dating some chick on the internet. Call her. You're…"

"About that chick…"

"I don't care. I'm not coming."

"Fine. I'll tell you. I found the lost log of Captain Kidd's first ship."

"In an abandoned papermill? In New Jersey, that part I could believe, but you're too far inland."

"It wasn't in the papermill. If I had lied and told you I was in danger, you would already be driving."

He was right about that. And if he hadn't told the cheap, easy lie, why would he tell her an extravagant one?

He said, "You'll want to see what I found. Whether you ever

want to see me again or not, you'll thank me for showing you this."

Dammit dammit dammit. "I'm on my way."

She hung up and wiped her hands on her skirt. The receiver wasn't paralyzing anymore, but it was still kind of gross.

Morgan glowered at her from the cash register. He'd already taken out the whiteboard marker.

"But I even bought a cell phone!" she protested. "I kept it charged and everything!"

"It only works for receiving calls if you actually give people the number."

"Oh. Right. Sorry."

"How long will you be out this time?"

"Just this afternoon." She headed for the back room. There was one thing she needed.

"It occurs to me," he said as he crossed out half the day on the calendar, "that I might have calculated the date wrong for your departure from this world. I'm worried about you."

She tucked the turquoise pendulum into her Tarot deck's black silk wrappings. "If I get myself killed, I'll haunt the shop full time to make all this up to you. No more pesky distractions of living to keep me from reading for clients, and I wouldn't need any of the proceeds."

"After this week, that's not funny."

"I'll be in tomorrow for opening at eleven."

"Here," he said, and tossed her a chunk of what turned out to be tiger's eye. "For luck. Be careful."

Ria bought a twelve-pack of bottled water, a big map of the Pine Barrens, and a box of fruit roll-ups at the gas station where she fueled up the amuletmobile. She tapped all her silver pendants in the proper order while she waited for the station attendant to top off her tank. Compulsive behavior, she suspected, so she checked her purse to make sure she had her meds. There was the Paxil starter pack, and nestled beside it the two Xanax samples.

If ever there was a day for Xanax, this was it. She popped open a water bottle to take one.

A bit later, about when she started seeing highway signs for various state parks in the Pine Barrens, she began to feel distinctly taller. Her posture had so improved that she had to adjust all her mirrors. "Curioser and curioser," Ria muttered. Yay Xanax?

The maple trees and orchards along the roadside gave way to pitch pines as she drove south. The soil, where she could see it, grew paler and sandier. Every turn she took toward the papermill got her onto a smaller, rougher, less marked road. Bridge after ever-smaller bridge over the tannic creeks clattered fragments of decayed concrete up as she crossed. When she finally found Frank's Jeep at an unofficial trailhead and got out to stretch, she discovered that quite a few of the beach glass blobs she had glued to the amuletmobile were knocked off for good.

Her hand rested on her necklace for finding lost objects, but really, was she going to expend that much magickal energy on a quarter pound of beach glass scattered over forty miles of back roads? Maybe she didn't need to keep absolutely every piece of luck she had affixed to the Saturn.

Here came the lost object himself. Franklin Lear crashed through the underbrush. He carried some kind of curved wooden plank over his shoulder. "There you are!" he called. "Wait till you see this!"

This turned out to be a worm-eaten timber from a rowboat. Frank loaded it into his Jeep alongside a dozen others like it. "I found a jolly boat from the *Blessed William*."

"This far inland?"

He shrugged. "The river must have had a different course back then. It's been a few centuries. Somebody was taking potshots at me a couple nights back, so I had to scramble into the underbrush and take cover for the night. When I woke up, the boat turned out to be what I'd hidden under. A very little digging, and voila, Captain Kidd's log."

"You can't seriously intend..."

Frank heaved the plank into the back of his Jeep. "Are you going to doubt me now? You, Ria?"

"That's not it. Of course Captain Kidd hid treasure in the Pine Barrens. When I was ten, my dad took me on a Halloween ghost tour at Barnegat Lighthouse. I saw Captain Kidd's ghost with my own eyes. If he didn't leave treasure around here, why bother haunting New Jersey, when he had much bigger grudges in London?" She tripped on Frank's hiking pack. He'd dumped it in the sand next to his car, perhaps to make room for more planks. "What I can't believe is that you're disturbing an archeological site. You could get scholars in here to confirm the find, and then nobody would be able to deny you." The plank for which he had rolled down the passenger window bore distinct traces of insect life. "Plus, you're going to get termites in your apartment building."

"I'll be able to buy a new apartment building with what I'm going to find. Don't you see, I'll be able to keep the magazine afloat this way."

"With a worm-eaten, three-hundred-year-old rowboat, some reassembly required?"

"With this." He opened the driver's side door and pulled out a bundle of very sandy oilcloth. "Go on. Take a look."

It weighed shockingly heavy in her hand. Inside the oilcloth wrappings was a crumbly old book—so crumbly that a chunk of binding fell among the pine needles at her feet. She swaddled it back up, as lovingly as she might have her own Tarot deck. "I can't. It's too delicate." Something niggled at her. What had she missed? "Wait. *Someone was taking potshots at you?!*"

"It was two days ago. They couldn't possibly still be waiting here. It's not like moving the rowboat parts has been an especially discreet process."

"You called me to meet you in a place where people were shooting at you two days ago?"

"You do make it sound pretty bad."

"Next you'll tell me the Jersey Devil found *you* and it'll be here to eat us in five minutes."

"I didn't get that good a look at it, but I don't think it's in any condition to eat humans anymore."

"That's it. I'm going home. You can tamper with archeological evidence while under fire in a cryptozoological hunting ground without me."

"Would you mind if I throw my laundry in your car?" asked Frank. "My whole pack would be even better. There's no room for it now that my car is full of jolly boat, and I hate to just dump such high quality gear. That's actually what I called you for in the first place."

A lifetime of celibacy was looking better and better. "I'll drop it off at your building," said Ria, with a calm she could only ascribe to psychopharmacology, "because I have to drive past it on the way home anyway, and I won't have you dumping who knows what in a fragile ecosystem. The land is sick, Frank. You can't treat it that way. And don't ever call me again."

Lost. Definitely lost. Driving faster didn't help, though she tried it for a while.

Something big flashed out of the underbrush by the roadside and banged against the hood of the Saturn. A shower of plastic trinkets popped loose from the car and flew everywhere. Ria braked hard. Whatever the thing was, it bounced off the hood and up, out of sight.

She pulled over, surprised she wasn't shaking. A vague memory of antlers in the blur told her she was lucky. It must have been a deer. If she had hit it at a different angle or speed, the antlers might have come right in through her windshield.

The engine was still running. So far, so good.

She got out to look at the damage, a huge dent in the hood. It amazed her that the car could still run.

Ria glanced around the road, looking for the animal. She'd have to report it. No way would she be strong enough to move the buck out of the road by herself, assuming it was even dead. If it was alive, it would probably impale her on its antlers.

She found it, flung all the way into the tall reeds on the other side.

Not a buck.

Not a buck at all.

It did not stir. Had she killed it?

In the fading light she saw its two cloven hooves and its two short arms that ended in something very like hands. The body seemed impossibly bottom-heavy, considering that it also had long, batlike wings. The wings looked serviceable enough, but to carry all that bulk? Ria couldn't imagine the mechanics working out.

To see its head she would have to get closer, close enough to bend the tall reeds out of the way.

The thing really wasn't moving.

Ria went back to the car for her broom. She wanted some reach if she was going to move those reeds, and she remembered an incident from the 1909 rampage when a farm wife had fended the Jersey Devil off from her dog by beating the monster with a broom. Ria's ritual broom, she was sure, packed even more of a wallop. Just for good measure, she backtracked to the spot where the creature had tried to cross in front of her car, and she swept at the black skids her tires had left smoking on the road. She had meant no harm, not even to monsters, so she concetrated on cleaning up the harm she'd done. She swept the hood of her car, which, now that she examined it again, had coarse hairs embedded in its scratched paint. She swept her own path, where she had first crossed to see the creature. At last, she held her broom carefully by the end of the handle, and brushed the reeds aside.

Antlers. She hadn't been entirely wrong. Antlers, on a broader, heavier head than any buck had ever carried. The eyes were closed, so she could not tell whether they glowed red as the old reports claimed. Its two hind legs looked mismatched. Maybe the car had injured one, or maybe the Jersey Devil just came that way.

She was close enough to hear its shallow panting breaths.

Weak though her aura sight was now, she forced the grinding shift, and staggered at what she saw. Two centuries could not have been enough to gather that collection of scars. It must be older. Much older. Jagged cuts in the etheric template glowed where the prana gushed out. The aura seemed to have more than the usual complement of chakras. Yes, nine on the front and ten on the back, conspicuously mismatched along the hara line. Who'd ever heard of a thing like that?

And what to do about its injuries? They were probably the reason there hadn't been a major attack since 1909. A prana leak that big would lay anyone—anything—very low indeed. Best to leave the etheric template alone. But Ria figured out which of the muddy brown chakras was most like a heart chakra. It looked as if it had been crushed in a giant crimper.

All the Devil's physical parts were mammal parts, as far as she could see, and any mammal would have a heart chakra worth fixing. Ria reached one of her prodding auric tentacles through the crack in the template and gave the heart chakra a little swirl, as if she were dialing a rotary phone. The chakra spun once, then stopped with a clunk almost audible. One more try. Spin. Clunk. Spin, half spin...

It started up like a creaky old lawnmower. The heart chakra spun, asymmetrically but in more or less the right place, and all the other chakras started humming along with it, some spinning forward, others backward. It was still a mess, but a much less ugly mess.

The auric vision faded, and though she tried, Ria could not get it back. Pain in the ass. It had taken her so many years of practice to learn an effortless shift, and now she'd have to learn it all over again.

Assuming she lived to get home, because now the creature's eyes were open. Red, though not glowing. They tried to focus on Ria.

At least I still have the broom.

The beast lifted its head, groaned like an undergrad with a tequila hangover, and lay back down on the crushed reeds.

And I'm still full of Xanax. More fear really would have been wiser. There was brave, and there was stupid brave.

Then I'd better enjoy it while I've got it. Only a few hours left, and I'll never feel like this again.

She wanted to turn away, but she gave the creature one more look, bottom to top, or almost top. Something stopped her, something she was surprised she hadn't noticed sooner.

Around its neck it wore a collar, like ones Ria had seen fastened on endangered creatures in nature documentaries. The band was of thick gray webbing, stencil-printed in large block letters with the words UNIVERSITY MARINE AND COASTAL SCIENCES CENTER. A small square plastic box, almost the size of Ria's fist, was affixed to the collar. That would be the transmitter.

The collar had worn a red, raw welt around the creature's neck. It hurt just to look at. No being should have to live with that.

But this was the Jersey Devil. The marauding, cattle-sucking, farm-despoiling, man-eating Jersey Devil.

If the creature was really as bad as all that, why had it been tagged and released instead of locked up? Surely even the state university, for all its budget cuts, would not turn loose the Jersey Devil, having once captured it, if it really posed a threat.

The creature moaned and tore at the collar with its tiny arms. Its claws appeared to have been trimmed. In a low, rattling voice, it said something that sounded like, "Treat?"

"Are you okay?" Ria asked. "I didn't mean to...are you hurt?"

"Treat?"

Ria rushed back to the car. If it expected a treat, she'd probably better give it one. The only treat-like thing in the car was the box of organic fruit roll-ups—or the remaining half of the box, anyway. Raspberry. She brought those, and her first aid kit.

The Jersey Devil ate the first raspberry roll-up. If it had eaten the livestock of 1909 with as much gusto, no wonder all South Jersey had been terrified.

"The rest are for later." She uncapped the tube of Neosporin.

It watched her hands with keen attention. "Treat?"

"Well, sort of." Maybe the Xanax was starting to wear off, because now she hesitated to touch the welts under the loose collar. This close, she could see fleas in the Devil's coat. Her first aid kit was not equipped for fleas. *I'm going to have nightmares about this for years. Oh, hell, I was going to have nightmares for years, anyway.*

She squeezed the whole tubefull of Neosporin into her hand and smeared it on the bare band of skin around the creature's neck.

It kicked a hind leg against the broken reeds at first, but soon settled into low crooning.

Ria had nothing she could use to wipe the residual ointment from her hands. Her fingers were sticky, and now she was going to handle food with goop on her hands, goop that was cultured from fungus. Fungus.

Oh, and the Jersey Devil was not a foot away from her. Yay Xanax.

"Treat?"

"Treat. Oh, right! Raspberry roll-ups. Here. You can have the rest of the box." She considered dropping it and running. No. This was a living being that could be hurt by a collar; the individual mylar wrappings from the snacks couldn't be good for any animal, not even one that had withstood two centuries. She peeled the remaining roll-ups open and put each one within reach of those odd hands with their trimmed claws. Some very brave person routinely got close enough to trim them. Ria wondered if it was one of her well-manicured sorority-girl clients.

As she backed quietly away, Ria wished she had a satellite phone. The University Center for Marine and Coastal Sciences ought to know their Devil needed a visit from the vet.

If she ever made it home, she'd call them.

She was about ten feet from her car when the Devil finished eating its fruit roll-ups.

Its voice drifted across the reeds and the road. "Treat?"

She turned and ran for the car's open door. Almost made it.

A hand grabbed at her ankle, and she half-stumbled into the driver's seat. Damn, that thing was fast.

The first aid kit slipped loose from her left hand, hit the pavement, burst open, and scattered bandages and ointment packets across the asphalt.

"Treat?"

But she still had the broom in her right hand.

Pivoting on the foot the creature held loosely, she raised the broom high and thwacked her captor with the bristles, right between the antlers.

Thwack! "Shoo!" *Thwack!* "Haven't I done enough for you?" *Thwack!* "I clean up your pus, and you repay me by—" *Thwack!* "—trashing my first aid kit and—" *Thwack!* "—ruining Xanax for me forever. Go away!"

It limped back a couple of steps on its mismatched hind legs. Ria clambered into her car, slammed the door, and blessed herself for leaving the engine running. She revved it hard and took off before she realized it was still in third gear. She must have been too startled from the collision to tuck the gear shift back into first. Whatever. The important thing was, the Jersey Devil was shrinking into the distance behind her. The rear view mirror didn't catch it at all now.

A pickup truck zoomed toward her, a blue emergency light spinning on its dashboard. A volunteer of some sort, someone not properly a first responder, then. Ria flashed her brights. She did not want to be responsible for some other poor bastard stumbling into the fate she'd just escaped. The truck was bright varsity scarlet with the university's seal painted on the side—Ria could just make it out as the two vehicles passed one another.

The other thing she made out was a rifle in a gun rack behind the driver. Might the Devil's researchers have been the ones taking potshots at Frank? She decided against turning around to chase the pickup for directions.

She turned onto a larger road, thinking surely that would lead her out, or at least to some signage, but the pavement soon gave way to sand, and the sand road ran on and on ahead of her.

The Saturn was not up to this. She really should have sprung for GPS on her new phone.

Still lost half an hour later, Ria pulled over to consult her pendulum. She held it over the map and said, "Where am I?" The pendulum swung in wild spirgraph swirls. Gibberish, which was the hallmark of having asked the wrong question. She put away the map and asked the pendulum simply, "Where should I go now?" She expected it to point her ahead or behind, but it pulled quite urgently toward the side of the road.

So Ria got out, stood beside the car, and said, "Seriously, into the pines?"

The pendulum swung to the right and stayed there—resolutely, impossibly perpendicular. Ria had never seen anything like it. Just for good measure, she picked the broom up and swung it over her shoulder like a rifle. It occurred to her that the Jersey Devil might be a species, not a specimen. She'd hate to meet a younger version of the desperate creature she'd cleaned and fed.

I should bring a knife.

The only knife in the car was her athame. She kept it, as the witches' proverb said, sharp as she wanted her wits to be, but her ritual blade was strictly symbolic, not meant to be a practical tool, much less a weapon. The ebony handle was inlaid with silver oak leaves. The blade's mirror finish had never suffered a scratch.

The Jersey Devil had wheedled for a treat because it was too weak to take one.

Ria plucked the athame from her glove compartment, loosened it in its sheath, and tucked it into one of her combat boots. Knives went in boots, didn't they?

Pendulum still in her right hand, she dowsed for whatever she was supposed to find. Mosquito buzz surrounded her. The emulsion of sand and wet pine needles under her feet clung heavy with water. There would be a creek soon, she could hear it. And, just under the creek's glossolalia, Ria heard too a distinctly human grunt, a scuffling with a small splash, and a moan.

The pendulum dropped. Was that supposed to mean she was looking for the person she heard, or that she was to stay still and hope he passed by? She thought it sounded like a man. The pendulum did not answer any of her silent questions. To ask aloud would be to make a choice. She stuffed the now-useless pendulum into her pocket and considered how quietly she could position herself to run back to the car.

This time the scuffling accompanied a muffled sob.

Ria forced the grinding shift into auravision before she peered around the tree. It was the one advantage she had. Whoever was out there projected a sphere of rose so bright it would have overwhelmed her entirely but for the speckles of gray, fear-gray.

No doubt what to do for an aura like that. "Hello down there," Ria called. "Do you need help?" She held the broom before her handle-first to part the underbrush.

A man knelt in the stream, dripping from the chin down. His hands were bound behind his back. He couldn't speak for the dirty strip of cloth tied as a gag. He'd been trying to drink from the creek. Such wide, wide eyes.

Ria crashed through bracken, flailing at branches with the broom. "I'm coming!" When she reached him, she pulled the athame from her boot and tried to figure out how to cut the gag without cutting his skin. Water had wicked all the way back to the knot, tightening it, but the knot itself was simple. As she worked it loose, she was glad to have lost her nail-biting habit. Yay Paxil. The knot that bound his hands behind him did call for the knife—he had pulled the rope far too tight in his struggles. While Ria sawed away, silently mourning her athame's mirror finish, she noticed he held something in his right hand.

A big chunk of tiger's eye.

She hadn't thought to look at his face.

"Thank you," said her banker's voice, again and again. It was hoarse, but definitely his.

The rope gave at last. The tiger's eye fell from his hand, and he turned with a cry to search for it in the creek bed. "Watch over me, Ria," he muttered as he found it and grasped it tight.

"I'm right here," Ria said.

He looked up. His nose had a new quirk to the left since she'd seen him last. "Are you?"

"Yes. Right here."

"If you happen to be real, would you happen to have any real food with you this time? I dreamed you brought me food."

"I might have some trail rations in a friend's pack. It's back in the car."

"You brought a car?"

"How else would I get here?"

He glanced at the broom.

"Oh, that. No, the broom's for fending off the Jersey Devil. It really works."

He laughed. She didn't. "You're serious," he said.

"I've had a weird day, even by my standards."

"Funny you should mention it. Once we get out of this creek, could you cut the rope on my ankles?"

She got his arm over her shoulder and helped him up. "You crawled into running water while tied up, hands *and* feet? You could have drowned."

"I think that's what the goon squad had in mind for me. I woke up in the creek this morning. I know *why* I got there, but I have no idea *how*. And I wish I knew whether I'm still alive due to their incompetence, or because somebody tried to do me a quiet good turn."

"I shouldn't have told you to do the right thing. I'm so sorry."

"Don't be sorry. It was worth dying for. And now I've faked my own death without even meaning to."

They sat on a log at the creek's edge. She sawed at the last rope while he shook the circulation back into his hands.

"So," Ria asked, "do you have a name?"

"Not for much longer," he said. "I figure by next year I'll be either dead or in witness protection. It's a damn shame, because

I think about you all the time, and now here you are." Which probably meant Ria could get laid if she decided to. "The sons of bitches who did this to me are going down, but right now it's probably best if you don't guess at any names, mine or theirs."

"I'm a professional fortuneteller. If I really want to find out, I won't have to guess."

"Don't go looking," he said. "Please. I've put you in enough danger already."

She put a steadying hand on his. "I won't go looking. But I have to call you something."

"Whatever you like."

"How about Rasputin?"

They laughed until he leaned all his weight on her shoulder. "Dizzy," he said.

"This way," she replied. "I lost my first aid kit, but I've got some other stuff. Bottled water, at least."

By the side of the gravel road she opened the pack and found Frank's rations. Rasputin devoured all the pemmican in the tin, several strips of beef jerky, and a handful of Altoids. "Ow. Curiously strong peppermints."

She passed him a bottle of water and picked out an energy bar for herself.

In another compartment of the pack was a big packet full of wet-wipes. Leave it to Frank to think ahead about cleanliness. What was that under it? A small box of condoms. Presumptuous sonofabitch.

Rasputin's clothes, under the layer of mud, were quite good business-casual things. Cotton. If he kept them on, wet as they were, he'd be hypothermic soon. She helped him out of them, handed him the wet-wipes, and offered him Frank's spare expeditionary wardrobe. Frank's clothes were baggy all over and too short in the leg for Rasputin. Ria found herself glad she'd never seen those garments actually on Frank.

Rasputin said, "You've got three days' worth of another man's clothes in your car. I apologize. I shouldn't have said anything."

"My ex," she said. "My very, very ex. Don't even ask what *his* car was too full of, that he asked me to bring this stuff back for him."

"As long as you didn't come to the Pine Barrens to dump his body, I've got no complaint."

She was about to throw the wet clothes into the woods, but he said, "Don't give the goons a reason to look for me again." So she stuffed the muddy things into a plastic grocery bag and put them in the farthest reaches of the trunk.

She had to unlace her sodden combat boots almost entirely to get them off. The socks underneath needed to be wrung out before she could bring herself to put them anywhere in the car. Barefoot, she walked gingerly over the hot sand to the driver's side door.

She wiped the athame on her skirt, sheathed it, and tucked it back into the glove compartment. There was the second Xanax. He wasn't looking. *I think about you all the time,* he'd said. She pushed the pill through its foil packaging and swallowed it dry. It was the only way she knew to be as brave as he was.

Rasputin walked around the amuletmobile, staring incredulously at the glued-on charms. "You drive this?"

"You got a problem with that?"

"No. It's just...not well camouflaged."

"How far were you planning on traveling in it?" She'd meant the question to be practical. It came out sounding like a pickup line.

"Not sure yet. Could I borrow your cell phone?"

"Yes. If you think you'll be looked for, we should get moving."

While she drove, he tried to text someone for a few minutes, then said, "Not a lot of signal out here. Can we pull over a minute?"

She braked too hard on the unpaved road. The Saturn skidded a slow, grinding skid and stopped up to its axles in sand.

"Sorry," said Rasputin.

"Not your fault," Ria replied. "What would you call hydroplaning on sand? Geoplaning, maybe?"

The cellphone chimed. "Finally, a reply!" Rasputin flipped it open and read. "You got a map?" he asked Ria.

She passed it to him. "Not that I'm sure where I am on it." While he checked its index, she stepped out to see how stuck they were.

"Is it bad?"

"Not too. Are you recovered enough to push, or would you rather take the wheel?"

"Pemmican works wonders. The wheel is yours."

It wasn't much different from getting out of mud or ice, except that there was no good surface to stop on so he could get back in. It took three tries and a great deal of wheel-flung sand before they were truly underway again, just before they lost daylight.

He rolled down the window and shook out Frank's spare hiking boots as they drove. "Sorry about the grit."

"You got us moving. I couldn't have done it alone." She could vaccuum later, at home. For now, she just rejoiced that the sand in the car bothered her less than it did him. Yay Paxil, yay Xanax, drug of drugs, hallelujah, hallelujah.

To either side of the headlights' cone, endless green sped by. Beyond that, evening's first darkness.

"What did your text say?"

"There'll be an FBI car waiting for us at Riders Switch. I didn't even know there was a place called Riders Switch. My contact loves shit like that."

Finally they came to a poorly paved road with a sign. She had to get out with her flashlight before she could read the name. Rasputin rolled open the window to confer with her as he examined the map. "Just one more hour, if none of the roads are closed."

Ria leaned against the passenger door of the amuletmobile. A bit of beach glass dug into her hip. "Last time I read the cards for myself, they said I'd be relationship material in about a year."

"I was just the object of a mob hit. How eligible does that make me?"

"So you're not in a position to be picky, is that it?"

"I didn't say that. I'm trying to tell you something like *carpe diem*. Or maybe *beware, beware*. You be the judge."

Her pulse beat in her ears. "How do you feel about latex?"

"Amenable."

"How do you feel about the backseat of my car?"

He bent to kiss her knuckles where her hand rested on the edge of the open window. She leaned in to kiss him back. Altoids. He reached his arms around her and pulled her in through the window altogether.

Morning reddened the horizon when they found the sign for Riders Switch. Ria and Rasputin had been quiet for most of the past hour's drive.

"This is it," she said.

Rasputin said, "I don't know if they'll prefer for me to testify in court, or to keep playing possum while they pick my brain about the case. They know better how to keep me alive than I do, that's clear enough now. Whatever their plan is, I'll go with it. They've got a lot of ways to keep me hidden. I don't know if those ways will work on you."

"How much could they really object if I found you?" Ria asked.

"A lot. And they'd have a point. You're not exactly inconspicuous. You're certainly not forgettable."

She pulled over and stopped the car. If the FBI wanted him, they could come to her to get him. She wasn't driving one inch closer to the place of parting. "We'll meet again."

"Have you foreseen it?"

"Not yet. But I'll look until I find a way."

They were twined awkwardly around the gear shift when a black car with no license plates pulled alongside them. It occurred to Ria that she might soon be the object of a mob hit herself, but Rasputin said, "This is my ride."

A man in a cheap rumpled suit came up and tapped on her window. She rolled it down. He had dark circles under his eyes and smelled of coffee grounds. "Ms. Santini, I presume?"

"Yes. And you are...?"

"I hear you have a working crystal ball."

"The crystal ball just sits there," said Ria. "I do all the work."

"No need to get testy," he said. "Your country may need you from time to time. I hope you won't mind hearing from me."

Rasputin gripped her hand tightly.

She replied, "I'll read as well for the FBI as for any other querent. Might you pass along the occasional message to your hidden witness?"

"That will be highly irregular, ma'am. Would be, I mean. Will be."

"More irregular than consulting a fortuneteller?"

The agent chuckled. "There's long-established policy for that. Get in the car, Ethan."

"Five minutes," Rasputin protested.

"Your one hour drive took all night," said the agent. "What more could you possibly accomplish in five minutes?"

"You're name's Ethan?" said Ria.

The agent cracked a smile. "Okay, five minutes. What the hell, take ten. Ms. Santini, your phone please?"

Ria handed it to him. Of course something would have to be done about those text messages.

She rolled the window up. "Ethan."

"Please just call me Rasputin. I couldn't stand it if the bastards who killed me found you."

"I have ten minutes to call you by your name. Look, Ethan, I'm not...I'm not brave, or reasonable, or even functional without these drugs I'm on..."

"If you were lying in a gutter shooting up heroin, I'd be in no position to judge you. You think I'm brave because I informed on a pack of killers, but first I had to make all the bad choices that put me in a position to know their secrets. I've laundered some very dirty money. At first I didn't know how dirty, but I figured it out. It was a long time before I was angry enough to stop. I have not been a good person."

"The person I am without Xanax could not have saved you."

"Would she have wanted to?"

"Of course!"

"Then I'm lucky beyond all deserving."

"See if you still think so when you meet her. Actually, the Xanax will be all worn off within the hour, and then I'll get to find out how much of my obsessive-compulsive disorder the Paxil can handle alone after our little adventure. You'll be safe from the mess."

"The mess. That's a problem I wish I could have."

"Maybe it's good we don't have time to see each other's failings with our own eyes. How much can I really screw up, if I only have five more minutes to be neurotic at you?"

"Can I propose a different use for those five minutes?"

The closest Ria came to thought in the time she had left was that she'd have to change medications. She was not giving up her libido now, not for anything.

The rumpled FBI agent knocked at the driver's side window. "The car, Ethan."

Ethan stole one last kiss. Ria opened her door and would have stepped out to follow him, but the rumpled man blocked her.

"Here," he said, and handed her a beautiful white smartphone.

"But, but radiation!" Ria sputtered as she tried to get past him.

The FBI man laughed. "That's a new one. Usually our newbies worry about privacy."

She harrumphed. "People are easier to track than they think."

"Indeed. You found Ethan with, what, a bead on a string?"

"More or less." She decided not to mention that she hadn't been looking for him.

"Like I said, your country needs you. The cell phone bill is on us. We'll be in touch."

Up the gravel road, Ethan leaned his head out of the unmarked car's window to look back at her.

"And him? Will he be in touch?" Ria asked.

"We have our policies for a reason. For your safety and his." The agent looked down at his feet. "Play nice, both of you, and we'll see."

Ria ate the last of Franklin Lear's camping rations on the drive back to Red Bank, then dropped what was left of the pack at his apartment building's front door. Before she'd even finished pulling the Saturn away from the curb, some guy slouching down the street sidled up and stole it. By the posture, it might have been Nils. Ria didn't want to think any more ill of Nils than she already did, so she kept right on driving. Not her problem anymore, either of them.

What a relief to pull the amuletmobile into her own driveway. She flung the plastic bag of muddy clothes from the creek into the trash bin. A puff of mildewy air exhaled from the bag. Ria reached up to close the bin's lid, stopped herself.

The contents of that bag were all she had that belonged to Ethan. Possibly all she would ever have. If she wanted to keep divinatory track of him, across what might be great distance and long years, the work would be a lot easier with something he had owned. And nobody she knew was in greater need of protective spells.

Dammit dammit dammit.

Ria tipped over the trash bin to extricate the bag. Gagging on the mildew stench all the way, she hauled it to the basement. Her own clothes were in better shape, but not by much. How had she managed to ignore that much mud on her skirt? She shucked everything and flung it all into the same washer load with a double dose of tea tree oil.

In the shower, she concluded her feet had never been so dirty in her life. Not the time she fell off the jetty and her clothes got full of sand, not when she was a schoolgirl with skinned knees, not in the years of her greatest gardening enthusiasm. This degree of grime did not feel triumphant. Drugs or no drugs, creek mud was still grimy.

She had just tucked herself into bed for a long day's recovery when she remembered she had promised Morgan she would be in to work at eleven. Dammit. A little nap, then. Just a little nap. She would reach over to set her alarm clock any second now.

The shop bells clanged her fanfare at eleven-thirty. Morgan looked up from his newspaper. "I see you meant it about coming back from the dead to do readings."

"Oh, come on, I must at least look like death *warmed over*."

"You got warmed over? When are you going to learn your lesson about Franklin Lear?"

Ria felt the smile pull at her face. Was she blushing?

"Ah. Not Frank, then. In that case, I officially don't mind that you're late."

Two housewives and a sorority girl wanted readings so familiar she could have given them in her sleep, so she more or less did. Querent One: *You need to make time for yourself.* Querent Two: *Your husband doesn't care about the stretch marks.* Querent Three: *Get thee to an eating disorders clinic!*

Reading for anorexics always made Ria hungry. She grabbed her bag and headed out for food. She was barely through the shop's front door when she heard Sebastian's voice calling behind her on the street.

"Hey, Ria! Up for lunch?"

Ria called back, "You guys read my mind."

Amber and Sebastian hurried a little to catch up with her. They grabbed her in a hug, and it didn't bother her in the least. The three of them got a table at a Cuban sandwich joint Ria had always been too symptomatic to try. Yay Paxil.

Over pork sandwiches Amber said, "We stopped by Transcendence Perfection to see if you were feeling any better. You haven't been answering your phone. What's going on?"

Ria wasn't sure how much of the business in the Pine Barrens fell under reader-client privilege. She'd think that through later. "I broke up with Frank."

"Again?" Sebastian asked. "Um, sorry to hear that."

"No, it's not *again*," Amber pointed out. "Usually Frank does the breaking up. So this time we say congratulations."

Sebastian said, "Now you see why she's the household etiquette and protocol officer. Congratulations, Ria."

"Thank you. I'm feeling a lot better. Oh, and I got a cell phone. See?"

"Ooh, pretty!" said Amber. "What's your number."

"Um. Hang on a moment. I don't call myself on it, so…" She fussed with the menu buttons. *Self-destruct sequence activated*, the phone's screen read. *Cancel?* Cancel! She'd have to get a manual from her FBI contact as soon as possible. "Here's the number."

"What about radiation?" asked Sebastian. "Wasn't that a big deal to you?"

"Yay Paxil," said Ria.

Amber finished entering the number in her contact list. A tiny tattooed fish wriggled down the coral fan of her forearm to nibble at her wrist. "Jane will have to eat some humble pie now. She's always maintained you would never get over yourself enough to buy a cell phone."

"Jane's sort of right. Chemical-me could do it. Non-chemical me couldn't."

"Jane's a mess," Sebastian said gently.

"Yeah, but she has it right about being a mess," said Ria. "Everybody who really cares about her knows her shit. She'll try not to say stuff out loud sometimes, but not because it's secret. It's because she's trying in her way to be nice. Usually you can tell what she's not saying, anyway." And now there were so many things Ria would not be able to say. She was used to keeping her clients' secrets, but the overlap between their secrets and her own was blurrier than it had ever been. And how would she ever make it right about all the lies over the years to cover for her OCD?

Amber gulped a big mouthful of pork sandwich and waved away a solicitous waitress. "So what, Ria? Where are you going with this?"

"So, that's what perfect love and perfect trust look like. Jane doesn't have to be perfect, or trust us to be perfect. She knows us as well as we let her, and she sees we're flawed, but she loves us anyway and trusts us with her flaws. The point is, I've never done that with this coven, or any other. Not even with you and Sebastian, though I'm trying. And until I can look you all in the eye and tell you the truth that belongs to me, I'm not entering the Circle in perfect love and perfect trust. The coven's not where I belong."

"Are you breaking up with us?" Amber said, incredulous. "It's one thing to break up with Frank, but Rugosa Coven..."

"Hang on, honey," said Sebastian. "Ria, I've been working on a plan. I think it's possible to de-escalate the situation with you and Jane, slowly, if..."

"If I can pull my head together enough to come back, you'll still be there to come back to. The rugosa rose is a hardy shrub. It's practically hurricane-proof. And I'm doing okay, actually. Jane needs you guys way more than I do."

"She'll feel awful about it, once you tell everyone," said Sebastian. "And the Baines sibs will try to argue you out of it."

"Who would it help for me to throw a big, final parting scene? I don't need it anymore. And the best gift I can give you all is not to subject you to it. Tell them for me, would you?"

Amber said, "It lacks aesthetic balance. Won't you regret making an incomplete job of it?"

"Not if I want ever to come back. Let it be incomplete for now."

Sebastian said, "What did the cards say about this?"

"I hadn't even thought to ask them," said Ria.

"Those are some powerful meds," he said.

"Yay Paxil," Amber agreed.

They divvied up the check and stood to hug, a little weepily. Ria held their hands and said, "Merry meet, and merry part, and merry meet again."

Lawnhenge shone in the slanting light of a windless afternoon. Ria considered the angles that would give her the most dramatic shadows, stepped back to include the new purple cyclamen blossoms in the shot, and pressed the screen of her smartphone. It sounded a nostalgic click and whirr, contemplated, and showed her what it saw. Perfect. If she'd been an ebay shopper herself, she'd have shelled out the bucks for that image. Somebody would, several somebodies—Amber was always right about that sort of thing, and the cards agreed. Henges would pay handily for therapy. Maybe eventually for the shop, too. No hurry.

She lay back on the grass to watch the clouds go by and rested a hand in her pocket, on the one talisman that mattered: a lump of tiger's eye tied in a man's worn dress sock. No hurry, no hurry.

Atlantis Cranks Need Not Apply

Jane packed away the altar tools. Rugosa Coven's ritual-in-a-box box was a simply organized Rubbermaid tub, full of cardboard dividers for compartments, and transparent Tupperware containers to keep the homemade incense from getting all over everything. She'd come up with their system herself.

When she was satisfied that she'd tucked the chalice and the blade away clean, with no traces of wine or beach sand left on them, she gave herself a moment with the birding binoculars she'd brought. Four kinds of gull circled, and a sandpiper ran along the waves' edge. Jane took in the wind in the dune grass and the light on the rugosa bushes. From Sandy Hook, she could see across Raritan Bay north to Manhattan. It was the Sunday afternoon just after Labor Day, and Rugosa Coven might as well have had the whole Jersey Shore to themselves. All to themselves, because they preferred the nude stretch of the beach. She got up to join her covenmates. The beach was never the same twice, and after what Hurricane Lorelei had done to Cape Hatteras, there was no knowing what Hurricane Nora would do to Sandy Hook. Already, the breakers were too big for swimming. Tomorrow the rain would come.

While Bob and Sebastian engaged in a futile attempt to play Frisbee in the sea wind, Sebastian's girlfriend, Amber, collected shells. Amber was always collecting things. When she'd run out of skin of her own for her collection of piercings and tattoos, she'd collected her tattoo artist. Casting her magpie eye over the sand, Amber saw something that stopped her stock-still.

Sophie dropped the bread she'd been feeding the gulls, let out a little shriek of horror, and pointed where Amber was looking. Jane turned to tease Sophie for how easily she startled, but then followed her roommate's gaze to a tangled pile of yellow seaweed at the high water mark.

Protruding from the tangle was a pale human foot. "Oh," said Jane, and a cold numbness descended over her.

"What?" said Bob, and when Sophie pointed, his face wore exactly the same alarm hers did. He went to his sister and put a hand on her shoulder to calm her.

Something had to be done, and with no lifeguards on duty, Jane might as well be the one to do it. She'd had the courage to leave her marriage, to drive Ria out of the coven, to sort out Sophie's taxes, and now she'd have the courage to lift aside a few fronds of yellow seaweed from whatever awaited her.

She had to get down on her knees and tug to clear the seaweed away, until the whole body was free and she could step back. It smelled simply of salt, so she took a deep breath to steady herself and looked.

Sophie said, "Pretty," and it was true. The pale body of a slender young man lay intact, if somewhat scuffed and lacerated, on the sand. His was a finely-shaped face under a tousle of curly black hair. How he had washed up naked and dead on a public beach, Jane could not imagine. Tiny crustaceans crawled over his cuts.

Then she saw it: a bit of seaweed that still stuck to his neck was actually caught under a flap of skin. "His throat's been cut," she heard herself say, as if from a very great distance.

Sebastian, who had the strongest stomach of any of them, knelt to get a closer look. He worked the frond of seaweed free. "Um, no."

"What, then?"

"See for yourself, Jane. You won't like it."

So she bent down to look again. Not a slit throat, no. "Gills," she said. "I don't believe it."

"You're looking right at it," said Amber.

"But they make no sense! He's a mammal. He's too big, they're too small. Plus, he'd freeze. Am I the only one who was paying attention in high school biology?"

Sebastian raised an eyebrow. A body modification artist needed to know anatomy, and Sebastian took pride in his work.

Jane wasn't having any of it. "He doesn't belong here. We should throw him back."

Sophie was aghast. "To be eaten by crabs? It's not right."

A hideous future played out in Jane's mind. "So we give the body to the authorities, and then what? Television news crews crawling all over Gunnison Beach, making lewd remarks about nudity. Journalists staking out our houses for comment on how we found the body, and you can imagine how they'll portray us, Wiccans naked on the beach. Bob, just think what your wife will have to put up with at Bible study. Bogus documentary filmmakers from the goddamn SciFi Channel staging episodes of the new *In Search of...* and demanding that we be their talking heads, and a whole generation of idiot Atlantis cranks rising up, and they'd be our fault, all our fault. We are not fluff-bunny Pagans! We are not Atlantis cranks! I am *not* going to be party to any of that." Jane kicked the body. "None of it!"

The body groaned, rolled sideways into a fetal position, and shivered.

It was Sophie who moved first, to touch the pretty man's hair. Typical. "Are you okay?" she asked.

The stranger's mouth moved, but no sound came out.

Bob ran back to the coven's heap of towels and returned with a bottle of water and a first aid kit. "Why couldn't he have washed up before Labor Day?" Bob lamented as he laid out the kit's contents. "There would have been lifeguards before Labor Day." He managed to get the stranger to swallow a little water from the plastic bottle.

There were alcohol swabs in the kit. Sebastian got to work cleaning the stranger's cuts and tweezing out the little crustaceans that infested them. "Hey, there," he said to the stranger, with the same calming voice he might have used with any client under his tattoo needle. "Where did you come from?"

A long run of syllables, short on consonants and heavy on pitch accent, failed to answer the question. The stranger opened his eyes to look blearily at Bob and Sophie. For Sophie, he managed a quite charming smile before the exertion of holding up his head was too much for him. As if it weren't trouble enough that he had gills, he had to go flirting with Jane's roommate. Jane was sure no good would come of it. No good ever came of Sophie's boyfriends.

"My name's Sophie. What's yours?"

The stranger tried another long run of vowels, waited a moment, then tried something different, something melodic but vaguely familiar.

Amber leaned over the stranger to listen, and said tentatively, "That's Ancient Greek."

Jane had to reassess her covenmate. "You know Greek, Amber?"

"I did a semester in college, skipped classes, and flunked because I was drinking absinthe and playing Starcraft. I was young and stupid. But I know the sound of it. Not that I remember much vocabulary." She screwed her face up in concentration until her eyebrow piercings clinked against each other. "This is so embarrassing. Um. Hoi polloi?"

Jane couldn't help laughing out loud.

"Hoi demoi..." said the stranger. After that, Jane could make out maybe one word in three. "Hoi demoi ... thalatteis," she thought she heard. He rambled for some time, flinching intermittently at Sebastian's tugs of the tweezers, and appeared to have difficulty keeping his eyes focused.

Amber said, "Well, I didn't get any of that except something that sounds like Atlantis."

"At least it still sounds like Greek," said Jane. "Maybe we can find a classicist."

Bob said, "We'd do better to find a doctor."

Sophie protested, "What do you think a doctor would do with an Atlantean? With gills? There would be dissections and government people and the Department of Homeland Security. You know what happens to foreigners from countries that actually have consulates. All kinds of badness, for no reason half the time. Who's got the authority to make sure his rights are respected? Us? A bunch of Wiccan blue-staters? He'd be safer if we threw him back into the breakers."

"She's got a point," said Sebastian.

Jane's head hurt. "Or she watches too much television. So if we don't want to throw him back, or leave him here, or hand him over to experts, what does that leave? That leaves taking him in, ourselves." Jane already knew where that was going.

Bob said, "I can't ask my wife and kids to deal with that on no notice."

Amber said, "Too many sharp things for him to come to grief on at our house," and Sebastian nodded.

Sophie looked up at Jane with big eyes. The house belonged to Sophie, but Jane paid rent. "We can take him, can't we, Jane? He can have the couch. Besides, our place is closest to the water. If he gets better, he can just cross the street and the seawall, and he'll be all gone."

All gone sounded good to Jane, even if the only way to keep the matter quiet was to install the stranger on her couch for a week. "All right. But I still don't think he's from Atlantis. He looks Greek, doesn't he? He probably just works on a freighter or a cruise ship, and fell overboard in the last gasp of Lorelei."

"Except for the gills," Sebastian pointed out.

Amber was still trying to remember her botched semester of language instruction. "Okay, I've got the principal parts of some verbs. Blapto, blapso, eblapsa, beblapa, beblammai, eblaben?"

"Eblaben," said the stranger. He gestured toward the waves. "Eblaben."

"He says he's been utterly destroyed, once and for all,"

Even Sebastian looked at Amber skeptically. "How do you get that out of one word?"

Jane said, "In a semester of Starcraft and absinthe, it would have been relevant vocabulary."

"Whatever," said Amber, and turned back to the stranger. "Agora?"

He shook his head no, and pulled the heap of seaweed back to cover himself. "Oux agora."

"Oh, come on," said Jane. "I could have done as well as that. You're just saying any old word that comes into your head."

Amber put her hands on her hips and said, "Well, it's a good thing you can do as well as that, since it's your couch he'll be living on. Nobody takes Greek because it's useful. You take it because it's beautiful."

"No agora," Sebastian assured the stranger, and pulled the seaweed off and got back to work with the tweezers. "No parasites, either. Goddamn sea lice. And what are these nasties? Mini trilobites? A warm shower would make this a lot easier."

So they packed away the first aid kit, and Bob and Sebastian propped the stranger up between them to carry him past the dune grass and the rugosa roses to the pile of towels, clothes, picnic baskets, and altar tools. The stranger shivered. Sophie bundled him in the dry towels before digging her garments out of the heap. "There, there," she said. "You'll be all right." They all gathered their things, dressed, and found that their cars were the last remaining in the parking lot.

"Good," said Jane. "No witnesses."

Bob cleared the child seats and plush toys out of the back of his SUV to make room for the stranger to lie down, and Sophie climbed in to keep him company. Closing the trunk on his sister and the stranger, Bob looked in through the rear windshield at the pair of them. He muttered to Jane, "No good will come of this."

"Oh, you're just noticing that now, are you?"

"Keep an eye on her for me, will you?"

"I've been keeping an eye on her since I moved in, for all the good it does."

They caravanned south, down Sandy Hook and through the narrow neighborhood between river and ocean, to the little teal house in Sea Bright. Though Jane tucked her Corolla as close as she could to Sophie's car, there was barely room in the gravel driveway for Bob's SUV to squeeze in behind Amber's silly little convertible. Jane rushed to the back porch shower—nearly tripping over Sophie's plastic shrine to Sulis, goddess of baths—and opened the hot water spigot all the way to clear the cold out of the line. Jane had time to hose the sand off her feet while the guys hauled the weight of the stranger between them.

Thank goodness for Sebastian, who was accustomed to keeping up delicate work for hours at a stretch despite the discomfort of his clients. Though he had to open all the stranger's cuts and scrapes up to do it, he tweezed out the sea lice, intoning a stream of soothing talk all the while. Sophie hovered outside the kitchen door, offering the stranger sips of water from time to time, while Jane took care of things inside. Fortunately, Jane had all the old wedding-gift towels and bed linens left over from her life with Nils, and she didn't especially care what happened to them just now. She pulled some stray sections of the Sunday *New York Times* off the couch and arranged a many-layered nest of sheets and blankets there. By the time she was done, her covenmates were bringing in the clean, much-bandaged form of the stranger.

The guest, now. Not a stranger anymore, the moment he crossed the threshold of her home. "Did you get a name out of him?" she asked.

"Not yet," said Sophie. "We've tried the me-Tarzan-you-Jane method, but it hasn't worked."

"We are not calling him Tarzan," Jane declared.

Amber still wracked her brain for traces of Greek. "Onoma, onomatos... Name, dammit, name. Oh, come on, meet me halfway, won't you?"

That garnered yet another long run of vowels. Nobody had any hope of imitating it.

"Fine," said Amber. "You look like the kouros sculptures at the Met. You get to be Kouros."

"Kouros," said the kouros, brightening a little. He pointed at Sophie and said, "Kore."

That cracked Amber up. "I don't know that I'd describe Sophie as a maiden, but you get the general idea. Damn, I wish I hadn't sold back my old textbooks. Jane, I'll see if I can pick something up tomorrow at Barnes and Noble. Do you need anything?"

"I have no idea what he eats."

Nobody else did either. Jane made her best guess and called the fusion Asian place two narrow towns down the peninsula to order sushi and fish broth for delivery. Lots of fish broth, plain, for which she paid too much for the privilege of diverging from the menu. When the delivery guy had been and gone, she and Sophie grappled the kouros by the arms and tugged him into a sitting position on the couch. While the rest of the coven ate sushi, Sophie insisted on spoon-feeding him the broth. The kouros appeared to be entirely unfamiliar with spoons. He just could not figure out what she wanted from him, until she demonstrated by feeding herself. He regarded the spoon with bright-eyed fascination then. The broth brought him back a little strength, and after he was fed, he insisted on holding the spoon, turning it in the light. He still held it when he fell asleep.

"All right," said Jane. Curiosity was a thing she admired. "Maybe this won't be so bad."

Bob, Amber, and Sebastian cleaned up after dinner, insisting that Sophie and Jane would have plenty to take care of after the three of them left. Once they'd gone, Sophie curled up to sleep in the reading chair beside the couch, the better to keep watch over her new pet. Jane shook her head at the inevitable before taking herself to bed.

In the morning, she called in sick to the H&R Block branch where she worked, and Sophie just blithely didn't show up for the lunch shift at Back to the Garden. It was a tried and true method for getting fired from waitressing gigs, and sure enough, it worked. Since she still had the small trust fund her parents had left her, and Jane's rent on half the house, Sophie wasn't too perturbed about it. What upset her was the Weather Channel's coverage of Hurricane Nora. Every town from Delaware to Connecticut might be ground zero. "What will we do if they tell us to evacuate?"

"Evacuate, of course," said Jane, as she checked that the flashlight batteries still worked.

The kouros stared fixedly at the time-lapse radar maps of the hurricane.

"Is that what happened to you?" Jane asked. He tried his hesitant Greek on her, then shrugged and gave up. She didn't have time to play charades about it, so she gave up, too. There was a basement to empty—a basement full of her old wedding china, her old table linens, bread boxes, toasters. They were wrapped in plastic against the constant damp, but wouldn't withstand immersion. As she stood at the top of the dark stairs, the flashlight showed the basement floor was already slick, as it always got at high tide. It would get much worse, but now that she surveyed these relics of her life with Nils, she couldn't bring herself to care enough to carry even one thing up. Let it all drown—her own little lost civilization.

Sophie found her sitting on the basement steps, running down the flashlight batteries. "You okay?"

"Better than I was back then."

"Need a hand?"

"There's nothing to be done down here."

Sophie kissed her on the top of the head and went back up to the kitchen. A few numb minutes later, Jane heard the kettle whistling. Sometimes Sophie got things right.

So they sat around the television, mugs of chamomile in hand, watching Hurricane Nora veer north. Everyone from Cape May south was in the clear, but Cape May was a long way down from Sea Bright. The Governor of New Jersey advised, but did not order, residents of Sandy Hook to evacuate.

The kouros was strong enough to hold his own mug now, and seemed to know what to do with one. He liked the chamomile, though Jane had misgivings about whether it was good for him. Now that he was clean and awake, the gills were hard to see. Jane caught herself staring at his neck from time to time, and whenever the Weather Channel cut to commercial, the kouros caught her staring, too.

The house was starting to feel small. The living room, with its huge picture window that, years ago, must have offered a stunning view of the ocean, yielded only a view of the huge concrete and aggregate seawall across Ocean Avenue. Walls and more walls, with torrential rain between, sealing her in with the kouros and his impossible gills. "I'm going out," she told Sophie.

"Is that a good idea?"

"Probably not."

"You're not sneaking a cigarette, are you?"

"And let Nils win his bet?"

"He'd never know."

"I'd know."

Jane threw on her raincoat, grabbed her umbrella, and headed out into the first reaches of the storm. Once across Ocean Avenue, she found the aluminum stairs over the seawall perilously slick with rain. She stood on the rickety platform at the wall's crest and watched the breakers roar in. She wiped the rain from her face and put thoughts of her life, her peril, out of her mind. The splendor of the storm, that was what mattered now. It was vast and utterly unlike herself, pitiless and incapable of malice. It was the raw power of the natural world, that which Jane worshipped, and which she doubted she could ever truly propitiate. "Beautiful," she told the storm, knowing it cared nothing for its own beauty. "So beautiful." She closed her futile umbrella and sat on the seawall in the presence of her Gods, until her raincoat soaked through and the shivering started.

No sooner did she get back and get the raincoat hung up to dry on pegs already laden with swimsuits and last week's beach towels, than Sophie said, "Ria called while you were out."

Through chattering teeth, Jane said, "She called us? Tell me you didn't call her."

Sophie gave her a reproachful look. "I didn't. She called to say she had the Weather Channel on, and was thinking of us, and read the cards. She said we don't need to evacuate."

"Funny, that's what the Governor said." Jane was not a big divination fan. "Convenient for her to know she's vindicated before the fact, isn't it?" She stripped off her wet things and settled for a slightly sandy beach towel. Freezing. She'd vacuum the sand up later, she promised herself, and then wondered what the kouros would make of the vacuum cleaner.

"Ria says we should stay put. The cards told her it's important."

"That's it, we're packing out."

And then Sophie took it where Jane had all along known she would. "Well, Ria was right about Atlantis..."

Padding barefoot to her room, Jane said, "Ria believed without evidence."

"You refused to believe, looking right at the evidence. How is that better?"

"I see a guy with gills who doesn't appear to speak English. That's it. Or is there an underwater city in the living room that I've failed to detect?"

"You owe Ria an apology."

Jane threw on jeans and a sweater. "The woman's a sasquatch cultist. A Loch Ness monster adherent. She never met a crackpot idea she didn't like."

"Oh, and you only have truck with the very finest, most fashionable crackpot ideas."

"Fuck you, Sophie."

"And after Ria brought you casseroles when you finally walked out on Nils."

"Bob's wife brought me casseroles, too, but that didn't obligate me to become a Methodist." She poured herself more of the tea Sophie had made for her. "Look, we're better off without Ria. Can you honestly say you miss talking theology with a person who fasted to purify herself so she could raise energy to heal the fairies of the Pine Barrens?"

"No, that was the last straw for me, too."

"All right, then."

"But you didn't have to be mean about it."

"We were never going to be of a like mind. Ria had to change or go."

"Sebastian had a plan."

"That would have taken another six months. And I'm not the only one who didn't have six months of patience left for Ria and her celebrity past lives."

Sophie laughed. "Cleopatra. Well, I guess the classics never go out of style. We're not really packing out, are we?"

Jane read the ticker scrolling along the bottom of the television screen. "Category Two, projected landfall in Montauk? Screw it. We've got candles and Sterno."

"And all that bottled water. And I don't think he can be moved yet."

Jane turned to assess the kouros. He looked bright-eyed and alert, if a bit pale and waxy. Maybe he was supposed to be pale and waxy. "Give him a couple days, and he'll be over the seawall and gone."

Sophie was crestfallen. "I guess he will."

A little past six o'clock, a pair of headlights turned in to the driveway, and Bob's SUV rumbled loudly enough to be heard over the pelting rain. Three laughing voices chattered their way around the house, and Sophie jumped up to open the kitchen door while Jane struck the television mute.

"Manhattan clam chowder," Bob announced. "Ricki and I figured he might eat that, and you will if he doesn't." He carried his vat of soup through to the stove.

Amber handed Sophie a plastic shopping bag. "A lexicon, and an intro textbook. Good luck."

Meanwhile, Sebastian went to the couch and gestured to the kouros that he wanted to take off the bandages. The kouros regarded him with absolute trust and started peeling the dressing off his upper arm.

"I closed the studio early and sent the apprentices home," said Sebastian, starting his hypnotic stream of talk, and he went on and calmly on about the body modification business, the condition of the county, the change in the weather, while he cleaned up the damage again. "We weren't going to get any walk-ins for branding tonight, not in this rain. Rumson and Red Bank are all closed down but the grocery stores, selling out of bread and batteries, and the mayors are ordering everybody to stay home tomorrow. Aha." He went for the tweezers again. "Come here, you little arthropod whatsit. I have you now."

Jane offered her empty mug for him to drop the creature into. "I thought you'd gotten them all."

"There must have been hundreds of them yesterday. Poor guy. But we're doing all right now, aren't we?"

The kouros didn't answer, but watched with fascination as Sebastian broke out the topical antibiotic and bandaged him back up. Adhesives intrigued the kouros, and they went through an extra half roll of surgical tape before the novelty wore off. The kouros's smile was markedly asymmetrical, and he tried to engage Amber in conversation, waving a hand covered with sticky tags of tape.

"I'm sorry," she said. "If you queried me in javascript, we might get somewhere. I just can't keep up with the Greek."

Sophie handed him the lexicon, and he promptly tore the cover with the tape strips on his hand. Apology was easy to recognize in his tone.

"It's all right. Can you read this?" She helped him de-sticky his fingers and flipped the book open.

What he thought would happen when he stroked the pages, Jane could not guess. He tried flipping the pages back and forth for a while, but the book's purpose eluded him. "Spoon?" he asked.

"Book," said Sophie.

He gestured feeding himself, as she had fed herself the day before to demonstrate the spoon's function.

"Oh! All right. What it's for." Sophie plucked the book out of his lap and read from the front matter. "'This abridgement of the Oxford Greek Lexicon has been undertaken in compliance with wishes expressed by several experienced School Masters. It is an entirely new work, and it is hoped ...'" Sophie sighed. "Look, I'm not good at this kind of thing. I'm not even much of a waitress."

The kouros tapped the cover with his fingertip and said, "Book. Book, spoon, Sophie."

"Yes, I'm Sophie." She tapped him on the chest to cue his name, but his reply—familiar now—was impossible to replicate. "Kouros," she said. "I'm afraid that's still the best I can do."

Jane brought two mugs of chowder and two spoons, and the kouros did just fine by himself this time. "It sounds more like whalesong than anything else."

At that, Sophie's eyes lit up. "Hang on." She went to rummage around in her room for a moment, and came back with her laptop.

Amber said, "Enjoy the wireless while you can. I'll be surprised if you still have phone and electricity by morning. We've got space for you at our house, you know. I packed the whole knife collection away in the attic before we came over. There's room in the SUV to get everybody across the bridge."

Bob said, "Ricki would rather the kids didn't see the gills, but aside from that, we'd love to have you in Rumson, too."

"We're staying right here," Sophie said, powering on her computer.

"Ria saw it in the cards," said Jane.

"You don't have to be all caustic about it," Sophie protested. "It's not like I told her anything."

Sebastian said, "I guess Ria was right about something. Who'd have thunk it?"

"Oh, yeah," said Jane, "and now that she's vindicated about Atlantis, let's all sign on for her theory that, in the second century, the Picts were practicing Kabbalah."

Sophie said, "Check this out." Whalesong poured from her laptop's speakers. The sound shut all of them up, and the kouros actually got up off the couch, quite uneasy on his feet, to investigate the computer. When the song ended, he tried singing it back to the computer, moan for moan, but it didn't answer him. "Would you like another?" Sophie asked. It was plain enough he would, so she downloaded a couple more. "Here."

The second song, he recognized, and sang with it in patient harmony to the end, then tapped on the laptop plaintively.

"More," she said. "The word you want is more."

"More."

Midway through the third round of whalesong, Bob noticed the updated radar images rotating across the muted television screen. "Oh, Gods," he said. "That doesn't look good."

Amber said, "There's still room in the SUV."

"Not going," said Sophie.

"I'm not abandoning them," said Jane. But she'd said that about Nils, the first two times he'd dropped out of rehab.

Sebastian recognized the trap Jane was caught in. "Sophie, you know what can happen to people who stay. And you don't have gills."

"It's a Category Two, and the Governor's still not..."

In fact, the Governor himself was on television, and Sophie hit the remote to let him have his say about severe flooding in Bergen County. But Bergen County flooded at every opportunity, and was an hour away, so Sophie wasn't much impressed.

Her brother watched the radar image in the corner of the screen. "I'd be a lot happier if you were coming. What would Mom and Dad have said?"

"Not helping your case, Bob," said Sophie.

"I guess not." She would not be moved, and the bright bands of color in the radar spiral made it plain that anyone who meant to drive over the bridge had better do it soon. With hugs and reproaches, the three mainlanders took their leave.

Not ten minutes later, the little teal house trembled under wind and rain. Though Jane steeled herself for whatever the storm brought her, Sophie and the kouros were afraid. So terribly afraid, they clung to one another on the couch.

"You might as well move him to your bed," said Jane. "That couch is so narrow, you'll be leaning on his wounds."

Sophie said, "I wouldn't presume..."

"I'm not the one to be coy with. We both know perfectly well you'll presume sooner or later."

Though she didn't deny it, Sophie stayed stubbornly on the couch.

In the morning, she was still there. Jane padded barefoot into the living room in the heavy gray light that seeped through the thin curtains. She thought it was probably ten o'clock, but her alarm clock was dead. So was the lamp on her bedside table. The television didn't acknowledge the remote. For her weather report, Jane stared at the seawall that filled the front picture window.

Power lines were down along Ocean Avenue. A fat, black cable thrashed on asphalt, spitting sparks. It would be hours before anyone would do anything about it. There was no going anywhere.

At least the gas still worked, and the refrigerator held its residual cold, so Jane lit a burner with a match and brought the chowder back to a boil. The plumbing worked, too, for the moment. She popped fresh batteries into the little radio she and Sophie kept for days on the beach. It was eleven a.m., and the good people at WNYC informed her that Nora's eye had made landfall in Montauk.

"Poor Montauk," said Sophie, rising blearily from the couch.

"Poor Montauk," Jane agreed.

WNYC kept up its chatter while the soup heated, and the kouros came to examine the radio. He was steadier on his feet today, and wouldn't rest until Jane carried the radio back to the couch. The radio interested him even more than the plumbing had—voices emerged from the radio, after all. He pushed all the buttons, turned all the dials, and put the antenna through its full range of motion. When he'd found, somehow, the WNYC signal again, he held the radio up for Sophie. "Book, spoon, Sophie?"

"Radio."

"Radio. Radio radio radio. More?"

So she turned off the news, powered on her laptop, and played him her downloaded whalesongs over and over until the batteries ran down. By then, the kouros could sing all of them, and he'd taught Sophie his harmonies. Even Jane could not resist, and droned along while she picked through her books, looking for anything that might help her.

When the laptop's batteries died, Sophie shrugged in apology and said, "No more."

"Radio book spoon Sophie more. More." He pointed to the computer, the coffee table, the lamp. Sophie gave him an afternoon of nouns until her voice brittled, and they slept again on the couch.

The gray light outside faded, and the rain pounded on. Jane lit the house with candles and laid out a stack of books and maps on the coffee table, flipped through them and marked the pages. If she had to use every Post-it Sophie had in the house, she'd prod her guest into giving her some answers. She checked the land line—still out. Her cell phone got no signal. The electricity was out, too, but at least the broken cable in the street had stopped thrashing, so someone was probably on the case. When Sophie and her kouros had had an hour's rest, Jane brought the soup back to a boil. The scent of thyme and tomatoes woke them.

"What's this?" Sophie asked, surveying the open atlases with their numerous tape flags.

"More!" said the kouros.

"Map," said Jane, unfolding a massive National Geographic work-up of the Atlantic's floor. She opened her history of the ancient world to the entry on the volcanic eruption of Thera and said, "Picture." She leaned back in the reading chair to see if he'd do better with pictorial representation than he had with text. "Where's home?"

"Are you *trying* to rush him out of here?" Sophie eyed her roommate suspiciously.

"Don't you want to know where he's from?"

"Why can't you just accept that he's with us for now?"

"One would think that, confronted with an Atlantean, you might at least try to make some refreshingly novel mistakes with your love life. But no. Same old, same old. Not enough questions, and the usual rush to give yourself away, and it's not like there's any ambiguity about whether this one will last."

"I'm sorry, Jane, whose habitual mistakes were we talking about?"

It was a fair cop. "You want some soup?"

"Yeah."

When Jane brought back her peace offering, she saw that the kouros had put aside the picture of Thera in favor of the sea floor map of the Atlantic. "House," he said, pointing to a spot in the blue.

"Oh, no," said Jane.

Sophie said, "Show me."

"Not the Bermuda fucking Triangle. Shoot me now."

"Nope," said Sophie, squinting around the kouros's finger. "Blake-Bahama Ridge, it says."

Jane leaned over her roommate's shoulder to see. "Not the Atlantis Fracture Zone?"

Sophie searched out the name and tapped at it. "Not here?"

The kouros held his hands out before him, palm down, thumbs together, and rubbed them against one another.

"Earthquakes?" said Jane.

"No house."

Jane considered the Blake-Bahama Ridge. "If that's Atlantis, how would anyone have known about it in Greece? It's practically a suburb of Cape Hatteras." She pointed at his home and asked the kouros, "Atlantis?"

He laughed. "No Atlantis. Atlantis." And he pointed to a spot between Gibraltar and Madeira.

"He's from the boonies," said Jane.

"Well, it has been a few thousand years. The Blake-Bahama Ridge could be a thriving metropolis."

"He didn't know what a spoon was. I think he's a hick."

"If you live in the ocean, what do you need with a spoon?"

"I still say his gills are too small to be functional."

All at once, the lights came on, and the refrigerator hummed back to life. The radio in Jane's alarm clock broke into a local news report. "Heavy rain breaking up by morning," it predicted.

Everyone in the living room startled. While Sophie soothed the kouros, Jane went to turn the alarm off.

"Intermittent power outages," said the radio, and all the lights went back out.

"Great," said Jane.

When she returned to the candlelit living room, Sophie and the kouros were liplocked on the couch. So Jane blew out the candles and sealed herself into her bedroom. A moment's scrounging in the bedside table's junk drawer turned up her set of earplugs.

Silence was no guarantee of sleep.

Several times over the course of the night, the alarm clock's red display blinked on, flashed twelve, and blinked back off. Sunrise came bright and clear and bounced off the house next door into Jane's window. She popped out the foam earplugs. No rain. No voices through the wall. Good.

Predictably, the kouros was absent from his nest on the couch.

Jane went irritably through her morning ablutions and dressed for work, just in case the roads were clear. The Corolla sputtered a bit when she turned the key in the ignition, but it started. By way of the car stereo, the good people at WNYC informed her of widespread beach erosion, devastated oyster beds, evacuees returning in droves to Montauk, lessons learned and a low death toll. The usual.

After what Lorelei had done to Cape Hatteras, after last year's wreck of the Gulf Coast, the old-fashioned usual was a relief, even to the oyster fishermen. So said *Morning Edition.*

All along Ocean Avenue, utility crews worked on cables, fallen trees, and drainage. The bridge was clear. At a traffic light where Rumson faded into Red Bank, Jane had a moment to rest her hand on the silver pentagram pendant she'd tucked inside her silk blouse. "Please," she said to the universe, "just let everything go back to normal."

Two traffic lights and a stop at 7-11 later, she was at work, with a donut and the *New York Times* for her mid-morning break. She didn't expect home delivery to pick back up so soon after Nora. The front page photos were beautifully composed, as disasters recorded in the *Times* always were. NORA BASHES MONTAUK; EVACUATION A SUCCESS.

Her boss and coworkers inquired politely about how she'd weathered the storm. "We're all right," she said, and they were satisfied. She'd taken the job two years before for its health benefits, to get Nils into rehab, so she was accustomed to keeping secrets from her colleagues. All any of them knew about her personal life was that her husband's name was no longer on the office's list of emergency family contacts. Today she was glad she'd trained them not to pry. Work was a relief. Aside from her donut and her *Times* break, the only distraction she wanted was a moment to send a two-line email to everyone she knew, saying the storm was no big deal and not to worry. So relieved was Jane at the tedium of her day at her computer and her solitary lunch at her desk, she almost resented Sebastian's phone call at five-fifteen.

"H&R Block, Jane Hirsch, how may I help you?"

"So you guys are okay?"

"I'm fine."

"You don't sound fine. Is it the storm?"

"We lost electricity. And the inevitable happened."

"That would explain why Sophie hasn't been answering the phone. It rings, but I get the answering machine every time."

Jane's heart started pounding. What if she'd been wrong to assume the Atlantean was only dangerous as some sort of cultural meme? "Should I not have left them alone?"

"Maybe I should call in the troops."

She stood and started gathering her things to go, the phone gripped between ear and shoulder. "Give me a chance to assess the damage first. I'll call you when I get home."

"If you don't call by six, I'm coming over."

"You rock."

"Good luck."

Jane signed out ten minutes early and ran to her car without saying goodbye to her coworkers. She'd accustomed them to that, too, in her early days at the franchise.

Traffic wasn't heavy, but the repair crews had blocked off the most direct route home, and Jane swore at the radio while she followed the detour signs. She should have made sure Sophie was okay before leaving for work. Should have thought to phone home from the office. Should never have taken their guest in at all. Jane turned the Corolla in to the gravel driveway and ran to the kitchen door, fumbling with her keys.

The plastic figure of Sulis gazed blankly from her shrine by the back porch shower. Somehow, the storm hadn't blown her away.

"I could really use some help here," Jane muttered to the little goddess. "Sophie?" she shouted at the window. No answer. She finally got the right key into the lock and shouldered the door open.

By the sound of things, the inevitable was in full swing again. The door to Sophie's bedroom was closed, so Jane had to consider the wordless voices.

Although it was her habit to flee the house and nurse her envy elsewhere when Sophie had a boyfriend over, Jane stood in the kitchen just a moment longer to make sure there was nothing unhappy in Sophie's voice. Louder than usual, she concluded, but nothing she needed to break up or stay for. Thank goodness.

Turning to go, she caught a glimpse of something bright in the living room. Despite a powerful wish to be anywhere else on earth, Jane took a step toward the brightness.

On the coffee table stood a model of a city, a model made of light. Jane sat on the couch rather more abruptly than she meant to—her knees gave out the moment she thought of sitting. The thing put her in mind of her old childhood Lego sets. Like Legos, only spherical and made of light. She reached a tentative hand to touch it. Her fingers went right through. She scrambled back over the couch and ran through the kitchen, slammed the door behind her, and stood shaking in the driveway.

A few breaths later, she was calm enough to cross Ocean Avenue and climb the rickety aluminum stairs to the top of the seawall. With all the storm damage, it was the only place in Sea Bright where she could be sure of getting cell phone signal.

"Sebastian?"

"Should I call 911?"

"No. Just come over."

His muffled voice said, "Amber get your things. I'll start the car." A moment of shuffling and a slammed door later, he said, "How bad is it?"

"There's a supernatural thing in my living room."

"There's been a supernatural thing in your living room for three days."

"Just come. I can't go back in there alone."

There was the sound of the convertible starting up, and Amber's curious voice asking something Jane couldn't quite make out. Sebastian said, "How's Sophie?"

"She's fine. She's taking the cosmos into her carnal embrace."

"Nice work if you can get it."

Jane had nothing to say to that.

"Just hang on. We'll be there in ten minutes."

"Twenty. Detours. A lot of trees went down."

"Yes, there's the first one. You'd think anyone who can afford to live on the Rumson side of the town line could afford to hire a fucking tree surgeon once a century."

"I'm calling Bob."

"Already called him to ask if he'd heard from his sister. If you call him in your current state, you'll freak him out even worse. Let me do it."

"Okay, okay."

"Hang tight. We're coming."

Jane flipped the cell phone closed and turned her back to the teal house to stare across the waves. So clear, the air after the storm. So clean, the salt scent. She tried to quiet her mind. The waves would soothe her if she let them.

She let them.

The horn of Amber's convertible snapped Jane out of her calm, and she clambered down the seawall steps. The honking of five passing cars accompanied her sprint through a narrow gap in Ocean Avenue's petty evening rush hour.

It was just as well Sebastian didn't wait for Jane before he opened the kitchen door. What would she have told him? That evil Legos from the deep had infested her coffee table? The house was quiet now, but for the hum of the water heater and the patter of the shower. "Sophie?" said Sebastian.

"Be right out!" Sophie's cheery voice answered through the bathroom door.

Amber caught sight of the city. "Ooh, shiny," she said, and sidled around the couch to get a better look.

Still hovering in the frame of the kitchen door, Jane said, "Serves me right."

Sebastian turned to look at her. "What?"

"I told her I didn't believe in Atlantis, despite him. I said, 'Is there an underwater city in the living room that I haven't detected?', something like that. And now there is."

Sitting rapt on the couch, Amber ran her fingertips along the edge of the city's walls. "Where can I get me one of these?"

"Hey there, Magpie Eye," said Sebastian. "I wouldn't mess with that."

"It's so beautiful."

Jane finally had to agree. "Yeah, but it shouldn't work."

Amber made a face at her. "You are the most magic-allergic Pagan I ever met."

"It's not magic I object to. A living universe, every stone ensouled? Cool. Change of consciousness in accordance with will? Hunky dory. No greater magic in all the world than that of love? Well, I guess I wouldn't know, but it sounds good. But this." She gestured hopelessly at the bright city. "This is the supernatural. I don't trust it."

"So beautiful," said Amber, and she contented herself with leaning around it to examine it from different angles.

The latch of the bathroom door clicked open, and Sophie emerged in her bathrobe, toweling her hair dry. Far too happy for her own good. Behind her, the kouros stood dripping wet on the bathmat, holding a towel awkwardly in his hand as if baffled by its function.

Sophie took in her covenmates assembled around the little city. "Pretty cool, huh?"

"Gorgeous," said Amber.

Sebastian said, "How did he make it?"

"Don't know. I pointed to his spot on the map and asked him to tell me about home. He sang, and there it was."

Jane finally figured out what it was about the architecture that felt wrong to her. "Why do they need slanted roofs? Not to keep the rain out. Not to shade them from the sun, at a depth of three thousand feet. And the tower..."

"Why do people get piercings and tattoos?" Sebastian countered. "If they want a tower to ornament their city, it's nobody's business to say them nay."

"I don't think you can reduce public works projects to private idiosyncrasy."

The kouros came into the living room, leaving a trail of wet footprints on the floor. He had something to say about the model, for all the good saying it did.

"Sophie," said Jane, "care to do something about the wet footprints?"

Unwinding the half-damp towel from her hair, Sophie said to the kouros, "We mop up." She dropped the towel onto the floor and scooted it along the trail of prints with one foot.

"Mop up," said the kouros.

Sophie beamed. "We got to verbs today."

"You certainly did," said Jane.

Just then, Bob peered through the window of the kitchen door and knocked furiously.

"Come in," Jane and Sophie said.

"What the hell?" said Bob as he opened the door. He looked at his sister, saw that she was all right, and turned his attention to the kouros, who stood naked and still not quite dried off beside her. Jane would not have traded places with the kouros for anything. "What did he do?" Bob demanded.

Amber said, "He made some art. Check it out."

Bob glanced at the city on the coffee table and turned back to say something. But then, the fact of the city sank in, and he stared at it, slackjawed. Eventually, he managed to get back to saying, "What the hell?"

Sophie said, "If you're all so worried about it, you know where we can get some answers."

"Out of the question," said Jane.

Amber said, "You can't avoid Ria forever."

"And you owe her an apology," Sebastian pointed out.

"The woman is a total whack job," Jane protested. "You all used to agree about that."

"Yes," said Bob, "but Ria can be a useful whack job when she wants to be. And we used to call her family."

Jane smacked her own forehead in disgust. "Do you really think divination is going to tell us anything useful here? It's fine for sorting out how you feel, but you'll never get outside your own head with it."

Sophie said, "It can't make things any weirder."

"Oh, now who's underestimating Ria?"

"After this, Jane, you'll find a Tarot reading from Ria reassuringly normal. Besides, I've made up my mind."

"If you've made up your mind, why get your fortune told?"

"I'm going."

"Fine. If you're going, I'm going. We'll see how well she can take an apology."

"Depends on how well you give it."

Bob interrupted the bickering roommates to say, "I left dinner boiling on the stove under the supervision of my ten-year-old. If nobody's bleeding or on fire over here, I have to get home."

"No blood," said Sophie. "No fire."

"Can I have a word with you in the driveway before I go?"

So the Baines siblings went out to have one of their hushed conferences. The rest of the coven tried not to think about what was none of their business.

Amber said, "I suppose she'll want to take our visitor with her. Show him off to Ria."

Jane had been trying not to imagine it, but now the picture was unavoidable. "Can't," she said. "He's got no clothes."

Sebastian said, "Surely there's something here he can borrow."

"The Red Bank police may not mind cross-dressers," said Jane, "but I don't think there's a garment in this house that'll stay on those skinny little hips of his. He'll just have to stay home." She wasn't sure which she dreaded more—the things Sophie might tell Ria if Jane didn't go along, or the supernatural mess she might come home to if she went with Sophie and left the kouros unattended.

Sebastian said, "He'd be swimming in any of my shirts, and nothing I've got for pants would stay on him. You want us to Atlantean-sit?"

"I don't know what I'd do without you."

Amber said, "Or... Hold that thought." And she went out to the driveway to interrupt the family conference.

Sophie came back alone, her eyes puffy and red. She sealed herself into the bathroom, and the cold water tap's shudder could be heard through the wall. Most unlike the usual Bob & Sophie Show. Maybe that was all to the good this time.

Out in the driveway, Amber and Bob opened up the back of the SUV, and they came back in with his dry cleaning. He looked at the kouros, looked at his plastic-wrapped clothes, and sighed. "I need to phone Ricki and tell her I'll be a little longer."

Sophie came out of the bathroom, all optimism again, to clothe her beloved, as if nothing had darkened her day.

The kouros could not be persuaded to tolerate pants, and in the end Bob resigned himself to parting with his utilikilt. "It's just a loan, now. I'll be wanting this back."

They needed one of Bob's shirts, too, and then Jane's winter scarf to cover the gills. For shoes, they had to resort to the big spare set of beach flip-flops.

The kilt hung a bit low on the kouros's hips, even with the belt cinched. Jane folded her arms. "It's an odd mix, but he doesn't look too bad."

"Nothing better than a man in a kilt," said Amber.

Sophie said, "Thanks, Bob. I don't know what else we'd have done."

"Ricki's hoping the utilikilt doesn't come home."

"Shows what she knows," Amber said.

Despite Jane's misgivings about taking the kouros out in public, she allowed Sophie to cajole him into the backseat of the Corolla and buckle him in. He objected strenuously to the seat belt. Sophie didn't want to press the matter.

"Fine," said Jane, "but if we get pulled over, you're paying the ticket. And explaining him to the police. I'm just giving you a lift, if anyone asks. Got it?"

Sophie paused between backseat kisses to say, "Got it."

After dodging work crews and following detour signs, Jane finally squeezed the Corolla into a metered spot right in front of the shop Ria now owned. *Transcendence Perfection Bliss of the Beyond,* the neon sign blinked. The name was unchanged, despite a long succession of owners. Jane had found the place back when she was in high school, had bought her first copy of *The Spiral Dance* there, and still made an annual supply run. For the past few years, though, she'd found herself cringing at the fluff-bunny white-light New-Ageyness of it all. And that even before Ria bought the place.

Nonetheless, Jane paid the parking meter, harried the lovers out of her car, and pulled open the glass door, setting off a tinkling of bells. Inside, the patchouli was so thick she paused with the door open to inhale one last breath of Red Bank's honest street air.

The girl working the cash register was chewing gum and wearing a pair of handpainted silk fairy wings. The wings were stretched over a wire armature and suspended on the girl's back with lacy shoulder straps. The fairy cashier looked up and said, "Can I help you find anything? We have a special sale on crystals today."

Jane followed the girl's gesture to a bin of assorted stones. The poor dears, all cut and tumbled and tarted up for sale. "We're looking for Annamaria Santini."

"Oh, you mean Lady Rhea." The shop girl breathed the H heavily, broadened the E.

Jane raised her eyebrows. "Lady Rhea? You've got to be fucking kidding me."

"Lady Rhea has an opening in her schedule in half an hour."

Sophie said, "But we need to see Ria urgently."

"The rates for her sessions are posted on the wall."

Jane consulted the chart. "I've paid less than that for marriage counseling. And to think, the coven used to be treated to her posturing for free."

The fairy popped her bubble gum. "Do you want the appointment or don't you?"

Jane glanced at the kouros, who had opened a jar of incense—a dollar fifty per ounce, according to the label—and had stuck the lower half of his face into the wide opening, the better to inhale the scent. His face wore a look of absolute bliss, and his topmost gills ruffled open, just slightly, above the edge of the scarf.

"Yeah," said Jane. "We'll take it."

"That'll be eighty dollars up front."

"When Morgan owned the place, he never demanded it up front. Did Ria get a lot of dissatisfied customers walking out on the bill?"

"Cash or credit card. No personal checks for divination."

Jane yielded up her Visa card and drummed her fingers on the glass case, while the kouros smelled, in turn, the contents of every single one of the herb and incense jars. He got to V for valerian, and his expression of shock and dismay at the smell made her laugh out loud.

"Name?" he asked, putting aside the valerian jar.

"Dirty socks," said Jane, and signed the sales slip. Her old signature, to match her old card.

The fairy cashier took the register copy of the sales slip and said, "Thank you, Ms. Hirsch-Sigurdson."

"It's just Hirsch."

"But your card says..."

"Please. Just plain Jane Hirsch."

"If you say so."

In the ensuing half hour, the kouros touched everything in the store, and licked several of the rocks in the crystal bins. Sophie giggled continuously and egged him on, draping him in cloaks and crowning him with diadems she pestered the shop girl into taking out of the jewelry case.

Jane pulled off the shelves every book she thought might discuss Atlantis. Several times, she interrupted the happy couple to show the kouros a picture and look for any trace of recognition in his face. Nothing, nothing, and nothing. Finally, in a biography of Dion Fortune, she found reproduced a sketch from one of the long-dead occultist's astral journeys. She showed the picture to the kouros, and was highly irritated when he snatched the book from her hands and began pointing to various architectural features and naming them in his not-Greek, and then in his pidgin Greek. Neither roommate knew the names in English for most of the things he pointed to. They weren't confident they knew what exactly a pediment was. At least Sophie's months of waitressing at the vegan restaurant had taught her the difference between a lintel and a lentil. Jane could have kicked herself for showing him that book—she was not interested in believing in astral projection. Not one little bit.

But the worst came when the door to the back room opened. The divination client, a gray-suited businessman, scurried away with a jangling of the front door's bells, obviously embarrassed to be seen there. Ria, however, stepped into the shop, her bearing a wavering imitation of regal attitude. She was weighed down by at least five pounds of silver necklaces over her black dress, and her every finger had its silver ring.

It took Jane a moment to figure out why the black dress annoyed her. It was the stereotypical black dress of widowed Italian grandmothers everywhere, though Annamaria Santini was barely forty and had lived single all her life.

"The goth crone look," Jane said. "Are you aware that you're becoming a caricature of yourself, Ria? Pardon me. Lady Rhea."

"If that which you seek, you find not within yourself, you will never find it without, Jane."

"A fine thing to say, decked out like you are. I propose a new witch-dunking test. Throw the lot of us into a swimming pool. The ones who drown under the weight of ritual jewelry are too insecure to advise anybody."

Ria leaned around Jane to ask the shop girl, "Do I have a seven o'clock?"

"They're it."

The fortuneteller laughed. "Did you pay eighty dollars to mock me for an hour? I may be a caricature, but you're a Monty Python sketch."

Sophie bounded up and gave Ria a big hug. "Jane came to apologize to you."

And Ria found that even funnier. Intolerable. But not as intolerable as what happened when the kouros came to see what the fuss was about. He looked Ria over, eyes flicking from one bit of New Age regalia to another, looked into the back room at the lit candles and incense, and then knelt before her, head bowed.

"Never mind the apology," said Jane. "I've just brought you what you always wanted. I'm done here."

She turned and headed for the door, but Ria called after her, "I'm sorry, Jane."

Curiosity got the better of her. "For what?"

"I should have gone the first time you asked me. It was never going to work out. I shouldn't have put you in the position of having to say all those horrible things. And in front of the others. You were wrong about everything except that I had to go, and I thought I had to stay to answer every charge."

"I was wrong about *everything* else?" Jane said. "Do you want to make the case for spoonbending?"

"You know, your marriage might have lasted longer if you'd been better at apologizing."

"My marriage might have lasted longer if Nils hadn't made the big jump from booze to crystal meth."

Ria's face fell. "Crystal meth?"

"Found it in the glove compartment when he got back from rehab the third time. And you know how it was with him. Isn't there a song about it? Who you gonna believe, baby, me or your lyin' eyes?"

Ria retreated a step into her incense-smoky sanctum. "Please. Come in."

Such thick incense, with a jasmine topnote that Jane knew from experience would give her a piercing headache if she stayed the full hour she'd paid for. No one could say Ria for stinted on her materials. The incense was heavy on essential oils, early pressings. Whatever kitsch she sold in the shop, only the good stuff made it to the altar.

"I didn't know," said Ria as she closed the door. "I must

have misread the cards. I thought the Devil trump was referring to you."

"How flattering."

"But it was him. Why didn't I see it? I was a poor coven sister to you when you were in need."

Sophie put in, "You tried. You sent casseroles."

"They were good casseroles," Jane admitted.

The kouros, meanwhile, stood with his hands carefully behind his back, examining everything on Ria's altar. Jane let herself notice that the altar really was quite beautiful. She'd always admired Ria's ability to create a sense of sacred space.

"Who's this?" Ria asked.

"Isn't he lovely?" said Sophie.

Jane said, "He's our houseguest. Turned up on the beach between hurricanes, not in great shape."

The kouros figured out they were talking about him, and bowed to Ria again and tried talking to her. The borrowed scarf unwound mid-bow, and between long phrases of his melodic greeting, his gills gaped open.

Ria's eyes watered and she choked up a little as she said, "Hail and well met, whatever you are."

"This is why," said Jane, "I maybe owe you an apology."

The kouros let out a startled yelp when Ria grabbed him in a bear hug as if he were some sort of lost kinsman returned. Fortunately, she kept a box of tissues in the room, so she was able to pull herself together before the kohl around her eyes ran too badly. "Usually it's the querents who need these," she said, daubing at her face with a Kleenex.

She settled in at her reading table and set her hands over her cards in prayer. Whatever crackpot ideas she embraced, at least she embraced them with her whole heart.

"Truth be shown, truth be spoken, truth be heard," she muttered, eyes closed. "So, which of you wants to shuffle?"

Sophie reached for the cards. "He probably should, but I don't think he knows how. We'll be here all night if we try to show him."

The kouros watched, fascinated, while she shuffled the worn pack. "Name?" he asked.

"Cards."

When Sophie had finished, Ria laid out the opening spread. That was even more intriguing than the shuffle had been

"Name?"

"Radio," said Sophie. "Sort of. It's full of news."

The kouros's face contracted in puzzlement, and he looked to Jane for confirmation.

"Game," she said. "Very pretty game."

"Veryprettygame," the kouros repeated. "Cards."

His skepticism raised him several notches in Jane's estimation.

Ria ignored the exchange. "Not too many Major Arcana. Lots of wiggle room for personal volition." She laid down a few clarification cards by the last card in the opening spread. "It's fast. Six weeks to the Singularity."

"I wish you wouldn't call it that," said Jane.

"It's the event we can't see past. Do you have a better name for it?"

Jane thought she did, several of them, but none were good follow-ups to an apology, so she kept them to herself.

"Everything on the table will be over by Samhain. The Broken Tower is in the origin spot. That would be Atlantis. The Two of Cups in the recent past. Sophie, you do work fast. Two of Wands crowned by the Ace of Pentacles for the present. You think you're waiting for one thing, but quite another is already happening. Near future's the Seven of Wands—confrontation. Up the pillar we have, hm... You're thinking Four of Wands, commitment. Everyone else is thinking Seven of Cups, self-delusion. You're afraid of the Queen of Swords reversed. That would be Jane." At this, Sophie nodded.

"Do you *fear* me?" Jane asked Sophie, aghast.

"Um," said Sophie.

Ria reclaimed the reading. "We end with Death, total transformation, clarified by Six of Swords, more transformation, and maybe a journey by water. Ace of Swords, for getting something right, and Ten of Swords reversed. Weird that there are so few reversals, but then, they generally indicate where people are being stubborn." At this, Ria looked at Jane. "So the Ten of Swords reversed is probably about you."

Jane was long past taking Ria's jibes personally. "From which you conclude?"

Ria tried laying more clarification cards at various points in the spread. "Sorry. We're at the limits of comprehensibility. The cards won't give me a straight answer past that."

"Total transformation," said Sophie.

"Also known as Death," Jane pointed out. "Whatever."

"Look, Sophie," said Ria, "if you were just some Rutgers freshman with the usual boyfriend, I'd know what to do with this. You're not, and he's not. If I thought I knew the answer, in this room, I could make you believe it, but I'm out of my depth. I'll have Daffodil give you a refund."

"Daffodil?" Jane said. "Why not Peaseblossom, while she was at it?"

"Not her fault," said Ria. "Her parents actually named her that."

Sophie said, "We don't need a refund. You did your best."

Though it was Jane's signature, on Jane's credit card, that Sophie was being so generous with, Jane decided to let it slide. She'd seen Ria admit to having been wrong, and then to being uncertain. For Jane, it was worth the price of admission. "Thanks," she said, and shut her mouth before she could fuck things up again.

So the two roommates and their guest went home to await Death, transformation, whatever, for the next six weeks. The shining city had vanished from the coffee table by the time they got home, and the kouros didn't rebuild it. Apparently, he had other things on his mind.

He went on collecting nouns and verbs, and eventually moved

on to adjectives and rudimentary sentences. Language occupied his days completely. As far as Jane could tell, he had no particular inclination to leave the house unless Sophie did. And Sophie didn't, much.

Nor did Sophie ask for her old waitressing gig back. There was no new one. She spent her time teaching the kouros English—all vocabulary, minimal grammar, no method. Sophie awaited the six-week mystery as a small child awaits Christmas morning, making lists of her hopes and counting down the days.

Jane assumed Ria was wrong, but resigned herself to the pointlessness of persuading Sophie to part with the kouros before the six weeks were up. For one thing, that was as long as any of Sophie's entanglements had lasted since her parents died. For another, it was Sophie's house, and Jane was the tenant.

So Jane concentrated on the practical realities of life. The IRS didn't care about the eruption of the supernatural into her household. H&R Block cared for the IRS and its shareholders and not much else. The groceries still needed to be bought. She went to work and worked hard, did her share of the chores around the house, and retreated to her room in the evenings to reread *Middlemarch* again for comfort. And then again. She stopped searching for Atlantis in her reference books, and couldn't bring herself to look at the Greek-English lexicon Amber had given her. Jane's greatest accomplishment that month was that she hauled the sodden wreckage of her bridal registry up from the basement and out to the curb for the special post-hurricane trash pickup. And she resisted the stupid nostalgia for cigarettes. They'd been a poor substitute for sex during the last year of her marriage, and she knew they'd serve her no better now. Sophie and the kouros provided many occasions for Jane to put in her earplugs to sleep.

With the crisis faded into routine, Jane had time to see if anyone had responded yet to the personal ad she had placed on SinglePagans.com. She'd had months to revise out the bitterness, one phrase at a time. The rant she'd opened with when she first posted it made her laugh now, but even with the rant gone, she wasn't getting any worthwhile replies—just lots of overseas people trying to marry into the U.S. Maybe there was some bitter thing left to take out. *Divorced Wiccan Female, 32, seeks realistic rebound guy. Petite and trim brunette. Enjoys the ocean, 19th century novels, long Sunday mornings with the New York Times. Atlantis cranks need not apply.*

It was Amber who had insisted she include the petite and trim bit. "If you make yourself sound like such a downer," Amber had said back at Midsummer, "whose eye are you going to catch? You've got to put in something good. And would it kill you to put up a photo?"

"But the ocean's good, and I *am* such a downer," Jane had replied, and then typed in her physical description anyway, in partial capitulation.

But now it was mid-September, and there was still no word from anybody she wanted to meet. Which was probably just as well, since Jane could neither rule out the possibility of Atlantis nor bring herself to cut that last line.

The Autumnal Equinox fell on a Saturday of the second week of the Countdown to Destiny—Sophie thought it was funny to call it that. She and Jane spent the morning and afternoon cooking for the Mabon feast, while the kouros petted the glossy photos in Jane's cookbooks.

"Pictures move and pictures do not move," he mused.

He didn't object to wearing Bob's utilikilt and shirt for the occasion. With a little prompting, he made himself useful, carrying some of the potluck dishes to the trunk of the Corolla, and sat himself in the backseat properly, but still wouldn't tolerate the seat belt.

"Your funeral," Jane muttered. Whenever they went anywhere together, Jane did the driving these days, since Sophie didn't have a job to pay for gas. *Just until the trust fund kicks in, at the end of next quarter,* Sophie kept saying. There was plenty to mutter about, not least Sophie's apparent determination to spend down her inheritance.

When it wasn't practical to perform their rituals on the beach, the coven usually held circle at Bob's house. The temple room he'd set up in the old Rumson manse was big enough for the whole coven, and then some. Ricki usually took the kids out to see a movie on full moon nights and holidays. This time, she hung around long enough to meet Sophie's new boyfriend.

"Is a pretty house," the kouros told Sophie's sister-in-law. Sophie had rehearsed him on how to make Ricki smile. "They are sturdy children."

"Thank you," said Ricki. "How do you like New Jersey?" The concept of New Jersey was lost on him.

Susan, the oldest of the three Baines children, kicked along on her razor scooter across the marble floor of the front entryway. "Who's the boyfriend, Aunt Sophie?"

"His name's Kouros," Sophie said, and plucked affectionately at his scarf to make sure his gills were covered. "He's from overseas."

Jane knew there were things Ricki didn't want to get into with the kids, so she changed the subject. "What movie are you guys going to see?"

Ricki gave Jane a big, appreciative smile. "Some film about wild geese. It's supposed to be like that penguin one."

"Yeah," said Jane, with one eye on the kouros, who was kneeling on the floor to examine the workings of the scooter. "I heard that, too. One of the accountants at work said her kids liked it."

Susan demonstrated proper scooter technique, and after a couple of tries, the kouros scooted in circles around the marble floor. He sang one of his whalesongs for joy, and just for a moment, Jane let herself see why Sophie loved him.

It wasn't a thing she could bear for long.

Ricki rounded up the twins, called for Susan, and took off. While Sophie showed the kouros around her childhood home, Jane carried the food in from the car. Rugosa Coven set a proper Mabon table, with a harvest thanksgiving spread that included everything they hoped to enjoy in the coming year. That, and an impressive array of Tupperware for divvying up the leftovers.

Over the years Rugosa had been together, everybody but Bob had had at least one lean season. Now it was Sophie's turn, again, to be the Mabon leftovers queen. The rest of the coven conducted a furtive gossip exchange while she was out of earshot.

"How's it going?" Bob asked, carrying out the plates.

"They're happy," said Jane. "I don't see any other reason why he wouldn't go home. He seems well enough. I tried asking him when he'd leave, but I don't think he understood me."

Sebastian said, "You're sure Sophie's happy?"

"I've had to use my earplugs so often, I actually wore out a pair and had to replace them. Is that happy enough for you? Because it's a little too happy for me."

That cracked Amber up. "You wore out your *earplugs*?"

"You'd be amazed."

"Well," said Bob, "I guess we can't complain about happiness."

"Again, you'd be amazed."

"When things go sour, you tell me right away," Bob urged her. "If a time comes when I need to run him off, I don't want to wait too long."

"Run him off?" said Jane. "Run him off to where?"

Amber said, "It worked on Nils."

Bob and Sebastian glared at Amber.

"It what?" said Jane.

"Um," said Bob.

Sebastian took a deep breath and said, "About a week after the time he stole your clothes, Sophie noticed him sitting on the seawall, staking out the beach cottage all day. So Bob and I paid him one last visit, to let him know that if he kept up the stalker bullshit, we would take it personally."

Jane pulled out one of the ornate dining chairs and sat heavily down. "You told him you'd take it personally? Maybe you should cut back on your *Sopranos* habit."

"It was the newspaper habit," said Bob. "Every time I read the police blotter page in the *Home New*s, I was afraid I'd find your name. Or that you'd be the next Jane Doe dumped at the next construction site. It was time to do something. And, blood kin or not, as far as I'm concerned, Sophie's not my only sister."

Now that she thought about it, the stalker bullshit had stopped pretty abruptly. "Catching him behind the beach house picking through Sophie's trash at three in the morning was pretty damn creepy. But after he burned our handfasting cords, I really thought he was done."

"See?" Amber said to Sebastian. "I told you you could just tell her."

Sebastian said, "It's not a casserole, but it was what we could think of to do."

"Thank you." Jane's universe was spinning, but at least it was orderly.

Everything happened for a reason, and reasons were knowable. Her ex-husband had stopped stalking her because her coven brothers would otherwise have beaten the shit out of him on their own initiative. The discovery was unexpected, yet downright Newtonian. Or maybe electromagnetic. It had been a long time since Intro to Physics. What a relief, after the past three weeks, that some part of the world made sense. "You probably did the right thing."

"What matters is, you're still here," said Bob.

Sophie flounced down the stairs with the kouros in tow and said, "Are we doing ritual, or what?"

Up in the temple room, Bob had already arranged everything. The candlewicks were trimmed. The incense charcoal was dry. The altar was dusted. Rugosa cast the circle hand to hand, acknowledged the elements, and welcomed the Gods. The kouros did whatever Sophie did, and gracefully, though he was a beat behind. He was all intention, with nothing of habit about him.

It was good to be six again, with Ria so long gone.

Amber started them on a wordless chant, just a soft drone, and one by one they named their gratitudes for the year's harvest. With Hurricane Lorelei on their minds, Hurricane Nora just behind them, and two months left in the storm season, it was easy to be thankful for every good thing. When the drone wound down, Sebastian said, "You remember Jon? From Chamomile Coven? He emailed me from the Red Cross staging area in Hatteras. Asked if we could send some energy. I should have mentioned before we cast."

Jane said, "Now, those are people who need a casserole."

"A really big casserole," Amber agreed.

"Well," said Bob, "what else would anyone expect from a pack of kitchen witches?"

So, bearing in mind the Charge of the Goddess's injunctions regarding both mirth and reverence, they closed their eyes—the kouros, game for anything, closed his eyes along with them—and visualized a glowing, restorative casserole for sixty thousand. Laughing, improvising a description together in layers of detail, they sent it where it needed to go.

Although it was usually Amber and Sebastian who, with chalice and blade, performed the symbolic Great Rite, Sophie volunteered herself and the kouros. She handed him the blade, picked up the chalice, and took a breath to talk him through it.

Jane braced herself for one of those painfully awkward moments that was occasionally the price of an improvisational liturgical style.

The kouros needed no explanation. He looked downright relieved, as if, for once, something familiar had been asked of him. Suddenly, the bit of bastardized 1940's-vintage liturgy, which the coven had adapted from a secondhand paperback book about a branch of Wicca they didn't even practice, shed the shabbiness it had always had in Jane's mind. Sophie spoke both the priest's lines and the priestess's, over the kouros's song, and the chalice and blade were joined. It was a tentative, delicate matter of absolute concentration.

So that was what people meant, when they said there was no greater magic in all the world than that of love.

Later, with the circle uncast, the Gods and elements hailed and farewelled, and the feast blessed and sat down to, it occurred to Jane to resent the kouros for validating a discredited theory of Wiccan history. She'd made her peace with the fact that her house was built on shifting sands. It was her house, to build where she liked. Why did he have to keep substituting rock?

Though Sophie resumed her Countdown to Destiny after the Equinox, marking the days on the kitchen calendar, Jane's sense of routine deepened. The kouros understood what a calendar was, as it turned out, and was able to comprehend the idea of a week. If he had to stay, Jane decided he ought to have a share of the weekly chores, since it was obvious he couldn't be asked to get a job. What would the immigration bureaucrats have done with him? He mopped up—he had words for that, and Jane showed him how to do it with an actual mop, rather than by dragging towels across the floor with his feet. He swept the sand back out through the front and back doors. Eventually, he got over his leeriness of the vacuum cleaner.

The next Full Moon circle came and went. It was an uneventful ritual, but that Sophie and the kouros had done the symbolic Great Rite so beautifully at Mabon, Amber and Sebastian were perfectly happy to defer to them for that bit of the liturgy. Bob's suspicions softened, and even Jane could forget, for an hour at a stretch sometimes, her annoyance at her roommate's still-vigorous courtship.

She was on her third pair of earplugs in a month.

In the fifth week of the countdown, Sophie took sick with a sore throat, and Jane thought miserably of the Death trump, and of her dim recollections from reading *Guns, Germs, and Steel* a few years back. It was mid-October, a perfectly reasonable time to catch an upper respiratory bug, but Jane nursed a sense of impending doom while she boiled water for tea. Sophie's lymph nodes were swollen something fierce, and she had no appetite, but still refused to see a doctor.

"You look awful," said Jane on the third day of Sophie's

malady. "I can take tomorrow off work."

"You've taken too many days off work for me already."

"Not as many as I took off last year, and better over you than Nils."

"I'll be fine. I'll just keep sucking on zinc lozenges, and it'll go away."

"But what if, without meaning any harm, he's brought something..."

"I'll be fine. No need to get all Homeland Security Department on me."

"More like the Centers for Disease Control. Besides, tomorrow's Friday. I'm ahead on my paperwork. They won't miss me."

No dice.

That night, Jane was so preoccupied she couldn't find her earplugs, so there was no avoiding the inevitable. She heard them through the wall. Even with a sore throat, Sophie sounded intolerably happy. It came back to Jane's mind in a rush, then—the moment she had let herself see the kouros the way Sophie did. How long had it been since she'd looked at anyone that way in her own right? She couldn't ask them to stop, and she couldn't abide hearing it go on.

Jane got up and dressed in the dark, and padded out quietly to the front door where her beach flip-flops and her windbreaker waited in the little foyer.

It was a windy night—too windy for the devotional candle in her pocket, so she didn't light it. She walked past the dune grass and the rugosa bushes, their blooms gone to rose hips. At the tide line, she stepped out of her shoes to feel the cold, wet sand under her feet. The waning moon shone in the east, and Jane gave her troubles to her friend the ocean. She needed it smaller than itself now, needed it nameable, but it was big enough to swallow up all the names she knew. Male and female created she it. "Manannan," she said, "Yemaya. Poseidon. Epona." Then she came to the one she knew she'd choke on. "Aphrodite."

An hour later, she was cried out enough to go home. The teal house was, mercifully, quiet.

Jane woke just a few hours later to the sound of pounding at her bedroom door. Not knocking, but a flat-handed, irregular drummer's thump, accompanied by a panicky jumble of the kouros's not-Greek.

She rolled out of bed and said, "Coming, I'm coming, for pity's sake, shut up, you'll wake the neighbors." She opened the door and found the kouros there, wide-eyed with fear. He grabbed her wrist and pulled her toward the other bedroom.

"Sophie! Sophie!" he said.

The light was already on in Sophie's room, and Jane squinted into it to see Sophie lying face down on her bed, and the sheets soaked with blood.

"Hi, Jane," Sophie said, somewhat weakly.

"What the fuck?"

"I figured out what the swelling's about."

Jane came close and pulled away the topsheet Sophie had pressed against her neck. She wiped down the skin with a clean corner. The skin had torn laterally over an opening that was, unmistakably, a gill slit, just under Sophie's jaw and tilting up to end behind her ear—like the kouros's gills, only bleeding at the surface. Lined up under the newly-open gill, four more distinct ridges and depressions under taut-stretched skin were red and angry. On the other side of Sophie's throat was a matching set of five ridges, the uppermost just beginning to tear.

"At least you'll be symmetrical soon," said Jane. With a trembling hand, she pressed the sheet back against the open gill. "You need a doctor, sweetie. I'm going to dial 911 now."

"No ER," said Sophie.

"We're out of our depth. You need help."

"No hospitals. What do you think they'd do to me there? What do you think they'd do to *him*?"

"I think they'd keep you from bleeding down your throat and drowning in your own blood."

"I don't consent to medical treatment. And if the EMT's come, I'll tell them the same."

"Then I'll knock you unconscious before they get here, and they'll have implied consent."

"You wouldn't."

No, Jane wouldn't. Damn it. "We have to do something."

"I want Sebastian."

Amber and Sebastian's place was on the way to the hospital, so Jane agreed.

She threw on yesterday's jeans and sweater, stepped into her beach flip-flops, and grabbed her bag. The kouros dressed himself in Bob's utilikilt without having to be asked. With his help, she got Sophie bundled in the fluffy terrycloth robe and shod in her Birkenstocks, and bustled her into the car. Somehow, they folded her into the backseat so she lay neck down on a clean pillowcase, so as not to bleed into her airway, with her forehead resting on the kouros's lap. Jane jostled him a bit to get the seat belt around him, and he accepted her ministrations without question. With hands crackled with a light crust of dried blood, he stroked Sophie's hair while he crooned her a new song for comfort.

Jane drove at stupid speed through the pre-dawn dark, cursing like a Jersey girl all the way, down Ocean Avenue, across the bridge, through Rumson into Red Bank, and onto Reckless Place to park, where she banged the Corolla right into the bumper of Amber's convertible. The convertible's car alarm went off.

"Are we okay?" Sophie asked from the backseat.

"I just trashed Amber's car."

Sophie coughed out a little laugh, and nothing could have filled Jane with hope better than that did.

Before Jane had even managed to get the kouros out of his seat belt, a negligee-clad Amber came storming out of the house, brandishing her electronic key at the convertible, which yipped twice and fell silent. When she saw who had come, and in what state, her jaw dropped. She turned and ran back through her front door, shouting, "Sebastian! Sebastian, get up! We need you!"

Amber disappeared into the house, and the lights came on all over the first floor, and then up in the bedroom. Sebastian pounded down the stairs in all his pierced, tattooed glory and ran right out to the curb to see what was the matter.

"Sweet Jesus," he said, when he caught sight of Sophie in her bloodied bathrobe.

"Well, why not Jesus, too?" said Jane. "We need all the help we can get. She won't consent to medical treatment."

"Sophie, that is the dumbest decision you've ever made."

"If a woman wants gills," Sophie replied, "it's nobody's business to say her nay."

The lights were starting to come on in the neighbors' windows. Sebastian looked up and down his block. "First, we get her into the house. Then, we call 911." He pulled her out of the car, picked her up in his arms, and carried her straight to the kitchen, where he lay her out on the table. "Good light here," he said, and went to wash his hands. "Let me get a look, figure out what to tell the dispatcher."

"No ER," Sophie insisted.

The kouros took her hand and said, "No eee are." He looked Sebastian in the face, as if he meant to do something about it.

"Right, then," said Sebastian. "We never know what we're getting with you, do we?"

Jane dug her address book out of her bag and searched through the pages of fellow Pagans. "There's an M.D. in Chamomile Coven. And didn't their girl in nursing school just graduate? Cygnus Grove's crawling with paramedics. I'd feel weird calling on Thane Kindred, but they've got cops, first responders, and they were kind to me right to the end. If we ask for a promise of secrecy, you know those Norse practitioner guys don't break troth." She looked at the empty ring finger on her left hand. "Well, most of them don't break troth."

Sebastian shook his head. "Everybody we could call is down in Hatteras with the Red Cross. It's all over the community blogs.

You haven't been keeping up with LiveJournal, have you?"

"I've kind of had my hands full."

"Sorry, hon. I wish it were otherwise, but if we're not going to the ER, I'm the only game in town." He lifted the bloodied pillowcase from Sophie's throat and stood speechless at what he saw.

Amber leaned around him to look. "Wow. That's very... vintage circus sideshow."

"Thanks so much," said Sophie. "Screw you, too."

Sebastian said, "The bleeding's not too bad. You've been pressing on it?"

"For a while."

"Okay, then. I'm going to touch your throat now. Ready?"

"Yeah. Hey, Jane?"

"Yeah, Sophie?"

"Can you call Bob?"

While Sebastian prodded the gills with his fingers, Jane braced herself to tell Bob what had happened to his sister.

"She what?!" Bob's voice shouted over the phone.

"Grew gills," Jane repeated. "It doesn't seem to be going well."

"I'm coming over."

"We're at Amber and Sebastian's."

"If you could move her at all you should have taken her..."

"To the ER. Yes, everybody but Sophie and her boy are in agreement about that. Come tell her yourself."

"Damn right, I'll tell her myself." And Bob hung up.

"Your brother's on his way, Sophie."

But Sophie had her eyes squinched shut with pain. She panted little shallow breaths, and tears were running down the sides of her face.

"Almost done," said Sebastian. "You're doing great. I've seen people break down a lot worse, getting inked. Just another second. Okay."

Jane said, "Well?"

"Well?" the kouros echoed.

"Look, I'm not a doctor. But I think the problem isn't that there are gills. The problem seems to be that the skin is tearing.

A clean cut, with sterile instruments, and sterile dressings to hand, and we wouldn't have to worry about infection so much. I'm really worried about infection. But see, over here, the top one on the other side's torn open more just in the couple of minutes I've spent looking her over. I'm thinking this is a time-sensitive thing."

Jane folded her arms. "If she refuses to consent to treatment, there's nothing anyone can legally do to make her accept it." Nils had afforded her many bitter occasions for learning about medical consent.

"I've got the tools to open them up clean," Sebastian said. "If it's that or letting her tear more, I'll do it. We'll need to move her to the studio for reasonably sterile conditions. Best to have her done and out of there before my apprentices come in at ten."

"But she's stable for now?"

Sebastian shrugged. "I'm not the person who could tell you."

"At this point," said Jane, "we should wait for Bob, in any case. Maybe he can get through to her. Anyhow, it's inflamed, right? That looks like inflammation to me. What say we put some ice on it?"

The kouros looked from one face to another, trying to piece together what was going on. In the thick of things, he seemed to be struggling to remember his English. "Ais?"

Amber opened the freezer and started scooping cubes into a two-gallon Ziploc bag with her hands, grimacing at the cold. "Ice," she said. She plucked a clean dish towel from a drawer, laid it over Sophie's throat, and then arranged the bag lightly so the cubes piled up on either side, over the gills.

The kouros pinched one of the ice cubes through the plastic, nodded, and said, "Ice is good." Then he went back to stroking Sophie's hair and singing his new song, with its long, long phrases. She looked up at him and smiled the goofiest smile.

Bob banged the front door open without knocking and ran into the kitchen, sliding across the tile to a stop against the refrigerator. He'd driven straight over in his slippers and pajamas. The pajamas were printed all over with a repeating pattern of teddy bears and baseball bats and blue ribbons that said *World's Greatest Dad.*

"Hi, Bob," said Sophie.

"Let me see." He lifted the ice and the dish towel tenderly to show the torn and bloody throat. Bob began to turn very red in the face.

Sophie said, "Don't. It's nobody's fault."

It occurred to Jane then that she'd failed him. Hadn't he asked her to keep an eye on his sister? And Jane had looked after her only enough to know that Sophie was pleased. *I'm sorry,* Jane was about to say, but she'd never seen Bob so angry, not with her own eyes. For the first time, she was a little afraid of him.

But it was the kouros he went after—lifted him by the borrowed shirt clear off the floor and pinned him against the cabinets. "Make it stop," said Bob.

"Surprise," the kouros protested. "Don't know! Worry. I worry. Ice is good. No eee are. What is no eee are? Sebastian tweezers. Okay?"

"It's not okay. Make it stop."

"Don't know. Surprise." The kouros sighed, slowed himself. "I am surprise. I am worry, too. Please don't. Down. Please."

That reasonable, soothing, measured way of saying please, with its edge of fear, was entirely too familiar to Jane. She thought she might throw up.

"Jesus, Bob," said Sophie, "he's not the captain of the fucking football team. Cut it the fuck out."

Sebastian said, "Bob." The practiced voice wasn't quite enough to get through to him on the first try. "Bob, put him down."

"He has to make it stop. He can't do this to her. Look what he did."

"Bob, remember whose kitchen you're in. Put him down."

Amber said, in a very small voice, "He is a guest in our house."

Maybe if Jane doubted hard enough that Bob had become a

person with fists, it would stop being true. She'd never seen him with fists before. She ought to be doing something. She had counted on his temper, but it wasn't right that Bob should have fists. She couldn't think further than that.

Bob looked at Sophie, whose throat was still uncovered. He lowered the kouros so that his feet were no longer dangling above the floor, but then knocked his head back against the cabinet. "You can't *do* this to her," said Bob, again knocking the kouros's head on the cabinet for emphasis. "You can't *do* this to us."

The kouros replied, "You can't *do* this." Something like a sound cracked the air, rattled them all in their bones. Bob staggered back as if the floor were rolling out from under him—his slippers weren't helping him any. "Please," said the kouros.

Bob landed hard on one knee and held tight to one of the tall chairs at the breakfast table to avoid going down altogether. He gasped for breath.

As if this were the most pressing time in the world for language lessons, the kouros asked, "What is no eee are?"

Sophie answered with a hesitant sweep of pitch-accented vowels. The end of her phrase of not-Greek petered out in coughing, but the kouros was satisfied with whatever definition she'd given him.

Shocked, Jane said, "I didn't know you could speak it."

"Just because you're not around to see a thing, doesn't mean it isn't happening."

The kouros nodded ruefully. "No eee are," he agreed. "Okay." He offered Bob a hand up off the floor.

"Okay?" Bob said. "Not yet, it's not. What did you do to her?"

"He doesn't know," said Jane. She hadn't expected to defend the kouros, but there it was. "What do you want him to do? Make up an answer? I don't think Sophie would be well served by speculation."

Sophie said, "I'd be better served by Sebastian's instruments."

"Soon, sweetie," said Jane. "Bob, are you hurt?"

"I don't think so. What was that?"

But the kouros wasn't telling. He looked to Sebastian and said, "Tweezers for Sophie, please? Do you have?"

"We'll have to go to them," Sebastian said. He plucked the car keys from their hook on the wall, then put them back, chuckling. "I almost forgot."

"What?" said Amber.

"To put on clothes before I leave the house."

Amber said, "Oh. Yeah. I guess we'll be right back down."

Jane had seen enough episodes of The Bob & Sophie Show to give the Baineses a minute to themselves for reconciliation. It was time to pry the kouros away from the kitchen table and back off. "Hey, you," she said. Even after all these weeks, it bothered her to call him by a name she knew wasn't really his. "Hey. Kouros." He looked up. "May I have a moment in the dining room?"

"What is a moment?"

"Just get over here."

He did, and The Bob & Sophie Show's opening credits rolled. All Jane had to do was get out of the kitchen, and everything would sort itself out. She didn't even have to be out of earshot. While the kouros considered the sleek, modern lines of Amber's dining set, Jane leaned around the doorframe to watch.

Sophie said, "Nice jammies."

Bob looked at what he was wearing. "Oh. Thanks. Ricki and the kids gave them to me for Father's Day."

"I figured."

"It's not like I like getting in the way. It's just, sometimes you could use some protecting."

"Not from him."

Things were about to get sappy, and Jane didn't need it. Meanwhile, the kouros was standing right next to the sideboard, with all the arty blown glass stuff Amber liked so much, and he wasn't touching anything "Are you okay?"

"I am worry."

"Worried."

"I am worried?"

"That's what you mean."

"Okay."

"Bob's a good guy." She said it as much to remind herself as to reassure the kouros, after the unsettling spectacle by the cabinets.

"Yes. Bob is worry. Worried. Everybody worried." He let go the brave face he'd kept up for Sophie. "Is she okay soon?"

Jane shrugged. "Who can guess?" And, because she couldn't think of a reason not to under the circumstances, she gave the kouros a hug.

Amber and Sebastian came pounding down the stairs in a rush, and after some confusion over which cars to take and how to arrange the passengers, they all six ended up together in Bob's SUV, with Sophie and the kouros ensconced in the vast carpeted realm in back. It was barely a three-minute drive to the studio.

Sebastian turned the neon OPEN sign on out of habit, and Amber let him settle into his work mind before she switched it back off for him. The clock by the dormant cash register said it was not yet six in the morning.

Amber fished a pharmacy bottle out of her bag. "Percocet," she told Sophie. "Good thing I didn't throw it out after my root canal. It's the closest thing to anaesthesia we could find in the house."

"I'll need an assistant," said Sebastian, switching on his autoclave. He flipped on the lights for his work space, and all the line and color of the flash art on the walls woke under the incandescents.

Jane said, "Let me." Bob was about to volunteer, but she said, "You shouldn't have to watch her get cut."

The kouros said, "Let me what?"

"Too unpredictable," said Sebastian.

Amber handed Sophie a bottle of water for the pills and said, "Not me. Sorry. After all these years of getting inked by him, I trance out when I watch him work on anybody. It's kind of Pavlovian."

Sebastian passed Jane the box of latex gloves and pointed her to the sink. "Scrub thoroughly first." He showed her the instruments he'd need, and made her say the names back to him twice.

Most of them, she could figure out, but she couldn't help saying, "What the hell is a Bovie?"

"Electrocautery pencil. You want to stumble over however many syllables every time I need it?"

"No, Bovie's just fine."

"Sorry."

"No, I'm sorry."

"Jane. Breathe." He shook a finger at her in mock-scold. "No freaking out allowed."

"Okay. No freaking out." She was starting to sound like the kouros.

Sebastian settled Sophie into the used dentist's chair and tilted her back. The Bovie was, indeed, the tool for the job. Opening the remaining gill slits went far more smoothly than Jane had imagined, but the smell of cooking flesh was one she knew she'd never forget. She got through it all by thinking of the episodes of *M*A*S*H* she'd watched as a kid. Nurse, scalpel. Nurse, gauze. The thing needed doing, so she did it. If the transformation Ria promised had to come to pass, Jane would witness it without looking away.

Through it all, Sophie bore up bravely, though the Percocet was obviously not quite enough. Sebastian intoned his way through one of Kipling's *Just So Stories* for her, the tale of an astute little fish hiding under the door-sills of the equator.

Afterward he instructed Jane on how to change the dressing, while he put the first one on slowly so she could see. "Get a fresh tube of topical antibiotics," he said. "A full course of systemic ones would probably be a good idea."

"I'll call my primary care guy and say the sinusitis came back. He'll phone it in without seeing me." Jane laughed. "Look at me, scamming a doctor to score drugs, and all I want is penicillin. Nils would call me an amateur."

They cleared out of the studio by nine, and Jane called in sick to work, pleading the recurrent sinusitis she'd defeated months ago. After more well-meaning contention about who would drive whom where, she reclaimed the Corolla and carried Sophie and the kouros home to the teal house. Once the lovers were tucked into clean linens in Sophie's bed to recuperate, Jane phoned her doctor's office.

"Jane Hirsch," said her doctor's secretary, before Jane even had a chance to say hello. "I never forget a phone number. Hope it's not the sinusitis again."

"Yeah, I need another round of antibiotics, but I can't take time from work to come in. Could you phone the pharmacy?"

"Sure, hon. Just a sec. Okay, usual questions. No new allergies?"

"None."

"Any chance you might be pregnant?"

"Um." That might explain it, though Jane couldn't guess just how. In the early days of the language barrier, would Sophie have insisted on condoms when she couldn't explain what they were good for? Why, no. For a moment, Jane was angry enough at her roommate, she hesitated to lie about what she needed. Besides, she would be lying to a secretary who had, without judging Jane, handled paperwork for every blood test for every sexually transmitted disease known to man, after Jane told her primary care doc about finding Nils's stash of meth—there was no knowing who Nils had screwed while zooming out of his head on that stuff. Jane trusted the secretary, but not enough to tell her about Sophie's new respiratory system. "I hadn't thought about it. Maybe. A remote chance."

"Should I put your husband back in the system as the person to contact in case of an emergency?"

"Oh, hell no."

"Good for you. Fresh starts all around."

"Got finalized back in July. The judge expedited my case."

"Congratulations. Dr. Patel will find you something suitable. The pharmacy should have it in an hour or so."

An hour or so later, Jane was at the pharmacy, picking up the prescription and a few other things. When she got home, she arranged the few other things in the bathroom for Sophie to find.

Aside from the changing of the dressings, the two roommates hardly spoke all day. What with the recuperation, the sleep deprivation, and the Percocet, Sophie was down for the count.

On Saturday, restlessness drove Jane across the street to the ocean three times before sunset, and a fourth after dark, until it got too cold to sit on the seawall. In between, she did half-hearted internet searches on vestigial gills. Though she gave hours to the effort, eventually she despaired of finding information of obvious relevance to Sophie's condition. Jane's own condition bore looking into, so she paid a visit to SinglePagans.com.

Finally, someone had responded to her ad in earnest. *Single male Druid, 34, seeks skeptic. Loves the ocean, loves Dickens, esp Tale of 2 Cities. I'd wager dinner at Martine's you're a George Eliot fan. For a few weeks on the rebound, could you stand a LITTLE Atlantis crankery? Call anytime.*

He was in the right area code. His profile said he lived in Holmdel—far enough away she'd be unlikely to run into him on the street after it was over, close enough that a few weeks on the rebound wouldn't be too complicated. She wasn't in the market for crankery of any kind, but damn it, he'd made her smile, and he had her pegged about George Eliot. She knew she'd call him, if only to ask how he'd guessed. So it was worth thinking about his picture, which could only have been an unretouched image—he was very plain. Good. No false advertising. Jane was satisfied that she'd learned her lesson about pretty men: the ones who weren't from the bottom of the sea were mostly jerks, drunks, or worse. With this guy, there was a risk that something good might happen. She put the number in her cell phone's contact list for later. One thing at a time. Though her mind now had even more to race about, she was weary to her bones.

Sunday morning, Jane woke from a night of fitful sleep, nearly as tired and restless as she'd been when she lay down. In the bathroom, she found Sophie's pregnancy test kit on the ledge of the sink. Bright purple positive.

Why anger, Jane's brain asked itself while she threw the toothpaste across the room. What business did she have being angry about this? She pounded the tiled wall with her fist, watching herself pound on it, until the kouros came to the other side of the door to ask, "Okay?"

"Okay," she said. It felt exactly like the time she'd nearly drowned—anyone who lived near the shore long enough would sooner or later have a drowning story—when she got caught in the undertow and the Avenel lifeguards had to fish her out. That same split: the animal panic, and the self that watched the animal panic, fascinated. She perched on the edge of the bathtub until she could will her body to breathe again.

Still too worked up to shower, Jane went to pick a fight with Sophie, but Sophie was stone asleep again. The kouros, sitting beside the bed to keep watch, looked so solicitous, Jane couldn't pick her fight with him. There was nothing for it but to dress and get the hell out.

Which she did, though once she was on the beach, she couldn't remember crossing the street to get there. Last time she'd blanked out with anger like that, she'd been packing out of her old place for the second time, stealing her own clothes back from Nils.

Jane stood on the beach a long while, watching the waves roll in, while her brain chattered to itself. The sun floated up to warm the day. Soon the beach teemed with well-insulated people, out to walk for the last fair beach day of autumn. No doubt the Weather Channel had sent them. Every one of them was happy to be there, throwing bread to the gulls and plucking dried rose hips off the rugosa bushes.

She wanted everything back like it had been. No. She wanted to burn down the teal house, and her ex-husband's house for good measure, and maybe the whole of Monmouth County just for kicks. But then, she wanted a quiet day alone with her Sunday *Times*. Except that she wanted a man in her bed—it had been over a year, damn it—and oh, Gods, she wanted a cigarette.

"Fuck that," she shouted into the wind. "No fucking way. Go ahead. Break my theology, break my world, break my household, break my heart, but I am *not* having a fucking *cigarette!*"

The sea wind blasted on. The ocean offered her no comfort, so Jane turned her back on it, and nearly walked right into a barefoot kid. The kid—his hightop shoes dangling by the laces from one hand, skateboard balanced over his shoulder with the other—let out a fearful little squeak at whatever he saw in Jane's face.

"I have become the scary crazy lady," said Jane. Well, now she knew how that kind of thing happened.

"Damn straight," said the kid. "Don't hurt me." And he skittered away.

Never had the beach looked more crowded to Jane than now, now that she was the scary crazy lady. Everybody was looking. Except the ones who were carefully looking away, which was worse. She might as well have been an Atlantis crank, a Loch Ness idiot, a sasquatch cultist. She might as well have been stoned.

She staggered back to the stairs over the seawall, gripping the railing hard all the way up, and crossed Ocean Avenue to home.

Sophie was in the kitchen, naked but for a chef's apron and the gauze taped over her throat, pouring the kettle out over prefab miso. The kouros sat, wearing her recently bleached bathrobe, at the kitchen table. They both looked inordinately pleased with themselves.

"I am the scary crazy lady," Jane announced.

"Would you like some miso?"

"I'll be moving out, as soon as I can find a new place."

"No, you're not. I'm leaving you the house while I'm traveling. It's time I met his family. So, miso? No miso?"

"What?"

"I'm making you half-owner, at least temporarily. Oh, come on, say yes. Bob found a lawyer to sort all that out. I've been badgering him about it for two weeks now, when I thought it would be just a few months' vacation. But now there's some urgency, since I don't know that I can find a suitable obstetrician up here. Bob caved in the minute I called to tell him he'd be an uncle. Can you take a long lunch Wednesday? Apparently we have to sign papers."

"I can't believe Bob would help you disinherit yourself."

"He's counting on you to pay the taxes on the place while I'm gone."

"So it'll still be yours when you come back." Jane nodded. "Good on Bob. I can live with that." There was a mug of miso in front of her, with a couple of ice cubes shrinking into the steam. "About this whole leaving thing. How do you know it's safe down there?"

"I don't."

"What if the gills close over when your baby's born? What if you can't carry it to term? What if his family doesn't like you? For all you know, he's got a dozen wives down there already. What if it wasn't a natural disaster or an accident that drove him up here? What if he has enemies? What the hell are you going to do in Atlantis, or the Blake-Bahama Ridge, or wherever...what the hell are you going to do if you have enemies down there?"

"Where there's fear, there's power."

"Don't give me that platitude. Maybe so, but sometimes the power isn't yours." She took a long drink of the miso. Just right. "I'm afraid for you Sophie. I wish you had the sense to fear for yourself."

Sophie pulled her chair around to sit beside Jane, and she tugged the Sunday *Times* across the table. "Look at these headlines," she said, flipping open the front page section. *CATEGORY 4 HURRICANE FORMS IN AZORES, BEARS NORTHWEST*, warned the *Times*. Color graphics projected a two-week path that curved north to Cape May. Turning page after page of calamity, Sophie asked, "How do you know it's safe up here? I'm afraid for you, too, you know."

All over the front page, laments of fresh disaster wailed in bold type. The headlines in the New Jersey regional section shouted of folly and horror. The Op-Ed section reeked of stupidity. And then there was the fashion section.

"Stiletto heels with baby doll dresses," said Jane. "The kinder-whore look is making a comeback. You're right. It's the end of the world."

Sophie said, "We'll need to charter a boat, something to get us out a ways. With someone at the helm who won't ask questions or report anything to anybody."

"And what's that person going to think, when we come back with two bodies fewer than we had when we went out? Do we want to do business with people who would refrain from reporting an apparent double homicide?" Jane clinked her spoon around in her mug, chasing the last bits of reconstituted tofu. "What if it's not a total stranger? What if we tell somebody the truth?"

"They'll stop us," said Sophie.

"There's a marine biologist in Oakbridge Coven. I don't know her well enough to have her number, but her reputation's impeccable. She's got a good-sized boat."

"Not Oakbridge Coven!" Sophie protested. "Snobby high episcopagans!"

"Would you rather deal with a snobby high episcopagan, or some real-life inspiration for *The Sopranos*? Those may be our options."

Sophie slumped in her chair. "If I make the call, Oakbridge won't help. I'm too...fluff-bunny. What am I supposed to say? My fiancé wants to take me home to the bottom of the sea, can you give me a lift? They'll hang up on me."

"I'll take care of it," Jane assured her. "How are you going to get by without me?"

"I've already grown a spine to go with my gills. What I remember about Friday is that everybody panicked but me. I said

I didn't need the ER. I said Sebastian could do what needed doing. I said I'd be all right."

Jane stood to get to work. "We all did what needed doing." The tears welled up. "How am I going to get by without you?"

"You'll figure it out," said Sophie. "And you won't be alone."

Sophie spent the rest of the afternoon in lessons with the kouros, working on her pitch accent. Jane noticed Sophie had stopped addressing him as Kouros, and could call him now by his right name.

Meanwhile, Jane worked the phone, negotiating years of collected contacts toward a discreet person with a boat, someone from a branch of the Craft that prized secrecy and took its oaths with utmost seriousness. It was a good thing Jane had driven Ria from the coven, and made sure every Pagan in the county knew why. Nobody could mistake Jane now for a fluff-bunny New-Ager.

By five o'clock, one of the hard-headed traditionalists of Oakbridge phoned, conjured up by a chain of favors owed and given down several degrees of separation that started, years ago, with Jane's having helped a Druidic charitable organization get tax-exempt status.

"Tell me," said the hard-headed traditionalist, "this isn't some kind of communing-with-dolphins thing."

"I promise you this has nothing to do with dolphins, the alleged fairies of the Pine Barrens, or my past lives."

"I'll call Maggie. Maybe she'll get back to you. Maybe she won't."

Jane had time then to commune with her newspaper at the kitchen table while she waited for what might never come.

The fashion section appealed to her morbid curiosity. What idiot thought it was a good idea to resurrect the kinderwhore look? Even Courtney Love had moved on. Jane turned to find the one page in the section that always interested her: Bill Cunningham's empirical observations of what people were actually wearing on the street. His collection of photographs of non-models spotted in the wild was the only weekly fashion trend report that wasn't reducible to secondhand hype.

There, arranged all over the "On the Street" page, were a dozen tall, slender, dark-haired people in the oddest combinations of clothes, photographed while minding their own business on streets all over Manhattan. Half the subjects were men, which was unusual enough for Cunningham's feature, and every one of the men wore a kilt or a skirt. The women had statuesque model builds, and yet total disregard for every fashion convention of the past century. Each of the figures wore a scarf of one kind or another, wound high up the throat—that, and the blank expression of people who have lost everything. Although Cunningham's brief text likened his subjects to the stars of the heroin chic era, they reminded Jane more of the hundreds of hurricane refugees from New Orleans who'd come north to settle in Perth Amboy the year before.

"Kouros?" she said. "You need to look at this."

"What to look at?" he said, and came in from the living room. She handed him the fashion section. He took it, then stood there a moment, stunned. "Maybe a submarine mistake. I know him." The kouros pointed to a man in a leather miniskirt and Birkenstocks. The man in the picture had very nice legs and regal posture, which was probably why Cunningham hadn't written him off as homeless. Squinting at the faces in the photos, the kouros said, "They're not okay."

"They're alive," said Sophie, stroking his hair to comfort him.

The kouros turned his attention from the faces in the "On the Street" pictures to the hurricane graphics on the front page. "It is a fast calendar," he said.

For the next hour, he sang up another arrangement of light on the coffee table, and Jane sat watching, until the phone rang and she remembered she'd been waiting for a call.

"Hi, it's Maggie, I hear something's double-dog-dare-you secret, and yeah, sure, why not?"

Jane said, "Hi. Well, I thought I had all the details, but it looks like I may need to get back to you."

"You want to make a day trip straight out and straight back, no questions asked, right?"

"Those are the basics."

"Before Hurricane Timothy passes the Chesapeake, right?"

"Sounds good to me."

"Well, quick to help my brothers and sisters in the Craft, and all that."

Jane said, "How long can we have before we go?"

"October twenty-seventh is the last day, assuming current NOAA projections hold. Can you be at the dock up on the Hook by noon on the twenty-seventh?"

"Yeah."

"And reschedule at the drop of a hat, I call you, don't call me?"

"Sure."

"You're not planning any criminal acts, are you?"

After all Jane had done to distance herself from her ex-husband, she was irked at being asked. "No criminal acts."

"Had to ask. Okay. Here's the big if. My first teacher in the Craft took vows of poverty, did the whole legal bit thirty years back, so she could start Eglantine Sanctuary and live there as caretaker. First Pagan land preserve in Jersey, yadda yadda yadda, you know the place, the one with all the standing stones? She's seventy-five this year, too sick to keep it up, and just relinquished her poverty-vow whatever-you-call-it status. Way out of practice, thinking about money like a normal person, and she's, like, burning up on re-entry, you know? Do her tax paperwork for her every year for the rest of her life—I'm afraid it won't be long— and you've got a deal."

"Holy fuck. I had no idea Lady Briar was in trouble." There were not a lot of witches Jane could grant the old-school titles to without irony, but if Briar had wanted to call herself Empress, Jane wouldn't have objected. That was one woman who had paid her dues. "Maggie, if you'd told me that out of the blue, I'd have done it for the asking."

"No shit?"

"No shit."

"I'll give you her number on the twenty-seventh."

"We'll be there."

"We?"

"There might be a bunch of us."

"Less than ten," Maggie said. "It's not that big a boat."

"You got it." And that was that.

Sophie said, "What did you just agree to? Tell me it wasn't awful."

"Briar Kendricks is sick and needs help filing her taxes."

"Is she still vegan? We could make her a casserole."

The kouros had finished building his whatever-it-was.

Jane looked it over. Long chains of small glowing spheres layered in spirals on the coffee table. "Is it dangerous?" she said.

"It's a phone," he answered.

"But we can touch it?"

He laughed. "Try."

It had no substance but light. "How do you do that?"

He shrugged, and opened his hands to a gesture that included the entire house. "How do *you* do *that*?"

"It's explainable, but I can't explain it."

He creased his eyebrows and repeated the sentence a few times to make sure he understood. "Yes," he concluded. "Yes."

While Sophie napped intermittently on the couch, he sat by her and talked to his phone. Still no answer by the time Jane turned in. When she woke in the morning, he was still there, conversing with a very faint, fretful voice that emanated from the glowing Pop-It beads. He had the fashion section and the front page of the *Times* draped over Sophie's hip, while she slept with her head on his lap, and he looked at the pictures of his countrymen. Describing what he saw, Jane guessed, to someone who wanted to identify them.

Jane kept her morning ablutions and breakfasting quiet, so as not to disrupt the call. When it ended, he tried to make another. And tried, and tried, his voice hoarse with repeating what must have been a greeting. At eight-thirty, he roused another answer from his strand of lights—several ragged voices shouting in what might have been desperation or relief. A mix of both, Jane thought, but she couldn't stay to ask, and wouldn't interrupt. She made a pot of chamomile tea and left it with a mug on the end table for the kouros before she went to work.

It was training day at H&R Block. Someone perky had come from corporate with a PowerPoint presentation on the tax code changes that would kick in as of January. Jane had been a good girl and done her homework about all those changes already. She stared blankly at the projection screen and shut out the PowerPoint bimbo by concentrating on a question that did not ease her mind. If the kouros had, all along, been able to build his phone, why had he waited? It wasn't that she suspected sinister intent—she couldn't picture the kouros being sinister about anything—but rather that there might be some reason he had avoided phoning home.

When she got back, she asked him. She pointed at the glowing assemblage of spectral pop-it beads and demanded, "Why now?"

"Why now." He cocked his head sideways for a moment. "You mean is not soon."

"Sooner," Sophie corrected him.

"Why now is why not sooner." He sighed. "Sophie."

"That's it? The ocean spits you out, you spend two months hidden among an alien people and you could be, I don't know, taking over New Jersey, spying on the Bush administration, saving us from global warming, passing on a message of world peace, and all you accomplished is getting my roommate knocked up? Some supernatural phenomenon you turned out to be."

"I don't think he turned out to be a supernatural phenomenon," said Sophie, scratching at the adhesive tape on her wound dressing. "Go figure."

Headlights flashed across the driveway.

"Oh," Sophie said. "Did you get my message?"

"Message?"

"Called you at work. I invited over the usual suspects. Thank you, bon voyage, like that."

"I was in training all day."

"Sucks to be you. Pizza?"

The kouros preferred his with no cheese, heavy on the anchovies. After several tries, Jane gave up trying to convince the geezer on the phone that she wasn't a practical joker. "Hang on," she said. "Sebastian? We need the voice." While Rugosa Coven waited for the delivery guy, no one could quite bring up the matter at hand, and after the week they'd had, small talk was hard to come by.

Bob said, "Surely something else has happened to somebody."

Amber said, "Jane, did you see those pictures I emailed to the list? There's a nice one of you on the beach I thought you might put in the personal ad. Your hair's doing that corkscrew curl thing in the wind. Nobody can resist a photo like that."

"Actually," said Jane, "somebody already answered." She blushed. She hated blushing.

"Even with the rant still up?" Amber was incredulous.

"I took the rant down."

"So, what's he like?"

"How would I know? I haven't called him."

Bob asked, "How long have you put it off? Is it weeks yet?"

"Just a couple days. And there was, you know, stuff going on."

"I dare you to call him right now," said Sophie.

"Oh, that's just mean."

Sebastian said, "It's a phone call. It'll only hurt for a minute."

"And leave a mark for the rest of my life," said Jane. "Isn't that how your studio patter usually goes?"

"If you don't like the results," he said, "you can always have the phone call removed with laser surgery. Or you can pop it out and the puncture will heal shut within a week. Keep it clean."

"I can't do this with everybody watching."

Sophie said, "Well, you haven't done it since you got the reply, with nobody watching, so what have you lost?"

"I'll just call to see if I like his answering machine voice. But if I get a person, I'm hanging up."

"Who's the stalker, now?" said Bob.

"Smile when you say that, Baines." Jane took a deep breath, grimaced, and dialed. Sure enough, the number dumped her into voicemail.

"Hi, you've reached Kevin MacPhearson," said a cordial recorded greeting. "Leave a message at the beep, and I'll…"

Jane hung up. "It'll never work."

Sophie started giggling.

"Fuck you, too, Sophie."

Sebastian put on the patient tone to ask, "How can you tell it won't work?"

"His name's Kevin MacPhearson. And he's a Druid."

Blank looks all around.

So Jane had to spell it out. "He'll be one of those enthusiastically Celtic types. If there's one thing I don't need, it's a Druid with a case of ancestor worship. I got my fill of paleopagan reconstruction with an Asatru-practicing Sigurdson. I've got no quarrel with Thor, personally, but now when I hear people hail Thor at festival, I get hives. So you know how it'll go. I bet you five bucks, this MacPhearson guy and I would spend the entire first date arguing about nineteenth century Edinburgh antiquarians and their wishful-thinking archaeology."

"Done," said Bob. "I'm taking that bet." He took a five dollar bill out of his wallet and waved it at her. "Witnesses?" They all raised their hands—even the kouros. "Go on, then, prove it."

"What?"

"Go on the goddamn first date, and if that's all there is to him, here, five bucks. See for yourself, Miss Empiricist."

"Besides," said Amber, "Celtic Reconstructionist equals *man in kilt*. And there's nothing yummier to look at than a man in a kilt. Right?"

With that, Jane could not argue. "Do I have to call him back right now?"

Clearly, there would be no peace under her roof until she did. She redialed. "Hi," said the cell phone. "You've reached Kevin MacPhearson. Leave a message at the beep, and I'll get back to you as soon as I can. Today's poem is by William Butler Yeats."

Jane cringed at the mention of Yeats. Enthusiastically Celtic, all right, and pretentious, too. Now she could justify hanging up. But the MacPhearson guy gave a very credible rendition of Yeats's "The Folly of Being Comforted," as if he really understood it. And then, the beep.

"Hi, this is Jane Hirsch. You replied to my personal ad on SinglePagans.com? If you're not scared off by the fact that I've reread *Middlemarch* three times in the past two months, give me a call sometime after the twenty-seventh. Things have been kind of crazy around here, but I think my schedule will settle down then. Unless Hurricane Timothy comes early and Sea Bright has to evacuate."

She was rambling. Must not ramble!

"Let me give you my cell phone number." Rattling off the familiar digits gave her a moment to figure out how to escape from the call. "Do you really change poems every day?" Click. Done.

Her parting question was a disaster. What if he called back before the twenty- seventh? So much for one thing at a time.

Unless he didn't call back at all.

But her friends were all rejoicing in the living room. They congratulated her entirely too much, and Bob brandished his five dollar bill and said something about poems, and then the doorbell rang. Saved by the pizza.

It was easier to be happy over Jane maybe having some kind of love life again someday than it was to be happy that Sophie was leaving, but once the pizza delivery guy was paid and gone, there was no avoiding the harder subject.

"But it *is* a good thing," Sophie insisted.

Bob said, "You're heading to sea in a hurricane."

"I'm heading under the sea, more than a week before a hurricane is expected to arrive."

"Remember what a mess he was when we found him," said

Bob. "If it's so much safer down there, how did he end up here in the first place?"

"Small submarine mistake," said the kouros. "Oops."

"That was a small mistake?"

"No. Small submarine. Just me."

Bob covered his face with his hands.

"You want big submarine mistakes?" the kouros said. "Check this out." And he showed them the page from the fashion section. "These guys? Big submarine mistake. Not just me." He pointed again to the Birkenstocked man in the leather miniskirt. "I know him. He's a good guy."

Amber considered the photographs. "Wouldn't mind seeing his look catch on, even with the Birkenstocks. But the stocking cap on the girl in the bedsheet toga, I could do without. Pity. She has great cheekbones."

Sebastian said, "That's my Magpie Eye."

"The accident could have happened to anybody, is what he means," said Sophie.

"Not helping your case," said Bob.

"I'm not afraid."

Jane said, "Bob, you're not going to dissuade her. You might as well give her a good send-off and hope for the best."

"Who are you," said Sebastian, "and what have you done with the real Jane Hirsch?"

"We've been nagging the girl to grow up and settle down for how many years? And then she goes and does it, and we try to nag her out of it. Okay, so she's going to sea in a hurricane..."

"An inaccurate description, as I already pointed out," Sophie protested.

"Into the great unknown. Can you live with that, Sophie? All right, then. We got what we asked for. No sense sabotaging it now. And besides, is actual love so easy to get, we should expect her to throw it back? Maybe it was easy for you guys, but not for everybody. Bob, no one gives you a hard time about having married a Methodist."

"That's hardly the same. Ricki is a lot more like us..."

Jane cut him off. "Ricki gets skeeved out by just thinking

about the symbolic Great Rite. I love Ricki. I would walk through fire for Ricki. But she is not more like us than he is."

Bob turned to his sister and said, "Could you at least take a year's supply of prenatal vitamins with you? And remember, fish are full of mercury these days. And call. Write. Come home to visit. Don't just disappear on me." He gripped her hand. "Don't just disappear."

Jane regretted having her say already. Never mind that it was right. Even if Sophie didn't disappear for good, the house would be empty while she was gone. Best to hold onto the practical details. "So, we're meeting the people from the big submarine mistake."

"They are finding us," said the kouros.

"And they're taking you home?"

"No, they're lost. I'm taking them home." He pointed east, to the water. "My Rugosa will pick up. There's room in their SUV."

"Your Rugosa," said Jane.

"Coming from Blake-Bahama. From home. My Rugosa. Like your Rugosa."

"Well, then. I guess everything will be all right."

In the few days that remained to them, cooking lost its urgency, though Amber promised gourmet vegan casseroles to send with Jane to Lady Briar, once the dust settled. All of Rugosa gathered at the beach house in the evenings, where they subsisted on take-out and Kleenex.

Tuesday night, Ricki brought her scrapbooking supplies and a huge cardboard box full of family pictures. Coven pictures, too, which she had kept carefully labeled and organized.

"Not that the results will withstand water," Ricki admitted. "I hope you don't mind if the scrapbook stays with us while you're, um, overseas."

"It should totally stay with you," said Sophie. "I'm coming back, though."

Meanwhile, the kouros worked on building a more durable

phone, something he could leave behind. He ransacked the house for materials, to no avail. Nothing he found was quite what he was looking for, and he couldn't explain what would be. Jane noticed that he no longer looked Bob in the eye.

On the twenty-sixth, Sophie went to the Rumson house for a last Baines family dinner, to say goodbye to her niece and nephews. The kouros stayed home with Jane.

"What is the very pretty game?" he asked her out of the blue.

She tried to remember if she'd ever seen Sophie play a game with him. "What do you mean?"

"It's not a radio. It's cards. You said it was a very pretty game."

The phone rang. Jane had a sudden anxiety that the Druid guy was calling her early. Or it might be Maggie, to say the expedition was off. Hurricane Timothy was sluggish in its progress across the Atlantic, but it was plenty big. Neither call was one she felt she could face just now.

Jane stared at the answering machine while it had its say. *Jane and Sophie*, said the answering machine. She'd have to change the greeting next week.

"Kouros? Could you pass the Kleenex?"

Ria's voice said, "Jane? Jane, I know you don't want to hear from me, but I've been throwing the cards about this next hurricane, and doing some pendulum work over the map. Election Day week, it would really be best if you boarded up the windows and got your ass inland."

At that, Jane picked up the receiver. "But the windows are storm-proof glass. Sophie was just showing me the care instructions, and..."

"Listen to me, Jane. Do right by the house, and it will still be fine when you get back. Just don't press your luck about bad drinking water, power cables, food preservation. I don't know exactly what it will be, but don't press your luck about it. When the storm passes the Chesapeake, you pack whatever you can't do without for a couple days, and you get your ass across the damn bridge. Stay with somebody. Stay with me, Gods help us both. Just do it. And whatever unfinished business Sophie has, she'd better get it settled soon."

Discomfited as she was by Ria's predictions, Jane said, "Hey, what are you doing tomorrow?"

"I thought you'd never ask."

So, when the day came, Ria met them at the dock. She discreetly admired Sophie's new gills, which had healed up just fine.

Maggie pretended not to notice the gills while she herded all of Rugosa Coven and its hangers-on into her boat. The *Aradia* was a tight fit for eight.

It was a clear, still day, with a pale sky full of raucous gulls. Once the *Aradia* was well around the Hook and out of Raritan Bay, Maggie called Jane aside and said, "So, that's what's so double-dog-dare-you secret, is it? Gills on a human. And that's why the scarf on the boyfriend, right? Gills. Never seen anything like that."

"It may not be the weirdest thing you see today."

"Cool. Will she mind if I look at them?"

"Probably not."

"Hey, Sophie! C'mere."

Sophie bounded over. "What?"

"Can I see them? The gills?"

She loosened her scarf.

"Nice."

"Thank you. I grew them myself."

The marine biologist prodded a gill slit with her outstretched index finger. "What's with the burn scars?"

"Sebastian had to use an electrocautery thingy, what was it called?"

"A Bovie," said Jane.

"To open them up. The top ones ripped, see?"

"Wild," Maggie said. "Does breathing feel different?"

Sophie looked thoughtful. "Did you ever go to the Rockies?"

"Drove cross-country once, sure," said Maggie.

"You get altitude sickness?"

"A little."

Jane said, "My first job sent me to Boulder once to do an audit. I was weak as a kitten the whole time I was out there. Awful."

"Bob and I used to go to Aspen with Mom and Dad on ski trips, when we were kids, and I'd always get altitude sickness. So, you know how it feels, when the plane touches back down at Newark, and there's real air again? Good, thick, chewy Newark air, and you feel stronger and smarter and more awake than you ever did before?"

"Fun while it lasted," said Jane.

"Having gills feels like that all the time."

The kouros came to confer with Maggie over charts, and Sophie stayed to help translate. It was frustrating enough for all concerned without Jane in the middle of things. She chewed a couple of Dramamine tablets in case of seasickness and went to sit next to Ria. Ria wore her goth crone dress, but no silver, no kohl. Jane couldn't remember the last time she'd seen Ria bare of ornament.

"Do you think they'll be okay?" Jane asked.

"Do you give a rat's ass what I think?"

"Maybe. Depends on how you think it."

They watched the lovers trying to give directions together, while Maggie thumped the chart in exasperation.

"Their odds are as good as anybody's," said Ria. "The future's unwritten. You want some love life advice?"

"No."

"Good. Don't follow any."

Jane stared at Ria incredulously. "How do you do that? Now, if I don't follow any advice, including from you, I'm following your advice not to follow any. If I do all right, you give yourself credit. If my life falls to shit, well, you offered me advice and I refused. You get to be vindicated, no matter what I do or what happens to me."

Ria smiled. "Missed you, Jane."

"I didn't miss you. I don't want you back."

Ria went right on smiling.

"But I'm glad you called," Jane conceded.

"This is exactly where I'm meant to be today."

Jane stewed. As self-deceptions went, that was a really tempting one. After several minutes of stewing, Jane decided to try it for herself. What was the harm in acting as if she were right where she was supposed to be? Know thy enemy.

It didn't feel half bad.

Bob was barely holding himself together. Amber and Sebastian were on the case, so Jane decided not to meddle. Until Sebastian broke out the picnic lunch, Jane managed to maintain the sense of being exactly where she was meant to be. But food meant talk, and talk generally meant telling the truth, and that was how the doubt got in.

"It's not too late to back out," she reminded Sophie.

Sophie kissed her on the cheek. "You'll be fine."

That was how it went for all of them. Sophie was high on her certainty. For Jane, the hours before sunset were excruciating. The kouros spent them asking Ria about the cards, about the card radio, the very pretty game, arranging for remote reading appointments at Solstices and Equinoxes, to trade news. "Because," he said, "no phone. I tried, but no phone. It's not okay."

"It's all right," Ria assured him.

"No, really," said Bob. "Let him tell it straight. It's not okay."

Death, total transformation, whatever, lurked under the water or over the horizon, or somewhere, without a trace on the bright waves. Dusk was a relief, after day's tease.

A waxing half-moon hovered over the last of the sunset, and by that light Maggie first spotted the tugboat.

Jane asked, "What's a tugboat doing this far out?"

"Don't know," said Maggie. "They're skittish on the radio. But it's not weirder than the gills yet."

"Wait for it," Jane assured her. "Kouros? Is this your carpool?"

He squinted into the darkness. "It is a right place."

When the tugboat drew close to the *Aradia*, it was wrapped in whalesong. Or, not quite whalesong, when the kouros sang with it. His language had come to sound like words now, even to Jane, though she doubted she would ever make sense of them. Many voices, in several parts, rolled from the rail of the tugboat. She looked up to see, but the larger vessel's lights blinded her. There were human forms, maybe twenty of them. Her eyes couldn't be sure of anything else. For all Jane knew, it might be the tugboat crew she saw.

Sophie knew the song.

The moon's reflection in the waves grew brighter, larger, bubbled up from the deep. Such impermanence. Jane would have preferred to see a submarine built from something more reliable than light and song. It was no wonder the kouros had washed up on Gunnison Beach, if that was how his people traveled. The wonder was that it didn't happen every day of the week.

"You're going in that?" she asked the kouros. "If you stop paying attention for ten minutes, it'll dissolve around you."

"Yes! Now you see. No trash pickup!"

For a split second, she saw it as he did, and for that split second, the vessel made perfect sense.

"I wish my Rugosa is meeting your Rugosa," he said. "Tonight, we hurry. Home before the Timothy. But it is a round calendar."

"A round calendar. You mean the Wheel of the Year?"

He nodded.

"What about it?"

"Mabon again. We are back for Mabon, staying in your house. Is it okay?"

"Anytime."

And then he had other farewells to say.

Prying Sophie loose from her brother didn't look easy. Sophie herself was the one who managed it, just long enough to say,

"Group hug." They all stood clinging together a moment, until they heard the shipwrecked submariners diving from the tugboat, their long forms breaking the water. "This is where I get off," she said. Without hesitation, she broke from her circle to dive into the waves.

"At Mabon, there is room in my SUV," said the kouros. He waved, flashed his asymmetrical smile, and jumped the rail of the *Aradia* to follow her.

Jane stood at the rail, watching as the swimmers converged on the rescuers from Blake-Bahama. She couldn't help thinking of the submarine as a recyclable SUV now. There were figures standing within the constellation of lights, to pull the swimmers through. It was a long, painstaking process—the kouros's friends made sure to leave no one behind. In the end, two figures stood waving in the vessel's highest chamber as it descended.

Bob wailed like a lost child.

While Sebastian started a low, wordless chant to soothe them all, Jane went to check on Maggie. Somebody had to get them home. The marine biologist waved farewell to someone at the rail of the tugboat. When she turned to Jane, her face was delighted. "We're even," she said.

"I'll still prepare Lady Briar's taxes."

"Of course you will."

"I'm not laming out on a sick elder in the Craft just because somebody else lets me off the hook."

"Of course you're not. But, dude. You and me? We're even. You want a lift to meet that crowd anytime? Just let me take notes, draw a sketch, something. If I have to see it again under a promise of absolute secrecy even from posterity, I think my head'll explode."

"I don't think they can stay secret forever," said Jane.

Ria said, "They never were."

"Maybe not," Jane replied, "but at least he didn't know jack about Kabbalah."

She spent the rest of the journey home huddled with her covenmates, wrapped in the shifting strands of their chant.

Sometimes a word drifted through their improvisations, sometimes a phrase from a familiar song. They were willing Sophie safe. Happy, she could take care of for herself. Maggie brought them around the Hook, and the chant turned to homecomings.

Once on the dock, they found their voices were shot, and they had to stand very close together to hear each other talk. It was hard to say whose idea it was first that they should take their own last swim for the year, however brief, in honor of the occasion.

"You do realize it's fucking freezing, right?" said Maggie. "And I've only got the one wetsuit for myself?"

Jane said, "If Starhawk can do it at the Winter Solstice, in northern California, in the Humboldt Current, we can last a few minutes in the Gulf Stream before Samhain."

"Is it a competition, now?" Ria asked.

"It's an excuse."

Sebastian said, "I've heard dumber excuses for dumber things. Let's do it."

They ransacked their cars for beach towels and made their way across the street and over the dunes. The rugosa bushes had shed their last leaves but kept their thorns, so the band of skinnydippers made their way carefully in the dark, now that the moon was set and they had only the light pollution of New York to go by. They piled their towels and clothes together and rushed into the froth.

Jane pressed through the cold, until she could dive right through the waves that rose to break over her. *Safe out and safe back,* she reminded the ocean. *That's what Sophie needs. Don't forget.*

A very little bit was enough for all of them. They came back to their pile of towels to find they'd been careless and half their clothes had gotten soaked.

"Told you to leave them further up," said Ria.

Amber barely seemed to register that she was wrestling herself into sodden jeans. The jeans were winning. "So beautiful," she said. "If I ever hear that song again, if I ever see anything like their ship, I'll count myself blessed."

Sebastian said, "Give up on those jeans, Amber. At this hour, nobody on our block will be awake to notice."

The necessity of putting damp clothes on, on a late October night, brought Bob back to the moment rather abruptly. "Maybe you guys can get away with streaking from the car to the house, but in my neighborhood? Not a chance."

"Nope, not even in Sea Bright," Jane said.

Maggie was the only one of them not shivering. "A wetsuit is not a luxury. I don't know why everybody doesn't have one. You guys gonna be okay getting home?"

"We'll be fine," said Sebastian.

"Regretting the dip yet?" asked Ria, whose goth crone dress was almost completely dry.

"Not for a minute," Jane said through chattering teeth as she shrugged on her dripping wool sweater.

In the parking lot they parted company, with quick hugs and plans for Samhain, and injunctions to one another to warm up and have tea and take care.

Something in Jane's car was beeping. Not the dashboard, not the stereo. She turned the key and let the Corolla idle a moment. It was too old to be beeping like that. What did it have that was new enough to beep with? Every sixty seconds, another beep, all the way out of the state park gate and down the narrow town of Sea Bright. It was only when she'd pulled into her own driveway and watched the tail lights of her covenmates' cars pass on down Ocean Avenue that she realized it was her cell phone, stashed in the glove compartment, telling her she had voicemail. Numbly, she pressed the button to hear her message.

"Hi, it's Kevin MacPhearson," said the message. "I just

finished reading *Middlemarch*. Just finished, like five minutes ago, and even though I'm supposed to give your schedule a couple days to level out, I had to call and say I liked it. Didn't think I would. I tried to get into it twice before, years ago, and it did nothing for me. But people kept telling me, just read a hundred pages in until the heroine walks to the end of the gravel path, and everything changes. At the end of the gravel path cool stuff happens, incognito secret uncles, renegade priests hiding in priest-holes, suspense. I didn't really believe them, but this time I got to the end of the gravel path, and, behold, cool stuff. Sorry to ramble at you. Anyhow, the point is, if your schedule ever clears, and Timothy doesn't wash you out to sea, I'd really like to get together for coffee or dinner or something. Would it help to say I do, in fact, change the poem every day? Hope you call me."

"To delete this message, press seven," the voicemail prompt said. "To save it, press nine. For other options…"

Jane pressed nine. "You read my book," she said to the phone. It was after eleven o'clock, way too late in the evening to call him right back and say that nobody, not even her mom, had ever read to the end of *Middlemarch* for her.

She tucked the phone into her handbag and climbed stiffly out of the car. So cold. She didn't want to track salt and sand all over the house, so she shucked the beach towel and her windbreaker by the kitchen door. And then her sopping wool sweater. She reached for the spigot of the back porch shower and opened the hot water up all the way. Once the line cleared of cold, she stepped under the stream and stripped off as many of her sodden things as neighborly discretion allowed.

She washed herself warm under the watchful eyes of Sulis and all the improbable stars.

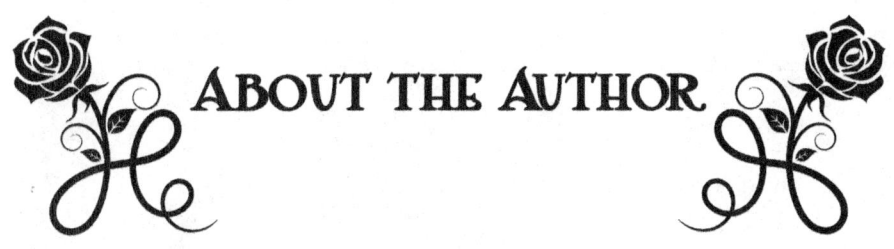

About the Author

Sarah Avery is an escaped academic with a Ph.D. in English and a happy private tutoring practice. Her stories have appeared in *Jim Baen's Universe* and *Black Gate*. She writes a regular column at *Black Gate*, as well as a personal blog, *Ask Dr. Pretentious*. An anthology she coedited with David Sklar, *Trafficking in Magic, Magicking in Traffic,* will be published this spring by Fantastic Books. She has lived in Japan and Germany, Kentucky and Korea, the DC suburbs and—for longer than anywhere else, to her surprise—New Jersey. She now resides in Maryland with her husband and sons.

The Novels that put the Dark...

The Eternal Cycle Series
YESTERDAY'S DREAMS
9781937051075
TOMORROW'S MEMORIES
9781937051082
TODAY'S PROMISE
9781937051099
Danielle Ackley-McPhail

SOUL BORN
9780983099321
BLOOD DIVIDED
9781937051242
Kevin James Breaux

AWFULLY FAMILIAR
Michael J. Tresca
9781937051532

FAERIE GAMES
B.E. Tartaglia
9781937051327

...into Dark Quest

THE HALFLING'S COURT
9780979690167
THE REDCAP'S QUEEN
9781937051068
Danielle Ackley-McPhail

THREE CHORDS OF CHAOS
James Chambers
9781937051396

DRAGON PRECINCT
9781937051280
UNICORN PRECINCT
9781937051150
GOBLIN PRECINCT
9781937051410
TALES FROM DRAGON PRECINCT
9781937051433
Keith R.A. DeCandido

Please see our website for further details www.darkquestbooks.com

Fantasy Novels

ECHOES OF OLYMPUS
Darrin Drader
9781937051549

LADY OF SEEKING
IN THE CITY OF WAITING
Jennifer Brozek
9780982619766

LORD OF WATER
Regina Glei
9781937051358

LEGENDS OF LONE WOLF
OMNIBUS ONE
9780982619704
LEGENDS OF LONE WOLF
OMNIBUS TWO
9780982619704
LEGENDS OF LONE WOLF
OMNIBUS THREE
9781937051174
Joe Dever and John Grant

UNEXPECTED ENLIGHTEN-
MENT OF RACHEL GRIFFIN
9781937051877
L. Jagi Lamplighter

I KNOW NOT
James Daniel Ross
9781937051105

THE LAST DRAGOON
James Daniel Ross
9781937051617

A TALE OF THREE CITIES
Elana Gomel
9781937051266

THE LAURIAN PENTOLOGY
ENDING AN ENDING
9781937051686
BEGINNING
9781937051693
BEGINNING AN ENDING
9781937051709
ENDING
9781937051716
Danny Birt

Please see our website for further details www.darkquestbooks.com